BABY OF
THE FAMILY

BABY OF THE FAMILY

A NOVEL

MAURA ROOSEVELT

DUTTON

DUTTON
An imprint of Penguin Random House LLC
penguinrandomhouse.com

Copyright © 2019 by Maura Roosevelt
Penguin supports copyright. Copyright fuels creativity, encourages diverse voices,
promotes free speech, and creates a vibrant culture. Thank you for buying an authorized
edition of this book and for complying with copyright laws by not reproducing, scanning, or
distributing any part of it in any form without permission. You are supporting writers
and allowing Penguin to continue to publish books for every reader.

DUTTON and the D colophon are registered trademarks of Penguin Random House LLC.

Library of Congress Cataloging-in-Publication Data
Names: Roosevelt, Maura, author.
Title: Baby of the family: a novel / Maura Roosevelt.
Description: New York, New York: Dutton, [2019]
Identifiers: LCCN 2018021291 | ISBN 9781524743178 (hc)
Subjects: LCSH: Inheritance and succession—Fiction. | Brothers and sisters—Fiction.
Classification: LCC PS3618.O683 B33 2019 | DDC 813/.6—dc23
LC record available at https://lccn.loc.gov/2018021291

Printed in the United States of America
1 3 5 7 9 10 8 6 4 2

Set in Guardi • Designed by Elke Sigal

For my parents, Ann and Jim

I have watched you in the dark of a yard
where we can only see each other by a lamp left on
some rooms away. . . . Two moths dust
the same screen for remembered light.
    —Jay Deshpande,
       "On Speaking Quietly with My Brother"

When I was young and irresponsible,
I was young and irresponsible.
    —George W. Bush

Whitby Family Tree

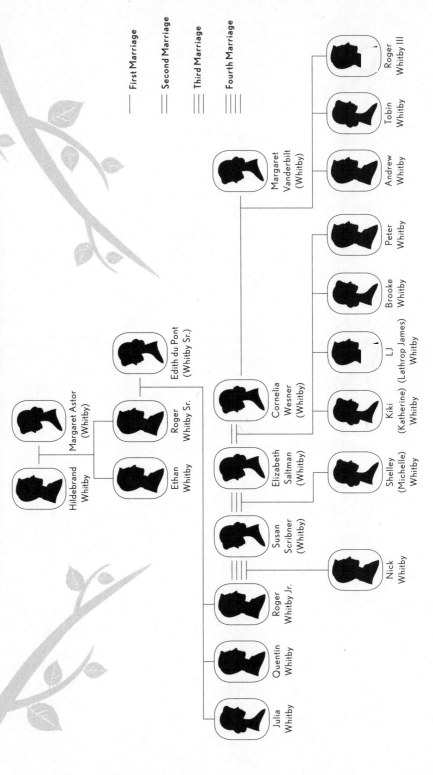

First Marriage
Second Marriage
Third Marriage
Fourth Marriage

Hildebrand Whitby

Margaret Astor (Whitby)

Ethan Whitby

Roger Whitby Sr.

Edith du Pont (Whitby Sr.)

Julia Whitby

Quentin Whitby

Roger Whitby Jr.

Susan Scribner (Whitby)

Elizabeth Saltman (Whitby)

Cornelia Wesner (Whitby)

Margaret Vanderbilt (Whitby)

Nick Whitby

Shelley (Michelle) Whitby

Kiki (Katherine) Whitby

LJ (Lathrop James) Whitby

Brooke Whitby

Peter Whitby

Andrew Whitby

Tobin Whitby

Roger Whitby III

BABY OF
THE FAMILY

Spring

| 2003 |

It all started with a rowboat.

—ROGER WHITBY JR.

1

There was a time when the death of a Whitby would have made the evening post. Two generations earlier, flags would have been flown at half-mast and taps played in town squares at dusk. When Ethan and Ethel Whitby perished after their Buick collided with a logging truck on Route 9 in the Hudson Valley, just weeks after so many of their pals lost their lives on the *Titanic*, a special announcement thudded onto doorsteps just before five. All across New York State and greater New England, women standing in their parlors shrieked at the news; men hung their heads over their desks in sorrow, removing their hats for these leaders of industry, these strong-willed, big-toothed Americans. When the plane carrying Ethan's son William and his new wife plummeted into the Atlantic two days after their wedding, all the major magazine covers displayed the couple's youthful images, mourning the country's great loss. But when Roger Whitby Jr. died half a century later, there was no such hubbub. On the night that Roger died, his youngest child, Nick, was completely unaware of his father's passing. Nick did not receive notification by newspaper, or even by phone. No, that night at midnight, Nick Whitby was off the grid: the twenty-one-year-old had left his cell phone in his desk drawer in New York City and was now standing under the stars in northern Maine, shaking, about to commit an act of civil disobedience.

As he beheld the construction site before him, Nick breathed too quickly and tried to muster up the fire—the fight—that he needed right now. Metal scaffolding encased the concrete frame of a six-story, half-built biotech lab, which was going up on the campus of Kennebec Valley Community College. He had done his research. The reports claimed that the lab would bring jobs to this empty expanse of rural vacation land. But Nick knew that it would also mess with the natural order of the world: once the walls of the lab were up, scientists would sit inside of them and breed mice with human ears, or manipulate corn so that it grew four feet high in two months and gave everyone who ate it cancer. This building was just one more development feeding the tumor that was the neoliberal takeover of America and the greater globalized world. Civilization itself was going to shit. Things were at a tipping point, and somebody had to step up and resist the destruction. So there he was, in the middle of the night in Maine, in line with eight other brave lunatics. He was taking a stand with a group of real anarchists from New York City. And as he took that stand, he couldn't help thinking about what a fraud he really was.

God, he was such a nerd. Clouds of his breath pumped out too quickly, and everyone could see. Soon they would know that he'd never done anything like this before. The air was very cold—even in a wool sweater and black hooded sweatshirt, with a beanie cap pulled over his forehead, he was freezing. For all purposes April was still winter in Maine. But Nick knew from his childhood trips through the state to the Whitby family reunions that in a few short weeks the sounds of bullfrogs croaking and crickets singing would emerge. He wished so badly for those sounds now; anything to cover up his huffs of panic. He was third in the line of people, and his comrades—or future comrades, as he was committed to showing he was just like them—were all dressed in similarly grungy jeans and winter hats, with bandit bandannas tied around their necks. There were no lights for miles: above Nick the sky was so clear and stars so bright that he could see the Milky Way. If he'd had time he could have named every constellation. He was good at things like that.

Big D—the lanky and unsmiling leader of this crew, the bearded man Nick had met only yesterday in the van on the way up—turned around and whispered harshly, "You all right, brother? Kever's going first, and then you're up. As soon as he gets into the bucket of the crane, you need to start climbing."

Nick nodded but said nothing. Then Big D's hands were, suddenly, on Nick's biceps. The guy's breath was redolent of the garlic-heavy stir-fry the farm owners had made them for dinner. "If you can't do this, walk away now. We need to act quickly once everyone is up there. If you're in, stay in. But if you're out, you need to get out. Now."

"In!" Nick barked too loudly, as if Big D were his drill sergeant. He focused on the machinery in front of him. It looked like one of those phone company cranes, but larger, and attached to a giant white construction vehicle. When he had agreed to be part of this action with this Earth Liberation Front group, he was told he'd just be a minor player—another body, a lookout. But when they'd gone over the plan on the six-and-a-half-hour van ride up there, they collectively determined that Nick was one of the stronger and fitter individuals involved, and therefore he was needed to climb the crane. He still wasn't the most crucial person in the action: the short guy in front of him in the line, Kever, would climb up the machinery first and then jump down onto the roof of the half-constructed building. Then Nick would climb up and stay in the bucket of the crane. Five-gallon Poland Spring water jugs, half-filled with ethyl alcohol, would be assembly-lined up to him, and he would then drop them down into Kever's tiny arms. Kever would strategically place the jugs around the roof of the unfinished building, then tie each one to another in a spiderlike web with gasoline-soaked rope cords. He would throw down the match, and they'd all flee the scene.

On the ground, as Nick waited in line, some of the women were spray-painting the sides of the other construction vehicle. That's where Nick's friend Devorah was, in front of a dozer with a ferocious-looking shovel on the front of it, painting a communiqué note claiming responsibility for this action. The spray paint would read: BIOTECH = CORPORATE CONTROL. DOWN WITH DEVELOPMENT! FUCK WAGE SLAVERY. STAY WILD.—ELF.

In the van on the trip up, Devorah had slept with her head in Nick's lap as they rumbled north on I-95. Nick was like a little kid at his first sleepover party, too excited and nervous to speak. This was the kind of adventurous life he'd been deprived of because of his freakish family, because of his adopted stepfather, Roger. Roger, when he was still his mother's secret boyfriend, hid Nick away at the hotel all those weekends of his childhood, then forced him to move out of New York and the only life he'd ever known. Because of Roger, Nick was always being taken away from something. He'd never had the chance to fit in, much less to be cool.

"Hey, you heard this one?" Kever, sitting beside him in the van, asked in a Southern-twanged accent. His studded jean jacket with patches of old punk bands on it looked child-sized. "Two anarchists walk into the bar. The bartender looks them up and down, sees their sneakers pulled from the trash, their homemade tattoos and ratty-ass sweatshirts. Then he asks these two dudes: 'What can I get for you?' And one responds"—he made his voice deep and cartoonish—"'That's not funny!'" He slapped his leg, howling at the ceiling.

Nick wondered if he'd misheard him. Was that a joke?

"And then the other—*hooo*—the other anarchist scoffs and says, 'That was *so* fucked up.'" He kept laughing, so Nick chuckled too, quietly and politely.

Devorah turned her sleepy face upward, and mock-groaned. "Get it? Anarchists have no sense of humor." Then she added, "Kever wants to be the first anarchist stand-up comedian."

"The punk-rock Jerry Seinfeld!" He winked. "But instead of talking about soup, I'll talk about, you know . . . smashing the state."

Nick laughed again, less softly. He was grateful someone even assumed he would get that joke. Devorah was the real reason that Nick was in that van at all. He had been in love with her since his freshman year of college, when she lived a few doors down from him in Hayden Hall. Devorah of the dark hair, of the East Coast professor parents, of the ring through the bottom of her nose. She was cool, she was into politics, and she was as far from the Orange County high school girls of his past as one could possibly be. She also claimed she was a lesbian. But Nick took that claim as a challenge rather than a hindrance, and followed her around to many

campus and citywide activities, waiting for his in. Nick Whitby—star sociology student, former swim team champion, only child of a middle-class,
middle-brow, anxiety-riddled mother—was uncannily good at many
things. This fact pleased him greatly, as he was also a perfectionist. And if
he could not do something perfectly, he was filled with an anger that tee-
tered on uncontrollable. Although six foot two and, if he did say so
himself, the proprietor of chiseled face and handsome physique, one thing
Nick was terribly bad at was girls.

His desire for females, for the feel of their smooth bodies and the as-
surance of their constant attention, was elephantine, and—he occasionally
feared—dangerous to his own health. In his miserable high school years he
was unable to talk to anyone of the opposite gender due to a sincere dearth
of confidence, but how could he have been blamed for that? He didn't fit in
anywhere. He wasn't a Californian, but was no longer a New Yorker either.
He liked hard-core music and punk bands, but he was in honors classes
and was too shy to introduce himself to the group of kids who smoked
cigarettes by the track field, wearing studded belts and dog collars. He was
even an outcast in his own family: when Roger finally married his mother,
after the years of living in secrecy, Nick gained the Whitby last name, yet
he knew he would never truly be one of them. Even though it didn't logically make sense, and even though his mother flat out denied it, he'd always
felt he'd looked suspiciously like Roger and his family, and therefore there
was a good chance Roger *was* his biological father. No one would ever admit
that to him though. So when he left for college, he decided to use the anger
he'd stored from his childhood as fuel, powering him to live the best adult
life he possibly could. And that life involved sex. At NYU, Nick talked to
every Converse-wearing, Elliott Smith–loving, Belle and Sebastian–
listening attractive girl he met. He tried, and kept trying. But in the end he
was wretched at engaging with them. They all had too many feelings—
feelings Nick didn't know what to do with and would eventually walk away
from. Now in his senior year, it seemed that the girls had begun talking
with each other too—lying to each other—and currently there was an army
of poetry readers out to get him, fueled by vegan diets and rage.

So Nick had returned to Devorah. She was the only one he'd ever loved anyway. And she was the only one he'd never even come close to kissing. When he was a sophomore, 9/11 happened just over a mile from their college. Nick and three hundred other terrified students had to evacuate their dorm building carrying as little as possible, a water bottle or a pillow, and run north on Lafayette Street as fast as their legs could carry them. It was 9/11 that had pushed Nick to truly care about politics, and when he joined the club Devorah started, SMD, or Students Mobilizing and Demonstrating, he became a star member. As with almost everything he attempted, he turned out to have talent as an activist: he organized teach-backs, led walkouts, and made speeches in Washington Square Park about America's unjust raids in the Middle East and why his university should divest from oil. It seemed that other college students wanted to listen to the tall kid with angelic dark blond curls. Even his wonky voice amplified through a megaphone did not deter people from gathering around and looking up at him.

But in their senior year, Devorah's activism started branching out beyond the college, and two weeks before they'd left for Maine she'd taken Nick to a citywide activist meeting held in the back room of the Alt Coffee in the East Village. The meeting was about the Republican National Convention protests—still a year away—and Nick sat through three hours of it, including four consensus-based votes about when to have the next meeting. When there was a pause in the agenda, his utter boredom compelled him to slip out of the front door and onto Avenue A.

On the street, as he flipped open his phone to investigate what hate messages he'd received from the poetry girls, he felt a tap on his shoulder. "You're Nick, right? The NYU kid?" It was the small, dirty-looking guy from the meeting. "Nice work y'all are doing over there."

Nick couldn't tell if this guy was making fun of him.

"You may have heard about *me*," the guy continued. "I've been going by Little D, or Little Dumpster. But that's changing now, so you can call me Kever."

Nick had not, in fact, heard of him, but they shook hands.

"Devorah told us you're friends with her. And we want you to be in-volved in, uh, a project with us. Can you come over to our place and talk about it?"

"Uh, sure, man. Love to."

Two weeks later, a van picked him and Dev up on the corner of Sixth Avenue and West Fourth Street, at two in the morning, in the wet spring cold. He had told no one where he was going: not his roommate, Amil; not his mother in California.

After the interminable van ride, Nick found himself in a sleeping bag in the loft of a barn owned by the radical art collective called the Ant Colony, a group that made giant murals explaining everything from the way NAFTA worked to the manner in which Zapatista communities divide household labor. Devorah and the rest of the crew appeared to be sleeping soundly beside him in the loft. By then it was daytime and both bright and icy in the barn, but something inside of Nick wouldn't let him sleep—testosterone or giddy excitement. The place reeked of the sleeping people: sweat and unwashed clothes and the yeasty scent of dried beer. It was as if he was on a field trip with a group of the most thrilling weirdos anyone could dream up.

Eighteen hours later they parked the van on a dark dirt road and played follow-the-leader through the woods, with Big Dumpster marching first, leading Nick into a state of near panic. He had a flash of being twelve years old and sitting in the cockpit of a helicopter beside his stepfather, Roger. The old man had urged him, with an unhinged laugh, to take over the cyclic stick. Nick's stomach dropped down to the shrinking toy island of Manhattan below them. He was not ready. "C'mon, kiddo," Roger had said. "You're the son I was always meant to have. You have the spark that made my family great. Be bold, kid. Captain this ship through the air!" Now, as twenty-one-year-old Nick recalled his own twelve-year-old hand shaking as it grabbed the cold, black helicopter lever, the pressure of tears pulsed behind his temples. It was pitiful, how much he had wanted that crass geezer to be proud of him. Since they had met when Nick was eight years old, Roger had kept an acutely focused eye on him, as if watching to see what Nick might accomplish or how he would live up to the man's strange expectations to perform adventurous acts. Thank God Nick was an adult now and didn't need that approval anymore. But as he realized that he hadn't spoken to Roger in months, the pulsing in his temples grew stronger.

At the exact moment that Nick Whitby marched through the woods in Maine, Roger Whitby Jr. lay in his bed in Pasadena, California, nearly as far away from his youngest son as he could be while remaining in the continental United States. In his bedroom, a single nightstand sat on the left side of a four-poster oak bed, the mattress harder than anything made in recent years. A mahogany bureau occupied an entire wall of the room, a piece he'd acquired in Boston at the start of his second marriage, old-fashioned even then, in the early sixties. The brass banker's lamp that he consistently forgot to turn off now illuminated a framed black-and-white photograph of two men in their early twenties, reclining on the bow of a wooden cigarette boat, grinning with the shared hilarity only siblings know. Their blond hair had been whipped in the wind; their ropy muscles protruded from rolled-up sweater sleeves. This photograph of Roger and his brother, Quentin, taken eighteen months before Quentin ended his own life amid the bearings of the Brooklyn Bridge, was the only personal relic apparent in the bedroom. No Dodgers banner nor child's sculpture rested on the bureau top; no local-business-owner award plaque nor John Singer Sargent print adorned the walls. At that moment, in that simple room smelling of dust and stagnant desert air, in that simple oak bed, a hemorrhage occurred in Roger's left cerebrum, and he suffered a stroke. He coughed once, then took his very last breath.

Although Nick had more than half a lifetime of rage built up against the man, and although he would never admit it, he also loved his step-father with the fierceness of a child ravenous for male affection. And Roger, in turn, loved his adopted son, and had outsize hopes for his future, which is perhaps the reason why, with Roger's dying breath, Nick became the only heir to the remains of a once-great American fortune. But perhaps there were other reasons as well. Perhaps Nick became the heir due to the scheming of his mother, who was rumored to have forced an amendment in the will, during Roger's final, unwell months. Or maybe in his old age, Roger harbored a private longing to see a continuation of himself carry on beyond him, a replacement for the youngest biological son, who died as a child, so many years before. Or it could have been Nick himself—the adopted son who looked so much like him—that induced deep guilt in Roger.

But Nick had no way of knowing the answers to these questions, nor the questions themselves. No one had ever informed him the inheritance was coming, and he was entirely unreachable as he stood in line before the biotech construction site. The clouds of his breath billowed out. Big D tapped Kever's shoulder, and Kever took off under the resplendent night sky, running toward the crane and jumping onto it. Once on the machinery, Kever resembled a ferret, steadily and stealthily inching up the long diagonal pipe that held the first extension arm of the machine. Nick followed the man's outline in the dark. Kever jumped up to touch the top arm of the crane; his hands gripped, and his little legs kicked up and looped around the pole. He was a gymnast, an expert. Soon he had shimmied far enough, and pulled himself into the crane's bucket. He let out a brief whistle, which meant that Nick was up.

Nick froze. This had happened to him before, like in the helicopter, when the task before him seemed too gargantuan to complete. At those moments, he'd had the overwhelming impulse to give up. Before swim meets he used to think: *I can haul myself out of the pool and chuck my rubber swim cap in the corner, then forget the whole dumb sport.* And why couldn't he do that now? There was no real reason for him to be here, in the woods, with these strangers. What was this action going to do, really? It was a minute resistance against a complex, multibillion-dollar industry. But they were all counting on him. Yes, he'd just met these eight people, but he'd made a promise to them. These were the people he wanted to be. Also, they were his ride home.

"Go now or get out, kid," Big D growled.

Nick took a deep breath. He was already in Maine. Devorah was probably watching. And, for no good reason, he'd been given too much in the world: white skin, a man's body, Roger's extravagant trips and dinners and the Whitby name and a paid-for college education. He was guilty. Whether he liked it or not, he was complicit in the demonic capitalist system. Now it was his obligation to resist. Nick had never actually walked away from a swim meet. And he wasn't going to walk away from this.

As he took off through the sparse grass, the cold air stung his cheeks. He jumped onto the ladder at the back of the white construction vehicle and climbed onto the flatbed. Soon his hands smacked the frozen metal of the lower bar of the telescoping crane. Two knees up, and he was doing it: climbing toward the bright stars, breathing evenly, focused. Blood pumped through his system, and he was wide-awake, invigorated. He had made the right choice.

His hands gripped the hard plastic of the edge of the crane's bucket, which swayed in the wind. He wasn't so far off the ground, but the wind really lashed around up there, forcing tiny tears to form in the corner of his eyes. Below him, everyone else was already working quickly and efficiently, and in mere moments they were handing him one gasoline-filled water jug after another. Nick dropped them down, one by one, and Kever caught each bottle without making a sound. Six bottles later, Nick stood in the crane's bucket and watched his new friend scurry around the edges of the roof, tying the soaked rope around each bottle's spout. Below Nick, Big D hung from his pelvis climbing harness on the crossbar of the crane, and flashed two thumbs up.

Nick was proud of himself. Finally. He was an individual now, making bold and courageous choices. Soon Kever would climb back into the crane's bucket and throw one strike-anywhere match toward what they'd been calling the "artery": the point where all the jute rope cords came together into one messy knot. Then Kever would shimmy down the crane, and all of them would run back into the woods while the rope caught fire and bottle bombs popped off, one after another. They would be safely in the van by the time the whole damn construction site burned to the ground, costing the developers and their evil biotech investors millions—billions?—of construction and research dollars.

From the crane's bucket, Nick thought about how every second, corporations were buying up America, seizing land and power, controlling minds, and ruining people's lives. They were murdering the environment in the process, but Nick didn't love trees so much as he hated greed. It was the gentrification of his childhood home that destroyed him: the old bodegas in Hell's Kitchen where the aging men had sold him single baseball cards were now being turned into condos. The neighborhood bookstore that he'd been terrified of—the one that sold witchy oils and potions in addition to used paperbacks—closed down, and the whole building became another bank. Nick had been forced to move away from New York when he was twelve, and the one thing that kept him going through those wretched last years of high school—when Roger had really left and his mother was desolate, literally moaning in desperation every night—was knowing he'd return for college. But when he did, the city was a different place. Within those six years, so much of the old New York grit and beauty had been erased. And Nick knew it would keep going. George Bush had been using 9/11 as an excuse to further ruin the world, to tie up the country into a web of evil oil money and disputes with the Middle East, to let every major economic center be overtaken by corporate control. What was Bush's response to the World Trade Center attacks? "Go shopping."

From the bucket of the crane, under the cover of the whipping wind, Nick said, "Fuck shopping."

It was then that he heard the shriek from the roof. Kever ran across Nick's eyeline, screaming. One orange tongue of flame shot up from the guy's right shoulder. He flung himself backward in a circle—a frenzied gerbil, howling—while white smoke and then flames ran down his arm.

"Take off your jacket!" Nick yelled down.

Below him he heard Big D hollering something, but the wind was too loud to make out the words. Kever's cries were curdling now. Then Nick heard a distinct hissing sound: a flame had caught on to one of the ropes.

A crackle and a hiss in the silent Maine night. Kever's jacket was off him: it lay on the roof engulfed in flames, two glowing orange arms without a body in it. But his screams were still there, his Southern twang ringing out into the air.

Nick had no choice. He pulled his feet up to the edge of the bucket, thought about the worried face of his mother, and asked for protection from whatever spirit looked out for him in his religion-free life. As he jumped down onto the roof, off went a soft pop. Then came the next pop, this one deafeningly loud. And a crash. Kever had accidentally set off the whole web of bottle bombs. The water jug in front of Nick broke apart at the middle, the top piece of plastic disappearing. The last thing he saw as his sneakers thudded on the blacktop roof was a yellow-and-red stream moving violently upward out of the bottle. It was a waterfall going the wrong way. Instead of water streaming down toward the earth, fire shot up into the heavens. A fear of the old Whitby curse flashed through his mind: Could he have been acting too much like the rest of his family, striking out too boldly and daring too far, and now the consequences were upon him? It wasn't until that thought that Nick realized he was screwed.

2

Brooke Whitby steadied herself against the side of her father's antique rolltop desk. A light wave of nausea ran through her—more like the floor tilting. She had felt a similar sensation yesterday, when she'd just arrived in California, and had wondered for a moment if it was a minor earthquake. But no, it was definitely nausea. A quiet question about what that might mean filled her head, but she shook it away: at thirty-seven she was too old to have that accidentally happen to her. It was very early in the morning, and she was jet-lagged, disoriented, and grief-stricken. Brooke, alone on the porch office of her father's Pasadena bungalow, was surrounded by a buzzing silence that occurs in the house of a dead person. The rest of the family—her full siblings and half siblings who had come in for the funeral, two of her father's ex-wives—had done a vulture's pass of the house yesterday, swooping and scanning to ensure that Roger Jr. really did not have anything of value lying around. When the other Whitbys found no Chippendale furniture in the living room, no Patek Philippe pocket watches or opal pinky rings in his top drawer, they promptly left, weakly thanking Brooke for all the packing and arranging and donating she was surely going to take care of.

Brooke was not like the rest of her family. She was smaller than the other Whitbys and naturally more responsible; she was earnest, she was giving—it was just her way. Her father had always told her that she was the one he counted on, that only she "could keep all these lunatics in line!"

But she wasn't doing a great job at the moment. Her brother LJ had tromped through the Pasadena house the prior afternoon, sporting his new frosted-tip haircut and never getting off a call on his cell phone. When he was standing by the front door again, he covered up the receiver with one hand and hollered to Brooke, "Mom says make sure to burn any letters from her!" He winked and left.

Brooke's mother was not coming to the funeral. Her mother, Cornelia, or Corney for short, was just like the rest of them: justified in her anger at Brooke's father but also using it as an excuse to be careless. Corney had surprised everyone by her toughness after the divorce, by her independence. But her overt self-respect also pushed her away from the whole Whitby family, including her children. And now she couldn't be bothered to leave Connecticut, where she lived with her elderly, money-managing, golf-obsessed boyfriend.

Brooke had always considered her own nuclear family to be Roger's real one. Her father had been married four times, and Brooke's mother was the second marriage. When Brooke was a child, her parents would discuss Roger's first family as an understandable mistake. He had married Margaret Vanderbilt when he was very young, at the same time as he flunked out of his senior year at Harvard. The couple then moved back to the upper-crust New York society from which they both hailed and quickly produced three towheaded children. Brooke had met poor Margaret a few times—she was silent and sullen, with a short blond ponytail poking over a pink-and-black skirt suit. It was as if she'd been pulled from central casting: someone couldn't have picked her out of a lineup in front of Brooks Brothers on Madison Avenue.

Roger married a Vanderbilt because it was expected of him. The Whitby family had made its way to the new world on the *Mayflower*, and then built their dynasty in shipping and importing. Hildebrand Whitby, Roger's grandfather and Brooke's great-grandfather, the industrious son of a family who still spoke Dutch at home, began a business at the age of sixteen, shuttling people across New York Harbor in a rowboat. Soon the rowboat business became a steamship enterprise, and by the time Hildebrand was thirty-one, he also owned several major railroad companies in the country. The family's later generations were also hailed for their ruggedness and cunning: when they got knocked down, they got up and tried another angle. Great American fortitude. Ethan Whitby, Hildebrand's youngest son, had been the biggest railroad magnate, but it was Brooke's grandfather, the oldest son, Roger Whitby Sr., who became a manager of the shipping and boating side, and had funneled his shipping money into real estate, thus crowning the Whitbys with the moniker "the landlords of New York." Indeed, the names of New York City landmarks—the Whitby Highway on the west side and Whitby Place downtown, the Whitby-Grand Hotel—were enduring reminders of this illustrious history. The original patriarch, Hildebrand, was more than a hero to the later generations of Whitbys: he was a demigod. Roger himself liked to repeat the phrase to his children, with wistful reverence, "It all started with a rowboat." But as each generation of children moved farther away from that demigod, they became more beleaguered by the expectations their last name carried. And marrying further into his social milieu had made Brooke's father, who was still a very young man at the time, feel stifled, anxious, and depressed.

After multiple failed attempts to work on Wall Street (whether it was two weeks or two months, he'd simply stop showing up to whatever office had hired him based on his last name), Roger took a trip to Boston to investigate a real estate venture, where he met the brash, dark-haired Cornelia Wesner. Cornelia was the antithesis of Roger's first wife: she was an effusive twenty-two-year-old who dreamed of being an actress. Whenever she walked into a room it began to glow, from her own freckles to the reddening in men's cheeks. Thus, the light in Roger's world started to shine once again. When Brooke was a child, her father proclaimed that her mother had saved him. Although the Wesners were in fact a staple of New England high society, by marrying Corney and moving to Boston, Roger was, in his own way, taking a bold stand against Whitby traditions. Brooke had always been convinced that if the tragedies hadn't happened, or if her father had simply possessed a heartier constitution and a more stable soul, then her parents' marriage would have been Roger's last.

His third wife, the woman he left Brooke's mother for, was the college roommate of Brooke's older sister Kiki. The marriage to Elizabeth Saltman was an impulsive reaction to Roger's personal upheaval, which was of course enhanced by the surprise pregnancy. But even though Elizabeth Saltman was more than three decades younger than Roger, in marrying her he was also returning to his roots. Although brown-haired and consistently shabby, Elizabeth was a sullen, New York–bred, Waspish preppy, who barely spoke. Her demeanor was more unsettling than that of Roger's first wife though; too pale and too thin, she consistently gave off an air of the disturbed.

Roger vacillated between silent women and boisterous ones; after a marriage to one kind, he'd swing to the other. The final wife was another act of resistance. Susan Scribner was a teacher from the Midwest or California or somewhere else foreign to East Coasters, and Brooke had to admit she was a real departure. Susan already had a child out of wedlock, and rumor said she had alcohol problems just like Roger. This final marriage was due to Roger's old age. It wasn't dementia exactly, but rather weariness that had allowed it to happen. All Whitbys had to put up certain defenses around themselves, to ensure that they were not taken advantage of by this exact type of wheedling personality. And Roger had simply let his guard down.

The saga made Brooke's heart ache still. She could see that those final two marriages were a reaction to the unfairness of the world. If circumstances had been different, Brooke's mother would be beside her right then, sorting through Roger's belongings. At one point, her parents had loved each other deeply. This was something Brooke was sure of. It wasn't just that they had held hands underneath the dinner table while jabbering on to all the kids, or that each would gaze with wonder at the other, at home or in public, as if they couldn't quite believe the perfect and pleasing configuration of the person in front of them. It wasn't just that her parents consistently touched each other's shoulders and elbows and thighs, but rather it was clear that each represented something grander to the other person. Brooke knew that jumping back and forth on invisible ions between her parents was the sincere belief that the other represented freedom. Each believed that with the other, he or she had become un-shackled from the standards and expectations placed upon them: Roger was absolved of his Whitby Wall Street duties, and Corney of her staunch Lutheran past. Together, they ventured away from the confines of their youths. It felt joyful, near miraculous, and was, in its own way, rebellious.

Brooke sighed and let her eyes scan the floor of the office, where the shiny oak planks were covered with file boxes. Roger Whitby Jr. had been dead for four days: he simply didn't exist anymore. How was that possible? She put a hand on her hot forehead. It had been just over a year since she'd seen her father. The previous February he'd sat on that very porch in his wheelchair, unspeaking but smiling. It was clear to her that it wouldn't be long before he passed; a nurse knows these things. But expecting some-thing and living through it are two entirely separate challenges.

A wave of queasiness passed from Brooke's throat to her chest again, and then her stomach churned back up to her pounding head. A smell that only emanated from homes in California overwhelmed her: burnt grass, dry air, ghosts of desert animals trapped in walls that should never have been built in this waterless, inhospitable land. She decided to lie down on the floor. She wanted to go home; she wanted to be in Boston, in her own old bed. And more than anything, she wanted to be talking to her ex-girlfriend, Allie.

The previous night, as she sat poolside with her chain-smoking brother at the Beverly Hills Hotel—the Whitbys had "their" hotel in every city that they went to, and someone long ago had chosen this particular one—she had looked around the dusky scenery and had the uncanny feeling that none of what was happening was real.

"Can you believe he's gone, LJ? I can't. It's like my body won't let me believe it."

The charcoal peaks of the Santa Monica Mountains floated above them, sprinkled with lights gleaming from mansion windows. Hot wind blew in from the east. Mexican fan palm trees surrounded the pool, their mile-high fronds outlined in navy. It was a dream landscape; surely they'd soon wake up to the sounds of traffic on the cobblestone streets where they grew up.

"Yes, I can believe it," LJ muttered while he lit another cigarette. The tip of it glinted along with the mansion lights, one more dancing gem in the dark. He stared at the surface of the swimming pool in front of them and chuckled softly. "Remember when he threw me into the water at that hotel on the Cape?"

Brooke laughed too, but only a little. Although the story had taken place before she was born, she knew it well: it was a quintessential Roger tale. Their parents had gone to stay at the Chatham Bars Inn near Hyannis one summer when LJ was four and Kiki seven, and Brooke just a three-month-old cluster inside Corney's belly. LJ had been crying and whining for the whole three-hour car trip, and while the family was heading to their suite—far past dinnertime and no one had eaten—LJ saw the kidney-shaped pool and began to shout, "I want to go swimming! Take me swimming!"

By that age LJ had been in multiple pools, lakes, and two different oceans, but he could not exactly swim. He could, though, be dragged around by his mother with inflated tubes on his arms while he exclaimed, "I'm an expert!"

"How much do you really want to go in the water?" Roger asked in his booming voice. He was so full of energy then, his large teeth bared in a constant smile, always cracking jokes. He was almost embodying the jolly and thick-skinned persona he had always aspired to.

"Realllly," LJ whined. And then, faster than Brooke's mother could register the actions, Roger picked up his son and threw him, clothes and all, into the pool. He let the kid sputter around for a long minute, his wife shrieking, her hands flailing in the humid air. Then Roger jumped into the pool himself, fully clothed. He lifted the boy out of the water and into the air, pumping the kid up and down over his head, as if he were a prize. Roger howled with laughter. He was proud of himself. He was ensuring that all his boy children would be resilient, always alert.

The handful of other guests milling on the deck had frozen in their tracks, astounded. "Never underestimate the element of surprise!" Roger announced to the onlookers. For a moment little LJ was stunned, quiet in his father's grip. But as soon as he saw his mother by the side of the pool, red-faced and horrified, he began to let out deep, gulping wails.

"No!" Roger said, placing his son on the concrete edge. "Stop crying, kid! I did that for you. I'm teaching you to be ready for anything—to be a man! This is a lesson to learn right now, Lathrop James: greatness cannot be achieved if you let your guard down. Remember the rowboat."

"I didn't want a rowboat," LJ wheezed, as his mother picked him up and swaddled him in her arms.

"What the hell is wrong with you?" Corney roared at her husband. "Are you mentally deranged?"

Now the child was heaving so hard he was sputtering, gasping for breath. Roger hung his head, receiving his wife's scolding with perhaps too much ease. "He's got to learn that he'll get what he asks for. He's my son, Cornelia. He's always going to get what he asks for."

In Corney's version of the story, LJ continued to sob for more than three hours and was finally calmed down with two giant pieces of chocolate cake from room service. But Roger was only present for the first fifteen minutes of his son's crying; after that he was stationed at the hotel bar, downing one Maker's Mark after another.

Now, from the distance of nearly four decades, on the floor of a bungalow on a well-appointed street in Southern California, it was hard for Brooke not to love that awful story, because it was so particularly Roger. Her father was always brashly himself: in his impulsivity, in his excitement, in his naive and dreamy intentions. He was always pushing. His motto, often stated in front of his children, was "Never let them see you sweat." Maybe it was because he got bored so easily, because he couldn't stand repetition, but he encouraged his children to never shy away from a challenge. Yet Brooke knew that these appeals came from his own vulnerable axis and a desire for his children to live up to the family name and not to be as easily broken as he could be. The other kids seemed to be following through on Roger's advice to make bold and illogical choices, but that had never been in Brooke's nature. In fact, she'd been consistently working toward the opposite for years now; she longed for staidness, for consistency. Perhaps that was why she was the one Whitby who had continued to show up for the man who had taught them not to.

What would her life look like now, if her parents had stayed together? There would have been no Allie. Brooke would have been more outgoing in high school and have gone to a better college, where she would have met a man with a steady, if prosaic, smile. They would have a summer home already, and she'd spend her days involved in her children's private elementary school. She would be living the life of the other people she grew up with, the ones who never encountered the disruption that made Brooke who she was. She wouldn't have spent so much time alone, grappling with her own skills and feelings and what to make of both, and she wouldn't have—under any circumstances—become a nurse. In many ways, Brooke was more proud of herself now than she would have ever been if her parents had stayed together. She was more valuable to the world, more unique, than she would have turned out otherwise. But she couldn't help but believe that if Roger and Corney had managed to stay married, although each stage of her life would have been unimaginatively prescribed, she would have been doing the *right* things, as opposed to the life she was living now.

Her cell phone began to buzz from its perch on a side table across the porch. The green-marbled file boxes were all around her, their letters and papers spilling out. Most of the yellowing paper had typewriter print on it, containing ancient, banal invitations to lunch dates between her father and her grandfather, or notes to a secretary about phone calls to make. But already she'd found some handwritten ones, including a Victorianesque love note between her father and his first wife, scrawled in looping script. At that moment, lying on her back with the phone ringing across the room, she held in her hand a letter from her grandmother Whitby, which urged her father to think of the family's reputation and stave off divorcing Brooke's own mother. *My dear boy, I understand your sorrows, and I side with you at every turn. But these problems you're experiencing in married life are precisely problems of married life itself and shall not amend themselves with a different spousal candidate. Do reconsider.* The words sped something up within Brooke's chest. They touched her, but in the form of fascination rather than sadness. Grandmother Whitby had known exactly what was going on.

Whoever was calling was doing so for a second time. Brooke hauled herself up. The phone's front screen revealed Armond's number. Her dear, old Armond. He was the family lawyer, a paid employee of the greater brood, but he and Brooke had formed a special bond years before, after her father left and everything she had grown up with was crumbling around her. She feared that this lawyer cared more about her than any of her aunts or uncles.

"Mr. Armond!" she exclaimed into the receiver. "Thank you for calling."

"Brooke, dearest." He paused. "Out in Los Angeles?"

"Indeed. I'm cleaning out my father's Pasadena place. You won't be surprised, but I am the only one here actually looking through his possessions and trying to figure out what to do with them." She sighed. When she complained to LJ or her sister, Kiki, or even to her mother or half siblings, when she reminded them that it was only she who took on the tedious familial duties, they'd all reply with nasal chuckles. *So don't do it, Birdie,* they'd snicker, using her childhood nickname. *You take this work on yourself. No one's forcing you to make yourself miserable. Just don't do it!* But if she wasn't there, categorizing the old letters into small gift piles, no one else would be. The family's little remaining history would be lost.

"Brooke, I've called you first among the children," Armond said in his overarticulated, obsolete transatlantic accent. He'd remained so much himself, all these years. "We have a matter of your father's estate to discuss, and I need you to be sitting down to hear this."

Brooke had already repositioned herself on her back on the oak floorboards. "Go on, Mr. Armond, I'm fine."

She was aware, as were the rest of her siblings, both full and half, that she would inherit little to no money. No one had expectations. It was well-known that due to risky business choices and bad real estate investments and, moreover, all the divorces, her father had blown through nearly all his inheritance from the Whitby fortune. (That was how the family had always referred to it: "the fortune," or "Grandfather's fortune." Perhaps it was a gauche name, but no one seemed to be aware of an actual numerical value attached to the money that her grandfather had amassed. And, of course, none of them would dream of uttering the word *fortune* to non-Whitby ears. Not even to Armond.) Brooke questioned: "Is something unexpected happening?"

"It's the houses, my dear."

"What?"

"The houses. They were all in Roger's name, and there is an amendment of the rewritten will that bequeaths all the assets—all of the money, and the property that outweighs the monetary assets—to one child alone. It's my duty to relay this news." Armond cleared his throat, as if to punctuate the importance of what he was saying. "It cuts everyone else out."

Brooke sat up. "What? All the houses? My house too?" The nausea had ceased rolling through her, but now there was pressure on her chest. Her breath caught.

Armond said nothing.

She knew, of course, that her father still technically owned the house on Beacon Hill, the same house he hadn't lived in for more than twenty years. But the thought of Roger repossessing it now, of him taking it back from beyond the grave, was preposterous. The possibility had not even occurred to her. Her voice cracked out high. She knew she sounded spoiled, but she couldn't help herself. "He gave my house away?"

"I'm sorry to bear this news. The funeral is tomorrow, yes? When do you return to Boston? Perhaps this is a subject easier discussed in person. I can show the documents to you—"

"Who did he leave them all to? Andrew? Andrew has more money than Midas. He wouldn't need this gift in a million years." Brooke was the nurse; Brooke was an underpaid and overworked nurse who dedicated her daily life to quieting the suffering of others. If anyone deserved this—

"No, no. It wasn't Andrew. He's left everything to the final child."

"He left my house to Shelley?" Her voice was loud now, amplified in the empty house. Shelley, her poor, misguided half sister, the youngest one of the bunch. She was a distracted hippie, but moreover, a child. Yet Brooke had always had a tenderness for her. All those summers on the Vineyard together. Although they were fourteen years apart, bred in different cities by different mothers, they were undeniably sisters. Brooke took a deep breath and let her heart rate slow: Shelley would let her keep her house.

"Pardon me, dear, it is not Michelle Whitby I'm referring to. The will marks Roger Jr.'s very youngest child as the recipient. Susan Scribner's son, Nick."

Brooke flinched. She had forgotten all about that kid. Nick was the child her father had adopted in his fourth marriage, in his old age, when his impetuousness seemed to multiply like cancer cells. At seventy-two years old, he'd discarded another woman and child, sending the members of his first three families into a state of confusion yet again, contributing to their acute need for therapy, which of course none of them would ever get.

"He's left everything to that accidental child?" Brooke was shocked; she no longer cared how her voice sounded. She had met Nick only a few times. He was tense and grim, angry even, with his knobby shoulders hunched around his ears. He hadn't even grown up with Roger—he had to have been at least ten when he was adopted. And Brooke had gotten the distinct impression that the boy hated her father deeply. "He's just a kid. Is it legal for him to take possession of a property?"

"He'll be twenty-two in December of this year," Armond said. "The papers state that in the event of his father's death, the money and the houses—Boston, New York, and California—shall be delivered to him in full. There's a waiting period, of course. But after being held in escrow for one hundred and fifty days, the entire inheritance will become Nick Whitby's legal property."

"What?" Brooke was yelling. She stood up quickly, her nausea replaced with rage. How could her father have done this? She was the only one who defended him for years, after all the disastrous decisions he'd made in the aftermath of their family's greatest tragedy. Brooke had been Roger's steady companion, and as far as she knew the only offspring of his four families who carried a shred of sympathy for him and the reasons why he had abandoned them all. But now he was doing it again: he was taking away her security, pulling her home out from under her feet.

Her mind was spinning. "But why would he do this?"

Armond didn't say a word.

"There was money too?"

"Hmm," Armond murmured. "We can discuss that in person, dear. Now I'm going to say something to you, and only you, Brooke. . . . Do not take this as coarseness, but there is a view in which Roger's death was timely, concerning the matter of these properties. I say this in your confidence, as you are aware I have, for years, had fealty to your well-being. . . ." Armond paused; that kind of admission must have been hard for a bound-up man like him. "The waiting period for the execution of this will ends by September. You have more than four months now, indeed a whole summer, to convince your half brother to gift these houses to the current residents. Is there any possibility of accomplishing that proposal?"

"Is he my half brother? I wouldn't know him if I passed by him on the street."

Her life had been so calm, so ordered in the past five, even ten, years. Her work was dramatic, so she kept everything else simple. She rented out the top floors of her childhood home on Joy Street and set up an apartment for herself on just the first; she had become a practicing RN, despite the disdain for her middle-class profession from both her family and everyone else she'd grown up around. She liked to wake up with the sun and walk her goldendoodle, Phoebe, down to the Common, then spend her day at Mass General taking vitals and inserting chemo ports in the chests of the very brave and very sick. She held her patients' cooled hands when their breath began to shallow, and allowed their spouses to cling to her after they'd received the news that the tumors had metastasized. It was quietly thrilling to Brooke to be good at her job, then be able to walk home to Beacon Hill utterly worn-out, and go to sleep satisfied. Within her routine she'd been able to protect herself, cocoon herself against the turmoil that her family caused.

It had taken her years, an embarrassingly long number of years, to crawl out from under the tragedies and disappointments of her childhood. But she'd done it. And at thirty-seven, she was fine. Everything had been perfectly fine, more or less, just a week beforehand. Now, still holding the cell phone, she clamped her eyes shut and pictured Allie. Allie's small, strong limbs; her black bushy hair that smelled of coconut. If Allie were there, holding Brooke against her petite, rock-climber frame while assuring Brooke that everything would be fine, life would stay tied to the ground. Then she remembered Marc: it was he and his tanned, masculine arms she was supposed to picture now, not Allie.

Her mother used to say it often during the bad years: the Whitbys were cursed. And Corney wasn't the only one who thought the shipping magnates dragged devastation around in their wake. All these disasters were colliding in Brooke's life. It was as if she were twelve years old again, when her little brother, Peter, died and her father left, and everything stable was snatched away rapid-fire, then disappeared. For years, she'd carried the fear that her life would one day unravel again, just as suddenly as it had the first time.

On the porch in Pasadena she tried to steady herself with a deep breath. This cluster of events couldn't turn out as poorly as they had when she was a child; she didn't have enough years left to recover again.

"I don't even know this Nick kid, Armond," she said into the phone.

"Well, I suggest you get to know him, Birdie."

3

Mrs. Susan Scribner Whitby winced as she glanced in her rearview mirror. The pace at which the sun was setting was painfully slow; why wouldn't it just get dark already? She let out another gulping sob and fixed her eyes back on the road in front of her. Her rented red Corolla sped up Route 9 to Poughkeepsie, going twenty miles over the speed limit. She was panicked. Her flight back to LAX was in less than twenty-four hours, and if she missed it, then she would miss her ex-husband's funeral, the event she was planning for a man whom she had seen only once in the past several years. Who was she crying for? Roger? She kept picturing the gorgeous face of her son, Nick, her little boy. When he was a toddler she couldn't walk one city block or cross through one aisle in the grocery store without someone stopping her to comment on his beauty. And Nick's good looks had only increased with age; he'd grown into his colt-like limbs, and his shoulders had broadened to those of an athlete. A stunning man.

Now Roger, to whom she'd devoted so many tears already, was dead and gone. She had known this day was approaching, yet it still knocked her down. Susan whisked the tears from either side of her face, then wiped a sweaty hand on her thick orange hair.

This inheritance was a second chance for her baby. It was, perhaps, the greatest thing that Roger had done: identifying that Nick was gifted and giving him an opportunity to truly fulfill his destiny. And it had barely taken any convincing from her. Yes, she and Nick had gotten into a vicious argument two months before. She would have never imagined she was capable of saying the things she'd said to him. While sitting in an Italian bistro near Washington Square, he had announced that he was considering dropping out of college—said he didn't want his final semester's tuition to contribute to *warmongers*, or some other insane blather. How dare he. After everything she'd done for him, all she had sacrificed. She had told him that he was *spoiled rotten*, which had prompted him to call her a "self-absorbed psychopath." As he'd stomped out of the restaurant—Susan having already paid for his dinner—he yelled over his shoulder, "Controlling bitch!" Now, as Susan played the scene back in her mind, more tears flowed steadily down her cheeks. She really should not be driving.

Nick was her angel, her savior, the best thing that had ever happened to her. When he was a baby it was just the two of them, in her tiny studio in Hell's Kitchen. She ached now for the warm, pulsing creature he had been. A scent akin to fresh baked bread rose off his perfectly smooth baby skin; she was able to put all of her body around all of his, protecting him from everything that could ever attempt to harm him. What year had he grown too large for her to surround him? Alone in the car now, she cried out the words, *"My baby!"*

Two days prior, Susan Scribner Whitby had gotten on a plane in California and come to New York. Nick had turned off his cell phone, and his roommates claimed they hadn't seen him in days. Although Nick's name was securely inked into Roger's will—she had gotten the changes in writing, of course—Susan knew that the Whitbys acted fast and fraudulently when money was concerned. She needed to get Nick to a lawyer as soon as possible and have his signature down on paper too. Plus she had a sinking feeling, call it a mother's intuition, that her son was getting into trouble. He was so passionate and so utterly brilliant in every endeavor he took on, but his problem was one of judgment. His decision-making capabilities had always wavered, and these days they were swerving wildly off any reasonable track. He was too emotional, with a temper. She'd pinned down all his NYU friends she'd been aware of, but had been unable to find him anywhere. Now she was on her way to Demming College to see if one of her recently deceased husband's daughters—Shelley, the loose one, who was probably some kind of addict by now—had any idea where her son could be. The two kids had developed a friendship for a short time period, a teenage attachment that Susan had never approved of. But Shelley was Susan's last recourse. Though who knew. Maybe the girl had dropped out. It was clear that the only reason the snide brat was even at Demming, after she'd spent a post–high school year of sitting idly in the house that still belonged to Roger, was that the college felt obligated to take on a legacy student. After all, the Whitby Student Center and the Whitby Auditorium had not been cheap endeavors.

The printed map on Susan's passenger's seat had directions to a dormitory called Senior House. She didn't have the slightest clue if that was where Shelley lived, but she should be a senior, and Susan didn't know where else to look. She stopped the Corolla in front of the redbrick building, No Parking sign be damned. Then she hustled herself out of the car, leaving behind the teal jacket of her pantsuit set.

On the second floor, a tall girl traipsed over the linoleum tiles wearing an oversize bathrobe, with her hair twisted into a towel turban.

"Hello!" Susan called. The girl didn't seem to notice her waving, so Susan grabbed at a shoulder of the robe. She was met by a high-pitched shriek.

"Listen." Susan did not have time for manners. She shook the girl a little. "Do you know Shelley Whitby? I need to find her immediately."

The girl's mouth dropped open, her hip cocked to the side, and she said nothing. Susan crossed her arms. Nick needed her. So what if she ended up missing the funeral. She would continue to wait for hours if she had to. That was a mother's job.

4

The Sunday after his death, Roger's youngest daughter—Michelle Whitby, or Shelley—was in Poughkeepsie Center working the end of a brunch shift. Outside, the air carried a weighty spring chill, but overnight the earth had popped bright green. Sun streamed through tree branches, marbling the grass and the sidewalks in yellow brilliance. Shelley looked out the window as she leaned on the Formica countertop of the Magic Mule Deli, famous for its pea soup and not actually a deli. The restaurant was a diner that strove toward the upscale, and the aging woman who was currently complaining to Shelley's boss was representative of the typical clientele: a midsixties salt-and-pepper-topped, tote-bag-bearing, flamingo-like frump. Shelley had plain forgot to put in the order of this woman and her shorter, plumper brunch-mate. The women were there for an hour without food, and then when it finally went in, the order got confused: one got bacon instead of sausage, the other's eggs scrambled instead of over easy.

The dissatisfied customer crouched over the old-fashioned cash register where Matt the manager stood. The woman pointed at Shelley. "She was the worst waitress I have ever seen, and on top of that, it is repulsive to not make a server wear a brassiere. Indecent! Visible nipple. Enough to put anyone off their eggs."

Shelley smirked and glanced up at the Elvis clock that hung on the wall. Elvis in his blue dinner jacket ticked his hips from side to side, checking off the seconds. It was one in the afternoon and Shelley had been at work since eight, on a little over four hours of sleep. She'd been light-headed all morning, which was something she truly enjoyed about waitressing—she could feel suspended in time. Her overcaffeinated body moved mechanically: pouring coffee, smiling at customers, carrying heavy oval plates piled with shaved potatoes and omelet creations. Her unwashed hair hung in a messy ponytail with small loops breaking out. In her V-neck T-shirt one could see, as she leaned on her forearms, the plump curves of skin that formed the inner side of each breast. It was then, when she was leaning over, that her cell phone began to buzz and ring from inside the half apron tied around her waist.

Matt looked at her with a softness he'd clearly come to feel for her in the two months she'd been his employee. But his look also said: *I don't blame you, but if you apologize to this pain-in-the-rear, we can all get on with our day.* Shelley rolled her eyes.

"Do not even tell me she is answering a phone call!" The frump crossed her arms.

Shelley flipped open her black Motorola. "Hello?"

"This is a call for Shelley Whitby," said an uptight, middle-aged man's voice.

"You're in luck."

"Yes, hello. It's Steven Armond." There was a long pause. "The lawyer."

"Oh—hello." It was a 617 number—Boston—so she should have guessed. She knew Armond. He came to Whitby family events, standing along the walls of the Christmas parties and at the farthest picnic tables at the clam bakes, silently. It was as if being employed by the family meant he was de facto related to them as well. But he might as well have been; Shelley was fairly sure his father had also been the Whitbys' lawyer.

"Listen, Shelley. This dispute over the estate and your father is getting heated."

"What?"

Matt's hands were on the counter in front of her now, and he mouthed the words: *Off. The. Phone.*

Matt was a rail-thin hippie in his early forties who enjoyed a cold Bud Light and seemed to love his two greyhound dogs just as much as he loved his own long ponytail. He was particular in his way, but at the core of it just like everyone else: after her first week of working there, he caught Shelley in the chilled air of the walk-in, cleared his throat, and said, "I've been meaning to ask. Are you *related*?"

The lawyer continued, "I know it's only been a handful of days since he passed, but this is the kind of thing that has to be picked up on right away."

"What are you talking about?" Shelley asked. "Passed what?"

The lawyer was silent then, but this was typical for him. Her mother once claimed Armond spoke so slowly in order to increase his billable hours. Shelley remembered now when she had heard this man speak before. Her father, Roger, had drunk too much at the end of a summer reunion dinner up at the Idlehour house, and he stood in the middle of the front lawn, unzipped his fly, and with a sheepish smile began to piss on the grass in front of everyone. It was the lawyer who had hollered, "No, Roger!" before speeding over and pulling him by the shoulders into the darkness of the south driveway.

"Shelley, when was the last time you spoke with your mother?" Armond asked.

It had been more than a month—perhaps six weeks—since the two had spoken. Shelley didn't exactly know where her mother was, although she had her private suspicions. The breakdown in communication was part of the reason that she was, at the moment, standing in the Magic Mule Deli. Shelley was still a senior at Demming College, slated to graduate in less than a month if she could figure out a way to make up five incomplete grades. Her mother had been supporting her throughout college by sending her substantial checks every three weeks. But the checks stopped coming regularly toward the end of that fall, and in February, after several unanswered phone calls, Shelley had yet to receive a check at all for the spring semester. She began to have trouble buying sweaters and notebooks and big Styrofoam cups of beer. Soon enough she couldn't even buy herself lunch, so she walked down Garden Street and into the Magic Mule and asked if they were hiring.

"I talked to her last week," Shelley lied to the lawyer. "I think she was on the Vineyard."

"Dear." The man sighed, but it was clearly a pitying sigh, directed toward himself. "Shelley, I'm sorry." A great pause. "Your father died of a stroke last Sunday."

The whir and hum of diner conversation muted in her ears. *No* was her first thought. She didn't believe it. The lawyer was misinformed. Her father was going to live until he was nearly one hundred, just as his father had. She must have displayed some sort of physical reaction, because in the diner the flamingo woman stopped her warble and lowered her pointer finger. Matt dropped the hands he'd been waving in front of Shelley's face.

She said nothing at all, so it would have been hard for the lawyer, who stood above his desk in his leather-swathed office in Boston's Back Bay, to read the moment. "Are you there?" Armond asked. "Did you hear what I said?"

Something in Shelley's chest began to quiver, threatening to split open. Instantly she missed her father in a physical way. He was so rarely there when she was small that his importance became amplified, at all times projected over her and her mother and her grandmother. When she did see him, it felt as if he were a giant. She wanted his body next to hers at that very moment, towering over her as he had when she was a child. She wanted him to be looking at her, calling her Secret Spell Shell.

Shelley waited. "What?"

"He was in his bed in Pasadena, and his nurse was in the other room. It was a quick affair."

She thought to herself: *This doesn't just happen without any warning.* When her grandmother Biddy had died a handful of years earlier, Shelley had witnessed her slow decline. But this news of her father came out of nowhere. She knew then that in the depths of her mind, she had never stopped believing that Roger would one day come home to her and her mother. A sense of injustice began to fill her with anger. She had so much left to deal with, concerning him. She needed more time. It wasn't fair that he could just be gone, like that, and never return. It simply wasn't fair.

An image of Roger's hand popped into Shelley's mind. When she was small she used to pick his bulbous fingers off the dining table, run her own hands over the edges of his square fingernails, then unfold these fingers into a flat plane and use them as a pillow. She would lay her head in her father's hand whenever she pleased, and it was as if he didn't even notice. He wouldn't so much as look up from his newspaper or ongoing conversation. Now, in the diner, Shelley touched her cheek to confirm she wasn't crying. No tears. She vibrated slightly though, in the region of her lower ribs.

Her father, Roger Whitby Jr., had passed eighty the year before. And his Parkinson's had gotten progressively worse, which was something Shelley had been told but hadn't witnessed, as she hadn't seen him in more than two years. The fact that she had never imagined him dying before was a testament to how young Shelley still was at twenty-two. But it was also a testament to her penchant for dismissing subjects that caused her anguish. This was her personal golden rule: if one stopped oneself from worrying about the effects of one's actions, then those actions never mattered. When all her schoolmates at Spence were concerned with getting As and Bs, Shelley smirked, aware that she was in on a secret that distinguished herself from her peers. When she received a D on a math test, she closed her eyes and imagined a large cardboard box with tissue-paper stuffing. She mentally placed the test in the box, crunched down the paper and folded over the sides, then pictured kicking it away. That was the end of the stress about the math test. Now she tried to see the disembodied image of her father's hand and place it into one of her old boxes.

She kept the black flip phone pressed between her collarbone and cheek as her boss and the woman stared at her. "Is that it?" Shelley asked the lawyer. The vibrating had risen through her torso and her voice had joined in on the matter.

"No!" Armond nearly hollered. "The reason I've called is that it seems Roger Jr. had created a trust for his children." Another pause. "But, Shelley, last year he signed the trust over to one beneficiary. He's left every penny to your brother. There were more pennies than we thought, and this child is going to have all of them. Every penny, every acre, and every house—including your mother's house." The man pronounced *pennies* in a Brahmin accent that was seldom still heard in this world: *pahn-es.*

Shelley's oldest half brother, Andrew, was basically an old man himself by now. He lived in Connecticut and took the train into the city every day to work on Wall Street. He had a herd of children, all of whom were much older than Shelley. Andrew was the firstborn son, the child whom the money would not make a lick of a difference to. Of course it was all left to him.

"I'll have my mother call Andrew," Shelley said, ready to hang up. Her pulse had begun to speed. A darkness—or a confusion, really—was falling over her. If her father was dead, everything in her life could change.

"No!" Such emotion from this dry cracker of a man. "It's not Andrew. It's the final child, Nick. Susan Scribner's son. He's going to inherit everything after the mandated grace period, at the end of the summer. And, Shelley, I can't get in touch with him. His own mother claims she can't find him."

"Nick?" She almost said, *My Nick?*

He was, of course, not hers. Nick was Shelley's younger stepbrother— no, half brother, not by blood but by adoption—and they hadn't even known each other until their early teenage years. But she'd come to think of herself and Nick as being on the same team. All of their other half siblings were over a decade older than them, from a different generation. She and Nick were not only the youngest but also the two kids from her father's haphazard, slapdash families. Nick always giggled when she said that; he preferred the term *avant-garde families.* They were compatriots in their circumstantial weirdness, and for that she loved him. She imagined Nick's broad face and unruly hair, then remembered the screaming fight they'd had when she last saw him, after she had bought him a Starbucks coffee and he poured it out on the sidewalk in a political stand against something she wasn't quite sure of.

Shelley hung up with Armond and found herself leaning on the Magic Mule's counter, feeling unhinged. Her father loved Nick more—he always had. Her constant fear, festering since her father had left when she was in the eighth grade, had been confirmed: Roger never cared enough to even notice her. She was shaking. It wasn't sadness she was experiencing but anger. It flashed in her stomach, then through her chest. It was finally confirmed: she had been a mistake, and her father had never wanted her. *Unwanted, mistake, nuisance.* Then without any effort, one of her mental boxes popped into her mind, and she shoved all those thoughts into it as fast as possible. There they would stay. Plus, she wasn't sure she'd been told all the facts. It was all invisible: first Roger's California life, and then his death.

If it was true though, if Shelley's father was dead and no longer existed in the world, she wasn't just unhinged; she was free. She was a cog that had made it out of the Whitby machinery. Her breath came in bursts, as if she was at the top of a roller coaster about to ride into a great plunge. A sharp cackle came out of her.

"Everything cool?" Matt the manager asked.

She tried to breathe in through her nose.

The flamingo frump had walked away and was muttering to her squat pal by the restaurant door. Matt came around the counter and sidled up behind Shelley, so that his pelvis pressed lightly into her buttocks. Once, as they both smoked by the dumpster, he had acted like so many others in her life and mumbled that Shelley was beautiful. She'd pretended not to hear him. Now he put both hands above her wide hipbones, thumbs falling into her steeped-in waist. "Hey," he said softly, by the side of her neck. "Everything okay, Shells?"

"Nope." She shook her head forcefully. It was unclear if the *nope* was an answer to Matt's question or just a general disagreement with everything happening at that moment. "Nope. I'm done with this job." She continued to shake her head, and then, giving the old bird by the door a slant-eyed stare, took two large steps away from Matt. "None of you people know who I am. And, what you don't know is that I . . ." These outbursts didn't happen all the time, but she certainly wasn't surprising herself at that moment. She reminded herself: consequences do not exist if you do not let them. She finished, "I do not deserve to be here!"

She pulled the string from the apron around her waist, balled it up in her hands, and threw it. The apron flew over the countertop, hitting the giant brushed aluminum tank of the coffee station. Two Bic pens soared out in opposite directions; some change clanked against the floor. "I quit," she announced. "I'm going home."

Shelley stomped out of the glass door of the restaurant and up Garden Street, back to Lathrop House. In her dorm room she pulled a giant suitcase from the back of her closet. She had thought about leaving Demming before. She'd barely been going to class since she began working at the Magic Mule. No one actually needed a college degree. A diploma was a meaningless paper symbol; she pitied her friends who didn't understand that fact. There had been thirty-one dollars of tips in her apron pockets, money that she could have certainly used, but she decided to preserve her dignity and not go back for it. She told herself she wasn't going to graduate anyway, with all those incomplete classes. There was nothing left for her there. In fact, she'd almost left school the previous week, when she had walked into her suitemate Aleisha's bedroom and saw Ollie, the boy she'd been sleeping with for nearly a year, shirtless in the other girl's bed. Shelley hadn't spoken to either of them since that afternoon, despite several phone calls pleading to let them "explain." It was not her father's death or her future career prospects as a college dropout, but rather Ollie that she focused on—his pale sunken chest with scraggly red hairs at the center of it—as she picked up heaps of unfolded clothes from her drawers and dropped them into the suitcase.

She did not think of her father at all until she was in a taxi on the way to the Metro-North station. The last time she'd seen him was two years before, in California. That was spring break of her sophomore year, and she'd been staying at the childhood home of the same suitemate, Aleisha. As a city kid, she'd never learned to drive, so she took an interminable cab ride from Santa Monica to her father's one-story house in Pasadena. Roger's petite Nigerian nurse had showed her to the screened-in back porch, where he sat in a wheelchair pointed toward a swath of California pines. Shelley sat beside him in silence, but for the final few minutes of the visit she had grabbed his hand and told him about college.

When she was small, Roger would occasionally make vague incantations that his other children were all brilliant and fearless and audacious, but he'd never once extended the comment to her. When she'd terrorized teachers at Spence and her parents had to go in for a meeting, Roger would return home and sit in the parlor, clicking on the television. Little Shelley skulked around the room, waiting for him to comment on her actions, waiting for one chuckle or one assertion of, "Definitely my child, you are." But she'd received nothing from him. Around that time Shelley had told her parents that she wanted to be an actress or a singer when she grew up, anything where she could take center stage. Her mother always hugged her tightly and told her she'd imagined nothing less. But after her father left, Shelley had dropped that dream and stopped picturing what her future would look like entirely. It was as if she was waiting for Roger to come home and tell her what to do. What she had wanted her whole life was for her father to ask her questions about what she liked and what she thought. In the past two years, Shelley had thought about those minutes on the porch in California often, although he hadn't so much as squeezed her hand back in response.

Now, looking out of the rectangular window of the Metro-North train car, she watched the Hudson River roll by. She hoped she never saw Ollie again and that Aleisha would return to California and be miserable in her shopping-mall-filled, parochial life. She pictured her half brother Nick with his constant scowl, hiding away in the Village, probably in some poor, susceptible NYU girl's room. Shelley wished him to stay there. As she considered all these people, the rage announced itself in the depths of her stomach again, collecting heat as it swirled and grew. She rattled back toward Manhattan, toward home, all the time looking out at the breadth of the Hudson River, recently unfrozen and deep muddy brown. Wide and unadorned, filthy and dull; that river was permanent and would never change. It was miserable and there was nothing she could do about it.

Back in the city, Shelley got out of the cab at the corner of Columbus Avenue and Seventy-Third Street. No, she couldn't afford to take another cab, but as she was standing in front of Grand Central, one rolled up in front of her—an old-school Crown Victoria with some dents on the bumper, which reminded her of her childhood. The driver was heaving her suitcase into the trunk before she could protest. Shelley "grew up in a New York that doesn't exist anymore." When she was a child her parents had a mart' at four, and left her with a nanny after that. When they could no longer afford the nanny, they simply left her alone. She had lived in the same apartment on the Upper West Side all her life, save for those three-plus years of college. But now the apartment she grew up in was empty: her father left when she was in the eighth grade, her grandmother died five years later, and her dazed and bespectacled mother, well . . . If she wasn't doing another in-patient stint, maybe she was actually on Martha's Vineyard selling Shelley's grandmother's, Biddy's, old house.

Now, Shelley bumped her suitcase against the cobblestones as she made her way up Strong Place. She liked to repeat that line, that she "grew up in a New York that doesn't exist anymore." Where she really grew up was in an apartment at the back end of an old horse alley off Columbus Avenue, between Seventy-Third and Seventy-Fourth Streets. Strong Place was a street so narrow a car couldn't drive up it, and the Whitbys' apartment, a duplex on the bottom two floors of a brownstone, was so narrow itself that as a child she couldn't do two consecutive somersaults across it without banging the crown of her head against the plaster. The walls were lined with built-ins, filled with classic novels and volume after volume of glossy, hard-backed art books. Her poor mother had cherished these, buying them at forty-five, fifty bucks a pop, without thinking twice. She bought them even when the cash on hand was so low that Shelley had to lure her grandmother Biddy into another room, the old woman's white topknot bobbling as she padded over the rugs, while Shelley's mother dipped into her purse. Although a Whitby, Shelley was her father's youngest biological child, and by the time she came along, it was only Biddy who had any dough. And after her mother's travel and the pills and primarily the long divorce, they burned through that money too.

The cold outside was biting and wet. It was below fifty, and she didn't have a jacket. The setting sun turned the air dusky as Shelley laid her eyes on her childhood home. When she entered she saw that the foyer light had burned out and mouse droppings speckled the white countertops of the first-floor kitchen. But the place smelled like comfort: dried pasta and old books, a tinge of dust that threatened a sneeze. She inhaled it all deeply, that particular scent of home. Then she put herself down at the kitchen table and picked up the landline telephone. Although Shelley had been avoiding facing the reality of where her mother really was, it was time to try to find her. The darkness from the diner was closing back in on her. She dialed her mother's cell phone, closed her eyes, and tried to imagine the most peaceful place she could think of. She found herself picturing the end of the old dock at her grandmother's Martha's Vineyard summer home. The phone rang and rang, and Shelley's mother did not pick up. Finally a high-pitched computerized voice announced: *We're sorry, but the mailbox you have reached is full and is not accepting new messages.*

It wasn't as if her mother had always been attentive, but disappearing for this long was new. Shelley felt the heat of anger rising again through her lower abdomen. She was still the child. She was the child, and her father was dead, and she deserved a little consolation. For years after her father left, her mother barely went out of the apartment at all. Elizabeth Saltman Whitby had just hummed around the overpacked rooms, her chin-length blunt cut rustling. She never said a word. She was, for lack of a better phrase, a woman destroyed. But in Shelley's final years of high school, she managed to get her mother out on the weekends, where they would sit side by side at the counter at Old John's Luncheonette. Shelley would order for them both: "Two plates of two fried eggs, and hash browns extra brown." No *please*, no coy appreciation. She would gulp her large orange juice, smack her lips, and let out an *ahhh*.

Now Shelley sat alone in the kitchen and wondered if it was time to cry. Any chance she'd had to become a part of her father's life was gone, forever. As she sat there in silence the tears didn't come, but irrational thoughts did. What if Roger was really alive? What if he had just gotten better and decided to leave California? Could he and her mother be hiding somewhere, making up for the years that they'd missed together?

After finishing a packet of soggy saltine crackers, Shelley went up-stairs for the night. The downstairs still reminded her of her father right before he left, slumped in the winged-back armchair watching the first televised discussion of the president's rumored affairs, his frayed shirt collar pulled up from his moth-eaten Brooks Brothers sweater. A Scotch tumbler sweated as he sat in front of the television for hours, unaware of Shelley and her friends traipsing around. He was already so old. His shade business, which he'd started when he'd retreated from the corporate and political aspirations of his previous marriages, was going under. The hobby-cum-company had catered to old homes, brick mansions in the city, and wide-windowed arts-and-crafts summer places in the far reaches of Long Island. Roger Whitby Jr. aimed to fulfill the needs of each house's intricacies. But Home Depot and Target had been pushing him out of the market; no one wanted to buy custom-cut shades from a local shop anymore. For years the Whitbys kept the tiny workroom and storefront, which was four blocks from their apartment. The place was nothing more than a closet with a counter in front of a few work benches scattered with tools and tacking nails, set on the ground floor of a dingy tan office building from the sixties. Her family kept the shop long after Roger had moved to California with Shelley's former teacher Ms. Scribner, truly sur-prising them all that he still had it in him.

Shelley lugged her bags up the creaking staircase, then climbed into Grandmother Biddy's old bed and pulled the nubby bedspread up to her chin. Roger Whitby Jr. had no doubt been ignored by his parents as well. And in turn, her grandparents must have been disregarded too. A lack of attention, but moreover parental rocking and petting was absent. This lack of parental love funneled through their family, a fissure hundreds of years old and ditch-deep. The absence of physical, bodily security traced all the way back to the *Mayflower*. Growing up, Biddy was the only one whom Shelley had touched regularly, and the only one with whom she could speak honestly. On one of those final days when Biddy was in bed, never to emerge again, Shelley had tucked herself in beside her grandmother. The old woman's halitosis overtook the room, and her pinched warble warned, "You know your mother, Shelley; she's not well. She's always been prone to untoward things."

Now Shelley thought about her personal golden rule, about her absent mother, and decided that she was entitled to do whatever she wanted. She pulled a pack of Virginia Slims out of the front pocket of her backpack and lit one up while lying in bed. She flipped on the television. Her shoulders were shaking slightly. Her father's hand no longer existed. If he really was dead, if the lawyer's report was right, perhaps there would be talk of it on the news. She began flipping from channel two to channel four to channel seven. Tom Brokaw discussed the new military base camp being set up in Fallujah, with a projected map of Iraq above him. Richard Schlesinger showed clips of George W. Bush blushing behind a podium, repeating the phrase "*Dubya-Em-Dee*, it stands for weapons of mass *dee*struction." Barbara Walters was doing a special on residents of the Financial District who decided to permanently relocate in the wake of 9/11.

A middle-aged man with dark Italian features looked into Barbara's eyes and told her, "It's the memory of the smell. Human bodies. I can't get that out of me." The camera cut to Barbara shaking her head without blinking once.

Shelley flipped between these stations, one after another, waiting for any sort of mention of her father, or her family. He was a Whitby. Wouldn't there be something? Wouldn't the news mention that another Whitby died from the ridiculous family curse? She kept flipping. She made it through six cigarettes, clicking at the remote control while a swirling ball of rage and despair swelled inside of her. It was then that Shelley cried. It was just for a minute or two: her perfectly balanced face distorted, and real, wet tears streaked down her cheeks and fell off the cleft of her chin. She was totally alone.

5

| 1994 |

The scent of pink lilies flooded the hotel lobby—sickly sweet, intoxicating the mind with each breath; one could think of nothing at all. On the other side of the automatic glass doors the morning was hazy and claustrophobic, like so many Los Angeles mornings. Nick Whitby was twelve years old. He wore a New York Yankees cap and a charcoal suit, too large in the shoulders and too short in the ankles. His mother clacked ahead of him on the mauve marble floor. "*Will* you hurry—?" She stuck her hand behind her as if Nick would grab it. His shoulders hunched up in humiliation. Although they lived only an hour away, Nick and his mother were staying with the rest of the family at the Beverly Hills Hotel. Today was Grandfather Whitby's funeral. The barrel baron, the king of capital, the yelling fat man in a wheelchair—he had fought off death for ninety-seven years, and came close to beating it.

A line of black town cars waited in the circular drive of the hotel, each car perfectly aligned with a potted queen palm, beside which stood a driver in black uniform and white gloves. In front of Nick, his mother moved at an alarming clip; the wide seat of her pantsuit waddled to and fro and into the back seat of a town car. Nick was the only child of this ex–third grade teacher, this half-hearted gardener, this piner after her absent, aged husband. He wondered if there was a car for each of his adopted father's wives: *"One, Two, Three, Four . . ."* Though Roger had just moved Nick and his mother to California, he was already living outside of their home. Every time they walked through the lobby of the hotel, Nick's mother's freckles burned as she looked left and right for Roger, her face brighter than the copious blooming lilies.

Grandfather Whitby had been an icon to many. Roger Whitby Sr. was the shipping king turned real estate mogul, the prize of American industry. The son of already prominent industrialists, he and his brother had surpassed their parents and created a true empire. His physical image had been reproduced wildly on pasted-up bills and magazine ads in the forties: two solid feet planted at the stern of a wooden steamship, hands clasped at his chest, collar tied up tight. The blade of competition gleamed in his eyes, underneath one-hundred-foot sails. Somehow Grandfather Whitby possessed none of the Whitby characteristics that his progeny and the subsequent bloodline upheld. No, Roger Whitby Sr. was a stout five feet nine inches tall, with a drum of a belly orbing from his egg center. His hair, when it still existed, was dishwater dark and wiry. Yet his children were ethereal WASPs: sullen and stretched-out, perpetually sunburned. And his grandchildren were all the more Waspish. It was as if Grandfather Whitby had produced this familial effect through hard-set will alone. Although Nick was adopted, and technically only a Whitby through legal means, everyone commented on how he looked like the rest of them. He was an angular kid, and tall for his age, with most of the height coming from the great length of leg that held him up. He would have looked older than he was, save for his head of fat golden curls. Mothers had cooed at his hair for as long as he could remember. It gave him a softness he couldn't get away from, and this fact made embarrassment boil in his guts. He knew he was cherublike, girlish.

During the funeral service at the chapel of Forest Lawn cemetery, Nick sat beside his mother in the second row of pews and didn't notice the girl there at all. His mother kept telling him that this was a "family event," but Nick understood that he was in a room filled with wealthy strangers, most of whom were suspicious of him and his mother, if they had any idea who they were. It wasn't until he was standing in the graveyard at the front of the crowd that he saw her. The service was a buzz of boring protestant platitudes until three notes from a bugle player cracked through the gray air and three marines marched out holding mahogany rifles. Two more marched behind, in white hats and dark jackets, but these men walked backward while their knees rose in time to the bugle as they unfurled an American flag. Nick wondered what he would feel like if all these multitudes of people really were his family—it would be like being part of a sports team, or an army, where you were always protected. The sheer number of them ensured this; all those people would not only know you but help you, and you could do anything in the world that you wanted. It was then that the girl at the front of the crowd began to produce embarrassing hound-like howls. Nick's adopted father was at the foot of the burial plot, eyes unfocused, turning his tongue over in his open mouth, holding a metal cane. He was getting sick. In recent weeks Nick's mother had tucked herself beside Nick in his bed and pulled her son close as she whispered that his father was an *adulterer.* Nick found this fitting. Roger was certainly an adult; compared to him and his mother, he was so very old.

One marine yelled: *Heeeeeh-up!* The three in the line twirled their rifles into position, expressionless. *Bang, bang, bang*: three shots rang out in succession. A three-volley salute for Grandfather Whitby. The other two marines held the open American flag at chest level, as the bugler began the first bars of taps. Nick's mother found his hand, and he let her take it. The bugle hadn't made it past "gone the sun" when the girl began her howls again. How many people were there? Hundreds? Many dabbed their eyes with tissues, but this girl was the only one making a scene of it. Nick looked again. She was older than him—fourteen?—wearing black corduroy pants and a blue paisley tunic. Hardly funeral wear. Then it came to him: he knew her. It was just before his mother had married Roger and they'd moved to California, when he had been sent unaccompanied on an Amtrak train from New York to Boston to go to swim camp. He had been sitting across the aisle from this exact girl, who had been reading a book. On the train she began to laugh loudly at her book every few pages—a squawk, to be honest—which forced everyone in the car to direct their attention to her.

Something about her face on the train had made Nick's eyes linger; he wanted to stare at it for hours, to figure out how it worked. The eyes, the lips, the nose, the mouth: all slight, unobtrusive oval shapes. Pale but not too pale. Freckled just barely. It was a perfectly plain face, but it tempted him. He had tried to turn away, to watch the View-Master scenes of New England click by the train window. The sun was setting into stripes of orange and purple, and the flat blue shoreline of Connecticut spread itself out. Boats filed perfectly into slips; sailboats, motorboats, wooden cigarette boats; one after another, row upon row. Nick turned back to the girl. Her lank brown hair hung over one cheek. His gut compelled him to go over and yank that hair, hard. He wanted to see what she'd do. He swiveled to the window: burnt bristle tree stumps stuck out of the water, a dam's stillness reflected back. Not an animal in sight. Bombed-out and boarded-up brick warehouses echoed the roar of the zooming train. No one in the car said a word. The girl squawked; Nick examined the curve of her waist, the plump funnel of her upper arm. To the window—the sky azure-ice blue, then water again: silver. Soon came the bridges of Rhode Island in the nighttime. Metal turning to stone; the hum of permanence. Her laugh.

In California the end of the burial procession had begun. It was time to throw handfuls of dirt over the coffin and set the old man to rest. The minister, in his white Episcopal robe, spoke in a monotone: "Ashes to ashes . . ." Multigenerational ex-wives, dressed head to toe in black, traded glances and raised eyebrows. They would settle a plan for who would throw in the first handful. Was it possible that Nick and his mother were the only people who didn't know everyone else there? The wives were mid-head-tilt-conversation, when the girl from the train marched ahead and picked up a fist full of dirt. She threw it into the hole recklessly. "Love you, Grandfather," she announced in a clear, strong voice. She shrugged and began her way back to the crowd when Roger seemed to snap into it.

His deep croak: "Thank you, Shelley."

Then the girl did an about-face. She put two hands on Roger's shoulders and bent to kiss the man on the cheek. "Love you too, Daddy," she announced, her face turned expectantly to the crowd.

Daddy. That's what she had called him. Nick had met the people who were now his other half siblings—the older ones, Andrew and Kiki, and Kiki's sister and brother. Many of them lived in New York with their multitudes of children. But this girl was younger than the rest, closer to his age. And no one had ever said a thing about her. Could it be true? Anger for his own mother boiled inside of Nick, and he dropped her hand. The word resounded within him. *Daddy*.

6

| 2003 |

"Well then, dear. All is not lost. Not yet." Armond nodded as he retied his maroon scarf. Brooke, standing on the banks of the rapidly thawing Charles River next to the aged but very upright man, tugged on Phoebe's leash to keep the dog away from a wandering duck. They were in front of the orange Arthur Fiedler footbridge, which would soon carry Armond over Storrow Drive and return him to his decorous home office on Commonwealth Avenue. It was before eight in the morning, and Brooke and Armond had just completed one of the early walks that they'd been going on a few times a year for the majority of Brooke's life. They'd been going on these walks together since Brooke's father left, right before she started high school. Perhaps Armond did this because she was the youngest of the brood then, and the most in need of a father figure. Or maybe it was because he saw himself in her measured, sincere ways. Both of them were early risers and serious walkers.

He tucked his hands up near his armpits as he often did when departing: a clear sign that he was not planning to shake her hand, and certainly not offer an embrace. His consistency was a comfort.

"Thank you, as always," she said. He nodded again and turned. She watched his charcoal-wool-covered back stride up and away on the orange ramp. How much she owed this now old man for walking with her over the

49

years, for listening to her troubles and triumphs and offering small snippets of guidance. She occasionally wondered if Armond regretted never having children of his own. He had not married and had always lived alone in the big Back Bay town house that had once belonged to his parents. He never acknowledged his personal life at all. Instead, Armond was a listener, and a good one. The frustration at her recently deceased father that had been churning inside of Brooke for the past week had just funneled out of her mouth and into Armond's quiet, receptive ears. She was furious at her father for disinheriting her and plagued by the questions of *why*, but her upset had also stirred her anger at him for leaving her family so many years ago. And now she was even mad at him for dying.

For nearly eight days Brooke had been legitimately fatherless. But of course, her father had been absent for so much longer than that. As she stomped again along the cracked river path in her L.L.Bean boots, she muttered to herself, "All is not lost," mimicking Armond's antiquated accent. But she felt the laces that held her together loosening at her center. She was terrified that everything was, once again, coming undone.

At least the dog was happy, panting and trotting along in the frigid morning as they walked toward the CVS by Charles Circle. Brooke wouldn't allow Saul's son, the pharmacist at the local pharmacy, Gary Drug, to ask her questions about the thing she needed to buy there. Her dizziness had dissipated, so she wasn't very worried anymore, but she would still buy the test as a precaution. By the river, a handful of poplar trees carried white buds on the ends of their knurled branches, and two runners sprang around her on the path—a couple wearing knit gloves and beanie hats. The air emitted the chlorinated smell of melting ice, but winter's knuckles were still grasping for a few more weeks of life. In Boston, not-yet-May was often still winter.

Armond had given her sound advice about the house problem: lay out the disparate possibilities of what could happen with the property, calculate the financial outcomes of each, and write down a plan for dealing with each potential outcome. It was a logical task, and she could complete it that morning. In a dream world she and her half sister Shelley would work together to pin down this Nick child. She knew Shelley better than any of her other half siblings, due to the summers they were both on the Vineyard. Perhaps they could convince Nick to simply gift Shelley's New York house and Brooke's Boston house to them, respectively. Maybe, if Nick was given all the rest of the money without a fight, he wouldn't mind?

A ridiculous thought. This child owed her nothing. He had no ties to her at all; why on earth would he just give her a property that was effectively worth millions of dollars? What was more likely was that Nick would take ownership of the house on Joy Street, the only place Brooke had ever been stable and happy, and live into his old age on all the remaining Whitby money he'd come into by the odd collision of coincidences. But still: What if? What if she went to New York the next day and she and Shelley worked together to find him and talk to him at least?

Perhaps that's what she needed, anyway, a New York trip to lift her spirits. In Boston, Brooke had always felt like a regular, if unlucky, person. But in New York she felt like a Whitby. It wasn't just the roads and the buildings bearing her family name that gave her that impression. It was the energy of the city that allowed her to step up into the role of heir, a role that no one really gave a damn about in Boston. But in New York, people noticed her. She was acknowledged.

When she was a child, her family would go to the city a handful of weekends every year, one of which was always the first weekend in December, for the annual Whitby Christmas party. They'd catch the early train and arrive in Midtown at the family hotel, the Whitby-Grand, just after noon. The hotel had begun as two separate hotels built next to each other, the Whitby and the Grand, helmed by warring cousins at the end of the nineteenth century. It was Ethan Whitby who had later joined them together, convincing the two sides of the family that if they kept the infighting within private residences and out of business deals, it would benefit all involved. And Ethan proved to be correct, even after his death: in the years following the merger, the hotel was known as one of the most luxurious and prominent in the nation, raising millions of dollars from events hosted in ballrooms—from benefits supporting victims of the

Titanic to Cold War–era peace conferences, where the president himself laid out plans to eliminate the counterinsurgents and communists who plagued the nation. But in the seventies, after their international hotel chain endeavor failed sorely, the Whitby success began to plummet and they sold off pieces of the New York hotel.

Now it was just another Davidson property, owned by modern-day wealthy people who still worked. But when Brooke was little, when it was still theirs, she felt that as soon as she entered the hotel, she was a Whitby princess. The grown-up guests smiled down at her, and the navy-suited staff asked her if she needed anything. The expansive main lobby varied its holiday decorations every year: one year giant red and gold bows dangled from the archways and staircases; another year, dozens of elf-sized Christmas trees adorned the balcony level, each overdecorated, creating a maze worthy of Charlie and his chocolate factory. The decorations changed, but every year, without fail, there were the great silver branches held in oversize urns set up in the entryway. Pinprick lights gilded the branches as they arched up and over Brooke's head, forming a shining dome. When she walked through that glowing Christmas arch, that was when the transformation happened. It was her favorite moment of every year.

The last year of the Christmas party, 1977, was also, possibly, the best one: it was when her parents decided to put on a show, for the rest of the family and whatever longtime friends and business associates who received their annual invitations. The party was in the ballroom as it always was, but that year it seemed there were more people in attendance than usual; faces peeked down from the stacked balconies, as if they were at the opera. Brooke's mother strutted up to the microphone in a strapless gold lamé gown, with a peplum jutting straight out from her narrow waist, while her father took a seat at the piano.

Later, Kiki and LJ would say they were mortified by the prospect of their father playing the piano and both parents crooning away, but Brooke, young and naive, had been thrilled by it. They looked perfect up there: her father leaning back at the baby grand Steinway in his red bow tie, wearing a Santa hat at an angle. Her dark-haired, mysterious mother beaming. The couple launched right into the beginning of "White Christmas," and as soon as they began, all of the partygoers fell into thunderous applause. It was a few hours into the event, but the older kids had yet to pull their inevitable prank. Brooke's older siblings and cousins had a tradition of completing a small prank every year, although their schemes had been growing over the years. It was more than exciting when all the cousins from the shipping side (the Rogers) and the railroad side (the Ethans) got together. It was joyous. During their daily lives at school and at summer camp, they were always set apart. They were looked at by other kids and parents and teachers with an edge of suspicion and an arm's-length curiosity; each child was an awkwardly plain yet semifamous specimen. So when they were in the same place it was a relief. They all felt giddy to be part of the norm, just one of the gang. And they channeled this giddiness into their pranks. But perhaps the tradition would be snuffed due to her cousin Theo Jr.'s pyrotechnics last winter: he'd set the Christmas cake on fire, causing the kitchen staff to revolt and threaten to not make anything for the coming year's party. It really had been ablaze, four tiers with flames shooting up from it. The adults who were not enraged seemed actually rather tickled. Was it kerosene? Olive oil? How *had* he managed to do that?

At the close of her parents' first song, Roger and Corney kissed each other. Screams of approval and whistles of pleasure resounded from the floor and all tiers of the balconies. Corney looked coyly around the room and said into the microphone in a husky, dampened voice, "Oh, who's coming to town? Who is on his way?" She put a hand over her eyes, as if to search the horizon, while behind her Brooke's father began singing, "You better watch out, you better not cry . . ." The crowd cheered and began to clap along to "Santa Claus Is Coming to Town."

Little Brooke, at the edge of the dance floor in her velvet-topped red plaid dress, found herself swaying along, grinning while holding her Shirley Temple. Where were Kiki and LJ? Where had all her cousins gone? It was the first Christmas party that her younger brother, Peter, hadn't come to. He was already very sick, although no one in the family ever verbalized the word *cancer*. But everyone was positive about his treatment then, and one of the nannies, Carla, was probably sitting beside him in his bed at Children's Hospital in Boston at that very moment. Brooke always had an empty feeling without her little brother, her constant playmate, around, like she'd forgotten to pack something important but couldn't remember exactly what it was.

It was after the second number that Brooke's mother stopped and announced to the crowd: "We have a very special song right now, for a girl who recently turned twelve, and has spent the past year being the best daughter and big sister a mother could ever dream of."

It took Brooke a moment to realize her mother was talking about her. All the faces in the ballroom turned, and her father got up from the piano and leaned into the microphone. "Birdie, where are you? Would you come up here and dance with your dear old dad?"

Everyone clapped as Brooke made her way toward her father, at the front of the crowd. He grabbed her hands and spun her around, before taking her fully into his ballroom-dancing-trained arms. Her mother began an a cappella version of "The First Noel," and her father swayed and twirled a giggling, blushing Brooke.

In retrospect, Brooke understood that her parents had enacted this charade because they knew how hard she was taking Peter's sickness. His death, which would occur a year later, would tear her family apart and forever change the course of Brooke's life. Her father would never totally recover from it. But at the time, Brooke had not envisioned that possibility. And it didn't occur to her to analyze her parents' motivation for the singing-and-dancing show. She was simply happy. Upstairs in the ballroom's balconies, her older brother, LJ, was in the midst of leading a band of Whitby cousins in what he considered the greatest prank they'd yet to pull. He and Theo Jr. had cooked up this plan over the phone, and two days earlier LJ had gone to Gary Drug on Charles Street. He'd told Saul, without blinking an eye, that what he needed was three cartons of condoms.

"Cartons?" Saul had leaned over the counter with eyebrows raised. "What do you need one carton for, LJ?"

"I just need them!"

Saul rolled his eyes. "And I don't suppose a quick call to your father would change this order?"

LJ's jaw set, and he stamped one foot. "This is illegal, Saul. I need three cartons of condoms, and I'm paying you for them. So just give them to me before I call the police!" He was a skinny and childlike sixteen—not someone who should, or by the look of it could, be using the condoms for their intended purpose. LJ continued, "And, if you really must know, these prophylactics are for a sexual-health class at the St. Paul's School, where I am an exemplary member of the student body. Ever heard of it, St. Paul's?"

Saul rolled his eyes so far back he looked possessed. "You are not paying for any of this, kid," he grumbled as he walked into the back room to get the products. He muttered *jackass* under his breath, but quiet enough that there was no way LJ could hear. The Whitby family account was the highest-grossing one every year.

Now, up in the balconies, four Whitby teenagers (Kiki had deemed herself too old) stood with plastic bags filled with wrapped-up condoms at their feet. The cousins didn't live in the same town or go to school together—they had very little shared experiences—and therefore these little stunts became a bonding mechanism. A joint life event; something to remember one another by. Theo Jr. and LJ were across the room from each other, motioning with their arms that the time was *not quite* right yet. In the balcony box beside Theo Jr. was Eliot (the fourth) and directly across from him, in her own box, was Anna, thrilled to be included.

At the end of "The First Noel," Brooke's mother hit her soprano's high note, and Roger picked little Brooke up underneath the arms and swung her in a circle while she shrieked in delight. This dance was the kindest thing her father had ever done for her. She felt more than special; she felt chosen. Just as she was spinning, LJ gave a thumbs-up to Theo Jr. and the boys reached down into their plastic bags. It was perfect timing: the father-daughter scene would be disrupted by a flitter, a flutter. "Snow?" the ladies in their heels and pearls would ask their bald, tuxedoed husbands, squinting upward. "How charming." Then *splat*—a condom would land directly on a glistening forehead. Then all around—*splat splat splat*—it would be raining condoms, disrupting their perfectly choreographed event. And although Roger would feign anger at that moment, although he'd probably yell a bit at LJ in front of Corney for show, he'd be downright tickled. Roger loved a successful prank.

But just as LJ dug his hand into the plastic bag, he was seized on either shoulder. He turned to see a mustachioed man in a black-and-white suit, growling. The hotel employee said, "Not this year, asswipe."

Across the ballroom, LJ could see that there was a fat man grabbing Theo Jr. in just the same fashion. A coordinated ambush! In the box beside him he heard a cracking voice admonishing Eliot, "You kids think this is a damn joke? Do you know how much more work you create for all of us?"

They were caught. The plan had failed. All the Whitby kids were being dragged away from the balconies.

Below, on the ballroom floor, Roger kissed the top of Brooke's head. As he returned to his place at the piano, her mother announced that they would perform their fourth and final number. Her father's shoulders bounced up and down as he pounded out a keyboard flourish, before the couple launched into a bopping version of "Joy to the World!" As Brooke walked to the back of the ballroom, one of her aunts squeezed her shoulder, to share in the excitement. Brooke could not stop herself from smiling. This is what happened in New York. She was a part of something bigger than just her parents and her brothers and sisters. That day was, perhaps, the happiest she had ever been.

Yes, even in Brooke's adult mind, New York was still a dreamland, where her family was charming, loving, and all together. A place of happiness. But if there was anything that adult Brooke had learned, it was that that kind of happiness didn't last. She tied Phoebe's leash to a stop sign pole and entered the electric glass doors of the CVS pharmacy imagining what *was* realistic, and what would really happen to her after her house was gone.

She and Phoebe would have to move to a depressing one-bedroom rental apartment that her RN salary could support, far from the hospital. *It shouldn't be that bad*, she told herself, moving into a smaller place and taking the T to work. It was a normal thing to do. But as she reassured herself, she began to panic: she'd constructed each part of her existence so carefully, laid the routine of her days down meticulously so that she'd never fall back into the hole of sadness she'd spent years crawling out of, after her brother's death and the subsequent dissolution of her family. In moving out of her home, she'd certainly lose the circle of friends she was still loosely a part of: all those born-and-bred Beacon Hill people, all the other St. Paulies who lived in their Back Bay town houses with their husbands and wives and golden retrievers. Brooke had managed to maintain contact with these people by having just enough extra cash to occasionally go to charity events on weekend evenings. This was the life that those people lived: black tie and white tie and cocktail attire; the Children's Fund or Friends of the Earth or the Mayor's Council. Brooke paid the property taxes on her house, but with not having to pay rent or a mortgage, and with the added income from her upstairs tenants, she could sometimes manage to buy a ticket to an event and show her face among the only group of friends she had ever known. While she never had much fun at these evenings, seeing all those familiar faces gave her comfort. If she stopped going altogether, the whole gang of them would surely forget about her.

She sighed loudly, walking down the drugstore aisle. Why did she need those so-called friends? The problem was that they knew her. Even if they knew nothing about her current daily life, as none of them ever asked a word about her nursing job, they knew her family and exactly where she was coming from. They didn't ask about her job because they simply didn't understand it. Most of the women didn't work now that they had children, and the men were by and large investment types or lawyers at the bigger white-glove firms. It was a full nine years ago when, during cocktail hour at a Kennedy Greenway Conservancy charity dinner, she had told a group of friends she'd gone to Beacon Hill Nursery School with—the Pickney sisters and Brad Waloff and a handful of others—that she'd gotten into Northeastern's nursing school and was planning to go. They'd all tilted their heads and narrowed their eyes in confusion.

Caroline Pickney had asked earnestly, "Why would you want to do that?" They had no conception of the need for money. It didn't occur to them that people they grew up with would ever have that need.

Brooke was aware that if she wanted to, she could most likely be married to Marc Costa within the year, and then all that financial worry would disappear. The rational option was to appease him, marry him, suck it up and move to a giant house in the suburbs. They'd been on and off for two years now, and at forty-two, he was frothing at the mouth to lock down a wife and have multiple children before his parents felt he was inappropriately old. What she liked about Marc was his ease and his ability to make her act in ways she never had, enjoying his cars and clothes and other material possessions. She liked these things, and Marc himself, as guilty pleasures. During their first few months of dating he'd wooed her by taking her on weekend sails out of the harbor in Newport, Rhode Island, in one of the many motor sailers he co-owned with his friends. It was their hobby to buy and sell these boats, but they only ever went out on the water with a captain. They had no interest in the hard work of sailing. Instead, they'd steer the boat for a few minutes before Marc would blend a drink in the cabin and hand it to Brooke, already sprawled out in her bikini in the bow cockpit. It was gluttonous, really, and fun. But could one marry a guilty pleasure? She couldn't shake the deep-seated fear that she was failing. When she was a little girl, her father would say to her, "You are my constant, Birdie. You are a rock. I know just the kind of life you're going to lead." And although living her life as a middle-class nurse wasn't what her father had envisioned for her, marrying into Marc's tacky family and living in the suburbs certainly wasn't either. It wasn't what she was meant to do.

Yet, if she broke up with Marc and she dropped off her social circuit because she couldn't afford it, she would be alone again during all nights and weekends, with no one to eat her meals with. Her only identity then would be her day job: Brooke Whitby, RN; Brooke Whitby, middle-class, lonely, average woman. In the middle of the brightly lit family health aisle, Brooke leaned down to examine the small white packages on a bottom shelf.

"Can I help you?" asked a chirpy teenage girl in a smock and cornrows. Brooke shook her head. She'd found the brand of pregnancy tests that they used at the hospital: four minutes, 99 percent accuracy. She wasn't worried. Biologically, the timing didn't make great sense.

Back outside, with the test tucked safely into her handbag, she and Phoebe made their way up Charles Street. Her friends would be ferrying their children to private grade schools in Brookline and Cambridge about now, waving from their Volvos and city-sized Subarus. She tried to compose herself, smile as though it was just any other morning and she was out to pick up a cup of coffee. But it wasn't any other morning. Her father was gone, and soon her home would be gone too.

As she and Phoebe huffed up the slant of Mount Vernon Street, she imagined becoming Mrs. Costa and still being invited to all the benefit dinners and charity balls. She would be able to, for once, buy a table. (She had, in fact, met Marc at the Humane Society dinner, where his good looks forced her to forgive him for his embarrassingly typical question of "So . . . are you *related*?") But with the image of being his wife, a shadow of misery encroached on her peripheral vision. What would she do all day in a pop-up mansion in Newton? When she had first met Marc, she had thought of their relationship as a kind of joke—a temporary vacation from real life, with an uncomplicated, pleasure-seeking, fun acquaintance. He was nothing like her, and therefore it was amusing to speed over to Newport in his Audi and care little about the problems of the world. But what had started as a slightly embarrassing dalliance had now been dragged out for so long. And the truth of the matter was that he did not know her. It made sense why he wanted her: a petite blonde, a Whitby, old enough to not make him a vulture yet strangely still single. But Marc with his gaudy taste; Marc and his perpetually surprised, childlike demeanor—he had a completely different angle on the world. He would never be able to see hers.

When her own house on Joy Street came into view, she saw a small figure in a bright green coat on her front step. Brooke nearly laughed out loud. It was as if by magic that she was there, someone who really, truly did know her. Allie sat patiently waiting.

Brooke's house was brick and three stories high, not one of the grander mansions in the neighborhood but stately with its gas lamp in the front yard and a whaling-era knocker on the door. Even now, when she approached it, she remembered the first twelve years of her life, those happy ones, filled with noise and family and Peter. There were multiple years between each of her siblings: Kiki was the oldest, then three years later came mischievous LJ, four years later was Brooke, and finally, five years after her, Peter had been born. Although she was significantly younger than Kiki and LJ, it was only Peter who seemed to be considered younger than the rest; her mother liked to call him her "most handsome surprise." Although they lived in the middle of the city, the family was a sports-loving one, and there were always ice hockey sticks and field hockey sticks, and footballs and cleats and crew uniforms strewn about the house. They'd had two nannies, Carla and Rosemary, both of whom walked over from the North End before breakfast and must have walked home again long after Brooke was asleep and her parents had returned from parties, disheveled and happy, holding high heels and cummerbunds in their hands.

One of the most awful parts about the divorce was the fact that before it, her parents had been so joyful. They were boisterous together: singing and kissing in the kitchen in the morning, dancing in the great room at night, causing their children constant embarrassment. Corney's upbringing in her severe, Lutheran family on the North Shore of Massachusetts clashed with her natural exuberance. She'd joked that she had left the North Shore for Broadway, but Roger had caught her in a net in Boston and she'd never made it to New York. Roger was jolly and energetic back then; whistling down to wherever his office of the moment was, the insurance business in Downtown Crossing or the brokerage firm at Government Center, challenging LJ to shoot pucks at him in their tiny backyard. He would take them on trips without any warning, loading her and Peter and their mother into the car, driving up to New Hampshire to pick up Kiki and LJ at boarding school, then going a million miles an hour on I-90 to Niagara Falls, or zipping back to Boston and taking a helicopter to Hilton Head Island or the Bahamas. "It's too damn cold!" He'd grin. "I can't let my family ice over in the New England winter!" This was what it was like, her family, when it still existed. One day she was a happy twelve-year-old girl, going to her progressive private day school in the morning and returning in the afternoon to a gleaming old kitchen filled with Carla's still-warm focaccia, milk and oranges, and sometimes a small piece of chocolate. By dinnertime her mother would swoop in, squeezing Peter and Brooke close to her. Then everything changed forever.

Now, thirty-seven-year-old Brooke—maybe not happy, but totally fine—let herself into her own front gate. Allie held up an offering of two cups of coffee in her white-and-blue mittens.

"I know I wasn't invited. But . . . cinnamon lattes?" Allie said, standing. She gave Brooke an impish smile. Her curly black hair was now whispered with gray, but her eyes were still childishly large and warm.

"I didn't know you were in town," Brooke said.

Allie made her way toward her as Phoebe whined, wanting to go inside. Allie ran a nonprofit that sent underprivileged girls on wilderness retreats throughout New England, mountaineering and sailing and sea kayaking, as well as school-year-based mentoring and enrichment classes. She'd founded the organization nearly a decade ago, and the main offices were in Woods Hole on the Cape, just a ferry ride away from where Allie had grown up on Martha's Vineyard.

Her arms were solid around Brooke now; she smelled of coconut, of comfort. "I'm so sorry about your father," she said into Brooke's neck. "I wish I'd known sooner."

Brooke felt the smoothness of Allie's chin knock into her own, then move toward her face. Was it possible that Allie was trying to kiss her, right there on the street, right in front of her own house at morning rush hour?

Brooke lurched back. "Come inside." It wasn't that their romantic relationship had been a secret. All those Beacon Hill people had known Allie since high school, and everyone was aware that she was gay. And for two years Allie had lived in the house on Joy Street with Brooke, which Brooke also assumed everyone knew. But Brooke didn't like the gay label. She simply wasn't a lesbian. It was undeniable that she was, or had been,

in love with Allie. But whatever they'd had was a one-off, a special relationship. And she didn't need to broadcast it on the street. Plus, Allie had
made it clear she was done with Brooke: Brooke wasn't interested in marriage, and therefore whatever had been between them would never be happening again.

In the high-ceilinged great room at the front of the house, Allie
crouched on the piano bench while Brooke sat on the robin's-egg-blue
rug, sipping her coffee and letting Phoebe off her leash.

"Want to tell me about the funeral?" Allie asked. And Brooke did. She
gave her all the pertinent details: LJ's obnoxious behavior; the cousins
who were there (Allie knew them all by name); the fact that Brooke's
mother hadn't shown up; how everyone in the family came to the whispering consensus that it would have been cruel to tell her father's third
wife—Shelley's sick mother, Elizabeth—about the death and the funeral.
All the Whitbys knew about Elizabeth losing her mind and her increased
stints in hospitals over the past few months.

Allie listened to the report with interest, nodding along in her solemn-
yet-thoughtful Allie way. Then she moved onto the rug too and sat with
her legs straight in front of her so that the sides of their feet touched.
"Well, you knew this was coming. And at least this chapter is over now.
Can you feel good about that?"

Brooke took a deep breath and leaned into the side of Allie's body. She
had shed a few tears at Forest Lawn cemetery while her father was being
lowered into the ground, in the plot next to Grandfather Whitby. But
sobbing was not in Brooke's precise nature. Since her father had died, she
had not, in fact, lost it.

"It's not over," she told Allie, her voice wavering with emotion. "It's not
over, because my father—he did something cruel, although I don't know
how cruel he meant it to be. He gave my house away."

"What?" Allie placed two hands on the tops of Brooke's knees. "This
house? How would he be able to give it away?"

"You know it's his," Brooke whispered, then explained the whole thing. She couldn't control her tears. Allie turned and held Brooke, her firm breasts pressing beneath Brooke's smaller and softer ones. Involuntarily, Brooke felt her sobs getting louder. In the past few months, she'd seen Allie less than she ever had since the day they really met each other, during Parents' Weekend when they were in their first year, third form, at St. Paul's. Now she could count on her fingers the times they'd been together that winter: a planned dinner at Sonsie, Jules's birthday drinks, and one accidental run-in by the Frog Pond skating rink. But here Allie was, showing up at the moment when Brooke needed her most, making the whole tilting world seem so much more stable.

Allie wove her warm fingers into Brooke's. Then she stroked the top of Brooke's hand, just as she'd been doing for years. Did they hold hands like this in high school, or had they waited until they were in their twenties, when their love affair had finally, totally begun? Now Allie's mouth was by Brooke's ear, kissing her lightly.

Brooke leaned back and caught her breath. "I can't, Als. Marc said he's coming over for lunch today."

Allie flinched.

"I need to pee," Brooke mumbled, and lugged her now leaden body up off the ground, remembering to pick up her leather purse.

"I'll be here," Allie said, grimacing.

Inside the white-tiled bathroom, Brooke perched for a moment on the side of the claw-foot tub. Everything was fine: she was still in her house; she still had her job. And Allie was there. Just like Armond said, "All is not lost." She took the pregnancy test box out of her bag and as she unwrapped the plastic, she noticed that her hands were shaking. This was ridiculous: she was a medical professional, good in a crisis. This was just a logical, rational precaution. She peed on the foam wick and four minutes later, after breathing deeply with her eyes closed from the side of the tub, she stood up and peered at the tiny window.

She took in the information clinically at first. Then a thought occurred to her: how funny that most modern women find out life-changing news while locked inside a tiny room, all alone. Perhaps at that very moment, millions of other women were looking down at these little sticks, shocked. There they were: two faint pink plus signs.

Her heart began to race. Her breath sped up. The biological chances of this happening were less than 20 percent. She knew this as fact, she kept track of her body. She looked again at the faded pink symbols and tried to inform herself of the news: *I am pregnant.* She heard footsteps in the hallway. Allie, walking toward the kitchen. Allie's footsteps landing on her floor.

She loved those footsteps. Now panic set in. She loved the fact that Allie's feet were in her house. And once Allie knew about this pregnancy, she would certainly leave forever. Brooke's hand went instinctively to the lower part of her abdomen. She was pregnant. With Marc Costa's child. Upon looking down at the plastic stick, she realized perhaps this was what she wanted to happen, but this was certainly not *the way* she wanted it to happen. It felt as though everything that had been secured to the floor was now blasted into the air, floating. She stumbled back onto the edge of the old tub. She felt her fear coming true—the Whitby Curse was actually returning. Despite Armond's assurances, it was all coming apart again. Soon she would have nothing to grasp on to.

7

It was two weeks after Shelley fled college and her waitressing job that she met Mr. Kamal. She'd needed money quick, although looking back, it was just a tiny sum. The shock of what we didn't know can impress us, over and again.

Shelley had never lived alone before. She was staying up late watching episodes of *E! True Hollywood Story*, sleeping until noon, then beginning her day with a tropical fruit juice and Stoli concoction. Why the hell not? This setup was temporary—it would end any day, whenever her mother returned. Occasionally she wondered if this was the lifestyle her mother inhabited, before she fell off the edge into mania. But Shelley quickly dismissed those thoughts; she wasn't like her mother. She was a kid, and this was normal behavior. She was happy to have left Demming, really. Not only was she wasting her time there, but with every plastic cup of beer and plate of french fries and matinee at the South Hills Cinema, she was unnecessarily draining her bank account. But now that she was away from that ineffectual yet busy college life, her days seemed longer than they'd ever been. The night after she'd arrived home, she had picked up the ringing landline phone, and thus been found by the shrill voice of Ms. Scribner, who had apparently talked to some random Demming girl and learned that Shelley had returned home. Then, of course, Ms. Scribner had told the lawyer, Armond, where Shelley was. Now she received phone calls from each of them on a near daily basis. Some days it was a mere check-in ("Heard from Nick?"), but other days there were thundering yells from Ms. Scribner and the occasional cry. She felt deadened to these outbursts. Since Roger's death, Shelley's life had been on hold, and it seemed that Nick's was too. He'd surely pop up when things returned to normal.

One Tuesday Shelley was up early: 11:52 a.m. The phone rang, and there was Ms. Scribner, inconsolable. "Is he dead, Shelley? Is my baby dead? Gone forever, lying in a park somewhere—murdered and cast away?" She continued like this while Shelley remained silent. The police had gotten involved. Nick was considered missing, but Shelley hadn't succumbed to the panic. It was just the kind of thing he would do, disappear so that everyone would pay attention to him. "You don't understand," Ms. Scribner wailed over the line. "You're too young, you've never even known anyone who has died." Shelley didn't respond, but rather felt a kick of sorrow in her stomach as she refilled her drink in a pint glass that read *50th Reunion, Exeter Class of '41.* The glass had belonged to her father.

Shelley hadn't spoken to her other half siblings, although Ms. Scribner said many of them were at their father's funeral. This confirmed two facts: that there had actually been a funeral, and that the other children had conveniently gotten the message about it. With this news, that kick became an ache lodged in Shelley's gut. Her half siblings were quick to forget her. They were so much older than her, living lives she couldn't imagine. Brooke was her only connection to them, and even she hadn't told Shelley about it. The other half siblings were more like distant cousins who only reached out when they had a personally pressing need. She imagined their distraction right now, the raging fires popping up in the houses of each of her semi brothers and sisters. They must have spent the past week calling each other late at night, wrapping strands of pearls around their fingers and crunching the ice from their drained tumblers. "He would do this to us, just one final smack from the grave. He would give everything to the one person who *isn't even a real Whitby.*"

Shelley's half siblings called Nick that on several occasions, whenever there was a family reunion or a wedding or a funeral that required most of them in attendance. Shelley was related to them by blood—half the stuff coursing through her was similar to half the stuff coursing through them—and to the older crew of siblings, this was enough to include her. Although Roger's marriage to Shelley's mother certainly upset and disrupted the previous families, his other children never seemed to hold it against Shelley personally. Of course, there was another reason she was included by her father's first two families. Shelley's mother was a Saltman: an East Coast–bred, putter-around-in-loafers, old, wealthy family. The Saltmans knew the Whitbys, always. But Nick's mother was simply a schoolteacher. She had grown up in California, where no one was really from. Ms. Scribner was uncouth, short, and heavy-set in the wrong places; she was clearly not their kind, and therefore, neither was Nick. Shelley imagined Kiki and Andrew, and all the rest of the lawyers and bankers and stay-at-home moms with Princeton degrees, scoffing through the phone lines: "Obviously that woman is behind the change in the will," which actually meant, *That woman is trash, trash, trash.*

As Shelley's lonely days in her mother's apartment piled up, she watched her physical pile of cash dwindle down. She paced her intake of Virginia Slims and bought the off-brand tropical fruit juice. Yet the money still went. Her mother, her sweet and well-intentioned mother, had been sick for years, but as far as Shelley knew, she really *could* be dashing back and forth from the Vineyard to Boston, talking to lawyers and "saying goodbye" to the old house. Although this was the longest stint, this was not the first time she'd dropped off. Elizabeth's previous disappearances had always been due to hospitalizations. After the first hospitalization, when Shelley was in high school and Biddy was still alive, Elizabeth had returned home and said absently, under her breath but very clearly, "I am no longer in charge." Shelley had stopped in her tracks in the parlor but had not responded. If they talked about the comment, it would become established, more true. Yes, her mother sometimes needed help. And if she was in the hospital now, then she was also being taken care of. Someone, at some point, would let Shelley know.

After a week of camping out alone, she'd finally called up some friends. Charlotte and Zoë were girls she'd gone to Spence with; girls she'd slept beside during sleepovers at their country houses; girls who, for their own reasons, were not in college but rather living in upper Manhattan with their families. They had met some trouble-making skateboarding boys in Union Square and brought them back to Strong Place on a Friday night with beers and rolling papers. Shelley accidentally fell asleep upstairs on Biddy's old elevated bed and awoke around five in the morning. She stumbled down to the parlor to see her guests kneeling around the coffee table with a beefy Latino man, snorting lines off the cover of an art book. The dealer had baggy jeans with one leg rolled up—he had ridden his bike there. They were all jabbering and smoking cigarettes with abrupt hand gestures when this rolled-up man lifted himself off the floor and down again onto the end of the powder-blue velvet settee, which broke under his weight. The foot cracked vertically in two pieces, and the couch fell on one of its haunches.

Shelley turned toward the accident: she was in a haze, confused. "Why'd th-that happen?" she stuttered. The man shrugged, and Shelley thought of her mother. Of all things she would care about when she returned, this was the most grave. Although technically it belonged to Roger, the house was the only beloved possession her mother still had. Elizabeth Saltman Whitby truly loved their four walls, their constricted rooms and ancient possessions.

"Bastards!" Shelley yelled at the crowd. The two girls and three boys in the living room giggled at various pitches, as if she were joking. She wiped her nose with the back of her hand and nearly spat. "Out! Everyone out, all of you! Now."

She pointed and pushed the drug-laden group through the kitchen and out the front door, then watched them descend the cobbled street in the predawn. Inconsiderate. Selfish. Not one of them had said a thing about her father. Neither Charlotte nor Zoë even knew that Nick was missing. Had she ever made a decent friend in her life?

Back upstairs in Biddy's bed, the sun rose as Shelley alternately pulled at the roots of her hair and released tears that resembled trickles of sweat. It was midmorning when she concluded that what she needed to do was make some cash and hire a professional to repair the couch before her mother returned. She went into the cramped office, turned on the old desktop, and went onto Craigslist. She'd thought of this work before; what occasionally broke young woman in New York hadn't? She perused the Casual Encounters section, searching *M4W* and *Paid* and responded to the first three bulletins. Then she clicked on the Etc. / Misc. tab, where the headline of the first ad announced: ASSISTANT TO BLIND PROFESSIONAL NEEDED, UPPER EAST SIDE. The body of the notice said: "Looking for well-educated young woman to read to clinically blind architect, in his home. Must have strong reading voice and be able to take dictation. Position available immediately."

She shot off another thoughtless message, which invented a college degree, before her drowsy head wavered and dropped to the shellacked surface of the rolltop letter desk.

Her cell phone's ring woke her; her back ached from having slept while sitting.

"Hello?" a deep voice inquired over the line. It was a voice that commanded a listener to follow it; a voice that believed it was owed another's time. Shelley was disoriented. Her email held messages from two of the three Casual Encounter requests she'd responded to. The voice on the phone continued, "This is Yousef Kamal. I have been told you responded to my ad for a reader." Each vowel of the last word was elongated, articulated individually.

"Oh, yes, hello." She was surprised that her pitch hit an octave higher than normal. She had never thought of herself as shy. At Spence she'd often sat in the wood-paneled office of the upper school dean. *Mr. Berneson, stop making the girls sing that banana song, it's perverted*, she'd said to her sixth-grade music teacher. *Mrs. Michaelson, if you didn't smoke cigarettes by the jungle gym you wouldn't have so many wrinkles and your husband wouldn't have left you.* Fourth grade, mandatory suspension. *The Fulbright committee called and said they'd never give you a fellowship, because you are so unbelievably average.* Dr. Kelly, seventh grade. Grown-man tears.

"Let me tell you about myself," the voice over the phone bellowed. "I am the master architect of two public monuments and multifarious classical buildings, both American and abroad. I was rendered into absolute blindness from an automobile accident at age twenty-four."

The first two emails back from her M4W responses were polite: "Looking for a freak, hope you fit. Let's play! Respond and I'll send location." And "Business man who can give a good spanking, fun and easy. If you're ready to have it I'm ready to give it. Fast cash—must respond now." But she had two more emails from the second man: "Meet at 5 at my office. My desk is waiting. I'll spread you over it. A sure $150." Then: "What's your fucking problem? I'm sick of undependable cunts. I need to leave my office soon."

Shelley opted to respond to the voice on the phone. "I see—"

He said, "I am looking for someone to help me, to read to me. How soon can you come in for an interview?"

Two hours later Shelley had showered and crossed the park. She found herself on Sixty-Eighth Street and Madison Avenue, standing in front of the Grisham: a mammoth stone building that fit into the dignified air of the neighborhood. She unfastened the safety pin that held her peacoat shut. It was a nice coat, really, it was just old. As soon as her mother returned from the Vineyard she would surely buy Shelley a new one. They'd probably go to the Patagonia store and buy one of those non-puffy down pieces, her mother hugging Shelley's body sideways as they descended the wide, crowded sidewalk on Columbus. But for now, Shelley took the safety pin out from where a button should be and put it in her pocket.

One deep breath, and she walked into the lobby. The doorman was shrunken; the starch of his black-and-gold uniform seemed as if it alone were holding him up.

"How may I help you?"

"I'm here to see Mr. Kamal."

He looked her up and down. "Top floor, ma'am. Press fourteen."

As Shelley ascended the stacked floors of the Grisham, she knew exactly where she was. She rose past locked apartments where children in sparse kitchens were tucked into highchairs, being fed dinners of cut-up hot dogs and brown rice by their tired nannies. The doorman was returning to his post, fixing his eyes through the glass door, onto the pavement's yellow traffic lines, dotted with brown maple leaves that had emerged from the late-thawing snow. Across the street at the Stylus Club, white-haired women pretended to smile while sipping lukewarm decaf in the drawing room, discussing their dead husbands.

The elevator opened directly into the apartment. Its low *bing* and the jut of the doors made Shelley sigh. It was familiar; just the same as the apartments of the Charlottes and Zoës of her life. How nice to return to the places you were really from. She swallowed, looked up, and there he was. In the foyer stood Mr. Yousef Kamal, almost falling into the open doors.

He had no eyes. He was Middle Eastern, in his midsixties, wearing a crisp oxford and belted khakis. His hand extended, waiting. He had sparse, wiry hair. Where there would normally be convex bulbs there were scooped recesses, largely obscured by drooping skin. The cornea, the pupil, the retina below, none existed—only two moonlike slivers of white were visible just below the eyelids.

For a moment she froze, terrified. He didn't look human. *Inappropriate,* she thought, even for her. She stuck her hand right into his. "Shelley Whitby. Nice to meet you."

"And you as well. I am Yousef Abdel Kamal. Please, follow me." He turned into the dimly lit front room. "Now, some of these rugs are more than two hundred years old. I ask that you remove your shoes." The rugs were beige and blue with intricate Persian designs. The grandfather clock swung into a chime. A wall of plates displayed colorful, geometric designs, a few containing looping Arabic script.

She kicked off her boots as he moved his stocking feet with deliberate shucks, his hands flexed about his hips. "Come now. Shall we go to my athenaeum?"

He led Shelley through the front of the twelve-room apartment, starting with the dining room, where the table was set with fine china, crystal glasses, and silver serving trays. A three-tiered cake stand stood as a centerpiece. There was no food on the table, but the places were set: it appeared a great dinner was about to be had and then abandoned. Something about this old room reminded Shelley of the empty apartment Grandmother Whitby had kept on Sixty-Fifth, the one that seemed to disappear after she died. When they reached the russet-glossed study, Mr. Kamal questioned, "Is the light on in the room?"

There were small lamps glowing behind an oversize wooden desk, though it was darker than what Shelley was used to. In the far corner of the room was a pristine white drafting table, tilted up. Beside it, a tall, glass cylinder rested on the floor, containing oversized scrolls of paper—blueprints or plans. "Yes, two lights."

Mr. Kamal sat behind the desk, and Shelley in front of it. He waited for her to stop shifting. "You went to Demming, I see. Now tell me, Shelley, what do your parents do?"

"Uh," she stuttered. Could he know she was one of *those* Whitbys? Her nerves pricked up one by one. She got the distinct impression that he knew more about people than others did; perhaps his lack of sight gave him other gifts.

Mr. Kamal waited with a stony face.

Shelley's mother had never had a job. The family lived off Biddy and her father's semipopular shop, Whitby Shades and Blinds, which he'd opened on a whim.

"Well," she sighed, "my mother's in real estate, and my father owned a shop."

He nodded. "And where do they complete these jobs?"

"I'm from the city."

"Very good."

When Shelley's father met her mother he was already on his second marriage and still the ambassador to the Caribbean. His eldest daughter from his second marriage, Kiki Whitman Whitby, had been a senior at Demming College, where she was the best friend and roommate of Elizabeth Saltman, Shelley's mother. Roger Whitby Jr., Kiki's father, would come to visit his daughter for a week at a time, as the trip from the island of Barbados was not quick. After his third trip to Poughkeepsie, he announced to everyone that he was divorcing his wife and marrying his daughter's college roommate, the young Elizabeth Saltman. They were married in December, right after the fall semester ended, twenty-one-year-old Elizabeth and fifty-nine-year-old Roger, on horseback on a Caribbean beach. It was a small wedding, about thirty people. Many of the guests were Whitbys—weddings were something they showed up for. Hats were big then, according to Biddy. Boxy ones adorned with peacock feathers and netting kept blowing off and landing in the sand. Biddy—who had been pleased, of course, that her daughter was marrying a Whitby, but had also expected nothing less—had recounted the scene to Shelley numerous times: as Elizabeth sat atop her horse, a large gust blew her empire-waist dress back against her body, and her four-and-a-half-month pregnant stomach was outlined in ivory crepe. Inside of Elizabeth, Shelley was growing at a healthy and rapid rate. The crowd squawked and clucked, though the bride and groom couldn't hear it over the wind off the water.

In his dim study, Mr. Kamal continued the interview. "I already know you are prompt. But are you neat? Would you say you are an organized person?"

"Very much so."

"And happy? As a child? Do you often have regrets?"

Shelley heard an uncharacteristic giggle escape from her throat, and then cut it off—he wanted her to answer. "Oh. As a child I was very happy."

"I meant these days. What's the most recent mistake you have made?"

Could he sense her eyebrows rising? She pictured her body passed out in a Z shape on Biddy's bed, while the party in the parlor clamored on.

"I don't often have regrets."

Mr. Kamal nodded, the horizontal line of his mouth taut. He was a powerful figure, a commander. But there was something strange about this squat man. "And happy, are you a happy person?"

"Very," she responded, growing weary of the questions.

"Fine. Now: What do you know about me?"

What was she supposed to know about him? She'd looked him up on the internet quickly before leaving the house but had only learned that he was blind and built many low-rise buildings and restored the National Cathedral in Washington. "Well, I've heard about you, and read about you. And I think—I mean, I must have been inside some of your buildings."

"Yes, well. I am the master architect of two public monuments. I am the winner of the Driehaus Prize, and I worked in conjunction with Prince Charles of England and the Royal Family. I attended MIT and taught at Princeton."

Shelley understood by the silent beat that she was meant to respond. "Wow."

"I was blinded shortly after beginning my London apprenticeship with the father of new classical architecture, Raymond Erith. Mr. Erith then took me under his wing and allowed me to plan and envision without the use of my eyes. It was he, and my first assistant in his office, who enabled me to design masterpieces through the use of touch, smell, and sound."

The speech sounded mechanical, as if he were expounding the long version of his name. "My assistants have always acted as my amanuenses. Do you know what an amanuensis is?"

Shelley scanned her brain. "No."

"John Milton wrote with an amanuensis. Andrea Bocelli composes with an amanuensis. And I build with an amanuensis. All of my communications, theories, and plans have been dictated to someone, who then physically transcribes my ideas. This person also acts as my first editor, because I will occasionally ask them how a line falls or a tower rises."

"I see."

"Now tell me, how does that sound to you? Do you think that is something you could do?"

"Yes, definitely." A trickle of cold sweat ran down the right side of her rib cage, but she made a point of smiling. Perhaps he could sense a smile, just as one knows if someone is smiling on the other end of the phone line. Her adrenaline was waning. There were other jobs.

"This is a unique moment in my career, as I am endeavoring something new. I plan to write my own narrative book, the first of its kind by a great architectural mind. Would you be interested in this becoming a full-time position, if you are up to the task?"

"Yes!" She perked up. "That would be wonderful. Fantastic." Writing was the one subject in school that she'd been okay at. She'd produced nothing gut-ripping, but opinions she was not short of, and her education had, if nothing else, taught her to record them correctly. Shelley had never actually visualized what her grown-up life would look like before. No one had expressed realistic hopes that she become any kind of professional. Shelley always assumed that ambition was something she'd get to later. And after her father left, that later kept getting pushed further and further away. Her half sister Brooke was the only one who had ever even inquired about Shelley's predilections and minor talents. While the other, older half siblings couldn't be bothered, Brooke seemed committed to the charade that the two of them knew each other better than they really did. And despite all her eye-rolling, Shelley accepted Brooke's put-on and the attention that came with it. But the older girl never seemed to accept that Shelley was not what one called a go-getter. She hated running, and couldn't be bothered to keep her bureau tidy or her bed made. What she did like were the old Grateful Dead CDs Brooke had given her years before. And rip-off bands like Guster and the Slip. Her mind flashed to an easy life of walking to the Grisham with earphones on.

Mr. Kamal's austere mask seemed to break for a moment, and his mouth contorted to something of a frown. "Now I must tell you something, because when you are looking me up on the World Wide Web you may come across it: a few years ago, I had a mentally deranged assistant."

"Oh." Then she offered, "Sorry."

"She was mentally deranged and wrote an article about me. A defaming article. Despicable. She accused me of everything—everything. From perjury to rape to murder."

The last word fell slowly through the dim, unventilated air. They were alone in the study with the door closed. Her mind raced to whether there was anyone else in the apartment.

Mr. Kamal continued, "I could not be a rapist."

She told herself: *He's a blind man. He is barely moving.*

"There's no way I could be a rapist. I won the Driehaus Prize!"

Now the word struck her as if she'd been physically hit. This was not the kind of crap she took. When an evangelical loon preached on the subway, Shelley was the one in the car who screamed, "You don't know me! Don't put your demon gods on me!" But Mr. Kamal was old. And his frame looked too small to truly crush her, if he tried. She took a deep breath and gripped the edges of the wooden chair. She visualized the broken couch leg, her MIA mother, and her own bank statement that read $41.50. Her high-pitched giggle returned. "That's terrible, I'm sorry."

"Yes. Well." His voice dialed back to its lower tone. "Will you choose a book, any book, off the shelf? Open to the middle of it, and begin reading to me."

Shelley stood and perused the floor-to-ceiling bookcase beside her. Her mouth was dry. All the books were reference: *The Encyclopedia of the Victorian World, The Economist Desk Companion, The Almanac of Famous Men.* Finally, on a lower shelf, she found something. "I have Shakespeare's sonnets here."

"No. Much too difficult. Choose something else. Perhaps you should look in the bookcase beside me." Moving across the room, Shelley realized that again, it was full of volumes of reference material. There was one non-reference book on the shelf, Freud's *The Interpretation of Dreams.*

"All I could find was Freud."

"Yes. Go ahead, read from the middle."

She sat back down in front of the desk, opened the book, and strained her neck in order to see the print in the low light. She took a deep breath. "'Illusions commend themselves to us because they save us pain and allow us to enjoy pleasure instead. We must therefore accept it without complaint when they sometimes collide with a bit of reality against which they are dashed to pieces . . .'"

When the interview was ostensibly over and they both stood up to leave the study, Mr. Kamal announced in his booming voice, "Shelley Whitby, everyone is deprived of something. I want to find out just what it is that you are deprived of." He grabbed her forearm. She resisted for a flash but then let him lead her out of the room and over his ancient carpets. The word *deprived* echoed through her mind, as if it physically ricocheted off the penthouse walls. She was all alone now. Her father was dead, and her mother might never come back. But on paper, she was a Whitby. The antithesis of deprivation. When this man found out, he would surely figure she didn't need the money and refuse to pay her. Her pulse sped up. She was, in fact, broke. Mr. Kamal moved toward the elevator a few steps ahead of her, his arm behind him, gripping hers tightly.

Why was she letting this happen? A meek voice emerged from her throat, offering a goodbye. "And thank you."

He hung there, sipping in small exasperated breaths. "I think you are a very nervous person," he said. "You seem too nervous."

That was enough. She thought if she put up with that interview at least she would be compensated.

"But I want you to come back tomorrow. I will give you another try. I will call you promptly at nine o'clock tonight."

The elevator door opened as Shelley was nodding, catching herself before she tripped over her unbuckled boots. She forced herself to say, "Thank you again."

As she rode the elevator down and then exited the building, she was shaking and wasn't sure why. She found herself released into the Upper East Side night, the street a spectrum of rotating taxicab lights and streams of people walking, directed, looking at no one. Who was that man? What had she just done? She struggled to hold her coat closed, but she soldiered on, making her way toward home.

8

From Marc's bed, Brooke heard the shower go on. She looked down at her bare, exposed stomach: it was pale and soft but very flat. She hadn't told Marc anything about the pregnancy, because she hadn't yet decided what to do. It was hard to believe that life had taken hold in there, that an organism had glommed on to one of her body parts and was now thriving and growing in time to her own heartbeat. But she was utterly exhausted every day and nauseated upon waking. She placed her palm below her belly button to check if, illogically, the skin was warmer there. A ridiculous thing for a nurse to do. She was unraveling.

Marc's apartment, on the twenty-eighth floor of the Prudential Center, might have been the highest residential space in all of Boston. Brooke leaned over a bedside table and held down a white switch, which made the wide shades raise on the wall of windows. Slowly a picture of Copley Square and the brown town houses of Newbury Street came into view, then Storrow Drive and finally the blue snake that was the Charles River. It was a sunny day, and a few triangular sails floated out on the water. Brave souls, it had to be frigid out there.

It was nearly noon and a Tuesday, but Brooke's work schedule was off-kilter that week because she'd covered for a colleague with a sick child. Today was her nurse's Saturday, and Marc could work whenever he pleased. He was a developer with his family business, Costa Construction.

He was one of those guys who walked around construction sites in a suit jacket, wearing a hard hat. Most of his business was in the dismal, far-out suburbs—Waltham and Framingham and Whitman. But he'd begun embarking on bigger projects on the Cape to turn unused land into strip malls, working with the Davidson Corporation, the same people who now owned her family's hotel. His work was unseemly, really, but Brooke didn't focus on it, or listen very carefully, when he reported on his day. From the bathroom she heard music go on, and then Marc's own cracking voice singing along with the gruff tones of DMX: "'*Stop! Drop!*'"

At forty-two, he was as mature as he was ever going to be: whatever she signed up for now with Marc was what she was getting forever. What had once been refreshing about him—his nonserious nature, his appreciation for indulgences, his long summer sails under the New England sun—was no longer. And the hope that she had for herself, that she could embrace his family the way she had Allie's, and become once again a member of a loud and loving clan, was quickly diminishing. She hadn't slept at Marc's apartment the previous night. She almost never did, as he was a late riser and didn't have the kitchen gadgets she needed for her particular blended smoothie breakfast. And now with the morning nausea, she certainly had to avoid it. But she had come over around eleven because they were going together to look at a house in the suburbs. Brooke had told Marc about her father's will and the mysterious, invisible boy who was slated to steal her house away from her. After she'd recounted the news, Marc hadn't asked one question about how it had made her feel, nor had he offered a condolence on losing her home. Instead, Marc had grinned. He was delighted. He wanted her to live with him. But how could this relationship that had begun as a distraction from her regular life become the rest of it?

His shower water turned off now, and she realized she only had a minute to try Shelley again. For over a week, Brooke had been calling Shelley's cell phone every day at various hours, to no avail. She just wasn't answering. As the phone began to ring, in came Marc with a towel tied around his waist and his tan chest exposed. He looked good for any age; the only sign that he was in his forties was that the small patches of hair above his nipples had gone slightly gray and bushy.

A voice on the other end of the phone line said, "Hello?"

"Shelley!" Brooke was taken off guard. "I haven't been able to reach you. It's Brooke! How's school going?"

"Fine."

Brooke watched Marc drop his towel on the floor and walk naked into his long, narrow closet. He wasn't listening to her call.

"Do you know about Dad?" Brooke spoke into the receiver, stumbling over the word *Dad*. Normally, she would only use that term with her full siblings, Kiki and LJ. With Shelley and the older Vanderbilt half siblings, she called her father Roger. But this was not a time to make anyone feel like an outsider.

Shelley sucked in a loud breath. "I know."

Brooke paused. What she wanted to say was: *Do you have this same hollowed-out feeling that I have? How would I feel right now if he had ever apologized to me? That's what I wanted to hear: I wanted to hear him say, "I'm sorry for all the trouble I caused. I have faith in you. You're making the right choices in life." Did you want to hear that too?*

Brooke said into the cell phone, "Then you know about Nick Scribner? And what's happening to our houses?"

"Nick Whitby, Brooke. His last name is Whitby."

"Okay. So you're aware that we're screwed, right?" She sighed. "You know the kid better than the rest of us. There's no logical way that he would give up these houses, right?"

"We're not screwed!" Shelley's voice rose into the middle ground between a shriek and a whine. "You and Armond don't know Nick at all. There's nothing to worry about. No one is fucking *screwed*."

"Calm down, Shells. I'm just trying to be realistic. Do you know of a way to get in touch with him? Armond says that even Susan can't find him."

Shelley didn't answer.

Brooke pushed on. "When was the last time you saw him?"

"I saw him over our winter breaks. But no, I haven't talked to him recently. He's fine though. It's going to work out. There's no reason it wouldn't."

Shelley was just the type of person who defensively, always, convinced herself that everything was fine. She was a magical thinker. What was happening with her right now was very far from fine—her house was going to get taken away too, and Brooke knew all about Shelley's mother's sickness. Shelley's grandmother, the only other person who had ever really taken care of the girl, had died several years ago. It was a sincere comfort to Brooke that although Kiki and LJ had basically divorced themselves from her family, they still existed. Just as their mother had disappeared into Connecticut postdivorce, her jaw set in determination not to be taken down any further by Roger, Kiki had fled to England after her father married her old roommate. And now, years later, Kiki was fully wrapped up in her own three children, whom Brooke could barely tell apart. They'd come to visit Boston every year or two, staying at the Copley Plaza and inviting Brooke on a Duck Tour or to a game at Fenway, where Kiki would occupy herself with baby wipes and juice boxes and snickering at the ugly footwear of Americans, as if she herself had been raised in the United Kingdom. On the rare occasion that Kiki's husband, Will, would pop up, he'd offer a handshake before burying his grimacing face in the business section of the *International Herald Tribune*.

LJ was another story. Brooke missed him, deeply, but knew that if he were around he'd just be disrupting her life. LJ, who seemed to only be friends with people like Marc now, lived in Las Vegas and appeared to be following in their father's footsteps by getting himself involved in one risky business venture after another. But he consciously distanced himself from all things Whitby, including the East Coast. And since they'd entered their thirties, Brooke had sometimes gone years at a time without seeing him. Still, he would call her when he was in trouble, as if she were the older sibling rather than the younger, and ask for advice and occasionally a loan.

Yes, her full siblings were difficult and largely absent. But they were hers. If she ever truly needed them, they would be there. Poor only-child Shelley was more alone than Brooke.

"When's your graduation, Shells? I'd love to come. And I think it would be good to see each other to discuss our plan about Nick."

"We don't need a plan. And I'm not going to graduation. It's a ceremony for corny losers, so I'm skipping it."

She was being more obstreperous than usual. "Come on." Brooke clucked her tongue. "You have to go!"

Shelley said nothing.

"Let me celebrate you."

"Just come to New York in the summer, when I'm back. Anyway, I gotta get off the phone. Big test coming up."

Brooke sighed and hung up the way they always said goodbye, since back in their Vineyard friendship days. "Ciao-ciao."

"Ciao-ciao," Shelley muttered.

Marc emerged from his closet fully clothed: sharkskin slacks, an electric-blue oxford, and shining leather shoes.

"Up and at 'em," he said with a wink. "Let's go check out Brooke in Brookline. Let's go see how hot you look in this mansion I'm going to buy for you."

Marc seemed happy. Or, more than happy, he seemed relieved. His father, Lorenzo, was also a developer, one who had made the right financial moves early in life and fought through connections with some of the toughest men in the city of Boston. (No one ever articulated the word *mob*, but it was clear.) When Marc was ten, Lorenzo had moved the whole family out of the immigrant-laden urban neighborhood of Dorchester and into a huge house in the sprawling suburban enclave of Natick, where it was widely acknowledged that the Costas had made it. Now Marc, the spoiled only son, the one who had made nothing for himself, might finally follow in his father's footsteps: he thought he was going to marry a Whitby and make it.

"Did you even hear that I was on the phone?" Brooke asked him as she sat up in the bed.

"Mmm. My man LJ? What kinda trouble is he stirring up now?" Marc let out a weak chuckle. He always had a vaguely distracted air about him, as if ready to stop listening the second a conversation got too complex or heavy for his liking. Occasionally she thought of him as a six-foot-tall toddler. He tossed Brooke her lavender blouse from where it had landed on the floor.

"No, it wasn't LJ." Just after the funeral, LJ had called her from Reno. It was six in the morning in Boston, which meant it was the middle of the night in Nevada. He claimed he'd had a small motorcycle accident, that his bike had been clipped by a landscaping truck. But why would a landscaper be driving around in the middle of the night? He'd clearly gotten into some fight somewhere and gotten himself hurt. Another notch on the belt of Whitby destruction. Brooke hissed at Marc now: "It isn't funny to talk about LJ like that. Plus that wasn't him on the phone. That was Shelley. Do you even know who that is?"

"Sure I do." Marc's hopeful expression fell swiftly. "We're gonna be late, Brooke. Let's go." He walked out of the bedroom.

She closed her eyes. She was the one being childish—petulant in front of a man who only wanted to help her. Brooke knew that the right thing to do would be to perk up, go look at this ugly McMansion, and try to gather the scraps of her life together as best she could. In recent years, she'd put the thought of having a child out of her head, as it had been too painful to accept the reality that she probably wouldn't have one. But now she let herself wonder: What kind of mother would she be? Attentive. Present, even if something bad happened, unlike her own had been after Peter died. She and Marc could have this baby, and the baby would have a backyard and a big bedroom to itself, and most important, a greater family of grandparents and aunts—Marc's sisters—around. Brooke would be a mother and wear a heavy diamond ring on her left hand. Her friends would giggle at its gaudiness, but they would still be there to giggle. Some of them would even drive out from the city for lunch in the summertime, bringing their kids to jump in the Costas' pool. It wasn't what she'd ever pictured. It was more gauche than anything the Whitbys did. But, even if slightly tacky, the baby could be surrounded by many loving arms. It was what she wanted for this baby. It was what she wanted for herself.

A wave of nausea rolled through her, and Brooke shot out of bed. She ran to the stainless steel bathroom and kneeled in front of the toilet, evacuating her morning smoothie from her stomach at an alarmingly forceful rate. Terrified that Marc could hear her throwing up, she tried to flush the toilet as it was happening. After the worst of the episode was over, she leaned her head against the stone-tiled wall. She would call Shelley back and ask to meet her in New York as soon as possible. They needed to talk, face-to-face. They at least needed to try to locate their half brother.

All of this was her father's fault. He had caused her life to fall apart that first time, and he was doing it again now. When she was young all the trouble actually began not when her little brother got sick, but when Roger attempted to run for governor. Brooke had pinpointed the beginning of the end to one particular day: that early-spring party, when her father had officially announced his campaign. All the Whitbys were there. Twelve-year-old Brooke stood on the steps of the Massachusetts State House in her heavy wool coat, just a few short blocks from her house on Joy Street, with her straw-like hair sticking out of her wide-brimmed Easter hat. Before the speech began, while she was trailing her father through the crowd, old men kept stopping her. "Never be surprised by what your dad chooses to do!" one bald guy said, with a wink. Another, with a raspy voice, "Your family did come across on the *Mayflower*, so your father is actually from Massachusetts more than the rest of us."

Roger overheard that last one and nudged an elbow into the man's arm. "Ah, Bob, I don't know what I'm doing!" Then he added with a wink, "Saw Judge Strout in back, he's looking for you." That was her father: simultaneously self-deprecating and name-dropping—saying he didn't belong, while making it damn clear that he knew everyone who did. Yet his children, especially Brooke, knew a different story. Roger's jolly-go-lucky attitude was genuine but also precariously thin. The surface of it could be pierced at any moment and Roger would fall through into a pit of gloom that no one could pull him out of.

Brooke thought she knew where this penchant stemmed from. Roger had often told his children the story of how the body of his brother, Quentin, was found washed up on the shores of the East River in 1956, in what was then a homeless encampment in Battery Park. The rest of the Whitbys upheld that Quentin must have been murdered. But after years of searching, the investigation closed without finding a culprit, and Roger always professed, angrily, that passersby had reported seeing a figure who resembled Quentin lurking at the edge of Brooklyn Bridge, looking down. It was a terrible story, but every time Roger told it, it was clear that he'd loved his brother, cherished him in all his tragic glory. And yet after the story, Roger would go dark, for hours or even days. Although it rarely happened in public, when it did occur it was a violently quick transition. But it hadn't seemed to happen once since he began his campaign.

As Roger began his speech at the temporary podium in the middle of the State House steps, little Brooke, lined up between her mother and Kiki, faced the crowd and scanned it for people she knew. Her uncle and cousins from New York were in the front; there were her older, mysterious half siblings from her father's first marriage; farther back were her great-aunts and second cousins and all these family hangers-on—"friends" and employees they had collected throughout the years. Behind Brooke the red-brick and white columns of the State House held up the massive golden dome, glinting in the sun beside an American flag, snapping in the April wind. The scene might have been a postcard of what the patrician pilgrims dreamed for their New England home. Behind the podium, her father smiled in his newsboy hat and open trench coat, which revealed a maroon bow tie, his signature style. He was large already back then, his face puffy and stomach solidly round. But that didn't stop him from being light on his feet, shifting and jumping up the steps while he talked in front of the reporters, the photographers, and all of the Whitby cousins.

His voice boomed: "This coming November, the great state of Massachusetts will face one of the most important elections in this century. And you might be thinking, what's this old New Yorker doing on our State House steps? Well, let me tell you. I have been won over by

Massachusetts—by its history, by its traditions, by its physical beauty. Although I might have been born in the Big Apple, I'm proud to call the Bay State my home. My home for now, and *forever!*"

He had been campaigning for months already, although unofficially. Brooke had already spent Sundays and weekday evenings being dragged to old-folks homes and elementary schools with him, or to the Gillette factory or the Squirrel Nut Zippers candy factory, and a few of the downtown hospitals. She had never seen her father in the middle of crowds like that before. She gathered, even at age twelve, that it was a new thing for the Whitbys, to try to endear themselves to the working masses. The previous men of the family had been eagle-eye-focused on business and industry, on watching the price of their stocks go up and down, on growing the gross profit from shipping of opium, shipping of whiskey, shipping of furs, building of train tracks, the transport of lumber, the invention of container shipping, the buying of houses, the buying of hotels, the buying of city blocks and parks and undeveloped forests. Typically, Whitbys couldn't be bothered with the duties of a public office.

Brooke's mother was clearly relieved that Roger had finally decided to commit to something, by running for office. He had never kept a profession longer than a year and a half, two at most, and paid all their bills through his Whitby trust. Brooke and her siblings were often unaware of where their father's office was, as it changed so often. But now he had decided that he was getting too old to waste any more time, and it was time to make his mark on the world, like the rest of his family had. He would dedicate his life to this new endeavor. All Whitbys were Republicans, but Roger was considered progressive, socially liberal and fiscally conservative. He told reporters he believed in taking care of the poor, in human rights for all, and, especially, in the preservation of the environment. But what he was really running on, in 1978, was an antibusing agenda. For four years, the city of Boston had been embroiled in a battle that began with legislation forcing children from black neighborhoods to be bused into schools in white neighborhoods, and vice versa. In the late seventies, while the rest of the country considered the civil rights era over, in Boston the movement was still taking place and being fought out daily. Once, while Brooke was safely protected inside her parents' Mercedes station wagon on the VFW Parkway, she saw a cluster of white teenage boys hurling rocks at a school bus. The Whitbys' car had sped by, but the force of the boys' throws, the sounds of their hateful epithets, stuck with her.

On the State House steps, her father's slower voice indicated that he was coming to the end of his speech. "The most important thing to know about me is that I am not a politician. But I am a leader, in business and otherwise, and I'm a strong manager and, above all, a preservationist. That's my plan for leading this great state: I will protect the pristine dunes on the shores of Cape Cod, I will fight the developers threatening our precious farmland around Pittsfield, and here in Boston . . . I make a solemn promise that I will restore peace to our city's schools!"

Brooke's mother now placed one arm around Brooke's shoulders, clinging to her in a way she didn't usually. Maybe it was because she usually kept her arms around Peter that way, protecting him in throngs of people. But Peter was still in the hospital just a few blocks away. It had been months now that he'd been there. Was he with the nanny at that moment, or alone? Perhaps he had told her parents he was fine there; at seven years old, Peter had a sense of dignity and fairness rarely found in a child.

Roger continued, "Boston has been one of the most successful cities in America since the founding of this country, and our city's success has always begun with strong education. As the next governor of Massachusetts I will restore the city to peace. I'm going to preserve our legacy as the bastion of thinking, as the champion of education within the whole United States. I, Roger Whitby, will return us to our former glory!"

As her father grinned, he appeared to be as large and strong as any man ever was; rather than being someone who was easily pushed over the edge, he looked then as if he'd protect his whole family, and the whole state, for the rest of their lives. Brooke had swelled with pride and the feeling that she was, physically and otherwise, extremely safe.

All the Whitbys, extended family included, were whisked into town cars and delivered to the stately stone building that housed the Harvard

Club. Although they could have walked, it was Whitby custom to hire a fleet of black cars at family events. Brooke was proud that her parents were finally the ones hiring the cars and hosting the event. She had always felt like a second-class Whitby, being from dinky Boston and not from "the City." But here was her own immediate family, finally doing something exciting and Whitby-like: a political campaign and their own party.

Inside the wide, square rooms of the Harvard Club, above the marble and crimson-carpeted floors and below the oversize chandeliers of this old boys' establishment, Brooke felt at home. She'd been going there her whole life and could tell all the other kids about the secret bathrooms on the third floor, and the camouflaged door under the grand staircase that led to the basement kitchen. Kiki seemed to be feeling the same way and strode into the club as if she owned it, directing people to the coat check and informing them about the crudité and cheese plates in the front salon. Kiki was finishing up her junior year at Demming College and had adopted an air of maturity and adulthood. Brooke could see through it, of course, but if Kiki's adult put-on came with her calling Brooke by her real name instead of Birdie, and treating her with an ounce more of respect, she'd take it. LJ was not there to witness their sister's act. He'd been temporarily forced out of boarding school for a drinking infraction, and was on a "trip" in Colorado, which was actually a three-week military-style boot camp in the desert, with scarce food and evil drill sergeants, meant to scare the pants off him. St. Paul's had suggested it. They used the camp with troubled children whom, due to promised endowments, the school could not afford (or so they thought) to simply kick out.

Inside the front salon of the Harvard Club, Brooke searched the crowd for her cousins, wondering if they had retreated to one of the hotel rooms upstairs without letting her know. She wished Peter were there. Viscerally, she felt the lack of his small body; it had always been there for her to track with her eyes or physically catch in her arms. If he were there he would be mashed between the arms or knees of one of their aunts or uncles, offering them a typical Peter story—a sincere explanation about how the portraits on the walls were actually superheroes in disguise, or how the grandfather clocks led to another galaxy. His imagination was astonishing. No one, not her parents or her siblings, had ever talked to her about their greatest fear, which was of course her fear as well. Although in the past six months they acknowledged the severity of his cancer, and spoke the word *leukemia* often, not one person would dare to say the word *death*. It was unimaginable.

An hour later, Brooke sat alone in a corner of the large dining room, sulking. Her cousins had gone somewhere else and not invited her. She couldn't find any of the kids. Surrounding her on the wood-paneled walls were oil paintings of white men: their old-fashioned faces were long, and they all wore black suits, ranging from pilgrim-era narrow to wide-collared seventies-chic. These presidents of Harvard University looked down on the crowd with stern and distant resignation. Would they be pleased that her father was running for governor?

Her parents ambled up to an upright piano, which the staff had brought into the dining room for the occasion. Now her mother tapped a finger on the top of the stand-up microphone and spoke into it one breathy "Testing." Both of her parents looked ecstatic. They must have thought that the Christmas concert had been such a raving success, why not do it again? Perhaps this is what their lives would become, if her father won the race: the Whitbys, heirs to a family fortune, state governor and his wife, musical duo, sure to liven up any cocktail hour on the Eastern Seaboard. In the Harvard Club's dining room, her mother giggled into the microphone, then flexed her hands in jazz-dance manner. "We thought we'd treat everyone to a glimpse of what it's really like to be in the Whitby family," she said in a husky voice, which was met with resounding chuckles. Then she added, "We like to keep things musical!"

Behind her, Brooke's father's low vibrato began, "'Oh the Wells Fargo Wagon is a-coming . . .'" Everyone cheered as he launched into the song from *Music Man*, and her mother joined in. The whole crowd began clapping along. As always, her parents were a hit.

That was when the protestors entered. There was a line of them, wearing jeans and T-shirts, some in multicolored winter coats. They marched in a line, all silent, into the grand crimson room. These protestors held handmade cardboard signs over their heads, reading: INTEGRATED SCHOOLS NOW, WE DEMAND AN END TO THE BIAS, and DORCHESTER NEEDS QUALITY EDUCATION. They were all black, with cropped hair or big Afros on both the men and the women. Brooke would understand later that they were also young, mostly college kids, but at the time she saw them as adults. There were so many protestors: Twenty? Forty? All of them were tight-lipped, staring straight ahead as if in a trance. As they entered the room, the Whitby-partygoers collectively gasped, abruptly halting their singing and clapping. But in the corner, Brooke's parents didn't notice what was happening. For several excruciating moments Corney and Roger went right along singing the song from *Cats*, for what they continued to believe was a sympathetic crowd. Brooke considered running toward them, but when she tried to move, her limbs locked.

The waiters and staff of the Harvard Club sprinted around the room; men and women, in black-and-white serving outfits, tried to yell while also whispering, "Call the police." "Get Al! Get a manager!"

A man with an Afro at the front of the line of protestors pointed to Brooke's parents in the corner, and they all began marching directly toward them. The appetizer-eating bystanders parted for this line of activists. The faces of her parents' friends are what Brooke remembered clearly: shocked but also unmoving. No one jumped in front of a protestor to stop him, no one shouted anything. Brooke's mother noticed the protestors first and cut herself off right in the middle of a long note: "'Mem-rieeeeeee—'" But her father kept on playing the piano for a few beats. Corney, just like everyone else, froze. The leader of the protest held his sign with one hand and picked up a walkie-talkie radio in the other. He muttered something into it, and less than a minute later—it happened too fast for it to make sense, really—the second line of protestors came in. But this line was different. This line was made up entirely of children.

These children were both black and white, not one of them older than eight years old. Each child had a large piece of cardboard slung around his or her neck with string. Their handmade signs read, HELP INTEGRATE OUR

SCHOOLS and DON'T I DESERVE AN EDUCATION? All of these kids wore party clothes: small gray suits and pleated pink dresses and shiny shoes. At first they looked bewildered. Each child had a hand on the shoulder of the one in front, but their little faces turned left and right, ogling the giant room they were walking through. Some offered a confused hello to the cocktail-holding crowd.

At this point Roger stood up from the piano, shocked. He paused with his hands at his side, mouth slung open, until the guy with the Afro in the front of the line planted his feet like a soldier. The leader placed his hands on his hips and yelled: "Mr. Whitby, these are the people you will be destroying by blocking the busing initiative." Then he reached one hand into the leather satchel that hung off his shoulder.

It took a few seconds at most, but the photographs of it would last forever. It was the photographs that ultimately did Roger in. When the protest leader stuck his hand in his shoulder bag, Brooke's father flinched and dropped to the floor in front of the piano. Roger, in his navy suit and bow tie, lay facedown on his stomach; two flexed arms protected the crown of his head, hands gripping the back of his scalp. The protestor pulled the aluminum can out of his bag. An air horn. He pressed the button on the top of the air horn one long time, and at the sound of the horn, the children, prepped to think this was some kind of game, squealed in delight and began running. When the horn sounded, they all ran toward Roger on the floor. Soon the adult protestors were laughing, overjoyed by their good luck. They directed the children: "Over there." "He's your man." And the children, with some of their neck signs swinging to their backs, surrounded Roger. Two of the smallest ones crawled directly onto his back, and a sweet-looking girl with French braids sat on his thigh and giggled.

The photographers swooped in. The protesters had brought two of their own, but the *Herald* had also sent one just to be at the Whitby party. When Roger heard the *snap snap* of the camera shutters closing, he looked up, confused. Then he heard Corney huff, "Get up, Rodge!" He peeked up to see tiny patent-leather shoes and knobby tights-covered knees sticking out from under party dresses. He understood what was happening, but it was too late. The image of Roger Whitby, cowering facedown on the floor while surrounded by a group of happy children, was captured. This picture was printed in both the *Globe* and the *Herald* the next morning. The *Globe* headline read, IS THE WHITBY WIMP READY TO GOVERN? It was mortifying. He was called a racist from every pundit on the local level, as well as by a few on the national. His bid for governor was over in less than two weeks. Martin O'Toole, the son of a deceased congressman from an Irish-Catholic family, joined the race and knocked Roger out of the running, thus returning Brooke's family to the second-class, everyday, Boston-based Whitbys they really were. That event—and that knowledge of their average status—was the first in a line of catastrophes that jostled Roger out of his seat of sanity and sent her family flying.

Bang bang bang: Marc's fist on the bathroom door.

"Come on, Brooke."

She shook her head, as if it could literally fling off the memory of the shame that began her family's downward spiral. As she flushed the toilet another time, she yearned to forget where she came from. She splashed tap water on her face, wanting to push the memory of her father and all his misguided actions out of her mind, at the same time as she wished so badly to be able to see him again.

"We're very late," Marc said through the door. "Mom and Poppa are waiting for us."

"What?" Brooke turned off the faucet. Marc was the kind of adult who referred to his parents without a pronoun. Never "my mom said" but rather "Mom said." It made Brooke's stomach turn, while also ringing up a note of sadness. There was no way she was close enough to her mother to say that.

"Why are your parents coming?" she asked from her side of the door.

He gave a squirrelly laugh. "They want to see the house! Shouldn't they get to see it, if they're paying for it?"

Of course his parents were coming. Marc's money was all from the family business. His parents would always be coming, to every dinner and holiday and movie and shopping trip, for the rest of her life. His mother was always touching Brooke's body, making comments about future children. His father was always grotesquely asking her about her salary, her family's investments, and the numerical cash value of her house. This was not how Brooke Whitby did things. Yes, in some shallow way Marc was soothing to her. Walking beside him into a restaurant, spending a night sipping cocktails as he bantered on to businesspeople, falling asleep under the mainsail as he and some other boneheads he went to the Noble and Greenough School with laughed and shouted among themselves. It was fine and comfortable. But it wasn't love. As she stared at the back of the frosted-glass bathroom door, her body literally ached for Allie's. She just wanted to touch her, to feel that Allie, the person who knew who Brooke really was, existed in the world.

The nausea returned, and Brooke could do nothing but lay back on the floor. She was astounded at herself that she hadn't yet made a decision about the pregnancy. She was normally carefully decisive. But now she just didn't know what to do. Although she was not a woman who'd ever fantasized about being a mother, she'd calculated the positive aspects of the role more than once. And this might be her last chance. Her visions of motherhood involved rolling a stroller over the cobblestones of her urban neighborhood and singing the baby songs her parents had sung together. But this baby also belonged to the man, the guy who was so unlike her, on the other side of the door. The only grandparents the baby would really know would be Marc's uncouth, money-obsessed parents. And the baby currently did not have a home to live in. "I'm not coming, Marc," Brooke said in the loudest voice she could muster, without getting off the floor. "Go on without me."

9

The personal history of Mrs. Susan Scribner Whitby—the forty-nine-year-old ex–third grade teacher, the frequent gardener, the long-estranged wife of a recently deceased man—was inconsequential in the scope of civilization and culture. No one knew this to be true more than Mrs. Scribner Whitby herself. Her insignificance did not just rankle her: it pressed on her chest morning through night as she puttered around a small house on a slanted street in Orange County, California.

Susan's personal history began thirty years before she was born. In 1924, in a state far removed from any Scribners, a young American named after his famous lyricist cousin sat down to write a book. Frances Scott Fitzgerald wrote *The Great Gatsby*, and it became a remarkable thing. Scott, as he was personally known, was twenty-eight when he made this remarkable thing, but Susan Scribner knew that in order to do that, he must have accomplished many more feats of daring during his prior twenty-seven years. Susan had known she was destined for remarkable things since she took her first breath in the world, but it wasn't until she picked up *Gatsby* in American Literature Review at Orange Coast College in 1972 that she realized it was only her own actions that would mark her as extraordinary.

She read the book cover to cover, repeatedly, until the binding was cracked and the pages began to fall from her paperback copy. What was it about the story that enticed her so? The moments she loved best were when the characters were in the center of the roaring city, clumped up in raucous, unlikely groups. Susan wanted to see the actions again and again: champagne bottles glinting in the moonlight, Wolfsheim winking through cigar smoke above a craps table. Nick and Jay, Daisy and Tom, Myrtle and Jordan, they were constantly drawn toward Manhattan and then repelled from it; the city was the throbbing nexus they couldn't handle too much of. Susan, in suburban California, fantasized about New York's machinery and strangers, about licentious liaisons in grand hotels and rented apartments, about chance meetings becoming thrilling action.

From a young age, Susan, who lived with her retired Air Force–captain-turned-power-plant-manager father and her homemaker mother, was always in trouble. An itch had tormented her most of her life; she felt restless, bored, and utterly companionless in these feelings. Her parents didn't know what to do when her teacher reported she disrupted class, or she got kicked out of Sunday school for asking unanswerable questions. At fourteen, she boarded a bus and traveled to Los Angeles by herself, in order to go to a vigil after the assassination of RFK. But she lived in a small town; going unnoticed was not an option. When she got off her return bus on Sand Canyon Avenue at dusk, her father was waiting with two indignant arms crossed over his chest. Susan's problem, simply put, was that she was smarter than most of the other people she grew up around. Therefore, a deep loneliness built up inside of her, and outwardly, she was unruly.

In college, when she read about Jay Gatz, he became a role model: he was a man who possessed the deftness and consummate will to remake himself. He wanted to become someone new and stopped at nothing until he had. Could a woman do what Jay Gatz did? Could she kick through all the roadblocks in front of her, jab down anyone or anything that attempted to hold her back, until she attained the thing that would make her finally, ultimately, happy? Of course, Susan had had no actual Daisy to pin her dreams to, and therefore her goal was more hazy than Jay's. She wasn't sure what she aspired to possess, but she knew that whatever it was, it was not waiting for her in Orange County.

She didn't understand then that her dislike of the place stemmed from her family. Her father wasn't exactly a violent man. Sure, sometimes he would get angry and throw his fist at things, including his loved ones. But his real vice was his sincere fury whenever he was not the sole purveyor of authority, in any situation. He controlled his three daughters, and he certainly controlled his wife. It was all up to him: what she ate and what she wore, who she was friends with and mostly who she wasn't, what she said and mostly what she didn't. When Susan was ten years old, her mother had shown up at a neighborhood kid's birthday party wearing a sunflower-covered dress with a slightly low dip at the neckline and a slightly high-on-the-thigh hemline, and her father had run into the neighbors' yard five minutes later. He screamed as he traversed the freshly cut, sun-scorched grass. "Get in the goddamn car, Marcy!" The other little girls had all clung to the cement edges of the pool, mouths dropped open. "No wife of mine leaves the house dressed like a harlot. And no wife of mine ignores my commands!" As he moved toward her, he raised his hand, winding up. But the birthday girl's father—Mr. Johnston was his name—caught Susan's father's hand as it stretched out. "Not in my house, Rick."

Her mother had hung her head and promptly walked out of the yard in shame, without so much as telling Susan to come along. It was then that Susan promised herself she would never, ever let her life be like her mother's. She would get out of Orange County, leave California, and refuse to crumple in the face of a man.

After high school, Susan continued to live with her parents, and once she had finished her classes at Orange Coast she spent her days teaching reading to elementary school students. Small children responded to her brusque and commanding manner: she was a symbol of authority one could depend on while still allowing a child to test out uncharted waters, a natural-born teacher. But Susan wasn't really interested in teaching. She was the oldest of three daughters, her two younger sisters already married and out of the house, each with a potato-like newborn to tend to. They were never leaving California. But as Fitzgerald had shirked his Minnesota homeland and made his way to Paris in order to write, Susan's gaze was set on New York City, sure that that was the place where the action of her own story would begin.

It took two full years, but in 1977 the petite, buxom, and officious twenty-three-year-old set out across the country with a copy of *Gatsby* in her father's bifold suitcase. She had won a scholarship to Teachers College by writing an essay for *Seventeen* magazine called "Women's Words: How Female Voices Mean More." Women's liberation was the hot-button issue of the time, although Susan wasn't particularly committed to it. She certainly believed in liberation for herself, but her beliefs didn't exactly extend beyond that. But there was opportunity in this essay contest. Getting her teaching certificate was just a means to a rent-paying end. She would start with the teaching, she told herself, and from there she'd look around for something else, something enlivening.

For the first year of living in New York, Susan eagerly clacked down the linoleum-covered hallways of Teachers College, attentive to her studies and focused on excelling. She lived in university housing but took the subway alone to galleries downtown and wine-and-cheese political fundraisers. There were men in New York who were nothing like her father; she was sure of it. She forced herself to smile brightly at every businessman and each long-haired wastoid on the subway platform; one never knew where opportunity would open its door. But as the months piled up, very few doors did open. She lived a solitary lifestyle and began to feel herself grow smaller in the big city.

After two years she'd finished her teacher-training program and her father called to announce that it was time to head home. The vice principal of Irvine High School had also been an Air Force man, and her father had spoken to him about a job. "We'll chip in on renting your own place, if you manage to get the position." But Susan felt she'd been cheated out of a New York experience, living in a women's dormitory and never missing a class. She refused her father, then also refused a full-time position teaching high school English at Spence, the prestigious private school on East Ninety-First, in order to have more free hours during the day in which she could really live.

It was 1980 when she found an apartment in the West Village, on Bethune Street. The neighborhood was dodgy, but "up-and-coming," and her "two-room studio" was cheaper than anything uptown. Occasionally needles lay discarded by the building's door, and she quickly learned that the man who occupied the apartment next to her, Anthony, was a pimp who dealt mostly in young boys. But she was twenty-six years old, she wore her orange hair in a retro flip in order to stand out, and she was able to live there by herself. The first five days in her apartment were spent scrubbing off a thick layer of scum that covered everything from the floor-boards to the galley kitchen to the window that faced into the air chute. She found a part-time elementary school teaching job at the Village Com-munity School on West Tenth, and had afternoons off to go searching for the elusive thing that she so desperately wanted and needed.

Susan didn't know where to begin searching, so she spent most after-noons sitting in bars around the Village, sipping cocktails and rereading her tattered copy of what she'd come to think of as *her* book. She wasn't sure if she was looking to find Jay Gatsby or looking to become him herself. Susan was aware that the most poignant paragraphs of the book did not involve Gatsby but rather Nick Carraway. Nick, quiet in the crisp West Egg air, under the belt of East Coast stars, looking up at Gatsby's mansion windows. Nick was the one to love, she knew, but Susan simply wasn't interested in quiet reflection and country air. She wanted to pour champagne herself, to steer a yacht farther into the sea.

So Susan waited for excitement, and as she waited she drank Cape Codders at Chumley's and at the front bar of the Ninth Circle. Sometimes she went to Ye Waverly Inn for a gin fizz. The other regulars were artists and writers and musicians, who found the fact that she was a teacher a real trip. On the way home from the Community School she'd pop into the White Horse Tavern or Cafe Minerva and drink a beer with the bartenders she'd become friendly with. A few blocks away, in Washington Square, the smell of marijuana wafted out of drum circles, teenagers danced around the defunct fountain with hair twenty years longer than it should have been. They seemed to have no idea that the 1980s had arrived. But over on the west side, everyone was aware of what year it was. With each passing month the gay revolution grew, and the streets of the Village became an urban Wild West. The partying did not only happen on the weekends: on Tuesday and Wednesday afternoons men walked by in assless chaps, and one could hear the rustle of blow jobs in the bushes by the pier. Once, at eleven in the morning, she walked into the women's room at John's Pizzeria, and a shirtless man on his knees in front of another yelled, "Get the fuck out, bitch!" It was unfortunate; her apartment was a fourth-floor walk-up, she was two vodka tonics in, and she truly had to pee.

Her neighborhood soon became a point of pride for her and a part of her identity: she was Susan of the West Village, the red-haired teacher who knew all the Italian grandmothers, all the drag queens, the names of both the white and the Puerto Rican children. She was the friendly Californian who was never without a drink in her hand. A billboard on Seventh Avenue stated boldly, GAY RIGHTS NOW, and it made Susan swell with pride at her chosen home. AIDS didn't exist yet, and male sex seemed to infect the very air everyone breathed—kinetic, but also containing testosterone-filled grinding and punching. The good and the bad of this air affected everyone. Straight men turned on sex signals left and right, and Susan hailed them down. This was not suburban California. She was in total control of how calm or how eventful her day would be, and how many drinks accompanied her various events. It was easy to bring men up to her fourth floor, or go to their similarly disarrayed apartments. Time passed quickly, and although she was frequently alone, loneliness and wanting were no longer a part of her personality. The itch that had tormented her for most of her life was lifting.

After nearly a year at the Community School, Susan began to show up late and then miss some mornings altogether. In an environment with very little respect for lesson plans, she had managed to break the rules. Her boss, Judy, was ten years her senior. When the formerly responsible Susan Scribner showed up to work for the first time all week on a Wednesday morning, Judy and her Coke-bottle glasses took Susan into the art-supply closet and fired her.

"We know you've been struggling with drinking," Judy said, her credulous eyes magnified behind the lenses. "We wanted to help you, hold you through the process of healing. But it's no longer fair to the children. You've already been drinking today, haven't you?"

Susan stormed away from the school, covering every ounce of embarrassment with the veneer of rage. She felt her childhood desolation rearing its head. She'd begun the morning with vodka straight, as she thought no one could detect the scent of it. But through her seething, she considered that perhaps this was a blessing. Now was her time to go after her dreams.

Susan Scribner continued her life on Bethune Street, but it would be hard to say it wasn't disrupted. Although she hadn't fully explained what happened at the Community School, her parents begged her to come back to California. Her nephews were growing old enough to miss her now. But 1981 came and went, and Susan subsisted in New York. She wouldn't, couldn't, give up the bone-deep feeling that important things were coming to her. Larry, a manager of the Village Vanguard, hooked her up with a gig as a "background actress" for television, mostly on police procedurals. Every few weeks she'd spend a long and cold day walking back and forth across one city block, being told to stop looking at the camera. This brought in just enough to pay for her rent-controlled apartment. But Bethune Street was changing. Some abandoned town houses across from her building were being demolished, and rumor had it they would be replaced by a condominium development.

Three months passed of her just barely getting by from her acting gigs and the small checks that her mother snuck from her father and mailed to her. She hadn't paid April's rent yet, and it was the eleventh. At three thirty in the morning, she'd gotten home from a man's rented room at the Chelsea Hotel—a tall and blond hippie who was at the end of his two-month stay in New York, about to hit the road again to continue finding himself. At home, Susan watched as the roach colony scattered across the counter when she turned on the light. On her square kitchen table sat a strawberry-vanilla cake from Rosie's Bakery in Irvine, which her mother had airmailed to her. The next day was her twenty-eighth birthday. The card read, "Another happy year for our city girl."

A tall stack of books sat on her wood floor, but she hadn't picked one up in months. She lay in bed, staring out the front window, then kept staring. When the metal alarm clock read 4:52, light began to break through the clouded sky and she could make out a water tower in the distance. Faraway sirens screamed. Then the sound was right outside her building: in and out, a panicked shrieking. She smelled smoke. Through the open window a fireman in a yellow suit stood spraying a hose on the roof of a building two doors away. There was a clatter, then a banging downstairs in her own building. Then: *bang bang bang.* A deep voice declaring: "Fire department! Everyone must evacuate. Evacuate the building immediately!" The voice repeated itself in crescendo. Then the scrapes of doors opening, the high-pitched barking of dogs abruptly woken. Through the door, voices traveled, all of them complaining. Italian grandfathers, young mothers speaking Spanish, the husband of that cool married couple.

Splayed on her threadbare sheet in ratty underwear and the white camisole she'd gone out in, Susan didn't move. Smoke seeped through her open window now. The din of her neighbors disappeared altogether. She coughed; the smoke was everywhere. It was as if she were paralyzed. She did not get up.

Had it been two hours or ten minutes? Would the fireman on the other roof be the last person she ever saw? Her apartment door began to jerk: someone was kicking it from the hallway. But the man who pushed his way in was not the rubber-coated fireman she'd expected. Standing in her kitchen was Anthony, her neighbor the pimp. Soon he stood over her bed, tall and thin as a greyhound. The only word that escaped her was a whining *no*. But he scooped her up in two arms and carried her like a bride through the stairwell and out the iron exit door to the roof.

Anthony lay Susan down on the cool black stucco, where she sat up but didn't thank him. She wasn't wearing a bra or pants. A morning breeze had kicked itself up; it was cool and sweet on all her limbs.

Anthony smiled sheepishly. "We got to move it from here. Firemen cleared the whole place." The two of them hopped over the one-foot gap between the buildings, and did it again, making their way onto the third roof. Then they sat on the curved slope, each person's legs outstretched. It was unseasonably warm for an April morning. They were safe as they watched the sun rise orange, turning the sky blue, lighting up the city.

Anthony took out a flat brown wallet, which had a tightly rolled joint in the crook of it. They passed it back and forth, letting the thick smoke curl out of the corner of their mouths. Anthony didn't touch her anywhere, or try to kiss her. She told him about California, and he in turn told her about growing up in the housing projects that lined the river on the east side of Manhattan. Then he offered her some life advice. "You need to find a new place, *cariño*. A place you'll want to run out of when the shit lights on fire."

Susan's eyes seeped with moisture, but she was too stoned to cry. He was right. But the vision of what her life would be if she returned to her family in Orange County strangled all the breath out of her. She could not go backward. She needed a chance to swing something in her direction, push her into a new place. It was pure chance that Nick Carraway had moved in next door to Jay Gatsby in West Egg. Perhaps this veritable stranger saving her life was the first event that would lift herself out of this dark chapter on Bethune Street.

Indeed chance struck again, three weeks later, when Susan discovered that she was pregnant. Sitting on the edge of the tub in her disintegrating pink-tiled bathroom, she held a glass test tube in two hands above the closed toilet lid. She'd bought the at-home pregnancy test kit that morning, and after placing three drops of urine in the test tube, she had let it sit in its holder for two hours. Now, the evidence was clear: a rust-red ring in the middle of the tube pronounced that her body was in the midst of an "active pregnancy." She didn't worry about which of the three possible men was the father. She didn't pause to consider if this was what she wanted; instead, Susan knew—her whole being knew—that this red ring was just what she needed.

10

After Shelley returned from her interview with Mr. Kamal, she had stood, briefly, in the first-floor parlor and stared at the disabled couch. She didn't like to spend time on the first floor, not with that ghostly image of her father lurking in his chair. The kitchen was on the first floor as well, but she preferred to collect her yogurt container and her tin of tuna fish and go upstairs. She did just that after returning from the interview, and upstairs she called her mother's cell phone, as was her custom every day since returning home. The call went right to the still-full voice mail, as it did every day. Then Ms. Scribner's voice floated into Shelley's head: *Is my baby dead?* Shelley's chest constricted. As air caught in her lungs, she shook her head and hands, physically pushing out the thoughts, banishing them into their boxes and kicking them away. Her mother was fine; Nick was fine. He was, she was sure, just holed up with a girl somewhere, trying to piss off his mother. She sat cross-legged on Biddy's bed and peeled the foil from the yogurt. Bad things don't happen all at once like that.

Mr. Kamal called her house phone at nine that night, to confirm the next day's meeting. He called her again, at seven thirty in the morning to decree: "Today at eleven, you will read me the newspaper." She lay in a swirled mass of bedsheets, wondering, *Was this odd behavior?* Surely it had to be, but then, Shelley had never worked as an amanuensis before.

At ten thirty, the April cold filtered through her coat as she crossed over the mud-bordered paths of Central Park. She was coughing by the time she reached the Grisham, but she was on time. Nodding to the doorman and making her way into the elevator, Mr. Kamal's bellow echoed within her—*I couldn't be a rapist.* Unbidden, the words *Mom, Mom, Mom* raced through her mind. As she rose through the floors, she pictured her mother's pale and pointed face. The numbers lit up one by one: *10, 11, 12.* Shelley could simply depress the *L* button and be returned to the lobby and delivered out of the building. Her encounter with Mr. Kamal could become just another secret and strange event of her life, like the time she stole the crotchless green silk body-stocking from the top drawer in Zoë's parents' bedroom. That lingerie was probably still crumpled up in the back of Shelley's closet. No one ever asked about it, and she'd never had to say a word.

The elevator doors pinged open: there he was. Shelley felt a hot sting in the corner of her eyes. He looked just the same as yesterday, in another set of khakis and a different, pressed melon-colored shirt. Mr. Kamal's hands were on his hips and his head bent forward slightly, displaying patches of scalp amid curly tufts. When he spoke, he seemed to grow larger.

"You are on time," he intoned. "Follow me to the library." The authority in his voice was reassuring.

A high-pitched croak issued from Shelley's throat. He turned his back to her and shuffled across the darkened foyer, hands poised at his hips.

Shelley struggled to unbuckle her boots and scramble after him. They passed through the ornate dining room, and this time she noticed a smaller gallery room that came off it, lined with cabinets containing different-shape glasses for varying wines and aperitifs. The glasses clinked with each of Mr. Kamal's steps. Nothing had been touched since yesterday. When they were almost to the library he said, "Did you bathe in the past hour?"

Was he speaking to her? They had nearly reached the room where they would be contained together, just the two of them. She produced a breathy sound that resembled a titter. Perhaps she'd misheard. "I got ready an hour ago," she mumbled, just in case she'd heard him correctly.

Shelley had made an effort to look nice for her first real day of work.

She'd run mango softening cream through her hair and pulled on green cargos and an embroidered tunic. She wasn't stylish in the least, but despite never having been inside a gym without being forced, she always looked healthy. She had inherited the Whitby height, but she was mousy brown, and uncontrollably hippy. Yet her entire life, her friends and their parents, drama teachers, and the occasional shopgirl at Gap had been telling her bluntly, "You're beautiful." As a child, these statements were so awkward that they often made her cry. But the frequency with which she received this comment had, at least partially, convinced her of the fact. And since puberty, she'd had an inkling that her figure was somehow comforting to men, as if they wanted to pour themselves into the spaces between her bigness and her smallness. As she stood in the doorway she wondered how much of her shape Mr. Kamal could sense.

The book-lined library was awash in late-morning light. "You will sit in the chinoiserie-patterned chair," Mr. Kamal commanded as he dropped down into a high-backed leather armchair. Shelley's shoulders relaxed. *Rapist* still reverberated in her mind, but it could be drowned out by facts: someone had told him what the pattern on the chair was. He must have other people around him here. A person was cooking his meals, turning radios on and off, picking up wet towels off the floor. Then Shelley realized a scent was overtaking the apartment. Freshly brewed coffee, with a tangy touch—spearmint or tobacco. Could Mr. Kamal have a family? She took her seat and genuinely smiled. All these nerves, and for what? There was probably a striking and distinguished wife lurking behind the weighted doors. Undoubtedly the wife wore designer clothes under a sumptuous silk headscarf. Perhaps a troupe of British-inflected young boys would come marching in after school, wearing navy blazers with gold buttons. No, Mr. Kamal was old: his sons would be grown and live in their own penthouses a few blocks away, their brown skin permanently crisped on the bows of sailboats during sun-speckled college days. They would wear their navy blazers to financial-management firms now, lunching with distinguished, disabled Daddy at least once a week.

To Shelley's right was the Greek-drama section of the library. Her eyes skimmed the spines: Aeschylus, Euripides. Mr. Kamal proclaimed with emphasis, "I haven't *looked at* one bit of the paper today." Now Shelley smirked at him, like her regular old self. She was beginning to understand this odd yet intriguing man's rhythms. The paper lay on a tea table between the two chairs. Mr. Kamal added, "We will have to see what you can handle. Begin on the front page."

She took a deep breath and began to read. He had an orderly process to getting through the paper. She started on the front page and read every headline, then began every piece. If he didn't like it he would shout: "No!"

The first time he yelled she had surged in her seat, then froze, waiting for him to apologize. But when the apology never came, she moved on to the next article. She was used to not being coddled. She was fine; her mother had barely said a kind word to her in the past decade. Soon she discovered a pattern in Mr. Kamal's "reading." After a paragraph or two, he usually ordered: "Cut to the jump!" and Shelley would have to skip to the continuation of the story in the middle of the paper. If she fumbled with the sheets, or took too long to find page A13, he would shout it again: "Cut to the jump!"

Reading the paper took longer than Shelley could have guessed. It was strange, sitting alone with another person for that long. Occasionally when Mr. Kamal shouted no, her own mind would jump to the chant *Mom, Mom, Mom*. She'd spent nearly four years of college without considering her mother very much at all, yet now she longed to touch the ends of the woman's gray-streaked hair, to curl up on the bottom of the hard mattress on Strong Place while her mother slept. As Mr. Kamal yelled, she reminded herself that this was just a temporary gig. How many days of this would it take to restock on fruit juice and crackers and then to fix the couch? She and Mr. Kamal had yet to discuss her rate.

Every forty minutes or so he put his palm in the air and uttered a firm "Enough!" Then he dropped his head forward in silence, his breath steady as a metronome. The first time this happened Shelley nearly burst into laughter. Was he a narcoleptic? Was she being paid to sit alone in a room with a sleeping man? His shoulders slumped forward and his brow knit, as if he was presenting his comb-over to her. Then it crossed her mind that he could be testing her, seeing how she would react. She became convinced he was a game player, consistently making the first move. His steady breath became louder, belabored, and she stared at him until a foreign feeling overtook her. Was this empathy? Perhaps his commands, his yelling bravado, perhaps that attitude was actually a thin cover for a person who needed help but sincerely did not want to need it. She was conflicted: Was he deceptively strong or surreptitiously weak?

When she couldn't look at him any longer, she examined the carpet and wondered what exactly it was that Mr. Kamal could see. Was her shape an orange blur to him, like a heat sensor? Perhaps his visions were charcoal and gray, one-dimensional moving lines, a depthless unending plane. After three or four minutes Mr. Kamal would sniff himself awake, make no apologies, and command Shelley: "Continue." She was able to raise her eyes and jump right back into reading.

When they had exhausted every section of the *New York Times*, Mr. Kamal rang a small silver bell that rested on a round table behind him. Shelley shifted in her seat, and Mr. Kamal said, "Tell me, where is it that you are from?"

"Here," she answered. "I grew up on the West Side. And I, uh, live there again now."

"Your parents are academics, I assume," he said, as if their conversation the prior day had never occurred. But before she could answer this, the thud of feet on hardwood floor sounded from the hallway. Another person! The heavy door creaked, and in came a large-busted woman. Shelley found herself grinning like an idiot. The woman carried a tray with a teapot, one teacup, and a plate with four blond cookies. She towered over both Shelley and Mr. Kamal, picked up the paper with one hand, and set the tray down with the other.

"Four Tahiti biscuits today, sir."

Mr. Kamal made a swiping motion through the air to dismiss her, and she left the room.

His two hands crept along the outer edge of the tea table, then cupped the small blue-and-white-patterned teapot with both hands. He found the handle with his right hand, then his left skimmed over the wood tabletop until it hit the side of the empty cup. His left thumb wagged in the air until it knocked into the handle of the teacup, and he finally grasped it fully.

Shelley's jaw ached from holding a forced smile while reading. "Would you like me to pour—"

"Quiet!"

She didn't jump at all at his command this time. Perhaps the yelling was a sign of respect, or an indication he thought she could handle his brusque nature. She was beginning to understand him.

A shaky stream of tea cascaded into the cup. The scent of hibiscus filled the room. He drank with loud slurps, then munched, biting off small sections of cookie at a time and chewing with his mouth half-open. Yellow crumbs trickled down the front of his oxford. He ate like a child, helpless, covering his body with food. He offered her nothing.

If he wanted silence, Shelley could give it to him. She was a goddamn pro. Many of the kids she grew up with went off to boarding schools in Connecticut and Massachusetts, and by the time they were in their second and first forms they came back to the city for the weekends, bringing more kids with them, from Chicago or Texas. They would rent out a room at the St. Marks Hotel or the New Yorker at Penn Station, and pick up three cases of beer. When the boys were just fucking her, it was easy. She wasn't sure why she did it—for entertainment, she guessed. Or for relief. It was like waitressing: after a while she felt nothing and her mind went blank. She'd kept herself totally silent and fixated on the beige paint chipping from the crown molding, and would only feel a few brief presses of a boy's weight on her sternum. These boys were never part of the host of people reminding her of her beauty. Instead, they were dismissive of her comfort and desires, just as her mother was. During the act, Shelley would notice the friction of the synthetic bedspread, the after-stench of his early-morning hockey practice, the even perforations of acne on his shoulders.

The boys didn't say much, but they saw her and physically gripped her. Afterward, she would feel better. One night, within two and half hours, she did three different boys from Choate.

When Mr. Kamal had finished his tea and cookies, he put his two palms on the tops of his thighs and stood. Shelley got to her feet as well. She figured they were headed to the office, where she would dictate his words for him, the writing portion of the job. This she was looking forward to: she would discover what was going on in his head, what his bizarre questions were really getting at.

"No," he answered, as if he knew she was opening her mouth. "You will leave now. You have not done well enough."

She shook her head ferociously. Hot pressure welled behind her temples. Who the hell was this guy? He had no idea who she was. He had no idea about anything at all. While she trembled with repugnance, Mr. Kamal managed to take two large steps that placed his body flush against hers: the oval cylinder of his torso lined up beside the vaselike cylinder of hers. The heat of someone else's body was enticing. Then he gripped her bicep with his two hands, as if to drag her down.

His voice lowered. "Do you need to use the bathroom?"

"No." She didn't step back. She didn't move. His question was bizarre and slightly repulsive. And yet she felt a bit honored that he was even asking about her.

"Very well." He cleared his throat. "You are still not precise enough, but I will give you another shot. You will come back tomorrow. We will read the paper, nothing more serious."

It was still midafternoon when Shelley returned to her apartment, a buzz running through each limb. The man could not be normal, but she did feel noticed by him; he cared enough to question. And really, what else did she have to do? Upon entering the front door, she stood in the kitchen and sneezed. The Kamal household emanated musky perfume, wool, and Pine-Sol. Her own apartment carried a particular stench as well, which she realized now was the stink of general dirt. Dishes stacked up in the sink, magazines dotted the parlor floor where she had absently dropped them, and dust creatures hunched under furniture. This was the first time in her life she had lived alone. It had been only a couple of weeks though, and when her mother returned she would sigh into her receding chin at the state of the place, shaming her into a measure of tidiness: "Shelley, please." Soon enough, all these troubles would be taken care of. Perhaps her mother would even work out this will and house issue with Nick's mother, settling the whole affair so that the children didn't have to, for once. But for now, Shelley wouldn't lift a finger. And she would smoke inside, whenever and wherever she pleased. As she stood at the counter, her stomach had an empty-pit ache, and she wondered again just how big her first paycheck would be. She made her way up the stairs and whistled for the sole purpose of hearing a sound travel through the silent and familiar rooms.

Walking through the uninhabited rooms of her apartment, Shelley thought of a time when they had not been. In her early years, her father was a looming presence, famous within his own house. Biddy, Elizabeth, and Shelley, they all tiptoed around him in his armchair, occasionally patting one ham-hock shoulder and refilling his drink. Shelley felt that she gave him a certain amount of contentment, as he would occasionally smile gently at her, or ruffle her hair as she passed. Back then, her mother was earnest no matter how hard she tried not to be. Her narrow shoulders squared above a steaming coffee mug for half the day, and then above a long-stemmed glass for the other half. She had become a mother at twenty-one and never been given a chance to find out who she could have been in this world. It wasn't fair.

Maybe things would be better now. This could be a second chance. It crossed Shelley's mind that her mother could potentially be happier, knowing that her father was dead. As soon as she thought that though, the truth behind it kicked her in the stomach. Yes, it wasn't fair: Roger's death, his life, the fact that he'd never paid a lick of attention to her and now had given everything to the one child not related to him by blood. She slid herself into Biddy's bed and wondered where her cigarette pack was. Her hand grasped fruitlessly over the rug beside the bed, until she gave up and pulled the covers around her neck. Perhaps everything could be different; she did have a new job. Mr. Kamal was distinguished and famous, in certain circles. And although he may have said harsh words, she had the feeling that he could, miraculously, identify something unique and special within her. No one had ever done that before. She wanted him to need her. She was invited back to his apartment the next day. *Yousef Kamal and his faithful attaché, Shelley Whitby.* She would be a calm caregiver, a cool-shouldered helper of the less fortunate. The headline would read, THE SHIPPING HEIRESS IN THE ATTIC: HOW A WHITBY WROTE A BLIND MAN'S BOOK. She smiled her family's big-toothed smile. She had never tried very hard at anything before. Think of what could happen if she actually worked at this job! Of all the things Shelley believed in—of finding peace on the beach by the Atlantic Ocean, of not judging anyone for their sexual or musical proclivities, of calling bullshit on religious fanatics and Holy Rollers of all kinds—she believed most strongly in herself. She would get him to admit that he was, in some way, *interested* in her. Soon enough she'd have Mr. Kamal wrapped around her finger.

11

_____

| 1982 |

Susan Scribner did not stop drinking immediately after she sat on the side of her bathtub holding the glass box containing the pregnancy test tube. But a week later, walking out of the doctor's office on East Sixty-Third Street with the confirmation that the red ring was not, in fact, a fluke, she vowed to dry up. She wasn't convinced that she would make it, but she didn't drink for the rest of that day. Her body revolted against the changes, and she threw up frequently for the next two weeks. It wasn't until she stopped drinking that she realized how much alcohol had been a root of the problem rather than an effect of it. So one Wednesday morning she cleaned herself up and took the subway to the Spence School to ask if there was any way she could accept the job they had offered her two years earlier.

The answer, from the headmaster Mrs. Frankel, was initially a re-sounding *no*. But the third-grade teacher had unexpectedly quit, and since Susan had the appropriate degrees, she was invited to fill the spot. Susan touched her belly and thought about how they'd have to find a replacement for a few months next winter. She said nothing of the baby to Mrs. Frankel though, and accepted the job. Over a month into her pregnancy, still sober, still nauseated, she found a new apartment in Hell's Kitchen. She called her parents and told them about the apartment and the employment, but not the child. Her father grumbled before hanging up the phone without offering a goodbye. Susan was delighted; she was an adult and was no longer subject to his rules.

The day that Nick was born—his full name was Nick, not Nicholas—she fell in love for the first time in her life. This child was the thing she'd been waiting for all these years. She'd been praying for a boy so that she could name him after the sensitive, stable character that she wanted to be, rather than who she was. And as soon as she saw her baby, she knew that he was her Nick Carraway. Her life revolved around Nick's tiny knees, his boiled and mashed carrots, his happy smile. She returned to teaching the following spring and spent mornings at Spence mindlessly administering vocab tests and miniature milk cartons, then rushed home to pick up her baby from her building super's wife, who watched him until the afternoon.

But over the next few years, that baby became increasingly independent of her and she began, too quickly, to feel again that she was missing something. She sought out men, this time not from bars or street corners but from personal ads in the final pages of *New York* magazine and the *Atlantic*. She was looking only for a certain type, these days. But drinkless dinner after drinkless dinner, through one bland tryst after another, Susan found herself uninspired. In the back of her mind she was aware that there were no speeding cars, there was no West Egg. Where was the commotion?

At a parent-teacher night in 1989, Susan's life changed again. The parents of one of her worst students—a sad and troublesome, loudmouthed eight-year-old girl, the kind who taught all the other children inappropriate songs and who frequently hid the glasses of the less celebrated children—came in to talk to Ms. Scribner about their daughter's behavior. The little girl was a Whitby. Susan had seen this before at Spence, with the offspring of prominent families, families whose money was so old and reliable that their wealth seemed a matter of public record. The parents strived toward nothing, especially not good parenting.

At a low table, in shrunken chairs, Susan made small talk with Roger and Elizabeth Whitby, discussing the Upper West Side and then California. The wife was a pale stick of a brunette, shabby from the tips of her

loafers to the tops of her tweed-covered shoulder pads. The father, decades the senior of the bland woman beside him, chuckled at his daughter's antics. "Yes, yes." His smile was alluring, his teeth large and his jaw
square. "It seems that bossiness and entitlement runs in our family. She's
destined to make a mark on this world, at least. We'll talk to her."

At the end of the meeting, Roger Whitby pulled his trench coat on and
corralled his stone-faced wife out the door, then popped back into the
classroom for his umbrella. "Hey." He leaned over the low table toward
Susan. "I'd love to buy you a coffee, even a wine if you'd like, and find out
your insider knowledge of Southern California. I have some business ven-
tures there. Tomorrow at eight? Gramercy Tavern?" Without waiting for
her response, he walked out of the room.

What kind of a man doesn't wait for a confirmation? The kind who
had never been turned down, Susan reasoned. A little bell went off inside
of her: this was a man who took risks, someone who went all in.

The next day, at a quarter to eight, Susan sat at the bar of Gramercy
Tavern, nervously munching from a dish of spiced pecans. She had never
been to the Gramercy Tavern before but felt smugly at home amid the
polished wood and soft music. In her seven years at the school, she'd had
one affair with a father, while the rest of his family, including the young
boy who was her student, had been at their East Hampton home for the
weekend. The whole event was awkward and disappointing.

That affair had been in the springtime. Now it was late March in New
York, freezing and sloshy outside, when all of the city's residents forgot
that sunshine existed in the world. Susan ordered a cranberry and seltzer
on the rocks. These were just the type of moments where she wished she
could drink casually, wished she possessed the ability to sip a glass of rosé
and simply relax. At five past the hour Roger Whitby made his way into
the darkened bar with his fast yet hobbling steps and sat down on the stool
beside her.

His hair was gray, thinning at the temples, but still very much there.
He took off his dripping trench coat to reveal a sack of flesh loping out
over his belt buckle. But there was something sturdy about his stomach. It

seemed to be made of hardened muscle. He placed a small yellow box on the stool on the other side of him, and without making eye contact with Susan, grumbled, "Thanks, thanks for meeting me." Of course this was not a date; he was a Whitby, and he was married and had a young child.

Roger launched right into his discussion of what his real estate business plans were in California, and how he wanted to get into developing West Coast shopping malls. He was a steady-stream talker, and she couldn't get a word in. He waved off the bartender a few times, but finally the guy slanted over the bar and interrupted. "May I get you something, sir?"

Roger looked up. "Bring us some of those little mushrooms with bread crumbs that you have. And escargot—Susan, do you like escargot? Of course you do, you look like a girl with good taste." He winked.

"And to drink?"

"Seltzer for me. Add some lime." Then he leaned into Susan and whispered, "I'm dry. A few months' stretch now, but it's been the best of my life." Then he winked again and said the strangest thing: "It's a great advantage not to drink among hard-drinking people."

Susan's heart dropped to her belly button. That was a line from *Gatsby*; she was sure of it. Roger Whitby, sitting next to her at a bar, both of them on the wagon, on a weekday evening in Manhattan. And he was quoting her book.

After an hour he paid the bill while she was in the restroom, and, kissing her cheek, began to leave just as abruptly as he had arrived. There was nothing explicitly flirtatious about their interaction. But for the few minutes that he had let her speak—or demanded her to, really, asking, "What's your favorite thing about California? Describe the air to me. What makes you desire it?"—he had appeared intensely interested in her responses.

Roger was old and overweight, but he had hopped off the barstool with the energy of a teenager. "Hey, thanks a lot," he said, looking toward the door like he had somewhere to be. "I learned quite a bit about the West Coast. And as a side benefit I got to learn about the beautiful Ms. Scribner."

Roger pointed to the flat yellow box on the chair, which Susan could now see had a professionally tied gold ribbon around it. "That's for you. When I saw it I just couldn't stop thinking about you. So thanks."

Then he hobbled out of the restaurant and, Susan could only imagine, into a cab that took him home to his family. Or maybe he had a driver. Perhaps all Whitbys were given a driver at birth. Susan gathered her things and the box, wrapped herself in her down coat, and went outside. Underneath a streetlight on the corner of Twentieth and Park, the slushy snow falling down on top of her, endless lines of cars went by, but not one taxi had its light on. Susan pulled the strand on the box's bow and let the ribbon fall to the wet sidewalk. She took something soft and smooth out of it and held it up in the foggy light. The purple silk underwear was a size small, with nearly nothing to it. A thong in the back; small glass beads the size of seed pearls embroidered onto the gold muslin strings. Naughty, to be sure. But there was also something lavish, celebratory about them. If she wore the underwear she may in fact look like a gift herself. The tag was still tied to a strap. It read: *Carine Gilson, $825.*

The affair began a few days later. Soon, Roger Whitby became a weekend staple in Susan's, and therefore Nick's, life. From Monday to Friday, Ms. Scribner made her seven-year-old SpaghettiOs or fish sticks for dinner, read all of the Chronicles of Narnia to him, and then started again at the beginning. She held his hand while they walked to soccer practice in Sheep Meadow, and kissed his forehead as he closed his eyes beside her at night. But come Saturday morning their lives changed. Roger would pull his black Lincoln Town Car up to the fire hydrant in front of their building, and then the three of them would drive fourteen blocks uptown to the Times Square Marriott, where Roger rented a three-room suite on the twenty-sixth floor. On these weekends, Roger often carried his favorite book with him in his overnight bag, a tattered first-edition copy of *Gatsby*. To Susan, this was more than a sign: it was kismet. Soon she was legitimately in love with Roger's bravado, with his large sheltering arms, and with the constant movement and shining gifts that now filled her life.

This hotel room became Nick's weekend home for the following three and a half years. Every Saturday they'd arrive at the suite, then his mother would disappear behind the locked door of the other bedroom, or zip off to a lunch with Roger elsewhere in the city. It was around this time that Nick began to be very curious about who his birth father was. Although his mother never wavered from her line that she truly didn't know, Nick found it suspicious that when Roger was in the hotel, he wasn't just attentive to Nick but focused on him. He had a sincere interest in the child and seemed to be amused by his thoughts and antics. But when Roger and Susan were busy, they seemed to think that the hotel staff was a good enough baby-sitter. If he were his real father, he certainly wasn't an ideal one. Nick's weekends at the hotel were the birthplace of his loneliness, the original home of sadness in his life. He spent hours wandering around the different floors, entering unlocked ballrooms and conference rooms, where he turned over the padded chairs, for lack of anything else to do. Five days a week, Nick was overwhelmed by his mother's watchful organization of his homework, his meals, his clothes, friends, sports, and books. But on the weekends, all of this pushy attention flipped right over to Roger. Nick would never have admitted it, but on Saturdays and Sundays, he missed her deeply. Roger told Nick to order himself room service for nearly every meal. Sometimes he'd get a burger and a waffle with whipped cream and a mini pizza, and only eat a few bites of each, then hide the uneaten food in various locations around the room. It made him laugh to think about the maid finding a little surprise of pizza behind a long curtain or a waffle underneath the couch. What he also did on these weekends was become a swimmer. From the very first day he spent in the hotel, he kept a strict schedule of swimming in both the morning and evening. In fact, during the hundreds of weekends he spent at the Midtown Marriott, he never missed his swimming regimen, not once. He'd do laps, he'd time himself, he'd work on his breath capacity. By the age of nine, he was serious and disciplined, teetering on the line of extremism.

Throughout these years, a dependence formed between Susan and Roger. From their first meeting at Gramercy Tavern, moving to California became a shared romantic dream, a mystical idea: for her, the glory of returning home a success, and for Roger, the allure of warm, pleasant days, following in the footsteps of his father, who had also fled west in his golden years. The way that New York had been a glowing goal for young Susan to attain, California became a beacon for her and Roger together.

By the time Nick was eleven he would often skip the hotel altogether to sleep at a friend's house. But when he was at the Marriott, he'd swim for hours every day, then order Playboy channel movies to the TV in his room. It was the fall of the year he was in the sixth grade when Susan showed up at Nick's classroom door at MS 44 on a Thursday, insisting that she needed to take him out of class for a "family emergency." At that time in the morning Susan was also supposed to be at school. As they descended the gray concrete steps, he'd wrenched his hand away as she'd tried to grab it. She'd come to get him because Roger was taking them on a picnic.

"I was busy," Nick complained.

Soon he and his mother stood on a paved helicopter dock by the Hudson River, next to the World Trade Center. The black chopper's propeller pounded steadily, and wind whipped their hair every which way. Roger sat in the pilot's seat, wearing sunglasses and large red earphones, and motioning to the two of them to come in. Yes, he was taking his mistress and her son on a picnic, but this picnic would be in Connecticut. Susan shrieked with delight for the entire ride to Greenwich. Turning around to Nick, who was strapped into a jump seat, she repeated to him, "How much fun are you having? How lucky are you?"

When the helicopter touched down in Connecticut, the old man put his hand on Nick's head and smiled roguishly. "How do you like adventure, son? I can tell you're made for it." Those words, said in Roger's rubbery low voice, would echo through Nick's mind for the rest of that day and many years that followed.

That afternoon, on a tartan blanket in the field outside a country house, Roger told Susan he had bought a house in Newport Beach, California. He was divorcing Elizabeth Saltman Whitby and wanted—very badly—for Susan to become Mrs. Susan Scribner Whitby. "Every other woman in my past has been holding me back from the grandeur I was meant to achieve. But you are different, Susan. It's taken me most of my life, but I've found you." He choked in what appeared to be a genuine sob.

Susan Scribner shook Roger by the shoulders. "Yes, yes!" she exclaimed. Nick sat dumbfounded beside them, as Susan began to calculate and organize. When the school year ended they would sell everything in their apartment and fly together, as a family, to California. They would begin again, all three of them unaware that their beginning would so quickly become another ending.

12

| 2003 |

Every day that week, Shelley received an early phone call from her employer. For the first time in her life, she trained herself to be awake by seven, as the time he called varied and she was afraid he would not approve of the sleep in her voice. She nearly jogged through the park on her way to the Grisham, wearing gloves and sloshing acrid deli coffee onto the recently thawed ground. Mr. Kamal was always waiting for her, unsmiling, at the elevator door. As the days passed, her duties were increasing. She not only read the newspaper but also began leading him on walks to Seventy-Ninth Street and back. Or, rather, he led her. He gripped her bicep and pushed her around children flooding out of schools and golden retrievers crouching next to parking meters. He sidestepped puddles and bore down on her arm while weaving in and out of scaffolding. Peculiarly, he said he "*liked to see* the afternoon sunshine best of all."

The first week passed, then the second. The April freeze softened into a wet and wicked May. When Shelley wasn't there to answer her calls, Ms. Scribner left voice mails on her machine without introducing herself. The woman jumped into her orders: "Try looking for Nick at a place called Bleecker Bob's, a record shop. It's right by the college and he told me more than once it was his favorite. And then this café that's open all night, on MacDougal Street. Esperanza? Esperanto? Nicky told me he was there at four thirty in the morning once. Tell me you'll go to these places. You have to look for him, Michelle—he's your brother."

Shelley listened to every word. She didn't call back, but she listened, and occasionally in the evenings she answered the phone and heard Ms. Scribner's huffs and shrieks of desperation. Ms. Scribner never once brought up the will or the money to Shelley. Perhaps she didn't know that Shelley knew. Brooke was also a frequent caller, and Shelley never told her about the conversations with Susan. That knowledge would just add to Brooke's own hysteria. Surely it would make Brooke hate Nick even more. Occasionally, in the midst of Ms. Scribner's telephone-line sobs, she'd blurt out, "And my baby's been through so much already. He deserves this chance. A chance!" This line was further evidence that she had manipulated Roger into leaving everything to Nick. That was the most logical explanation, Shelley told herself. It wasn't the money that bothered Shelley; she'd never cared about money at all, as long as she had enough to subsist on. What she cared about were her father's intentions. Even if he didn't love Shelley more, Roger had to have loved her just as much as he loved Nick. Didn't he? She was his flesh and blood. Ms. Scribner also insisted that the police would be in touch with Shelley, interviewing her about Nick and where and when she had last talked to him. But no police ever called.

Shelley was determined to focus on her job with Mr. Kamal. She went to the Grisham Monday through Friday, sometimes for two hours, sometimes for six. They were falling into a rhythm, she and this older man: she read to him in the morning, watched him eat his cookies and drink his tea, then moved to the office to answer his emails and organize his files. In the afternoon she often took the subway to Midtown or Wall Street to bring sealed envelopes to accountants' offices. On the way out of Mr. Kamal's apartment Shelley would occasionally halt in a darkened room to say hello to the cook, whom she learned was named Clova. Clova appeared to sporadically enter and exit the apartment, but as she said, she "had been with the Kamals" for twenty-four years and could do what she pleased. When Clova was there, though, she could usually be found in the kitchen watching a miniature, muted countertop television. But other than Clova, he appeared to live alone.

As her daily work duties increased, Shelley let nearly everything else fall away. She consistently refused Charlotte's and Zoë's invitations to movies and parties. She didn't have time for them. She was captivated, by both her increasing desire to do a good job for Mr. Kamal and her extreme urge to hear him say that she had. Mr. Kamal maintained his habit of questioning: Had she eaten eggs for breakfast? Did she use mouthwash that morning? He seemed particularly attuned to his nose, and Shelley adjusted her bodily behavior accordingly. She never smoked before going to the Grisham, and she made sure to toss her pants into the washing machine at night. In the two-plus weeks she'd been there, she hadn't been an amanuensis at all, but rather a gopher, acting as the man's eyes and hands and feet. She was a mere fetching agent. Occasionally Mr. Kamal would grumble that she was "not yet ready." Shelley had begun to take these jabs not as insults, but as challenges. She was challenged; she was trying. Instead of responding as she would have for the previous twenty-two years of her life, with a phrase akin to "Choke on a bag of dicks," she offered him one diminutive "Thank you." The exact number of weeks since she'd spoken to her mother wasn't clear now, but if she had counted she would have reached the number nine. Over two months without a word. She did know, though, that this stretch had been too long. It would surely end any day.

Mr. Kamal slipped a check into her hand at the end of each Friday afternoon. His own hand was smoother and colder than she'd expected, but his touch was also more tender. Shelley accepted this touch willingly, in the same way she accepted her rate of nine dollars an hour. She deposited the checks on the walk home, feeling not only accomplished but also energized. She would then immediately stock up on the staples that sustained her: Stoli, soy milk, tuna fish.

The news, which Shelley read aloud every day, reported impending economic collapse in all financial centers, American and otherwise. For interminable minutes she listened to her own voice, high and faltering, recounting pundits' conjecturing that the United States was conducting secret drone attacks on Iran and that southern India was sure to get involved. Editorialists riled with the fear of another great depression and what would happen domestically if America declared war in all parts of the Far and Middle East.

On occasion Mr. Kamal made smacks and snorts in response to the articles, but he never shared his opinions. Public policy was not a cup of tea Shelley had ever cared to taste either. Nick was the only person in her life who had ever talked to her about current events. On their walks Mr. Kamal continued to ask her "What do your parents do?" as if he had never mentioned it before. Was he testing her? Did his memory fail? By now she knew he would not call her on her consistency, so she changed her answer every time. Sometimes she said they were in politics, sometimes she said hardware. On those days she waited for the line *So are you related . . . ?* But the question never came. What he knew of the Whitbys—of where she fell, at the bottom of the illustrious line, of her father now buried in the ground, of her half brother nowhere to be seen—was a mystery.

Mr. Kamal and Shelley developed a unique rapport: beside him in the library, she followed his low and controlled commands and didn't attempt small talk when he didn't initiate it. Now, in his pauses, she would examine him: his brown skin was quixotically smooth. Small white flecks marred the bottom of his cheeks, but he had no wrinkles, neither smile nor frown lines; his mask was heavy, contemplative, and set. The stillness of his physical features was frustrating. There was no way to read him. But the stillness gave him a statuesque quality; he was solid and permanent, not handsome exactly, but closer to beautiful. The more cool and unmoving he was, though, the more Shelley squirmed and twitched in front of him. Could he be doing this on purpose? It seemed a favorite pastime of his to inquire about her need for the bathroom. He would also frequently question, "Are you feeling hunger?" with no offer of nourishment to follow. Once, as she was reading aloud the obituary of Daniel Winthrop Strang, the publisher of Blackrock Books, Mr. Kamal rested his hand on the arm of her chair. "Your head is aching at this moment, yes?"

In response to that question Shelley offered a small and quick "Not at all." But with each odd question, she blushed. Later that same morning she pulled the strap of her underwear aside and scratched at the groove of her pelvis. She could have sworn a satisfied smile crept across Mr. Kamal's face.

She thought, *Sick*. And yet, she was smiling too. As the days grew, Shelley found herself relaxing in his presence. He was so insistent about what he deserved in life, so sure of his worth. Mr. Kamal thought of himself as a great man, and this was, in fact, reassuring. He was someone to depend on, and she was determined to get herself into a position where she truly could.

This was the pattern, the two of them primarily alone, primarily in the library. It was a dull yet comforting pattern, until the day she stepped out of the elevator just as the bells chimed eleven o'clock and to her surprise, there was movement in the penthouse apartment. A private yoga class was taking place in the dining room. The table, still set, had been backed into a wall, and a squat German woman in a one-piece spandex suit was directing a more svelte, even lanky woman into the downward-dog position. As Shelley removed her shoes, the woman rose from her posture, her shoulder-length auburn hair settling itself as she ignored the German's orders. She walked right over to Shelley with a smile clenched in her cheeks.

Could it be—the wife? Mrs. Kamal was a white, athletic American. She moved with a brisk step, her outstretched hand preceding her. Her stare rose from Shelley's feet to the roots of her thin, blow-dried hair. "Nice to meet you. I'm Jillian," she said, as if conjuring a challenge.

Shelley was stunned. The woman had to be in her late forties or early fifties. Following introductions, Shelley began to move toward the library when the woman called after her, with hands on the hips of her flared yoga pants.

"You went to Demming? I graduated from a Seven Sisters school too." She shifted her weight. "That was right after Yousef won the Driehaus prize. When I met him."

Shelley maintained a smile and answered, "That's nice." Mrs. Kamal turned back to the German instructor and promptly assumed the lotus position. Why had the wife shown up? And where on earth had she been for the last three weeks?

Shelley said nothing to Mr. Kamal about the encounter, and he not a word to her. The morning and afternoon passed as usual, with her reading the *Times* and traveling downtown to deliver a parcel to a secretary in a skirt suit. When she returned to the Kamals' apartment Clova told her to wait in the library, for Mr. Kamal was engaged at that moment. In the library, on the side table where the morning paper usually lay, was a blocky white laptop. The laptop was open, but the screen was dark. After twenty minutes of sitting in silence, Shelley placed a finger on the touchpad, and the screen illuminated an Internet Explorer page open to the website *Gawker*. Black text on a white background read: UNCOVERING SCANDALS FROM THE PAST!

Below the headline were three hyperlinks, written in neon pink:

TRUE STORIES OF THE KENNEDYS' DISTURBED DAUGHTER!
INTERVIEW WITH THE MOTHER OF ROMAN POLANSKI'S TINY TART
INSIDE SCOOP: I WAS YOUSEF KAMAL'S SEEING-EYE GIRL

That was it. That must have been the article he'd mentioned in her interview—the one defaming him. Had he left the laptop there for her? Or was it the wife? She stared at the screen until it went dark again. Then she sat waiting. The grandfather clock chimed lightly for the quarter hour mark and then more heavily at half past. The minutes ticked by and eventually Shelley leaned over and skimmed her finger against the touchpad again. She clicked the third pink link, which revealed a retro black-and-white photograph of a young woman in a cowl-neck sweater. A brunette with vulgarly crooked front teeth. The headline on this page read: HOW KAMAL'S SEEING-EYE GIRL CAME TO HER SENSES.

Her eyes fell to the first paragraph. "One morning in his downtown office, he sat beside me and said: 'I can hear your polyester skirt rubbing against the skin and hair of your vulva. Why have you foregone underwear today?'"

Shelley clicked the page away and lowered the top of the laptop; it closed with a soft *snap*. She would not be caught reading that. She sat quietly in the library for the next forty minutes, at which point Clova curved her head in and told her she could go home. She would surely be paid for her wait time.

The routine of Shelley's evenings at Strong Place now began with eating a dinner of tuna from a can while standing over the trashcan and flipping through *Rolling Stone*. That day she hustled home with a plan to go right to the internet though, now that she knew where to find the article. As soon as she entered the chilly kitchen, she grabbed a package of saltines from the counter and made her way to the cramped office on the second floor. Dropping her pants, she kicked them aside and arranged herself cross-legged in her underwear on the hard office chair.

Outside, a few car horns blew on Columbus; the setting sun cast the room in an azure wash. As the gray desktop computer booted up, Shelley felt strangely giddy and giggled aloud in the empty room. So Mr. Kamal had ignored her today. That would happen, on occasion. She imagined, briefly, that this was exactly the life she wanted but had never known it. A daily routine, an undulation of intrigue: new news, old books, ornately decorated office-building lobbies. A walk across the park, a familiar penthouse. "Well, here I am," she said to no one, "a grown-up."

When the computer was on, she found herself clicking around to various websites. She checked out the Live Journal page of her old roommate, Aleisha. She downloaded a few songs from the Slips' new acoustic album. Outside, the sun had fully set. She did not go back to the article on *Gawker*. After an hour, she decided she truly didn't want to read it. There was no need for her to know those things. She would get up the next day and return to the job; her body had become accustomed to a clockwork rhythm. Shelley stood and walked away from the old desk. She wandered through the quiet rooms of her childhood home with a certain aloneness that reminded her of an empty Saturday afternoon, as if there was something she kept forgetting to do. This was a feeling she had nothing but fondness for. It wasn't that she was happy—no, she suspected this was not what happiness felt like. It could be, though, that this was what it felt like to be content.

Three days after their mid-yoga meeting, Shelley glimpsed the back of Mr. Kamal's wife's leather tote bag exiting the dining room and slipping behind the heavy door to the hallway that led to the family bedrooms. Mr. Kamal had already made it clear that "help is not allowed in those quarters." In the three preceding days Shelley had heard, several times, the patter of quick steps and the door to the family quarters shutting. It appeared permanent: the wife had returned to the apartment from wherever she'd been. The internet revealed that the wife was actually Dr. Jillian Hollingsworth Kamal, PhD in—strangely—Far Eastern rather than Middle Eastern art, and head curator of the Asian wing of the Metropolitan Museum of Art. Would it all change now?

But although there was a bit more breath and light in the Kamals' penthouse, as the work days passed, Shelley's fears were assuaged: it was still very much the staid apartment where she had been interviewed. She and Mr. Kamal's routine remained, but she had yet to write one word with him. Occasionally he would reference their future together. *When we begin writing, you will sit in that chair. Our writing, when it happens, will take place in the afternoon.* Yet each afternoon he kept her busy with emailing and filing and delivering. Day in and day out, Shelley watched him and something akin to admiration grew for this serious, particular man. Although he didn't seem to be working on anything—minor or major—at the moment, he had spent his life working toward being extraordinary, which in itself was extraordinary. She felt not just that she knew him but also that the two of them were on the same team. Perhaps all colleagues felt that way: extraordinary, together.

May chugged along, still cold, and perturbed New Yorkers anxiously asked one another, "What happened to spring this year?" Above Fifty-Ninth Street, various summertime plans were being sorted, East Hampton and Amagansett already booked from June 15 through Labor Day. Shelley spent her nights at home with her magazines and her ancient boxy television. She supposed some of her childhood friends would be returning to the city for the summer, but she had no interest in seeing them. Zoë had left for a two-month-long outward-bound sailing trip, which her parents sorely hoped would dry her out, and Charlotte had been sent to live with an aunt in London for the summer so that her parents would not have to bear witness to her nascent lesbian career. Armond's calls were lessening greatly but were being replaced by an increase in Brooke's calls, who now appeared thoroughly obsessed with their father's malevolent will. Brooke was trying desperately to set a date to visit her in New York. Shelley could have cared less about the actual money, but she was worrying a bit about Nick's whereabouts. It had been too long. Ms. Scribner still rang daily, and was threatening a visit too. Her whispered voice rose from the receiver, "What if Nick has done something, Shelley? What if he's mixed up in something horrible, something violent?"

On a Friday, Shelley and Mr. Kamal were sitting in their usual seats when he made his request. He poured tea from the porcelain pot and said, "I want you to accompany me to Rhode Island next week. I will start working on my book project, and I would like for you to be part of that work."

A blush rose from Shelley's navel to her décolletage, to her faintly freckled cheeks. Finally, to write for him! He wanted her to be with him. Air squeezed through Mr. Kamal's nose, whistling slightly, and she nodded in the dim air. She did not stop to consider the fact that the next week was her twenty-third birthday, for there was no one else for her to spend it with. Rather, she thought: *I am winning. I have been working hard, and now I am succeeding, just like my teachers always said.* "Thank you," she blurted. Then she cleared her throat. "I'm fairly sure I can come, yes."

He made a spitting sound. "Stop thanking me! And you shouldn't be *fairly* anything. Be more decisive. We'll leave at half past eight on Sunday morning and we'll return on the following Sunday."

After work, Shelley walked all the way down to the central branch of the library on Forty-Second Street. She hadn't been to a library once throughout college, and probably not in high school either. The last time she remembered going there was when her father had taken her to a Literary Lions dinner when she was ten, where the glow of the electric candelabras had cast an enchanting light in the great marble function room. As she entered the main hall now, her body reflexively relaxed. The hollow pitch of library silence was soothing, sedative-like. She found a computer, looked up the location, then made her way to the portion of the stacks where books about Yousef Kamal were shelved. She was looking for a biography or at least some interviews—something to prime her for the memoir work she would do the following week. She was ready to read about Egypt, about a healer he'd met on the shores of the Nile, a mystic who'd told him he was blind due to sins of a past life. But Shelley found nothing of the sort. The shelf contained at least fifteen volumes about him, but they were all large-format art books, containing photographs of his buildings, as well as some of the design plans. One showed the perforation machine he used to create tactile blueprints. The closest she came to personal knowledge was a preface in one book that reported:

> Yousef Kamal was blinded at age twenty-four, in the summer after he'd completed graduate school at the Massachusetts Institute of Technology. Directly out of school, Yousef was hired as an apprentice for Raymond Erith and went to work with him in London. It was his third week in London when, riding in the passenger's seat of a hackney carriage along the Aldwych, a lorry carrying construction scaffolding lost hold of its cargo. A scaffolding pole went through the windshield of Yousef's vehicle, piercing his skull and causing severe brain trauma that damaged his optic nerve irreparably.

So that was what had happened to him. And it was at the start of his career. It was undeniable: the man had accomplished fantastic feats. As Shelley flipped through the photographs of brick and stone buildings, skimming her hand over golden domes and long windows, she considered that he'd built his first private home when he was already blind, and then went on to build structures all over the world. He'd traveled throughout Europe and the Middle East by himself, with a mere cane to guide him, dreaming up these edifices fit for great men and brilliant minds. As her eyes skimmed over the photographs, Shelley felt a peacefulness overtake her; she envisioned herself writing down the details of his struggles and his triumphs, learning more about his past. Perhaps he would continue to tell her details as she led him on bucolic evening walks through the fine Rhode Island sand, deer peeking out of the brush behind them. She would listen well and write well. This was a skill she could master, this was a real job—one that had nothing to do with her family and the trouble that came with it.

13

On the last day of her junior year of college, Grace Kamal was un-characteristically hopeful about the future of not just her academic life but also, strangely, her social life. She stood behind a podium on the darkened stage in the Whitby Auditorium, thrusting her chin out and trying to stay focused on the debate, while the corpuscles of her cerebral cortex buzzed with the knowledge that the next morning, less than twenty-four hours from that very moment, she would be sitting inside a car with Shelley Whitby. It was simultaneously mortifying that her parents had arranged for Shelley to be injected into their lives, and thoroughly mirac-ulous that they had. Since Grace had arrived at Demming, Shelley had been the most frequently discussed, gorgeous yet mysterious, iconic screwup on campus. And after Shelley unexpectedly disappeared from school earlier that spring, the talk of her had only increased. And now Grace—Grace!—was going to have the inside scoop on just what hap-pened.

"Ahem. It's time for your closing argument, Ms. Kamal."

Crap. Grace nodded at the moderator and shuffled the papers on the podium in front of her, buying some time. She needed to focus. They were in the final debate of the eastern championship: Demming versus Wesleyan.

Grace cleared her throat and dived back into her argument. "A few moments ago my opponent from Wesleyan produced the sophisticated line: 'The last time I checked, more freedom was better.' While I'd argue with his casual debating tone, I'll grant that his statement is hard to contend with."

Breathe-breathe-smile, chin up. She cleared her throat again and tried to look to the back of the room, but she couldn't get past the front-row grins. It seemed that no matter what she did, people were always chuckling in her presence.

She was in the coda of her closing argument. Her team needed this win. She pictured the outline of her father in the back of the room, his slumped shoulders and exposed, listening ears. Her ability to debate people, primarily men, came directly from him and his commands. "Describe *Judith and the Head of Holofernes*." Or: "What was the motivation for Dustin Hoffman to run into the wedding chapel? How was the tension built?" Although she wasn't a talker on a sports field or in a high school hallway, she was trained in her father's presence to craft concise and forceful verbal depictions. If she was lazy, or incorrectly depicted Klimt's use of metallic, he would bark: "No! That was not evocative. Begin again." It wasn't until Grace was ten or so that it occurred to her that he was just assuming it was a poor description, as the man could not, after all, see the thing being described. But her father did have an uncanny ability to understand what he could not see. He was a blind architect, for Christ's sake. And although some might call him difficult, Grace knew that underneath his barking exterior, he was a kind and reasonable man, at least when it came to her. He barked those orders because he loved and cherished her, more than any other person or object or idea in the world. And he lavished unwarranted amounts of praise on her, as well, and embraced her more than her cold mother ever did. Grace was fully confident of her father's bottomless love, and that this love impelled him to teach her the thing at which he himself was an expert: endless, detailed knowledge of the world. Because of that, and because of him, she had the ability to be sharp with her verbal offense.

A few times, in the car on the way to Rhode Island or while waiting for the check at LuHan Grill, she had told her parents that she wanted to be a Supreme Court justice. She'd try to jostle some humor out of them with a crooked smile and a "Just aiming low." But they would sip their tea and nod, aloof as ever. The truth was that as a junior in college she didn't want to be a judge, even on the Supreme Court. It was a secret she kept in the pit of her stomach, one she'd never let see the sun, although she knew it to be the very clear truth. She wanted to be president. In the spring of 2003, that was her goal: to one day become the first female, nonwhite president of the United States.

Grace couldn't share her aspiration with her classmates and certainly not with her parents. The infuriating thing was that her parents didn't realize that her attachment to politics came directly from them. She was the only child of an interracial couple, one half of which was disabled. When she was growing up, her straw-headed classmates had asked her curtly, "What *are* you?" The eyebrow-pierced shopkeepers at Urban Outfitters had followed her around the store, pretending to straighten up stacks of baseball tees, in order to see if she would pluck a bracelet off the shelf and shove it into her pocket. On her family's summer trips to Cairo and Alexandria, she would walk in between her parents as they passed clusters of homeless children whose rib cages were the largest parts of their bodies. Jillian and Yousef would float right by them, discussing Puccini and the latest piece by Adam Gopnik. It was rage inducing. But what disturbed Grace the most— what convinced her she would never, ever be like them—was their reaction to 9/11. The attack had happened on the first day of her freshman year of college. After she heard the news she had called and called her parents from the Demming dorm phone, getting only busy signals. When Jillian finally picked up, Grace was wailing and thanking God that they were okay, which her parents found quite amusing. The way they said they were fine, the way they did not act deeply disturbed, it was as if they were spectators to the tragedy that happened in their own city, comparing it to Greek myths. They didn't go downtown, they didn't give blood. When Grace had pressed her mother she had pursed her lips and used her father's blindness as an excuse. "You know it's too risky to bring Yousef into that situation." Although he had nothing to do with religion now, her father had been raised Muslim. And he didn't seem bothered by anti-Islamic fervor. Her family was awkward and complicated, and thus Grace herself was not easily understood by an outside observer. It wasn't fair. If she had been born someone like Shelley Whitby, everything about her would be easily recognizable.

Now, Grace took a breath and pulled out her final trick of the morning's debate: the gender card. "My opponent tells us that 'a woman with a gun is eighty-three percent more effective at preventing rape.' But in response to that I ask you: How much more effective at committing rape is a man with a gun? This issue is about the value of each and every human life. Personally, I have hope. Hope for a future where each of these lives is cherished and given opportunities to grow up safely, to change the world, to fall in love. We need to act on our hope"—she paused for dramatic effect—"and take responsibility to create a safe future for every valuable life."

Chin high, she finished, nodding and thanking the crowd. Then to her astonishment, everyone in the Whitby Auditorium stood up for her— the handful of students watching, the four professors, the parents of the Wesleyan debaters. Even her three opponents were on their feet, holding straight, clapping arms in her direction. Grace couldn't help herself; she was beaming.

By the time she had packed up the last of her bags from her third-floor room in Lathrop House later that afternoon, she was once again reverberating with the knowledge that she was going to spend her first week of summer break with Shelley Whitby. Her parents didn't know that while everyone at Demming was familiar with Shelley, Grace had an eye trained on her this past year while they lived in the same dorm. Grace had awarded Shelley the label of Disheveled Equestrian. This DE tried to let herself fall with the commoners; she was a bad student who couldn't muster a care about her future, a cigarette smoker with a sneering attitude, a probable pothead who wore whatever clothes she found crumpled beside her bed. Yet Shelley's elegant finishes—her ruddy cheeks, her glossy hair, her collar that popped itself—shone through. Her very DNA gave her awe-inspiring posture and a body odor of freshly cut grass. Shelley was akin to a celebrity to her, and thus Grace was fascinated.

After Grace helped her roommate, Vanshi, board the college van for JFK airport, she returned to her packed-up room and slipped a pair of scissors out of the end pocket of her giant duffel bag. The idea had come to her three days beforehand, when her mother informed her on the telephone that the new amanuensis was coming with them to Little Compton. Grace knew she needed to do something to get Shelley's attention, to make it clear that she herself did not carry the uptight staleness that hovered around her parents. She didn't have time to go to a salon before the trip, but she was still going to go through with it: with a pair of orange-handled paper shears in one hand, and a beat-up *People* magazine that she'd found backstage in the auditorium, she went into the coed, multiunit dorm bathroom in order to cut off all her hair.

Someone had just taken a shower, so as Grace scrubbed out a circle on the bathroom mirror, she saw just how young and inelegant she really was. Her light-brown skin was spotted with acne eruptions, and her big mouth revealed her goofy, overlapping teeth. When Grace came to college, she took her eighteen years of failed social interactions and used it as fuel: she began to talk. Now she opened up to everyone, all the time. It took a few months, but by November of her freshman year she was even saying her jokes out loud, puns and one-liners that she'd always constructed in her head. And often, people got them. Since becoming a Demming Blue Jay, she had impressed the sociology and English faculties (double major), her dormmates and clubmates, and, if she had to admit it, she'd impressed herself. Emerging from one's shell is not easy work. By junior year she was an associate editor of the *Demming Howler*, the captain of the debate team, and the secretary of the Campus Democrats. She also did stage lighting for the opera club, because she felt the ol' résumé could use a bit of art and culture. She was, after all, Yousef Kamal's daughter and a Hollingsworth on her mother's side. She was excelling on the professional side of life, but she couldn't help the anxious, uncomfortable pressure building up inside of her, convincing her that she was missing out on the most exciting parts.

But this was her summer to begin to really live: to make friends, to go to parties, and, yes, to have sex. She had had sex exactly three times before, with a debate team member named Arun, twice in her dorm room and once at his parents' house in Port Washington. All three occasions could be categorized as banal. Shelley coming to Little Compton with the Kamals was a major opportunity: Grace would enmesh herself with Shelley; she would construct the girl to be her Marquise de Merteuil and allow Shelley to lead her gallantly into her world of mysterious and attractive men. She could finally have a boyfriend. Tomorrow, a short-haired Grace would walk into her own house and sit down beside Shelley Whitby as an utterly different person.

14

As Brooke's sandals tapped over the salmon marble tiles in the entryway of the mansion on Hammond Pond Parkway in Chestnut Hill, she couldn't help thinking about the Whitby Curse. If she had already found this Nick kid, there would be no way she'd be walking through this house right now. What if the silly curse was real? What if the Whitbys were destined to destroy themselves, again and again? In the internet age, it was very difficult for people to go missing. Nick could be dead. His death would be another family tragedy, and she reasoned logically, it certainly wouldn't help her keep her own house. It had become a nightly ritual for Brooke to search for Nick on the internet, scouring Friendster and Myspace and other internet sites. She'd located his pages, but he hadn't been active at all since before her father had died. Every few days, Brooke reported her findings to Shelley on the telephone, who didn't seem concerned in the least about the absence of their fake brother. It was disturbing and certainly pointed to the fact that Shelley knew something about what Nick had been getting into. Or maybe she was colluding with him somehow.

The nasal voice of Marc's mother, Candy, resounded through the living room and into the foyer of the mansion the older Costas were considering buying for their son. "Oh no! That bathroom is tiny! It would have to go. We'd just *have* to knock the wall out—double the size."

Marc's father gave a small *mm-hmm* of acknowledgment. Brooke grimaced. She had once had hopes about the Costas, that they could fold her into their family the way Allie's parents had. But it turned out the Costas weren't actually interested in her, in the end. This house tour was the last place she wanted to be.

The house had just gone on the market and disconcertingly had five bedrooms. Brooke was heading toward forty; how many children would they even be able to have to populate these rooms? Not that she had said a word to Marc about the pregnancy. She had told no one, and had scheduled an abortion appointment for a week from that date. If she was to go through with it, she had to do it soon. The procedure was scheduled at Newton-Wellesley Hospital, as far from her coworkers at the General as possible.

"This place is really something, huh?" Marc said, smirking at the lavishness of the foyer. Everything else in the house was either white or varying forms of gleaming gray: stainless steel appliances, charcoal bathroom tile, cold iron handrails on the stairs. The place came with a three-car garage, an extra-long faux-marble kitchen island, glass-walled double showers, and all the closets were walk-in. It had been built two years beforehand. It was, Brooke thought, an abomination.

From the other room, the real estate broker hollered, "You can do major renovation in here. Really, you could level the inside and remake it as your dream home."

"What do you think, babe?" In the foyer of the mansion, Marc positioned himself behind Brooke, wrapping his two arms over her stomach, holding her protectively. For the past couple of weeks it seemed he'd been staring at her petite body with wonder, his eyes glassy, as if he knew what was going on inside of her. But there was no way he could know. A few times she'd been so exhausted in his presence that she'd had to leave to take a nap, but she'd simply blamed it on work. His arms squeezed her now, and she tried to let herself relax. She should like this. But when her mother had met him, she'd rolled her eyes and gave one skeptical "Really, Birdie?" And her father would have detested him, of course, immediately dismissing him as a weenie. Yet Marc's arms around her—it was normal.

It was the logical thing to like. If she could simply enjoy it, the seams of her life would not break apart.

"Are you ready to live in this manse? Ready to be Mom and Pop in this castle?" he chuckled. "Costa babies would race up those stairs like maniacs."

Brooke wriggled out of Marc's suddenly repulsive grip. It was hot in this gauche, heinous house. Living there with Marc as her husband would mean not only financial stability but also familial stability: she could keep the baby. And what other option did she have? Living in a rented apartment as a single mother, friendless and exhausted, barely able to afford day care?

And yet. "All this marble, this glitz. You know it's not my style," she said.

"Oh, right. Extreme luxury isn't your style, I forgot. You'd rather live in a crumbling box from another century."

"Goin' upstairs!" Candy Costa yelled in her Boston accent, as she clacked back into the foyer in her three-and-half-inch heels. "Those upstairs bathrooms bettah live up to their advertisement." Her highlighted brown hair was blown out into its signature orb around her unmoving face; there had been a nose job, an eye tuck, a neck lift, Botox.

"This might be the one, baby," Candy said in a faux whisper as she passed her son. Before ascending the stairs she squeezed his shoulders briefly and didn't so much as rest her eyes on Brooke. Brooke might as well have been a mannequin to her.

Marc's father, Lorenzo, tall and slim with his shock of white hair, nodded at his son and Brooke as he followed his wife up the stairs. Brooke had a soft spot for Lorenzo. He had been the mastermind behind pulling his family from the ghetto to grandeur, yet he was always melancholic, as if he was deeply disappointed by something. Although Lorenzo was clearly a striver, he didn't remind Brooke of her own father. No, Roger was much too loud. But the quiet Lorenzo exuded sometimes reminded Brooke of Allie's father, Thomas. It was clear they were both kind, although Lorenzo seemed too shy to really enact his kindness. As she watched the older

Costas walk up the stairs, the beige-suit-wearing broker woman scrambling behind them, Brooke wondered what Allie's parents were doing at that very moment. A slice of sadness cut through her middle. She would lose them forever, surely, along with Allie, if she moved into this house. The Whitby Curse: everything that you can lose, you will.

"You know I don't want to live in the suburbs," she mumbled to Marc. But it was becoming clear to her that the truth was she didn't want to live in the suburbs *with him*. Maybe her problem was inherited from her father. What if it was in her blood, the fact that she couldn't be content with a perfectly good spouse?

He snorted. "Well, sometimes a person has to face reality, Ms. Whitby. What option do you have? You're going to have to move somewhere. Let's look outside. Brochure says there's a tennis court and a pool."

A wall of glass doors in the kitchen led them to the yard, where the sun had nearly set. Small but bright stars twinkled in the graying sky. Beneath Brooke's feet the thick grass gave off a pungent odor; it was real grass, freshly laid.

One hundred yards in front of them, a swimming pool shone with tungsten underwater lights. The weather was still cold, so Brooke guessed the sellers must have filled the pool specifically for the Costas' visit. Recliner patio chairs circled the pool. Marc sat on one side of them and pulled a pack of cigarettes out of his pocket. From the third floor of the house, across the vast green expanse of lawn, they heard a pop and then a round window opened on the top floor. Candy squawked from inside, but it was hard to make out her words.

Marc lit his cigarette, and Brooke noticed that his hands were shaking. "Want one?" he asked through clenched lips.

She did want one, badly. She shook her head.

Was he nervous?

"Lemme ask you something, B," he said, swinging the cigarette as he gesticulated. "I need you to tell me something honestly. Why the hell isn't this good enough for you?" His eyes looked bloodshot in the darkening air. "I'm going to give you all of this, and I'm going to be your husband, if you'll let me. I'll ply you with gifts for the rest of your life, you will never have to work another day, never touch another IV or old man's dressing gown if you don't want to—"

"Stop, Marc. You don't get that—"

"No, you stop!" His voice crossed into a higher pitch and took on a stronger Boston accent. "Why isn't this good enough for you? Goddammit!" He stood up. "Anothah woman would kill for this, Brooke! Why the fuck can't you be happy?"

She was quiet for a moment. She focused on the steam coming off the heated pool water, and pictured Allie, a young Allie: her face in high school, when it was already so wise and so calm. Allie's broad cheekbones; Brooke could meditate on those cheekbones alone and feel better. But what could she really say to Marc about her? He knew they'd been together, he knew that Allie had broken up with Brooke when Brooke said she would never marry a woman, even if it were legal. Instead, Brooke pivoted to her job. "I like being a nurse. It's what I was meant to do, and it's something that I'm good at." Her jaw was beginning to set. Why was she defending her life choices to him? "And I thought I'd live in the city forever. All of this—this house, and your parents, Chestnut Hill—it's not what I ever pictured for myself."

"And what did you picture for yourself? Whatever weird shit you were doing with that rock-climbing woman? Give me a fucking break."

She closed her eyes and thought about the sheer beauty of Allie's cheekbones. "This is not about Allie."

"Then what the fuck is it about?"

From the oaks behind the tennis court, a robin sang out in the dusk. In the next house, separated by half an acre of landscaped lawn, the lights on the top floor turned on one by one. Brooke said nothing.

She kept her eyes closed and remembered Parents' Weekend during her first year at boarding school, when her own parents didn't show up. It had been a crisp October Saturday on the verdant, stone-building-covered campus. The leaves on the trees exploded into flames of orange and red. Over the playing fields, a breeze was slight yet noticeable. Students trudged up paths with equipment bags hanging from their shoulders, leading middle-aged couples with their pearls and boat shoes through the stately, ancient buildings. Brooke herself—how small she was, how very like a defenseless bird—wore a plaid scarf and a fleece jacket over her choir robe as she made her way back to Brewster dormitory. She was crying, but it was a silent act; she was never one to wheeze or sniffle in public. It had been a strange few months: in September, she'd been deposited at the school by her mother, then forgotten about. The first few weeks in New Hampshire she had been so utterly terrified that she didn't speak for stretches of days, save for two-word responses to questions from her roommate or the dorm parent, a French teacher named Madame Tournet.

As September progressed into October though, things had been on the upswing. Brooke had begun to realize that being at the school, surrounded by people her own age with her own interests, was at the very least more interesting than where she had been for the previous year, in that bleak, foreign Caribbean city with her now silent mother.

Brooke hadn't spoken to her father since she'd gotten to school, and when she'd told her mother on the telephone that the weekend of October seventeenth was parents' visiting weekend, Corney hadn't even bothered to make up an excuse about why she couldn't come. Since Peter's death a year and a half earlier, grief had rendered her mother silent. That was what the fourteen-year-old was thinking about as she entered the heavy wooden door of Brewster dormitory: the windowless hospital hallway where she'd overheard the doctors' yelling as Peter's small body lost its remnants of vitality. And her mother's bloodcurdling cry, right before she crumpled into a heap of limbs on the linoleum floor. And then the next year, that night in Barbados, the smash that came with it, the breaking of glass and her father's back walking away through a hurricane. At St. Paul's, involuntary tears accompanied the images. She pulled on the heavy oak dormitory door and noticed a girl was coming out at the same time, but didn't look up. Then someone grabbed her elbow—forcefully.

"What's going on?" Allie Wainwright asked.

Although they lived in different wings of the dorm, Brooke knew who she was. Allie was a star field hockey player, a freshman on the varsity team, and one of the only non-white girls in Brewster. Brooke wasn't sure what ethnicity Allie was. She had darker skin, but she didn't eat breakfast or lunch with the cluster of St. Paul's black kids who traveled around campus in a small but consistent clique. In fact, Allie didn't seem to be close friends with anyone.

"I'm fine," Brooke mumbled, and tried to wriggle her elbow out of this girl's imposing grip.

"Where are you going now, Brooke?" Allie asked, holding tight.

"I'm just going to my room—I'm, ah, not feeling well, and I'm going to take a nap while my roommate is out."

Allie began to shake her head. "It's no big deal if your parents couldn't make it to campus this weekend. I'm about to go out to eat with mine though. You should come. We're leaving right now."

Brooke, although secretly thrilled that Allie even knew her name, shook her head. Why would she go out to eat with a stranger's family?

"C'mon, you can leave that choir robe in the car." The girl was now grinning, revealing perfect white teeth. She still wore her green field hockey skirt and a white collared sports shirt under a sweater.

Soon Brooke was sitting in the back seat of a blue Volvo station wagon, behind two of the calmest people she'd ever met, and beside Allie's little brother, Charlie, who smiled goofily at Brooke before returning his face to his comic book.

At the dimly lit, rustic-chic restaurant in downtown Concord, Brooke got a better view of Allie's parents. They both generously offered their background to Brooke, as if she was someone who mattered. Allie's mother, Paula, was a former ballet dancer turned painter. Her father, Thomas, was a psychiatrist—the only full-time psychiatrist living on Martha's Vineyard year-round. Charlie, who had donned a Red Sox cap and continued to smile, barely said a word. He read his comic book stack, which had some-how grown to three.

Brooke ate pumpkin soup—she always remembered that—and the steam from it warmed her face as she answered Mr. and Mrs. Wainwright's questions.

Now why did you want to sing in the chorus? . . . How wonderful to come from a musical family.

What were your favorite classes at your school in Boston? . . . As a painter myself I'm very glad to hear that. Some people just think visually.

Brooke was taken aback by how these adults listened so thoroughly to what she said; they seemed to care about her words and responded thoughtfully. It was a feeling she had nearly completely forgotten about in the past two years, this level of care. And Allie, devouring a chicken pot pie, didn't seem embarrassed by her own parents' questions at all. Back then Allie tied up her wild curls, and Brooke was able to clearly observe her earnest expression, nodding along with her parents, seeming to be just as interested in Brooke. They continued their battery of kindnesses.

It's a shame you've never been to the Vineyard. You're welcome at our house any time.

Vacations, weekends, whenever.

I suspect you'll love it.

It was one simple dinner, but the mere existence of the solid, caring couple stuck with Brooke throughout the night and into the next day. It was as if something bigger had happened to her, something redemptive. And when Allie plunked down across from her in the dining hall the next night and began to make fun of the biology teacher Mr. Movious's corny jokes, a few of the lights in Brooke's contained universe turned back on. She was, suddenly, un-alone. It was years before it occurred to Brooke that the Wainwrights' behavior that night of Parents' Weekend was a reflection of just how much they loved their daughter. They saw how lonely Allie was underneath all her success and wanted to help her make a friend. This was what a good parent was: someone who took the burden upon himself to help his child. Brooke didn't have that anymore. A lump grew in her throat that remained there, ever afterward.

The rationale behind the Whitby Curse was that there were so many tragedies in the family—so many unexpected deaths and other catastrophes—because the Whitbys were too bold and too greedy. They flew faulty planes when they didn't know how, sped down highways at the farthest edge of the speedometer, opened risky businesses, and bet on slim odds. They had been given too much, and thus assumed they were invincible. But Brooke knew that her family's misfortunes weren't due to extreme daring but rather to frenzied, panicked, striving: they engaged in impulsive acts in order to live up to those who had come before them. What was so miraculous to Brooke about Allie's parents was that they were content with their relaxed island life. They had time to pay attention to their own daughter and to ask Brooke about herself. While Brooke was more stable than either of her parents, the Wainwrights were the real thing. They were the adults she had never encountered.

The lump in Brooke's throat was there as she sat in front of a screaming Marc, in a suburban backyard, at age thirty-seven. While his own parents were inside potentially buying a house for Brooke to be a prop inside of, he was stomping on the ground with one foot, throwing an adult-sized tantrum. "I'm not good enough for you, Brooke *Whitby*. No matter what I do, I'll never be good enough for you. Goddammit! I'm too old for this shit." He hurled his still-lit cigarette behind him. "Should I give up? Tell me now."

At least he had been sharp enough to question how much of her hesitation really was about Allie. Strangely, this made Brooke soften to him.

He hissed again, "Do I need to give up, Brooke? Tell me, and I'll walk the fuck away from you and never look back."

She focused on Marc's tan face: he had lovely features. A thin nose, smooth and easily tanned skin. His child would be gorgeous, no matter whom he had it with. For a moment, she considered possibilities: she could fill the pop-up mansion behind her with her family's rugs and collected antiques; she could keep her day job, and Marc could pay for a nanny. But this man—this angry, wealthy man and his money-obsessed parents—would never feel like home.

Behind them, from the open glass door to the house's opulent kitchen,

Marc's mother's voice carried across the yard. "The upstairs isn't big enough! And a lot of construction, Marc. A lot of work to do here!"

Brooke's queasiness spiked up. The older Costas, although they frequently told waiters and coat-check girls and ticket-takers that Brooke was a "real Whitby," had never wasted a moment asking Brooke about herself. What would the Wainwrights think now, of the predicament she was in? Over the years she'd gotten into the habit of letting them advise her. In high school, when they called Allie nightly on the pay phone in the dorm's common room, they often asked if Brooke was also there. Brooke would chat with them for a few minutes, Thomas and Paula on different extensions in their long and low island house. They'd ask who got the solo for the choral performance at Taft, and how the physics class she was struggling with had been going. The girls did end up visiting their house on the Vineyard often, and soon it became Brooke's second home. On that first Thanksgiving break, the Wainwrights had driven all the way to New Hampshire only to pick up the girls and drive them back to Woods Hole, where they put their old Volvo on the ferry. But in the following years the girls were allowed to take the bus to the Cape and then board the ferry themselves; the Wainwrights had always already bought them tickets, which were always held at the glass window.

Brooke didn't address with Allie the strangeness of her involvement with the Wainwrights. If she had, she would have had to verbalize that with each growing week that her own parents didn't contact her, she felt more abandoned, more like an orphan. She was entirely grateful for Paula and Thomas, and more mortifyingly grateful to Allie for letting them come into her life. But Brooke could never speak those words, not even now. And Allie, always toughly mature beyond her years, didn't seem to mind sharing her parents' watchful eyes and interested affection. In fact, she treated it like it was the most normal thing in the world.

Over a decade later, when the girls were officially a couple, Brooke had been terrified to tell the Wainwrights about their relationship. What if they thought it was sick? She had basically grown up in these people's house, acted as a surrogate daughter to them, and now she was sexually entwined with their biological daughter. Allie and Brooke had fought about telling her parents for over two months, until one day Allie went against her wishes and simply called up Thomas. It was another rare moment when Brooke had truly cried, involuntarily. But four hours later, hours she'd spent actually shaking with fear, the doorbell to her Beacon Hill house rang, and standing on the front step were the Wainwrights. "Sweet child!" Thomas had gushed, enveloping her in his arms. After the phone call, the Wainwrights had headed straight to the next ferry with bottles of rosé and oatmeal pull-apart bread and gingersnap cookies from Humphreys bakery. They were there to celebrate, to share in the love.

But what would they say now? Brooke was pregnant with this man's child—this man who valued stainless steel and glass-walled double showers. Even after she and Allie broke up, the Wainwrights would call her to check in and occasionally send notes and holiday cards, small gestures and mementos to show they still cared for her. But of course their own daughter would always come first. Allie was their priority. They would never speak another word to Brooke.

Marc was walking away now with his hands thrown above his head in exasperation, back toward the lit-up house and his parents. Although different from most of them, Brooke was a Whitby. Leaving Marc would be reckless. Having a child without him would be extraordinarily irresponsible. Maybe it ultimately cursed them, but her family also taught her that if you didn't push for your dream, there was no chance of achieving it. Brooke noticed the large dark stain on the concrete bottom of the otherwise pristine pool. This was not the life she was meant for. She said firmly and clearly, in her best nurse-delivering-the-truth voice, "Yes, Marc, this is over. It's time for you to give up."

15

On Sunday morning Shelley walked away from Strong Place toward the east side, with a red Patagonia duffel slung over her shoulder. In front of the Grisham, in the loading zone, sat a black Range Rover with its engine off. Dr. Jillian lounged in the driver's seat with the window down, as the doorman loaded monogrammed canvas totes into the trunk. Of course. The possibility that the wife was coming had occurred to Shelley, yet she'd pushed away the thought as soon as it popped up.

The woman looked briefly at her husband, who was sitting up too straight in the passenger's seat, then offered Shelley a tight smile. "You can sit in back."

Shelley mimicked Dr. Jillian's smile and handed her bag to the doorman. The drive up to Rhode Island was slated to be four hours, but she was now sure it would feel longer. Shelley opened the car door, and to her surprise, there was already someone else sitting back there—a girl about Shelley's age, who was sleeping.

After settling herself, Shelley was able to see that the girl, although more unkempt than her parents, was certainly a Kamal: even sleeping, she displayed the poise and upright control of any prep school graduate. And underneath the girl's grimace and acne, there was something frighteningly pretty about her face, lingering just above her pronounced, round cheekbones.

"Shelley, meet my daughter, Grace Akila Hollingsworth Kamal," Mr.

Kamal articulated. The girl opened her eyes, raised her eyebrows a minuscule amount, then returned to her semi-curled position.

A daughter? Shelley was dumbfounded; she had never imagined a daughter, never mind one her own age. After an hour in the car, Shelley wondered if this family always said very little to one another or if their silence was on behalf of her presence. Not that she and her mother had said very much on their long car trips to and from the Idlehour family reunions, but the atmosphere in the car had been so much more relaxed. Shelley had played her own mixtapes, while her mother drove in companionable silence. The few times she could remember having her father in the car, he was telling family stories with relish and humming along to corny, old-timey music he'd bring with him, or, it was just as likely, if he was in his other kind of mood, everyone had to be silent. Those were Roger's unspoken rules. In the Kamals' Range Rover, opera played on the radio as she stared out the window, squinting to make the highway-side evergreen trees blur. How could Mr. Kamal have done this to her? She knew particular and intimate things about him: how he digested a news story, when he needed to talk and when he needed to think, the unique gait and the pace he kept on an afternoon walk. And yet, he knew nearly nothing about her. If he'd cared to consider it, he would have known that she would never have signed up for a family vacation. The air-conditioning numbed her limbs and filled the car with the slight scent of chlorination. She certainly was not paid enough to be sitting here. Grace had a copy of *Harper's* on her knee, and occasionally read it for a moment before glancing at Shelley, then dozing off again. When she was jostled awake, she would turn to Shelley again, staring, then lean forward and squeeze her father's shoulder, sometimes stating out of nowhere, "Love you, Yousef," easily using her father's first name. Each time she said the word *love*, both of her parents flinched. Other times she just stroked her father's shirt-covered arm.

The interaction made Shelley's stomach curl. But perhaps this kind of contact is more typical when one's father is blind? She would never have touched her father like that, for fear that she would have disturbed his driving or made him flip into a dark mood. Mr. Kamal was different from

Roger, yet there was a darkness to him, as well: a secret place he seemed to retreat to in his mind, that Shelley could not access.

At half past eleven, they stopped at a "crab shack," where Shelley and Dr. Jillian and Grace all ordered lobster salads, and Mr. Kamal ordered a hamburger, well done. He ate this with surprising agility; no crumbs, no munching to be seen. Dr. Jillian sat beside him calmly and took on the tending duties. She pulled out his napkin and positioned it on his lap, took his hand and put it on his soda in front of him, wordlessly. Everything about her was precise: her bell-shaped russet hair; her rail-thin body; her slender, sharp nose. Mr. Kamal easily accepted his wife's tending. Their bodies touched each other with great comfort, but in a nurse-patient manner.

After lunch, the opera music transitioned to *All Things Considered* and Grace had fully woken up. To Shelley's horror, it quickly became clear that although she'd never seen Grace before, Grace could in fact know her. The clues piled up fast, as it turned out that the girl was quite a talker: "My roommate, Vanshi, is touring Europe this summer with the Night Howlers, you know, the a cappella group—" "We were in the middle of a mock debate in the Whitby Auditorium, when our coach got a call that his wife was going into labor!" The panic inside of Shelley grew. Mr. Kamal's daughter, sitting on the other side of the back seat, was a student at no place other than Demming College. Soon one of the Kamal parents would mention that Shelley went there too, and then details would be parsed, and it would be discovered that Shelley had lied to Mr. Kamal: she had never graduated. It wasn't as if she needed a degree in order to read him the newspaper. But everyone in the car would know she was a liar and one of those Whitbys.

How could she get out of this car, out of this trip? For a flash, she wondered if Nick would come get her. Since her early teenage years, Shelley had relied on Nick's being there for her. Not that the two of them saw each other very much, but she knew that whenever she called him, he was likely to drop everything. More than once when she was having a lonely weekend in Poughkeepsie, she'd suggest he visit and he'd arrive on campus within hours. He'd proceed to follow her around to whatever parties were happening in the field or the co-op houses, then crash on the floor beside her extra-long twin bed. She understood now that she had taken his relentless attention for granted. In the past few weeks, in moments when boredom overcame her or a small reminder of her father popped up—an old man with a bow tie, a cheesy one-liner said by a character on television—Shelley reached for her cell phone to dial up Nick, before remembering that she wouldn't be able to reach him. It was in those sporadic moments that she imagined the worst, for a split second. The days of him missing were piling up. But before these thoughts spiraled and grew, Shelley would promptly box them up, kick them away, and distract herself.

She closed her eyes and pretended to sleep. There was nothing she could do for Nick while she was on this working vacation. Mr. and Dr. Kamal listened attentively to everything Grace said, and it became clear they'd been doing so for the girl's entire life. The crab shack wiping and helping between the couple had not been evidence of a connection but rather a service. Yet this joint cooing over their daughter was a connection; it was the first sign of shared interest—the first electric jolt—between the two of them. Shelley was unsure of the ratio of service to spark one was supposed to have in a marriage though. The idea of sharing so much of yourself with another, to routinely sleep with your body next to another's, to eat the same meals and have your cells nourished by the same organic matter, it was unimaginable. And then to orgasm on top of that very same person. Utilitarian, the setup of it. Sickening, really. With her eyes closed, Shelley pictured Dr. and Mr. Kamal on a bed, she straddling him, upright with her two fried-egg breasts tilted toward the ceiling. No, it would be her bent over the side of the bed, totally naked, and he fully clothed with his trousers merely hanging to his knees. There was no other way.

But Dr. Jillian did not kiss her husband in front of Shelley, not even on the cheek. And after lunch her hand had gripped his forearm forcefully as she led him back to the car, face turned away from her husband, her mouth puckered, resembling revulsion.

Soon they arrived in Little Compton. Off the main road was a gravel one, marked with a sign in the shape of an arrow, nailed into a tree. The sign read HOLLINGSWORTH HOLLOW. A bit of kitsch for the country. Shelley was told that the house in Rhode Island had belonged to Dr. Jillian's family for five generations. "We're the American side of the British artistic family, the Hollingsworths." Dr. Jillian stared over her shoulder to the back seat, her eyes vaguely pleading while she relayed the information. "My great-grandfather was John Tate Hollingsworth, the Impressionist painter?" Something about her little limbs and unfussy face implied everything about her upbringing: both staunch and plush at the same time.

The gravel road dissipated and became sand-covered, approaching a marshy field with a rocky vista in the distance, and the gray ocean beyond that. They came upon a grandiose white-shingled mansion. Black shutters cloaked every window, and a rotunda was off to the right, enclosed by crosshatched glass, festooned by azalea bushes. The house had a slope-eaved roof with a cupola on top and two chimneys on either side. Beside the big house, separated by a path, was a smaller and squarer white-shingled house. The whole complex was weatherworn and salt-washed; a little English seaside glamour. From the Kamals' car Shelley saw a gardener in white shorts crouching by a cluster of primroses. He turned and waved to the family.

As the car stopped, Grace squealed, suddenly an energetic little colt. She skipped out the door, singing, "My true home!" and sauntered inside without touching her luggage.

Shelley dropped out of the car too, quaffing in the salty air. Gulls squawked overhead. Her family were Vineyarders, but this was so very close. And of course she'd been to Rhode Island plenty of times, with cousins or with schoolmates. But which ones? At twenty-two, her whole childhood was already a distant, dreamlike blur.

"You'll be staying over there," Dr. Jillian said, pointing to the smaller of the two houses. "We had the guesthouse built when the place became ours, and each of the five bedrooms has an en suite. Choose whichever one you'd like."

Mr. Kamal opened the passenger-side door and was feeling the inside of it for a handle to grip. "Shelley does not stay in the guesthouse basement?"

Dr. Jillian pursed her lips. "We usually have the help sleep in the basement. But as there's no one else here, I don't see why she can't have her pick." She turned to address Shelley. "We just ask that you be tidy. We don't hire a cleaning crew to pick up after our staff."

Shelley nodded and walked toward the smaller house. She didn't offer to help with the bags and left Mr. Kamal, mouth agape, by the open door of the SUV.

Inside the guesthouse the mountainous cool of clean marble overwhelmed her. "Hell-o," she said in a ghoulish voice, just to hear it echo against the walls. The living room had a U shape of overstuffed beige couches, and each bedroom had a queen-sized four-post bed with bolsters and shams occupying half the length of it. She chose a room on the second floor with a deck overlooking the ocean. Lying facedown in the middle of the bed, all of her misgivings about the trip—all of her bitter feelings—were forgiven. She hadn't been back to the Vineyard for two years, and was only now aware that she'd missed it so. She ached to sit around with Nick in the old basement rec room, or to run into Brooke on Lobsterville Beach. It was nearly summer, the time to do nothing in a natural setting, next to a body of water. When had people stopped bringing her to country mansions in New England?

She was still lying in bed, humming a bar of that song "Uncle John's Band," when she heard someone call, "Shelley?" It was a deep voice, but distant. Then she heard an electronic buzz, and his voice came into her room. "Shelley, are you there?"

Mr. Kamal spoke from a white intercom installed next to the bed. She sat up and pressed the TALK button. "Yes, Mr. Kamal. I'm in one of the upstairs bedrooms."

"Very well. Dinner is at seven forty, and we would like you to attend. It is in the dining area in the main house."

Shelley was silent and lay back on the bed. She no longer had a family.

They were all selfish: each one of them had left her behind. But, now, she had Mr. Kamal, and all that came with him. He needed her.

The intercom buzzed again. "You must answer me, Shelley."

"Oh." She stretched one arm out to hit the TALK button, without leaving her comfortable perch. "I'll be there."

Dinner was in the glass-encased rotunda. Through the south-facing windows the ocean lapped against the rocky shore, the cloudless sky fading into the water. The oval table had four places set at it. Water sweated in ice-filled glasses, and inside two wicker baskets, rouge cloth napkins swaddled cranberry-walnut rolls, keeping them warm. Mr. Kamal sat beside Dr. Jillian and offered Shelley a "Good evening" as she entered the room. The married couple was distinctly relaxed. Here in Rhode Island they were like children, protected by previous generations who had sat in the exact same spots. They might as well have been swinging their feet in the air on the Acme Versailles dining chairs.

Dr. Jillian spoke to her husband. "The gallery system is slow to catch on there, and when I gave my talk to the council of investors in Shanghai they had quite a problem understanding why beginning artists would want to hang their work in such small spaces . . ." She wore a sea-foam-blue silk shirt, buttoned but untucked, and breezy linen pants. As Shelley approached the table, Dr. Jillian gave her a brief once-over, lingering on her shorts and sandals, then continued discussing the site of a new building at a university in China, which she seemed to have a part in forming. So that's where she had been in April. Grace moseyed in next and took the final seat, still wearing her black T-shirt and flip-flops.

A small woman wearing a black-and-white polyester maid's uniform began to fill Shelley's glass with white wine—a light bubble to it—and she found herself smirking at the Kamals' daughter. There was something endearing about the extreme openness the girl displayed. She seemed to have used some sort of waxy cream to make her short, choppy hair lick out to all sides. Shelley wondered if Grace was *alternative*, like Nick. Mr. Kamal cleared his throat and asked the table, "What shall our topic of the evening be?" No one answered him. He put two palms on the table, waiting. Where had the maid come from? Shelley had been served by a household staff before, of course, but never one wearing a uniform.

Dr. Jillian folded her hands on the tabletop too. "Shelley, we like to promote intellectual agitation at the dinner table by picking a topic before the meal. So if you're going to join the Kamals for the time being, you'll be expected to participate in cultivated discussion with us."

Shelley almost laughed, before she realized this statement was meant in earnest. She nodded.

A man marched through the open-arched doorway with a tray of something in his hands. Again, a black-and-white uniform. This was too much. Shelley wondered, remarkably for the first time, why on earth she had been chosen to assist Mr. Kamal. Surely there were people trained in helping and reading to the blind? The Kamals had money and could buy whatever service pleased them. Why put an ad on Craigslist and hire an unskilled laborer who had been unable to hold even a waitressing job? Why was she sitting there?

Despite Grace's flip-flops signifier of normalcy, Shelley observed that she did not look embarrassed by the presence of the servers. The tall man announced what was on his tray—"Roasted duck satay with pickled ginger rémoulade"—then bent beside Dr. Jillian to serve her first. She took her time choosing the appropriate stick. The female maid waited with her hands folded in the corner of the room, until the server reached Mr. Kamal. Now she picked two skewers up for him and placed them on his plate. A staff of two in order to prevent any fumbling for Mr. Kamal.

Grace piped up and said she wanted to discuss the "violence of the colonizer." She had been impressed the past semester by a Fanon scholar at Demming. She looked over at Shelley with widened eyes and said, "I was so lucky to get into Kolb's class. Did you ever take him?"

Shelley almost gasped. She had not told this girl that she'd gone to Demming, which meant someone else had. The Kamals had been talking about her. "Ah, no. Never took anything with Professor Kolb," she croaked. In fact, she'd never heard of that professor. Shelley had ended up being an art history major, mostly because it was a major that required the least number of credits. She hadn't done well in her classes but found that the lectures she'd made it to were tolerable and occasionally interesting. She liked the decorative arts segments the best. Now, the Kamal family stared at her, apparently expecting some more contribution on the topic. What on earth was there to say?

"Well, we've been reading about a lot of violence in the newspaper. I mean—I've been reading," Shelley mumbled. Is this what they meant by colonizers? "The weapons of mass destruction, the search for them from Islamabad to Jerusalem. The suicide bombers."

Mr. Kamal shook his head across the table and slid a chunk of duck off the skewer and into his mouth. Dr. Jillian said, "You know what they say: the lowest discuss gossip, the middle discuss news, and the highest, they discuss ideas." As she sipped her wine, Mr. Kamal nodded in response, and Grace let out an awkward laugh, perhaps hoping to cover up her parents' rudeness.

Mr. Kamal let his right hand grope about the center of the table, where a small silver bell sat. His fingers knocked into it and he gave it two quick rings. In came the man in the uniform, this time carrying the main course, a whole white fish: "line-caught monkfish," which was covered with sliced almonds. Shelley looked at her wrists, her hemp bracelet, her two silver rings, on her thumb and middle finger, respectively. She felt an ache of homesickness and wished she were on the Vineyard with people like her, or at least at home alone.

The Kamals began to discuss the march of history toward progress, Walter Benjamin and intertexts, then Homer, and "the elemental need of literary figures to return to a mystical homeland." This family was finally talking to one another, but Shelley had no idea what about. As a child, her family dinners mostly consisted of Roger discussing the homes he was retrofitting with custom blinds, or the real estate and for-profit college business endeavors that he wanted to go in on with various Whitby relatives. As the Kamals carried on their near debate, out came gold crescents of roasted new potatoes, lying in a bath of sweet-onion reduction. Then bundles of pencil-thin asparagus—"Naked save for a touch of lemon"—wrapped in a belt of prosciutto crudo. When the gently fried goat cheese croquettes with local blueberries and delicate greens arrived, Dr. Jillian paused her oration and exclaimed, "Oh! Lettuces from our garden!"

Mr. Kamal broke in. "You have been too quiet, Shelley. Tell me, what do you think of the adventure narrative's trope of finding home?"

She had been rendered speechless by the food being placed before her. When Biddy was alive, her family would occasionally go to her grandmother's favorite restaurant, the Russian Tea Room. But by the time Shelley was in high school they could afford only to order cup after cup of oolong and share one plate of blintzes, while convincing the server to bring over extra bowls of the gloppy purple lingonberry jam.

"Uh . . ." Shelley cut a potato quarter into an eighth, buying time. She wasn't entirely sure what he meant by *trope*. "It seems pretty sentimental, if you ask me. So you're kicked out of your home. Move to a new one—start again."

"That's quite egalitarian of you. And rather agnostic as well, Shelley *Whitby*," Dr. Jillian said. Shelley winced. So they had been discussing her when she wasn't there and were aware that a Whitby was now a lowly, underpaid, servile employee. Is that why Mr. Kamal paid her so little, because he thought she didn't need it?

His plate was clean and his fork and knife rested demurely on the right edge of it. "In these modern times, society has set itself up a certain way for valid reasons. Things move so quickly now, and all these children—blowing themselves up over there, the ones marching through the streets like fools here—want to disrupt the very structure that has been in place for thousands of years. It was put into that place because it *works*."

"Will the government impose a draft soon, Yousef? What do you think?" Grace asked.

Shelley hated the sound of Mr. Kamal's name coming out of his daughter's mouth. It was too familiar the way Grace said it, as if she was friends with her own father. Mr. Kamal rang the bell again, loudly and sternly, then began expounding on how the days of a military draft were history. The dessert course was chocolate mousse served in individual scalloped-edged glass bowls. The mousse was at once buttery and smoky; it melted on Shelley's tongue. With each spoonful, her mouth warmed from pleasure. When her bowl was empty she felt flushed and tired, and wanted to lie down.

"This is why we keep Sheila around," Dr. Jillian said coquettishly. "Her mousse is like no other." Then she leaned in. "A lot of immigrants from the Sudan here, and they acquired fantastic French culinary techniques."

Shelley tapped one of her silver rings against the tablecloth, and stared out the big picture window. It was uncomfortable, being the help while also sitting at the table. Never once had she pictured herself in a position like this. Outside, the sun had nearly set and the ocean's line was entirely indistinguishable from the sky.

Dr. Jillian asked her, "Your family was never drafted, were they?"

Here it was. The truth was that the Whitbys weren't drafted. Her grandfather and the other men from his generation had enlisted themselves because that's what prominent men did at the time: joined the military. They had gone overseas, but they were in charge of infantries and slept in officers' quarters and clubs. But this was all information that Shelley did not know. It was disappointing, that Mr. Kamal would be just like everyone else, assuming that she knew information about her family history that no one had ever cared to share with her. What she did know was that some Whitbys had been in the marines. "I'm sure some were, at some point."

Grace got out of her seat and went around the table to sit directly on her father's lap. Her legs hung sidesaddle off his, and she looped her arms around his neck as if she were a small child. Dr. Jillian ignored them. Mr. Kamal flushed red. He looked unattractively diminutive and fragile beneath his daughter.

"I love to have you here, Grace Akila," he said.

Grace put her head on her father's shoulder and muttered, "I missed you while I was at school, Daddy." An acidic reminder of the almond-crusted monkfish announced itself in Shelley's throat.

Mr. Kamal cupped the back of his daughter's head then, and he said clearly, "What is this?"

When she didn't answer, he roared, *"What* on earth have you done?" His voice was absorbed by the rug and the leather chairs and the drapes, but still loud. Dr. Jillian remained expressionless. Shelley was confused.

Grace jumped up and stood before his chair with her arms in front of her, as if she could push back the air around her angry father. "It's nothing. Just a new style. It will grow back."

"Your hair will grow back magically by the end of the week?" Mr. Kamal's hand swung frantically in front of him, fingers curved into claws, groping for his daughter's body. His arm lurched too rapidly and with too much weight behind it. Grace stepped away, her body tensed against the golden drapes.

"How could you do this? You have turned yourself into a boy," he yelled.

There were small tears in the edges of her eyes. She said, "Please stop, Yousef, it's just a haircut."

"It is ugly," Mr. Kamal said more quietly. Shelley saw that there were tears below his blank eye sockets.

Dr. Jillian, poised in her seat, only raised her eyebrows at her daughter, as if she had expected this exact scene. Then she flicked her fingers toward the door, motioning for her daughter to leave the room. Grace looked mortified by her mother's motion.

"I cannot forgive you for this desecration of yourself," Mr. Kamal said.

Grace made eye contact with Shelley, then turned back to her father. Her voice hit a high piercing note. "I don't need your *fucking* uptight, out-of-touch forgiveness!" She stomped away, taking care to make each step loud and vibrating—perhaps that was a fit-throwing technique children of a blind parent master at an early age.

Shelley was stunned. She couldn't help but think of the giant, reassuring presence of her own father, the roughness of his bulbous fingertips on her cheeks. She had never screamed at him like that, not even when he deserved it. She'd gotten into a zillion fights in her day, but never, ever had she spoken to one of her parents as Grace just had.

Mr. Kamal began to push himself up, then let himself fall back into his chair. "My only daughter. My progeny," he said. His face was wet, and he covered it with his right hand. Shelley remained still, watching him. Crying about a haircut? Why would anyone care so much about what their daughter's hair looked like? Then she recalled the shame of her youth, and the purple dress. How old was she when her father said he would take her to a party at the Museum of Natural History, and then never showed up? Twelve? She was just one of many to Roger. And a girl to boot, one who could not carry out a legacy in his likeness. When he was alive he had, she was sure, never cried over anything she had done. Now, she stayed perfectly still in her Acme chair and watched as Mr. Kamal shook and sniffed behind his hand for quite some time. To have a father who paid attention like that, who cared so deeply. Shelley would never have disappointed him.

16

The family reunion where Nick got to know Shelley happened when he was thirteen. It was during one of the brief stints in his teenage years when Roger and his mother were getting along, and Roger had insisted that Nick come to the gathering and "be a part of his own family." The move to California had not resulted in Nick's being around more extended family members than he had in New York. Susan's middle-class parents were definitively not impressed by Roger and his stench of money. They thought him not dependable and not a decent choice for their oldest, bravest daughter. Susan had gotten into a vicious fight with her own mother about this fact soon after they arrived in Orange County, which had turned not only her parents but also her sisters and their children against her. As a result, Nick lived near his mother's family but almost never saw them. So the Whitbys were what was left for him, and his only chance to see them was at large gatherings on the East Coast.

Perhaps back when there were balls and galas and dinners, every weekend was like a Whitby family reunion. But by the midnineties, the two sides of the family—Roger Sr.'s shipping side and Ethan Sr.'s railroad side—had been feuding for years, primarily over the failed international hotel chains. According to Roger, this reunion was a grand reconciliation. It took place on an island just over the Maine border, into Canada, at an

old house named Idlehour. Nick was not pleased to be there, although to
sweeten the deal his mother had taken him to visit his friends and his favorite diners in New York before making the long drive up with Roger.
Nick grumbled, but he went. And, it had crossed his mind that the girl
from the train could be there.

The Canadian island was called Caribou-Munroes Island, and the
named house, Idlehour, was giant and drafty and made of wood, and
closer in size to a hotel, with beds for all thirty-plus of the shipping and
the railroad Whitbys who'd shown up. To whom did the house belong? It
seemed, like much of the greater Whitby family property, to belong in
some way to the state. Nick and his mother and Roger arrived at cocktail
hour, which consisted of clusters of people shifting their weight on the
grand lawn, clinking ice in their glasses while wearing varying shades of
beige and pink pants. Nick saw her right away, standing next to her mother
in a crowd of people he'd been told were now his half brothers and sisters.
He kept an eye glued to her location as the first cocktail hour was about to
move inside to a drawing room, where it would become a second cocktail
hour, where sweaters would come off and a few of the older people would
surely swerve as they walked.

Roger hobbled over the grass beside Nick and his mother, until they
found a low table to sit at. Nick inspected the gray fat congealing on top of
the salmon paté dish at the center of the table. Shelley was in the corner of
the lawn. Her mother had disappeared, but she and the crowd of her—
his—half siblings congregated just outside the open doorway of the parlor.
Every minute or so the group of blond and once-blond heads would flick
around in his direction, then cackles would arise. Nick understood that
he was being talked about. He was the first adopted child in the Whitby
family and, he realized, the only person in the room without a divine
blood right to be there.

At the table beside him, apparently aware of what was happening,
Roger put his arm around Nick's shoulder. He leaned into his adopted son
and, quoting *The Great Gatsby*, as he was wont to do, whispered, "They're
a rotten crowd, kid. . . . You're worth the whole damn bunch put together."

Nick wriggled out from under Roger's arm, looking down. It was mortifying that Roger would be aware of his exclusion or the fact that he cared about it. Weakness was the fundamental trait that Roger hated. Nick watched as Shelley's half sister Brooke ambled over to the group by the door. Brooke, in a polka-dotted headband and shiny flat shoes, enthusiastically kissed Shelley on the cheek, then leaned in to the center of the circle. What Nick couldn't hear was that she whispered, "Can you believe Dad brought that woman and her child? The poor, miserable kid. He knows he doesn't belong here." This was the first time that Roger's older children had ever really focused on Nick, and now a thought that crossed through each of their minds, a thought that not one of them verbalized: the kid resembled Roger. Or, at least, he carried the characteristics of a well-made Whitby. But it couldn't be true, could it? A grim coincidence, each adult Whitby child concluded.

Brooke pulled a pack of cigarettes out of her bag. "Want one, Shells?" Shelley, although well over a decade younger than the rest, was included in their banter. Andrew and Tobin and Roger III (LJ was back in the city, and Kiki refused to come) all clucked their tongues in mock disapproval of the smoking, although a few of them joined in, puffing away under the rapidly appearing northern stars. The now-aged Vanderbilt wife was there somewhere too, but the second wife—Corney—refused to ever attend a Whitby event. "I can't believe you don't have a sport, Shelley," Tobin laughed. "We'll get you playing field hockey soon. Remember when Kiki was an all-star goalie at St. Paul's?"

Brooke faux-smacked her older half sister with the back of her hand. "She would be so embarrassed that you remember that!"

Before too long the siblings' discussion turned toward their father, as it always did, their comments lighting up like fireflies in the night.

He looks better.

Much better.

I set him up with a specialist, some Iranian out in Chicago.

Can you believe he dared to bring the teacher?

The word *gold digger* flickered through the air. This, of course, was the assumed motive of the marriage between Roger and Susan, even though it was widely known that everyone's capital had depleted after the Chinese hotels disaster, and that Roger specifically had burned through most of his money with his hobby shop on the Upper West Side, and all of those foolish California strip malls he'd sunk millions into. Most of the extended Whitbys were not doing as well as they once had, but a few had invested, and a handful had even found ways to generate their own income: they were money managers, retail owners; one was a personal assistant/consultant for a wealthy Taiwanese family. But there was also muffled talk, always, of lost money, hidden money, Roger's Swiss bank accounts and family heirlooms unexpectedly popping up at Sotheby's.

Later, when dinner had given way to the third cocktail hour and the older Whitbys poured one last nightcap in their rooms before lying down to let that evening's self-induced amnesia take hold, Nick was alone in the small servant's room he'd been placed in, listening to his Discman. In his hands, he turned over a blue porcelain jug that had been on the bedside table. His heart beat so loudly in his chest he felt his skeletal frame pounding along with it: he had seen Shelley go into her room three doors down. It took forty minutes to get his courage up, but finally he walked over, and, standing in front of Shelley's open doorway, holding his Discman and headphones, with the hood of his blue sweatshirt pulled up over his head, muttered toward the floor, "Hey."

"Hey, yourself." It was clear she knew exactly who he was.

"I was wondering. Uh. Do you like hard-core music?" He half-heartedly waved his headphones in the air.

Shelley giggled. "No!" But then she smiled, the same joy radiating out of her that he'd felt years before, on the Amtrak train. "Like punk? Ew. But come in."

Nick and Shelley sat on the wooden floor and listened, on the loudest volume, to a band called the Gorilla Biscuits, each holding on to one side of the foam-covered earpieces. She kept shaking her head and giggling. It turned out she was a year and a few months older than him, and had just turned fifteen. She was slender and composed, and, Nick couldn't help noticing, fully developed. "What do you like about this?"

"If you listen more, you'll see," he mumbled. The two of them played the rest of the album while sitting on the floor. They didn't say much else that night.

Just before Nick was returning to his bedroom, two hours after he'd entered Shelley's, Shelley said to him, "My dad will think it's fun that we're friends."

Nick's self-consciousness ignited and ripped out of him in a growl: "I don't give a fuck what he thinks." He grimaced at his own outburst, mortified that Shelley might have been aware of just how much he did care, just how much he wanted Roger's approval. He headed quickly down the hall, leaving Shelley in a state of surprise.

Later, during one of their marathon telephone calls, Shelley would tell Nick that what she had liked about him most that night was his anger. He never smiled, and his eyes—as long-lashed and bright blue as they may be—were perpetually unimpressed. And moreover, something under his surface was always ready to attack. When Nick heard Shelley say this, months later as he lay on his bed in Orange County with the phone receiver cradled against his jaw, he was rendered speechless. It felt like someone was paying attention to him for the first time in his life. Was this what having a sister was like?

The rest of that Idlehour family reunion was primarily made up of meals, which actually meant drinking and schmoozing. But on Saturday after breakfast (Bloodies) and before lunch (wine spritzers) a short sailboat race was being put on. The Whitbys were, after all, boat people first. It was just three men competing in this race: Nick's oldest half brother, Andrew; a cousin from the railroad side who Nick was fairly sure was named James—it was hard to keep all the names straight—and Roger, who had insisted on joining. The older man could barely walk, but he showed up at the dock with navy swim trunks hanging over his spindly legs. Andrew all but carried his father through the low waves and onto the bow of a Laser

Radial boat. They were racing to the island and back. Of course, Andrew, who was from the boating side, beat James by at least fifty meters, which meant that Roger had also won.

Nick watched the race from a boulder on the shore, where he crouched by himself in a hooded sweatshirt. When the men got out of the water Roger appeared to be disoriented. With his half-bald head and red star-bursts speckling his lifelong drinker's face, he looked older than his seventy-four years. A few people clapped, and someone let out a whistle, and then Roger, in front of everyone, marched straight to Shelley's mother, put his two hands on the back of her tweed pants, and kissed his ex-wife. It was a dramatic, triumphant kiss. The feckless bird of a woman remained entirely still: she did not pull back; she did not walk away. She let herself be kissed on the patch of sand, by her aging ex-husband, in front of his extended family and his current wife.

From the back of the crowd Mrs. Scribner Whitby roared, *"Ro-ger!"* Then she pushed through people young and old. Roger had stepped back but was grinning. Either he didn't yet realize it was a mistake, or the kiss was, in fact, not a mistake at all. But it was not her husband Susan took aim at. When she began to wiggle to the front of the crowd of Whitbys, it was clear that Nick's mother was moving directly toward Shelley's mother. The new wife pushed the old wife with two hands, on the shoulders, so that Elizabeth stumbled backward and nearly fell. She caught herself, but her glasses managed to land on the sand.

Susan turned toward her husband, as if she were yelling at a bad dog. "You are very confused, Roger! You were not feeling well this morning!" Roger's face dropped. He put both of his hands into the pockets of his swim trunks, and Nick's mother dragged him away toward the house.

At half past six that evening, Nick was in the chilly, expansive dining room eating a bowl of Rice Krispies, when Shelley's mother shuffled by with a pair of car keys in her hand. A cousin (Ginny, who lived in South-ampton) had loaned her a forest-green BMW convertible. Soon enough Shelley came down carrying a flower-print duffel bag. She marched over to Nick. "Have you seen our da—Roger? I'm leaving now, and I can't find him to say goodbye." Her eyes were rimmed with red, and her face was splotchy.

Nick's stomach dropped. "I haven't seen him. Or my mom. What if you . . . you could stay?"

"Can't. I've got eight hours of car time with my mother ahead of me. Woo-hoo."

"Do you want to call me?"

Shelley gave him a smirk, so he quickly added, "I mean, whatever, when we're both home. You could call me. I'll have my guitar, and I can play that Rancid song I was telling you about."

The half siblings traded phone numbers, and, each grinning, nodded goodbye.

And so the two teenagers got to know each other, primarily on the phone, which they spoke into from their respective bedrooms across the country. How could anyone spend that much time on the phone? They'd talk into the wee hours, two or three times a week. Nick would struggle to stay awake until eleven, occasionally nodding off with the receiver beside him on his pillow, even though it was two in the morning for Shelley at that point.

They'd argue about the music she liked. (*The Grateful Dead? I'm grateful they're dead.*) But always, by the end of the night, they would turn to the mysterious subject of Roger. It was usually Nick who began the discussion. During their first phone call, when Nick was still up at the Idlehour reunion, he had admitted that Roger had been around for years before his parents got married. Although Nick never dared to admit that he'd always wondered if Roger was his birth father, he told Shelley everything else: all about his weekends at the hotel and the fateful helicopter trip to Connecticut. Upon hearing this information, while she lay on her stomach on her bedroom floor, Shelley's response was a singular, deadpan *ha*.

They both conceded that they hated the man. That's what they told each other, that they hated him for what he had done, or was doing, to both of their mothers (whom, they conceded, they also hated). Roger was their most significant topic of conversation, and thus their greatest bond.

It was as if they thought that if they went over every interaction with the man, then they might crack the code that would let them understand him, and grasp what their father had really thought of them. Shelley said she was relieved to learn about Nick's years of living in the hotel on the weekends. It solved the mystery of where the hell her father had been for so much of her childhood.

Neither kid ever cried or even got emotional, save for one time, which became carved on Nick's psyche. Shelley told him that Roger left once, for a few months, when she was twelve. "Was he with you the whole time?" she'd asked. But he wasn't. At least not during the week. And if Roger had moved into the hotel full-time, no one had filled Nick in. After weeks of twelve-year-old Shelley not seeing him, she was told that her father wanted to take her to a gala at the Museum of Natural History. Her excitement was blatant, and Biddy gave her a credit card in order to buy a dress for the event. The Monday before the gala Shelley had walked, all alone, through the gray slush for nearly twenty blocks and then east for five more. It was totally dark when she arrived at Bergdorf Goodman. After the preteen girl announced to the saleswomen that she was armed with a credit card, they plied her with attention, three of them bringing out dress after dress that was suitable for a black-tie gala with one's distinguished father. Shelley's top choice was not the choice of the women though: it was a purple empire-waist dress made out of crushed velvet, with intricate satin roses adorning the waistband. She felt as if she were a princess when she wore it, a Whitby princess who would float to the ball. She didn't even look at the price.

On Friday evening the snow came down fast and small, piling quickly. Roger was supposed to pick Shelley up at seven, but she was ready in her purple dress by five. At six forty-five she began watching for him out the window in the kitchen. She was still kneeling—not moving a muscle—on the kitchen chair at seven forty-five. By a quarter to nine Biddy sat beside her, in silence. The twelve-year-old refused to cry, but it took all her concentration and resolve.

It wasn't until ten o'clock that Shelley gave up looking and accepted a bowl of oatmeal from Biddy. Roger didn't come. Her mother simply passed through the kitchen emotionless, saying, "What did you expect of him?" That statement almost pushed Shelley over the edge into tears, but she gulped them back. She wanted to yell at her mother: *I am a child!* But she swallowed that too, pushing it down while promising herself never to expect anything from her father again. As teenagers, Shelley told Nick all of this in her regular, even tone. But then her voice cracked. An odd sound came over the receiver. Was it a sneeze? "I never needed him anyway. It doesn't matter. He doesn't matter. But I'm still pissed that I never got to wear that dress. It's still hanging in my closet, unworn." Shelley was crying. Nick was silent on the other end. He had no idea what to say. Anger rang up inside of him—the particular, trenchant anger of being guilty of something you had no way to control.

17

| 2003 |

Brooke stood outside the emergency room entrance of Mass General Hospital in her light-green scrubs. It was warm for an evening in mid-May, and the circular loop by Parkman Street was hauntingly quiet. She was early. Allie was usually early too, but Brooke had shown up a full fifteen minutes before they'd planned to meet for their walk. A rock of nerves weighed down her chest: the abortion was scheduled for two days later. She'd asked Allie to meet her that night, on her break from her late shift on the oncology floor, so that she could tell her what was going on, including the information about the appointment. She'd had a lightened, energized feeling since breaking up with Marc. Perhaps it was the self-destructive, manic happiness that comes with knowledge that your normal daily life was on the edge of destruction. Maybe this is why her father had such a penchant for leaving people behind. Perhaps it was for the high that came with it.

A burgundy Chevy made its way around the driveway, and a pregnant woman, face contorted with active labor, stumbled out of the passenger's seat. Perfect timing. As the woman went inside, Brooke heard the noise of the emergency room briefly emanate from the electric doors. She loved the sounds of the hospital: the rushing of doctors and other nurses, the beeping of machinery, even the cacophony of cries from patients. She felt as if she were entering another world when she went to work. She put on her scrubs and became a different person, someone who was useful, someone who was seen; she became someone everyone was looking for. This she cherished about her job. Years earlier, when she'd begun her nursing internship on the same oncology floor, it took a while for the other nurses to realize the person Brooke became at work. The nurses she was assigned to shadow took one look at Brooke's pearl earrings and preppy little sweaters and dismissed her as a short-term intern. She'd once heard an older woman named Betta complain to the nurse manager, "Why are you sticking me with this twig of a child?" But Brooke was determined. She changed bedpans without flinching. She inserted catheters quickly and efficiently. She could find a vein in the arm of any man, woman, or child, no matter their obesity or wrinkles or history of intravenous drug use. Brooke, within the four walls of the hospital, discovered something she had never known about herself: she was tough as nails.

But there was a caring side to nursing too, one that humbled her and astounded her that she was able to do well. In a hospital, so many people are huddled into themselves, both patients and their loved ones, with shoulders crunched around their ears, and pain, both physical and emotional, coursing through their limbs. As Brooke stood outside in the humid and luscious spring night, so many of the people in the building behind her were living the worst days of their lives. She remembered those weeks before her brother Peter died, when she was beside her mother leaning on the hallway walls and sitting in the plastic cafeteria chairs of Children's Hospital. The last time Brooke had seen her little brother was in a darkened hospital room. For months, the nurses had been urging her to go in there and entertain him. *Try to read him story books. Show him a puzzle or a drawing you made.* Brooke was instructed to do anything to stimulate his mind and lift his spirits, and she took her instructions with the utmost gravity. Every time she went to the hospital, she packed a special bag of items to share with him. At first, earnest Peter had tried to be interested, but as the months progressed, when she'd take out a Slinky or a yo-yo, he would shake his tiny head and then turn away from her in bed.

Although seven, he appeared to have actually shrunk down to the size he was when he was three or four. His hair was sparse on his head, growing back in after the latest round of chemo. Even the freckles on his nose and cheeks that had once been so pronounced seemed to have faded. The last time she saw him he wore a diaper and a *Star Wars* T-shirt, rather than the usual hospital gown. She took out the *Fantastic Mr. Fox* book and began to read to him.

"I don't want to hear that," he said in a breathless voice.

"You'll like this one," she reassured him from the leather chair pulled up to his bedside.

"I told you to leave!" he shrieked. It was unlike him to be that commanding.

As soon as she stood up, Peter's face took on an alarmed expression. He looked down and threw up, quickly and violently, only he wasn't throwing up vomit but blood. He looked up at Brooke as if something had just happened to him rather than in him. "Why did—?" he began, but then his body started convulsing, and he threw up more blood. Brooke ran into the hospital hallway.

"Help!" she called out. "Help us!"

A heavyset nurse with a dark perm came running. "Go to the lounge," she yelled, pushing into the room. Brooke ran down the hall and into the elevator, and then through the lobby of Children's Hospital and out the electric glass doors to Longwood Avenue. That was the last time she saw her brother. He was taken back into the ICU and died the next afternoon.

Brooke harbored a secret knowledge that her adult choice to spend so much of her days inside a hospital was intimately connected to those few terrible weeks preceding Peter's death. When her family was still a family. The only person she'd ever revealed her true disturbed nature to was Allie. In bed one night, she'd admitted to Allie that she was afraid a part of her wanted to relive those final weeks of Peter's life. Perhaps her subconscious thought was that if she went back to that scene, something would be different. Allie's response was a head shake. "No, no, sweetheart," she'd said. "There is nothing wrong with you at all. You are wonderful at what you do. And don't all people who love their jobs have an, uh, extracurricular reason they love it?"

Brooke smiled, remembering that word: *extracurricular*. She glanced at the black plastic Casio watch she wore to work—9:35 p.m.—and when she looked up again, she realized that she might soon face the other side of the coin with Allie: Allie was unambiguously dedicated to her friends, but she was resolutely unforgiving when she thought they had done something wrong. The woman could be cold. Allie had walked away from many friends and never looked back. After her breakup from the college girl-friend, she removed herself from the whole Middlebury scene in Boston, without so much as blinking an eye. Brooke tried to brace herself. There would be no greater pain for her than to be excluded from Allie's inner life forever. But she needed to take that chance.

Her watch said 9:37 when the outline of Allie's voluminous curls moved down the darkened street. She gave a wave. Why is it thrilling, to simply watch the person you love moving toward you? How many years had it been, now, that Brooke had watched Allie walk toward her with this excitement? They had known each other for thirteen years before they fell in love in their late twenties. Or perhaps they were falling in love the whole time before that. Brooke had been struggling to find stability since college, and at twenty-seven, she had still felt like a kid. At that point she'd been working as an as-sistant for the Yamaguchi Gallery, a modern-art gallery on Newbury Street. She hated the job and only worked there because it was something her family did: buy paintings, look at them, sell them. She had been deeply bored all summer, and Jessica Yamaguchi hadn't given her the past three paychecks, so she'd taken two weeks of August off to go to the Vineyard. It was in the Wainwrights' royal-blue kitchen where Brooke had taken the phone call from LJ, delivering the news that their father had left yet another family. Brooke remembered her brother's words: "The bastard did it again, Birdie. Got restless and then fucked a bunch of people over. He supposedly moved to California with another woman who already has a child."

Brooke nodded and tried to remain impassive, as she was fully aware that Thomas and Paula Wainwright could see her from where they sat in their living room, with open books in their laps. She could feel their concerned eyes on her.

When she hung up the phone, Paula called from the other room, "Everything all right, sweetie?" It had rained that morning, and the earth smell bounced up from the banks of the island road and into the house. From the kitchen, Brooke could hear the invisible frogs croaking and the insects humming in the low-slung bushes.

Brooke had been seeing her half sister Shelley often that summer when they were both on the island—the girl's grandmother from the Saltman side had a house on the other side of Chilmark—and Shelley hadn't mentioned a word about their father's actions. Was it possible she didn't know?

Brooke found herself hollering to Paula as she slipped out the side door in the kitchen, "All is fine, thanks!" Then she was walking down Menemsha Road in the dusk. She had no jacket, no wallet, no key to the Wainwrights' house. She'd just left. She was compelled toward the other side of town by the knowledge that there was suffering there, suffering that she might be able to appease. By the time she reached Shelley's grandmother's house, Brooke wrestled with how her father's actions affected her. It didn't make a real difference to her whether he was in New York with one woman or California with another. It occurred to her, briefly, that this could be a vindication: this was proof that her father hadn't just hated her and her siblings and her mother. The reason he had left them all those years before was because of something restless and sad that lay inside of him. Brooke understood that about her father now. But Shelley was young; she wouldn't know that.

Brooke followed the stone path cutting through an overgrown and disarrayed front lawn, then banged on the front door of Shelley's grandmother's gray-shingled captain's house. Little Shelley answered, gawky and long-legged in her jean shorts. Her braces took up half her face; it appeared she couldn't close her mouth fully around all the metalwork. But Brooke could tell even then what a glamorous, ethereal beauty Shelley would be one day.

Her face lit up at the sight of Brooke. "Hi!" she squealed. "Did you come to see me?"

How a child's naïveté can break your heart! From the doorway, Brooke surmised that although Shelley certainly was going to be much taller, they did share many sisterly qualities: the same eyes, the same prominent cheekbones and wide forehead.

"I wanted to talk to you," Brooke said. "Is your mother here?"

"No, she's in New York. Just me and Biddy here now"—that must have been the grandmother's name—"and she's downstairs watching *Sixty Minutes*. C'mon."

They sat at the round table in the kitchen, and suddenly Brooke whispered, "What do you know about Roger—about Dad?"

"Huh?" Shelley picked up a box of crackers off the counter and began shoving handfuls into her mouth. She spoke while chewing. "He's not here either. He's in New York."

She was thirteen, just a year older than Brooke was when every stable thing around her had split wide-open. One had to be very gentle in this approach.

"What do you do here all day?" Brooke asked, pivoting topics. There were dishes stacked in the sink and crusted pots on the stove.

"Go swimming, read magazines. Hang out with my grandmother. We've got a great dock. Want to see it?"

Soon they were out on the end of the dock, which was the only one in a private sand-covered cove. They sat side by side with their legs hanging over the final warped plank. Dogwood trees arched out over the salt water, and beach plum bushes grew to the sand's edge. The tide lapped in rhythmically.

"I just heard that our dad is moving to California," Brooke said.

Shelley simply shrugged.

"Did you know about it already?"

Shelley shrugged again. "It's no big deal. He's never home anyway."

"Is your mother okay?" Brooke asked.

Shelley gave the slightest shake of her head, then caught herself. The two girls were silent for a while.

Shelley asked in an off-puttingly chirpy voice, "Do you want to smoke a cigarette?"

"Where the hell did you get cigarettes?"

"I have my ways."

Halfway through the thirteen-year-old's cigarette, Brooke asked for one too, and then the half sisters sat beside each other, smoking. It was getting late but still bright out, and gulls swooped over the water, looking for fish.

"When he left my family, I was around your age," Brooke offered.

Shelley let out a *huh*. Brooke waited for more, but nothing else came. What did she expect?

"It's fine," Shelley mumbled finally. "It's between my parents, and I don't even care. Everything's fine."

As the two of them walked back toward the house, Brooke felt a pang of responsibility. Whether the girl knew it or not, Shelley needed her. "It's probably not going to feel fine all the time, Dad not being there for you. You can call me, or come see me, if you ever want to talk about it."

Little Shelley shrugged and didn't make eye contact.

It was getting dark when Brooke trudged back out to Menemsha Road, confused and unsure if she'd done the right thing by going to see Shelley. It took her a moment to remember which way she'd come from, and as she stood looking from left to right she heard a quick *beep beep*—someone hitting a car horn lightly. Fifty feet away was Allie, in the front seat of her parents' blue Volvo, waving. How had she known where Brooke had gone?

When Brooke approached the car, Allie grinned through the open window. "Need a ride?"

It wasn't that surprising to see her there; it was just like Allie, to know where Brooke would go and then show up and wait. It was in that front seat, as they sat parked on the bank of the road by Shelley's grandmother's house, that something changed between them. Allie, in her navy Middlebury sweatshirt, turned toward Brooke and held her forearms in a strong grip.

"What happened?" This was just around the time when Allie had the idea for Urban Adventurers and was planning how to get the seed money, the initial investments, and how to set up the first few outdoor trips with the girls. She had been holed up in her parents' office for most of the vacation.

Brooke told her the whole story, about LJ's call and her father's most recent action, and little Shelley's reaction.

"And how does all of this make you feel?" Allie asked, her hands still on Brooke's arms.

She thought awhile. She would never have this conversation with anyone else in the world. But she was able to be more honest with Allie than she was even with herself.

"It makes me feel unhinged. Like maybe I've been freed from bearing the burden of something. The question of why my father left us. But . . ." She thought for a few silent minutes, and Allie waited, holding her arms. Brooke continued, "It also makes me nervous that I'm going to slip back into the way I felt when I was a kid. My dad is leaving Shelley at the same age he left me. I'm afraid I'm going to get upset for her and be sucked back into that darkness."

Allie nodded, taking in the information. "Well," she reasoned, "you're an adult now and you can control your own actions."

That was when Allie moved in toward Brooke in a way she never had before. Allie had a series of casual girlfriends in the past several years, all of them jocks without sensitivity or any kind of taste. And she had seriously dated a woman in college, a rugby player named Kate, whom Brooke couldn't stand. Although Allie had been in Vermont and Brooke in Boston, they saw each other frequently in their college years, on weekends and vacation breaks. Brooke suspected Allie never really liked Kate, as she almost never spoke of her. And, in turn, Brooke barely mentioned the men she'd occasionally end up in bed with after a party or a night out on Lansdowne Street. None of them had been remarkable, and she had refused to date even one. Her roommates had constantly poked fun at her for having too high expectations and waiting for the perfect man.

It had never once occurred to Brooke that she and Allie had the option of being romantic with each other. Of course she thought Allie was stunning, but any living person would have thought that. In the Volvo, Allie leaned over from the driver's seat, her earnest face next to Brooke's, and moved her nose into the crick of Brooke's neck. The women stayed like that for some time, as if in a silent understanding that whoever made the next move would determine the course of events. It was Brooke who moved. A burst of energy, something hot and forceful, broke inside of her, and she kissed Allie on the mouth. Then Brooke paused. The thought crossed her mind that she should have felt like she was kissing her sister. But she didn't—not at all. Soon her legs were over Allie's, and then she twisted her small body until she was totally on top of her, face-to-face. It was so surprising that Allie giggled, and then Brooke giggled, and then Allie pulled the lever beneath them to make the driver's seat shoot backward, giving them room.

It was beautiful. In both the moment and years later, when they thought back on that evening, neither one of them could deny how joyous it had been. While they were parked on the side of the leafy island road it started to rain slightly, and scattered drops tinkled on the roof. They were laughing, slightly, while they were having sex—at the surprise of it happening, and the wonder that it could be so good. It felt like they were laughing in wonder for years after that, as they continued to athletically dive into each other's bodies late at night, as they spent the next two years weaving a cocoon around themselves and the beds they slept in, as Allie moved into the house on Joy Street and the room they shared became bathed in the light of something special, nearly holy for both of them.

The oddest part of their relationship was that Brooke was not, in fact, gay. Brooke had dated only men before Allie; she liked the physicality of a man's body, how her small frame could tuck into his and she could thrash against his firmness. She had always maintained her straightness, which was something that Allie could never get over. In their late twenties and early thirties their love continued, and Brooke whispered to Allie in the mornings that she was a miracle, that she was the greatest gift that life had given her. There was talk that gay marriage would soon be passed in the state of Massachusetts, and Allie had proposed that they do it. But the fact was that Brooke Whitby could not imagine herself married to another woman. Her father had always told her that she was the bedrock of their family, she was the one who would keep the generations in line, keep the Whitbys going. She simply couldn't do that if she married a woman. That must have been what Roger was thinking, that horrible night when he found out about her and Allie. When she definitively told Allie she wouldn't get married, that was it. Allie was done. She packed up her possessions from the house on Joy Street and left, quickly and firmly.

But Brooke knew now, entering the final years of her thirties, that although she was attracted to them, she had never actually loved a man. As she stood outside the hospital where she worked, she watched Allie walking toward her and thought to herself: *Holy shit, I love her. Here she is walking toward me, and when I tell her what's really going on, she's going to turn and leave again, just as quickly and just as firmly.* Brooke put a hand on the lower part of her belly and tried to muster up the courage to tell the truth.

W hat Brooke didn't know was that at that very moment, as she stood outside the hospital on her shift break, Shelley's mother was less than four miles away, inside a room at the Charles Hotel in Cambridge, screaming. Elizabeth Saltman Whitby was in the midst of a medical situation. Frenzied, feline shrieks issued from the room's door, spliced with occasional frustrated grunts. Other guests on the third floor had rung up the front desk, and at the present moment the manager and two security guards stood outside the room on the gold-patterned carpet.

Elizabeth yelled, "Get them out. Keep them out." She broke into a whine. "Get them *ouuuuut*." Then came the sound of buzzing, or, really, drilling. The sound was an electric screwdriver. Elizabeth was running holes through the doorframe.

The hotel's manager banged on the door, with a security guard right behind him. "Ma'am, we need to help you. Please open the door, ma'am."

She was a frequent guest of the Charles Hotel, and the staff knew her well. On the other side of the door she screwed in brackets, securing herself inside. "Call an ambulance," the manager uttered, and the security guard nodded and walked down the hallway, grasping the cell phone clipped to his belt. "Let me in, Mrs. Whitby," the manager said in a soothing tone. Then he pounded again.

In response to his pounding, Elizabeth let out a terrified, guttural bawl. "They're telling me to keep them out. Get them out!"

It had happened before, voices in her own head saying someone was trying to harm her. Or was it the voices she needed to lock herself away from? Soon enough the ambulance and fire department arrived, leaving their vehicles in the U-shaped hotel driveway. Upstairs, two rubber-suited firemen took the door down, and then EMTs carried out Shelley's mother, thrashing, on a gurney. While she was lying in the back of the ambulance cab, her face the color of rotten berries, she paused for a moment and took two short breaths of air. "Mass General," she told the medic. "Whitbys only go to the General." Then she continued to wail and occasionally yelled out, "No! Stop!"

As Allie and Brooke walked between the now-empty office buildings of Blossom Street, Brooke retied the cable-knit sweater around her neck and relished the eerie silence around them. Allie stuck her elbow into Brooke's side with a smirk. "Nice pearl earrings, Birdie."

"I think so," Brooke shot back. Allie knew how the other nurses now made fun of her, calling her Perfect Polly and cracking up whenever Brooke said something overly polite or prim. Allie also knew how happy this made Brooke. Giving each other a hard time is how nurses show love. It was a way to be a family and to lighten the air on the oncology floor. As soon as the other nurses started laughing at her to her face, Brooke was elated. She was accepted.

Allie and Brooke turned onto Cambridge Street. Although most of the businesses were closed, the traffic was still heavy. Just as Brooke was about to dive into it, Allie said the very words that were about to come out of her mouth. "There's something we need to talk about."

"Wait!" Brooke screeched. Was there any way Allie could know? Brooke didn't think she looked pregnant at all, although perhaps Allie knew more about what her body normally looked like than she did. She couldn't believe how nervous she was. They were in front of Papi's sandwich shop, which was open late. "Let's get something to drink before we talk."

When they were back outside, each with a paper cup of lemon-chamomile tea, Brooke looked at her watch. Eighteen more minutes until she had to be back on the oncology floor.

"I know," Allie said, and Brooke nearly spit out her tea. "Caroline told me about it. I just, I think that you need to consider—really consider it."

"I have been considering it. That's why I've waited so long."

"Don't you know what you'd be getting into by marrying Marc?"

Brooke stopped walking. Laughter pealed out of her. "Marry Marc? I never even liked him." Then she clapped a hand over her mouth. She hadn't totally known that until she said it.

Allie looked confused. "You're going to move in with him but not marry him?" She was never one to let her guard down quickly.

"You know about the predicament I'm in with my house," Brooke said. "The only reason I was even going to see those houses with him is because I might be homeless in a few months if I didn't make other plans for myself. But you know—" She grabbed Allie's hand and then immediately felt guilty. She should be honest with her before she touched her. But she didn't let go. "I broke up with him. I told him I'm not going to marry him. And I'm definitely not going to move into some tacky house with him. Everything with Marc is totally over."

Allie moved in closer to Brooke, and a softness returned to her voice. "You're not? But Caroline said you've been looking at houses in Chestnut Hill every week."

Brooke shook her head. "Marc's gone."

"Move in with me," Allie said, astoundingly quick.

At those words tears sprung into Brooke's eyes. "What?"

Allie's hands were on Brooke's shoulder's now. Her face was so close to Brooke's that she was whispering. "I mean. I know my place is tiny, but with our combined incomes we could maybe even sell my Boston apartment and buy a bigger one. And I know—"

Something leaped inside of Brooke. Hope?

"If you want to move in with me and just be my roommate, that's fine. I mean, I know you don't want to go back to the way things were before. And I get that. I'm okay with that." Allie had a timid smile on her face. Her cheeks were red and shiny. "We'll just find a place and then see how it goes. I mean, live together and—"

Brooke couldn't help it; she kissed her. They were under the flood of streetlight on the corner of Grove Street. She was kissing her, and Allie was kissing her back. More than romantic, it was redemptive, like an apology and a homecoming at once. Then Brooke remembered what this walk had really been for. It briefly crossed her mind that she could not tell Allie about the pregnancy at all: she could have the procedure done and then simply never tell her, and they could ride this reunion out in peace.

But soon she was whispering. She couldn't muster the strength to speak in a louder voice. "Als, the thing I wanted to talk to you about actually does have to do with Marc. But only a little bit." She tried to say it as quickly as possible: "I'm pregnant, eight weeks. The baby is Marc's, and I have been considering getting an abortion, but if you were back in my life and you wanted to do this with me, maybe . . . Maybe we could?" She was shaking with fear.

The corner was silent then, with no cars or people passing. Neither woman said a word. As Brooke looked up though, Allie was taking a step back from her.

"Marc?" Allie said loudly.

Brooke nodded, but she immediately wished she hadn't. She was familiar with the tone Allie's voice had taken on.

Allie took another step away. She stared at Brooke's stomach now.

"I haven't told Marc yet. And if I keep it, maybe I don't ever need to tell him. It's not his business."

"It is his business." Allie's voice was quiet but stern. Her eyes were cast down toward the sidewalk.

Why had Brooke been so naive to think that Allie would easily warm to this news? Brooke was pregnant with someone else's child. A man— someone she had deemed more acceptable to be with than Allie.

"But I haven't decided if I'm definitely keeping the baby."

"Do you want to do it?" Allie asked. "Do you want to be a mother?"

"The problem is that I just don't know what to do," she said, but even as she spoke, she was nodding, thinking about the future she and Allie could have together. What was her father's silly line, that greatness had to begin at home?

"I want to be a mother too," Allie said, and then took another step away. "But not like this."

"What do you mean, Als?" Brooke's voice was high and cracking.

"This is Marc's child. I cannot be involved in this."

As Brooke heard Allie say those words, she tried to not believe them. But her face was deadly serious.

"If you want to have a baby, you should have it. I think you know me well enough to understand that there's no way I can do that with you."

Disappointment speared itself all the way through Brooke's body. Of course moral, cut-and-dried Allie would never want this. Brooke tried to think of the appropriate words to say, but nothing came out of her mouth. Allie was Allie; she was never going to change. They stood under the streetlight in silence. When it became clear that neither woman had any- thing else to add, Allie put up one hand in an unmoving wave and turned around, leaving Brooke alone on the corner.

She was stunned. The thing that she'd wanted was nearly handed to her, right before it was crushed forever. Brooke tried to flex her stomach muscles. Could the baby feel her emotions? Devastation could not be good for a fetus.

As Brooke entered the emergency room entrance of the hospital, Robbie, one of the security guards, looked at his watch and said, "Where you been, kiddo? Why you look so sad?"

She grimaced and mumbled, "Just taking a break." Her sneakers—white Reeboks, like every other RN who valued a healthy back—squeaked on the linoleum as she headed to the elevators. When she went upstairs, she would take the vitals of her prostate cancer patient, Alfred, for the second-to-last time. He had finished his treatment, was stable, and was set to be released from care in the morning. A reminder that good things can happen in the world.

But soon she considered what would happen if she didn't have the child and Allie didn't come back to her. She imagined her home packed up into boxes. She imagined waking up alone in a strange and ill-equipped apartment. Sadness threatened to hollow her out; she felt sick. If she had the baby, she wouldn't be alone in the new place. No, it wasn't appropriate, it wasn't logical. But, she thought as she punched the elevator's up button, her daily life was already nothing like she had imagined. No one ever tells you that as a child: you cannot control what the world will throw at you, and it is the unexpected that will shape you.

Allie had walked away from her, most likely forever. But wasn't that reality? People always leave. As her heart pounded, a patient's scream sounded from beyond the double doors that led to the general waiting room. Instead of being distressed at the sound, the muscles at the back of Brooke's neck loosened up. A scream meant a problem, a problem meant work, and therefore distraction. The double doors opened and two EMTs rolled in with a woman on the gurney. Brooke wondered if being a nurse would make a person a better mother, or if the coarseness of the profession would actually taint her abilities. As the EMTs passed, someone said, "Brooke—hello. Brooke!"

It took her a moment to register the words. The voice was hauntingly calm. It was coming from the gurney. Brooke stopped the elevator doors from closing. She pivoted on her heels and sped up to see who it was: a thin, older, middle-aged body. A mess of greasy brown hair with streaks of gray. Eyes clamped together again, red-faced, now screaming again. Was this the person who had said her name?

"Nooooooo, get them out!" the woman wailed, and then her eyes popped open.

It couldn't be. Brooke made eye contact with the disturbed, howling woman.

"Elizabeth, can you understand me?" she said. She commanded the EMTs, "Stop here. Guys! Stop for a minute."

As the gurney slowed, Shelley's mother ceased her screaming, and her dazed eyes fell on Brooke's face. Brooke saw no sign of recognition now, no indication that the woman was lucid enough to know who she was.

"Do you know who I am, Elizabeth? Did you just say my name?"

Red blood vessels had popped in the woman's unfocused eyes. It was unclear if any of Brooke's words had registered at all. But then Elizabeth Saltman Whitby ordered in a cool voice, "As you can see, I'm in a situation here, Brooke. Call your father immediately and ask him what, exactly, his plan is. Ask him what he wants all of us to do."

18

Shelley was surprised that the next few days at the Kamals' house in Little Compton were strikingly similar to her days at home, only now she had a prestocked kitchen. And being on vacation, or at least out of town, granted her immunity from worry about her mother or Nick. She certainly wouldn't be able to do anything for either of them until she got home. In Rhode Island, she was buzzed by Mr. Kamal over the intercom in the morning and read to him in his sun-filled office until lunch. In the afternoon, she sat beside him on the low-and-wide office couches underneath the skylight, as she corresponded with businessmen and accountants on the laptop, about his investments and other money matters. Each morning her stomach pounded with the possibility that today would be the day: she would finally write for him. Wasn't that why he had brought her there? But for such a prolific creator, Mr. Kamal never seemed to do any real work. She wasn't invited to family dinner again but rather made herself simple meals from the stocked fridge in the guesthouse, and found herself wandering the empty guesthouse in the evening and strolling along the deserted beach, covertly smoking cigarettes as she stomped through the sand alone. The routine involved a loneliness she'd become accustomed to; this loneliness was delicate and peaceful, occasionally lovely.

It was Thursday after lunch when Mr. Kamal traversed his large Rhode Island office more quickly than usual and called over his shoulder to

Shelley while he moved, "This afternoon we will do something different." He found his way behind his off-white desk and proclaimed: "I must write."

Shelley nodded—there was no time to consider the statement—and she opened the computer stationed at her side. She closed her eyes, preparing to fall feetfirst into this dark well she'd been dreaming of, but Mr. Kamal had already begun speaking. He spoke softly but quickly. She opened her eyes. His face had turned to the ceiling. It took her a moment to realize that this was it, this was him writing. Leaning over the desk in order to hear more clearly, she began to type as fast as her fingers would move; surely she'd missed a few sentences at the beginning. After two minutes of speaking he paused, and his tone of voice changed. "I can tell that you are wearing a perfumed scent. It is distracting. You must never wear this again, while you are my *amanuensis*." He said this last word with great emphasis, resettled himself, then fell back into his stream of words.

Shelley nodded but didn't verbally respond. After ten minutes she was finally hitting enough of a rhythm to register what she was transcribing. He was speaking about houses, describing the interior of houses in New York City. She was transcribing words about urban American WASPs in the early twentieth century and how these people arranged their quarters.

"The idea to break down the wall between the two town houses on East Sixty-First Street came from Edith Vanderbilt, mother of the new groom, as most decisions in that family did. . . ."

She could not help but be disappointed. When he described this book, she'd assumed he would be writing about himself. She thought his writing would be personal, and that she would be swept into the hot desert wind of his imagination, through the Byzantine arches and white-domed buildings of his youth. Perhaps, though, the topics didn't really matter. Here she was, finally doing her real job. Shelley wanted this. She *desired* to do well at this. She typed quickly yet gently, following the rhythm of his voice with her fingers. He kept talking, seeming to have fallen into a sort of trance. It would have been comical, really, if there wasn't the raw edge of tension in the room. However boring his sentences, he was trusting her by speaking them, and she was receptive and open to this trust. She was able to keep up with the sound of his voice, undulating in and out, as if she were playing a grand piano.

After a full hour and a half Mr. Kamal dropped his head. "Yes—that is enough."

Shelley rested her hands and noticed the pulsing veins visible through her translucent skin. Her fingers ached around the knuckles; they had never worked that hard. She raised her head. The room seemed dimmer than before. The abutting windows in the corner had steamed slightly, although she wasn't sure if it was from the Rhode Island weather or their breath and bodies.

Mr. Kamal's head hung over the rectangular desk as she watched him shamelessly. Slowly, he got up and shuffled around the furniture. Standing above her he asked, "Did you enjoy that work?"

"I did. Thank you." She was being honest. It wasn't the content that she liked but the act of writing it down. It shocked her, this new knowledge of herself: she liked taking directions, doing as she was told.

"*Thank you, thank you, thank you.*" His balled-up hands hit the top of his thighs. "I do not want you to thank me! Not here, and not at home."

Shelley choked in a gasp, then let it out as an awkward cough. She said, "Sorry."

"May I touch your hands?"

She shook her head.

Mr. Kamal took both of her hands into his. The door to the office was slightly ajar. Dr. Jillian was probably downstairs. "We worked very well together. I was put on this earth in order to create, and this book will be my next great creation. You have helped me achieve my divine purpose."

While she had been prodded and pushed by him, they had never touched like this before. His hands felt softer than the hands of most older men, and were scented with a lotion. She felt surprisingly honored, as if she had won something. Was this what he had wanted the whole time?

Was it, she questioned, what *she* had wanted? Her pulse went into her eardrums, and her shoulders eased down.

Mr. Kamal moved his hands out of hers and placed the pads of his fingers over her eyes. His nails caught briefly in her lashes and the dip beneath her lower lids. He brought the tips of his middle and forefinger over her eyebrows, in measured time, and around to her cheekbones. Onto the bridge of her nose now, he let them rest for a moment, quivering, before moving to the inner, vulnerable section of her cheeks.

Her own skin felt smooth when he touched her. She was inundated with his musk; it overtook the pine-scented air that freshened even the inside of the house. For a flicker she relaxed her oblique eye muscles, closing her lids and letting the heat of new skin touch hers. Perhaps this was him finally seeing her. She was convinced that throughout her life, most people had only cared about her for her looks—it was the one thing friends and strangers had consistently praised her for. But she was unsure if she wanted Mr. Kamal to join everyone else. All eight of his fingers moved slowly down to her mouth. As the pads of his middle and forefingers passed over the vermilion border, Shelley parted her lips slightly, and his nails hit against the enamel of her teeth. Was this an accident? Perhaps he was clumsy with facial layout. But on instinct, Shelley opened her mouth and her movement shifted his fingers. She took him in: his fingertips touching the moisture, the inside. With that he turned in a violent motion toward the back wall—his hands moved away from her mouth, her face. Then he cleared his throat. His right hand went to his temple, and he announced, "Very well, I'll see you again. Tomorrow."

That was all. Had she done something wrong?

Shelley rose slowly and left the room, teetering slightly. To her great relief, there was no one in the hallway—no Dr. Jillian and no Grace—and no one visible from the grand foyer of the big house. Not a soul could be seen outside either, on the path between the two houses. The air was heavy with the pressure of impending rain, and it filled Shelley's head. Although she saw none of the Kamal clan, she felt as though everyone must have known what she was doing. What had just happened could not have been a normal occurrence.

Inside the guesthouse, buzzing with self-consciousness, she went up to the kitchen on the second floor and put her hands on either side of the sink, letting her head hang down, breathing in the cool of the stainless steel. She breathed in and out for some time, and then, a floating sensation overcame her. She stood up to an embracing calmness, a calmness she hadn't felt since before her father's death. Mr. Kamal had wanted to hire her, he had wanted to work with her, and now, he had wanted to see her. There was a whole uncooked Cornish hen in the fridge, and Shelley decided to roast it by herself. She adorned it with slices of lemon, sprigs of rosemary, and small pockets of butter, and even found some kitchen twine to tie it up with. The bird roasted to perfection, and she consumed every bite of it, alone at the narrow guesthouse dining table, watching the unmoving trees from the side window. She did not overthink what had happened in Mr. Kamal's office but rather turned her mind off and let the scenery simply soothe her. That night she went to sleep before it was fully dark, quickly falling into the slumber of a runner who had just won a race.

In the morning it was raining steadily. Shelley was up early. She waited for the intercom to buzz, but by eight o'clock the buzz hadn't arrived. She drank a cup of coffee out on the deck, leaving the door open in order to hear the machine's call. As she watched the rain drizzle into the ocean, she remembered the view of the cliffs of Gay Head in Martha's Vineyard, which she could walk to from her grandmother's house. The grand and majestic sweep of the rocks, the white caps on diminutive waves. Of course, even the name Gay Head had been changed now, the politically correct police dubbing it Aquinnah to honor some long-since-disappeared natives. A disgrace.

By ten that morning she decided it was time to go into the big house and inquire. The door to Mr. Kamal's office was closed, and she heard his voice in there. Although he often read tactile images for work, he couldn't read braille. He had refused to ever learn. So he must have been in there with another person. Dr. Jillian?

Was this it? Was she being fired, without notice, while in *Rhode Island*? When the red ants of anger receded, shame flooded her bloodstream. Why had she opened her mouth yesterday? Why didn't she let him control the situation? Perhaps his touching was just something that blind people did; perhaps she had misread everything. She could be just one of many, just another one of the standard young women helpers he'd had over the years, entirely unremarkable. She stood outside the door listening to the voices, sipping very cold coffee she had brought over.

"Oh no," Sheila said. The maid had come up behind her in her black-and-white uniform. "You can't bring a mug from one house into the other, confusing the system. Mrs. Kamal would never abide. No, no. Take it out."

Shelley smirked. It was *Dr.* Kamal. "Do you know where she is?" Shelley asked in a surprisingly high-pitched voice.

"She's in there reading to her husband, and I suspect they'll be there all day. I'd go back to the guesthouse if I were you," Sheila said, shaking her head from side to side.

Shelley descended the stairs, but instead of returning to the guesthouse, she decided to explore the rest of Hollingsworth Hollow's main house. Her footsteps smacked through the silence of the first floor as she crossed through the kitchen and the pantry and back to the formal living room, off of which sat the glass-encased sunroom and dining rotunda. Just beyond that, there was a large room with floor-to-ceiling wooden library shelves. The room emitted the sour dairy stench of aging paper. The first several books Shelley pulled off the shelves were copies of children's literature from the 1950s: *The Hardy Boys: The Crisscross Shadow*, and something called *The Desire Years*. A bit more searching brought her to the classics though: Austen, Dickens, the Brontës. The few hours she'd recently spent in the Fifth Avenue library had brought a feeling of peace she wasn't accustomed to. And there might be a sense of accomplishment with completing the task of reading a whole book, cover to cover. It was an appropriate time for some self-improvement: the following day was May 23, Shelley's twenty-third birthday. Her eyes landed on *The Great Gatsby*. The Kamals' copy had the same haunting cover, the blue one with floating eyes, as the copy her father had loved and cherished. He'd kept his prized first edition on his nightstand in each home he lived in, as he moved from city to city and family to family. Although Shelley didn't know it, Roger's *Gatsby* book even lay beside him in Southern California, as he took his final breath in this world. She picked up the Kamals' copy now. Although she'd examined the cover many times, she'd never actually read it.

At three thirty that afternoon, Shelley, who had returned to her bedroom in the guesthouse, heard a buzz on the intercom. "Shelley?" It was Dr. Jillian's voice.

"Yes, I'm here." She dropped the novel into her lap.

"Shelley, we're having guests this evening and we'd like you to join us for dinner. Please be at the main house promptly at seven forty. And, Shelley, please, this time, no shorts."

At a quarter to seven Shelley went out for a walk along the beach. She had just enough time to smoke a cigarette, then pop into the shower before dinner. When she walked up to the edge of the icy water in her flip-flops, clusters of rubbery, coral-like seaweed lapped onto her toes. The rain had stopped, but the sand was still damp, all the way up to the grass and the trees behind it. A putrid smell drifted in the salt air, and she turned up the coast to see where it was coming from, only to find Grace's bare arms and T-shirt-covered back walking along the waterline. Grace bent and picked something out of the water, a shell or a rock, then lobbed it, underhanded, farther into the sea. Shelley headed toward her. She hadn't seen Grace for any substantial period of time since the Sunday night dinner disaster. Perhaps the girl was avoiding her.

"Hey—"

Grace turned in surprise, and grimaced when she saw it was Shelley. So this is what it feels like to be a hired hand. Shelley Whitby, servant.

"How's it going?" Shelley asked.

"I'm walking down to the old dock," Grace said, turning away.

"Oh yeah, let's go."

They began to amble down the shoreline. Grace did not smile but asked Shelley earnestly, "So why are you doing this job for my father? Do you want to be an architect or an artist or something?"

"Ha!" Two gulls circled overhead, their squawks seeming to echo Shelley: *Ha, ha.* "No way," she added. But now that Grace had brought up the subject of her father, Shelley saw an opening. "Does he, like, have a lot of girls come and do this for him? Is there always someone like me around?"

Grace didn't take the bait. "I don't want to be an artist either." She bit a hangnail off her pointer finger and squinted into the distance. "But so many people are graduating from Demming and just going to work at investment bank after investment bank. It seems so . . . common."

Shelley nodded, thinking about Ollie and Aleisha and the rest of her college friends. She didn't know one person who wanted to work at a bank, investment or otherwise.

"When did you leave school?" Grace asked.

Shelley realized that she was being stared at rather intensely. "Mmm. Early. I finished in December."

"You know, I remember you. From, like, Lathrop House. And the hangout spot by Harkins Field."

Shelley didn't respond. Perhaps this walk had been a bad idea.

"So what's your plan?" Grace asked. The big white house loomed behind them. Although the sun had yet to set, the windows inside were lit up and glowing orange in the mist.

Mr. Kamal would never see a mansion—his own mansion—glowing. He could hear the waves, smell and taste the salt that infused the air, but did he ever actually know where he was? Shelley fingered the outline of the pack of Virginia Slims in her back pocket. She should really walk away from Grace now, she thought, but the girl was a receptacle of information. "What's it like to have a blind father?"

Grace rolled her eyes and scoffed. "I'm sorry, but you have no idea how often people ask me that question." A low rumbling sound came from around the curve of the beach. "I like to answer: 'What's it like to have a lawyer father? A white father?' There's no answer to that question—it's just the way it is." Grace then looked down quickly, apparently embarrassed by her outburst.

Shelley couldn't keep herself from smiling. Grace! Sassier than she looked. She thought of the constant refrain from new acquaintances that she'd heard most of her life of *Are you related?* "Hey, do you want to smoke a cigarette?"

Grace shook her head.

Shelley lit hers anyway. "Dude. Have you ever asked your dad what it is that he sees?"

The noise sounded again, a low growl, followed by a high-pitched bark. Was it coming from the trees? No, it was farther down the beach. "What was that?" Grace asked, brushing a glop of wet sand off her ankle. The girls picked up their pace, and moved farther in from the waterline.

Grace continued. "I know what my father sees: nothing. Not blackness, not darkness. He told me when I was little, but I'm not sure I've wrapped my head around his perception ever. It's total absence."

Shelley tried to imagine an empty hole, but she couldn't. She kept picturing a well, a dark and cool space.

"You won't be able to do it," Grace said matter-of-factly. "It's like death. We just can't imagine it."

They rounded the outcropping of pine trees that grew over the point. Twenty yards in front of them was a cluster of animals. Two dogs—or wolves or coyotes—were side by side eating from something dead that lay on the sand.

"Holy shit."

The dogs were small and grayish brown, the color of rabbits. Both Shelley and Grace froze, and one of the dogs looked up, flashing the whites of its eyes. Dark blood rimmed its mouth and jawline, and as it growled, it displayed two tiny rows of teeth.

Shelley's limbs locked, and she heard herself scream. She wasn't prepared for this; she was from the Upper West Side. One animal dived back into its meal, jawfirst, and now both dogs were eating from a dead deer. Its fur was golden brown and its head faced up and back, the neck twisted until it had snapped. The dogs chewed at the very center of the deer's chest, which resembled a ripped leather bag.

Shelley puffed on her cigarette, the rest of her body stick-still in the sand.

"Help!" Grace screeched, although the animals did not seem interested in the girls. Then thudding sounded from up the beach. Out of the trees came the outline of Mr. Kamal, barreling across the wet sand shoulders first, head down. He was moving at quite a clip. In a plum-colored cashmere sweater and nubuck loafers, he had one hand protectively tensed in front of him, and he cradled something in the crook of his other arm. The very sight of him made Shelley's intestines drop. She hadn't seen him since she'd left his office the day before.

Grace yelled, "Yousef? Daddy? What are you doing?"

Grace and Shelley were alone between the animals and the ocean. Mr. Kamal kept moving toward them. Shelley flung the nub of her Virginia Slim toward the water. "Out of the way, girls!" He huffed as he yelled. As he approached, the two dogs looked up and growled. Shelley could see now that the thing in the crook of Mr. Kamal's arm was a large rock, the size of a softball. He must have picked it up by the trees when he heard them screaming.

Grace began to lunge in the direction of her father but halted as one of the dogs looked up. "Stop, Daddy!" she cried. "Don't come any closer."

Now Dr. Jillian was sprinting out of the tree line and onto the beach, wearing her linen pants and another shiny top. She ran with the lightness of a marathoner and was soon grasping for the back of her husband's sweater. Shelley realized the problem. Mr. Kamal wouldn't see if a dog was charging at him; he couldn't protect himself.

The dogs seemed to understand they were under attack. Both stepped away from the deer and looked up at him. One began a frenzied, high-pitched bark.

Grace whimpered like a child. Mr. Kamal had run around the animals and reached the girls. He put his free hand out, grasping, until he caught on to Shelley's shoulder and patted it, pressing into the skin around her tank-top strap. Then he put his whole body in front of her—and only her—protectively. Dr. Jillian reached them too. It was a split second, but Shelley felt the woman's eyes dissect the situation: her husband was standing in front of his young aide rather than his daughter. Mr. Kamal leaned back to gain leverage, apparently ready to lob the rock toward the dogs, but as he moved, Dr. Jillian stuck one leather-sandal-covered foot out in front of her husband. The top of his foot caught on hers, the rock spun left in an arc, and out went his legs behind him. Both of his feet kicked back in the air, and Mr. Kamal's face and arms beat against the wet sand as they landed. His legs fell next, in unison.

Although the rock bounced on the sand nowhere near the dogs, one let out a cry. The other barked twice, then ran, diagonally across the sand and into the woods. The remaining dog sniffed cautiously around the deer's corpse, then wiggled backward. Turning its svelte body, he too ran in a woozy curve toward the trees. The animals were gone.

From the ground, without picking up his head, Mr. Kamal groaned.

"Daddy! Are you hurt?" Grace rushed to him, and he lifted his torso and slowly turned onto his back. His face was stern, and he didn't say a word as he lay there. An uneven ring of wetness from the sand crept up both pant legs of his olive khakis.

Dr. Jillian, who had been fiercely focused on Shelley, dropped her gaze and went to help her husband as well. As the other Kamals pulled Mr. Kamal to his feet, Dr. Jillian shouted over her shoulder at Shelley, "He was protecting you."

"But we were fine, Yousef," Grace whined as she wound her arm around her father's back. "You shouldn't have done that."

"My shoulder," he croaked. He was audibly short of breath. With all the hissing and growling gone, the beach was eerily quiet.

"We need to get you to the hospital," Dr. Jillian said sternly.

The air was cool on Shelley's bare arms and the tops of her feet, everywhere but on her shoulder, where Mr. Kamal had touched her. She was stunned still. What had she just witnessed?

He said solemnly, "I must go to the house. Now."

"Grace, take him," Dr. Jillian commanded.

Behind the group the sun hung low above a canopy of clouds over the water. As Grace led her father away toward the well-spaced pine trees, Mr. Kamal's cashmere-covered arms vibrated evenly, as if he were on a train.

Dr. Jillian said to Shelley, "Needless to say I'll be canceling our dinner guests for this evening. The kitchen in the guesthouse is still fairly full, I'm sure." She was dispassionate and upright, as if she had done nothing wrong.

Shelley crossed her arms over her chest. "That was not—"

From her tight quiver of lips, Dr. Jillian said, "Yousef could have gotten himself into a very dangerous situation there. That may have been a wolf, although there is no way to tell. Wolves are an endangered species in Rhode Island. If Yousef had killed one, he could have gone to prison. You must not mention this to anyone. Ever." Then she turned and walked briskly back toward the main house, leaving Shelley, mouth agape, on the beach, listening to the *shuck shuck* of the middle-aged woman's natural-fiber pants. A seagull swooped in and circled around the dead deer and the grooves in the disturbed sand, then flew away across the water.

The next afternoon Dr. Jillian put Shelley on a bus back to New York City. She hadn't been explicitly fired by Mr. Kamal. She hadn't even seen him. That morning, Dr. Jillian came up to the second floor of the guesthouse and, rather gently, told Shelley that Mr. Kamal had dislocated his shoulder and his only priority was to recover. Therefore he was "done with his writing work for this vacation" and she would be driving Shelley to the bus station in a few hours. Dr. Jillian said nothing of import in the car; at the bus station, she simply paid for Shelley's ticket and handed it to her with a finely calibrated lack of emotion. The edge of aggression that Shelley had felt the day before was entirely gone though. Dr. Jillian was just a boring middle-aged wife, sexless and frustrated. Shelley assumed she would not know her, or the rest of the Kamal family, for much longer.

On the bus, Shelley felt as if someone had hollowed out her middle.

She kept the stolen copy of *Gatsby* on her knees, taken with the hope of unlocking some secrets about her father. But she didn't open the book. She simply looked out the window at the passing highway, the sedans and SUVs that sped by the Greyhound. In her mind she thought to herself, again and again, *What am I going to do?* She had no one to turn to for advice, and no obligations to follow. It had been a bad few months. Her mother would have said it was the Whitby Curse. But, Shelley thought, someone way back had gotten the curse wrong. It wasn't that her family was plagued by random misfortune. The Whitbys of the last few generations were rather afflicted with the sincere and problematic issue of not knowing what the hell to do.

Hours later, back in New York, Shelley meandered up Broadway and away from the Port Authority. Shelley wondered if she could live her life alone, build a force field around herself that was impervious to anyone else's advances. She wouldn't care who she talked to. She didn't need anyone to touch her. Wasn't that what her mother had done? But Shelley wasn't like her mother; she wouldn't ever let herself be. She hadn't told anyone, so she couldn't be upset that no one had wished her well: that day was her twenty-third birthday.

By nine Shelley was meandering up Strong Place with her duffel bag slung over her shoulder. At home she would prepare herself a birthday drink. She had nothing, and therefore had nothing to lose. This was twenty-three. She was turning her key in the lock when she saw something move out of the corner of her eye.

"*Hey, hey—*" A whisper shot through the darkness. Something seemed to be moving toward her. A person.

Shelley screamed. It was striking and high-pitched; the same involuntary scream she had let out on the beach the day before, one of a mammal under attack.

"Shush! Stop it, Shells. It's me." The figure pulled a black hood down from his head to reveal a jumble of golden curls. He stood right in front of her face: skinny, dirty, and petrified.

"Nick?" she yelped.

He crumpled into her arms. Something like joy sprung up inside of her and she felt the pressure of tears behind her eyes. But as soon as she let herself feel this happiness, a hot, liquid dread leaked into her brain: he must know. He must know about Roger and about the house. That's why he was there. She realized how much she did not want to talk about the inheritance, or think about any of it. Her father's death was a fact that had been packed away already. All she wanted to focus on was why she had just been sent home from Rhode Island and how Mr. Kamal had moved his hands slowly down her cheeks.

But there Nick was, warm and alive and standing in front of her. Shelley shoved his shoulders in the dark. "Where the hell have you been? Your mother calls me every day. People have been looking for you everywhere."

"Shhhh," he whispered. "We need to go inside."

Summer

| 2003 |

When opportunity trots by, lasso it
round the hind and hold on for dear life.

—ROGER WHITBY JR.

1

Nick Whitby awoke with a start in the twin bed in Shelley's old childhood bedroom. For the week that he'd been staying in the apartment, he hadn't been sleeping well. A recurring dream had wormed itself into his brain, where women's bodies appeared ghostly and fractured: Devorah's naked back, the thighs of one of the NYU vegetable-eaters who hated his guts—Abi—looped over his shoulders. But then that common dream had morphed into a disturbingly visceral vision of holding Shelley's face in his hands and kissing her deeply, while standing on the beach in Martha's Vineyard. That was when Nick's eyes had shot open in a panic. He shook his head. He tried to remind himself that Shelley wasn't even his biological relation. But he still hated himself for it. Of course now, with him having to hide out from the rest of the world, with the news that Roger had died, his perverseness would rear its pernicious head. If it wasn't the Whitby Curse afflicting him, he must have his own, individualized curse. There had to be some greater force making all these disasters transpire at the same time.

Nick hadn't exited the front door of the apartment once that entire week. He couldn't, it just wasn't safe. He had spent a few nights in those cramped rooms in the past—weekends early in college, when Shelley was home and had invited him to stay over. But on those trips, the rooms had merely been a stop in his hectic, New York City college-kid life. Now these rooms would be his entire world: until he figured out another place to go, until Shelley's mother showed up or he came up with a plan to make some cash so that he could leave town, he was stuck there. There could be cops or FBI agents anywhere.

The week had been a strange, slow-motion blur. On the night he'd arrived, Shelley had told him that Roger was dead. The news shouldn't have been shocking, of course, the old man was not in good health, but Nick still couldn't believe it. It didn't seem possible that Roger would ever die. Since he'd heard the news, Nick had felt constantly nauseous, and although he and Shelley hadn't spoken much about the man's actual death, it felt as though they'd spent the past many days holding their own private wake for their father. Most afternoons they sat on the floral couch in the parlor or on the floor in front of the broken blue settee, half watching some crime-scene-investigator show Shelley was obsessed with, while drinking gin out of plastic cups and telling each other Roger stories. The time Roger brought Nick to the Legends Suite at Yankee Stadium, or when he sat in the jump seat as Nick heli-skied in Tahoe, or their trip to northern Argentina to hunt blackbuck antelope. Well, maybe Nick was doing most of the talking. Maybe he had more to say than his sister.

One thing Shelley did keep asking him was where the hell he had been for the past several weeks. But for her own good, he wouldn't tell her. When he and his comrades had left Maine, they'd all agreed to scatter to different parts of the country and not reveal that they were part of the botched action to anyone, ever. Now, Nick slowly gained awareness and looked around the childish features of Shelley's bedroom: the ornate white dresser; the band posters of Phish and Crosby, Stills, Nash & Young; the plastic picture frames decorated in puffy paint. He missed the abandoned building he'd been staying in since he returned from the action in Maine. It was an old community center on First Street and First Avenue, the place that Kever and Dumpster had set up as a squat. Nick had been hiding there since his arm had healed enough for him to safely leave the farm. Even if the squat didn't have electricity or running water, at least it had reading materials to keep him interested. He'd read the CrimethInc. collective's handbook; twelve zines covering the topics of punk bands, sexual assault, and unoppressive flirting techniques; the majority of Bakunin's *God and the State*; and another novel-length zine about primitivism and the tree sitters of the radical environmental movement in Washington State. He had begun to peruse a book of Emma Goldman essays several times but had kept getting distracted and would end up taking out a Sharpie and drawing portraits from memory of his mother, Shelley, and Devorah on the blank pages at the end of the book.

A week earlier, he'd walked out of the squat to a bodega on the corner of Second Avenue and Fourth Street. He had a debit card, but there was no way he was going to use it and let the government track his movements. The only truly risky thing he'd done was send his mother that postcard. He'd drawn and mailed it out of an aching of guilt over how much she might be worrying. But even though he didn't sign it, he understood now that he'd made a big mistake. She couldn't be trusted. He was dumb, and now he was also broke. In the bodega, after buying two big bottles of Nestlé water (he couldn't even look at the Poland Spring bottles, didn't want anything to do with that company now) and one *New York Times*, his remaining cash totaled four dollars and three quarters. He had $4.75 to his name.

As he stood in front of the deli counter, the clerk said in a thick accent, "How's your night, brother?" Nick didn't answer the man. The sound of his voice would just be more material to identify him with. Instead, his eyes rested on a newspaper headline on the lower half of the front page. The headline read: ACTIVIST ARSONISTS CHARGED AS DOMESTIC TERRORISTS. Nick pulled the hood of his sweatshirt over his head, and, outside the door of the deli, read the rest of the piece. The three paragraphs described how a task force between the FBI and the Bureau of Alcohol, Tobacco, Firearms and Explosives had arrested three "dangerous individuals" in various states across the country and were in active pursuit of other suspects involved in an arson of a biotech construction site in Maine. The article stated that these individuals were coconspirators, with networks that traveled across state lines, who referred to one another as "the Family." Thus, the government's joint-task-force operation was nicknamed "Operation Family

Values." The article was short but it reported one striking fact: all members of the Family would be charged as terrorists.

Nick had trembled as he rolled up the newspaper and shoved it in his back pocket. On the corner was a double phone booth, the new kind with no doors, and he dipped into it. He put a quarter in and dialed Shelley's cell phone. He'd been doing this: calling Shelley every few days and not saying a word. Normally she'd answer with a confused "Hello?" Her voice was usually low and annoyed but so very Shelley-like. She'd ask, "Who's there? Is this Armond?" Nick would never speak; the sound of her voice, the confirmation that she was somewhere not too far away, being herself, was all that he'd wanted. After these phone calls he would briefly feel less wired and less bewildered. But that night the call went right to voice mail. He tried again. He waited two painful minutes, then spent his third quarter on a third call: no answer. That's when he began walking uptown.

Going to Shelley's house had seemed like a good idea, seven days ago. It hadn't felt safe to go back to the squat, where these accused terrorists had certainly stayed at various points. Shelley had to be home from Demming by then, and he needed to see her. She was his truest confidant, his safest haven, and the only person who could possibly begin to understand the weird history of his life. He could trust her wholly.

Now, a week later, Nick lay in bed wearing only his blue plaid boxer shorts and wondering what on earth he should do. The nineties-era alarm clock announced it was 7:32 in the morning; Shelley wouldn't be awake yet. He looked at the red and scaled skin that streaked his left forearm and wondered if he should call his mother. She, and others in their extended family—and the lawyer—had been calling Shelley consistently every day; the house phone was always ringing. But Roger was dead. His mother didn't need to deal with Nick's disaster now. He was doing her a favor by not calling her. He would take care of the problem himself.

With that resolve, Nick jumped out of bed. Pulling on his Carhartt jeans, he made his way to the parlor. There was a tangy smell pervading the room—garbage? The whole place was, in fact, filthy. After checking two closets, he found an ancient pea-green Hoover vacuum. He'd vacuumed the entire top floor and was standing on the stairs letting the giant machine suck up clotted gray dust and balls of shed hair, and even, strangely, an onion skin, when he noticed the newspaper he'd bought at the bodega that night, folded and pressed against the wall. It must have fallen out of his pocket and landed there a week ago. There was the headline, staring up at him in black print: the word *terrorists*. Nick dropped the vacuum handle while it was still running and lay down on the carpeted stairs. He kept lying there for God knows how long. The vacuum started smoking. It was as if he were paralyzed: everything was still except for his breath, which pumped in and out of him at an uncontrollable rate. He repeated one line in his head, again and again: *I don't know what to do.*

Of all things that Roger would be ashamed of, this was the greatest. Roger had believed in Nick. He had believed that Nick could be strong, and bold, and brave, and had told him so many times. But now Nick was revealing his true colors. He was weak. Roger would want his youngest son to take charge of this situation, to turn the bad luck around and make these circumstances work for his own advantage. Nick couldn't continue this powerless existence. He had to plan something, make some move. He stood up, took his multi-tool off his belt loop, and set off to find all the phone jacks in the house, as well as the modem internet line. Cutting them off would be his first step to bring himself back into action. He would stop the constant phone calls and then be able to really focus. Now that Roger was dead, Nick strangely desired to make him proud. He would figure out a plan.

Shelley lay in Biddy's old bed and stared at the ceiling, while she wondered what the hell to do about her mother. She had been woken up by a strange humming noise. What could Nick be doing? Whatever it was, she didn't really care. Although she didn't tell him, she was entirely grateful that he'd shown up when he did. It was some kind of sign, his being there when she needed him most. It was miraculous, really. She was no longer alone. The day after she'd been banished from Rhode Island and Nick showed up, she had received a phone call from Brooke, who had run into Shelley's mother in a hospital in Boston. Brooke had delivered the news that Elizabeth Saltman Whitby was truly unwell. As Brooke recounted the whole tale, Shelley couldn't help remembering the words that her grandmother Biddy had said about her mother, years before: *She was untoward, indeed.*

Brooke had implored Shelley on the phone, "Come to Boston immediately. I'll buy you a train ticket in the morning, when we'll know more about the treatment plan."

But every day that past week, Shelley would watch her cell phone ring three or four separate times, with Brooke's 617 number flashing across the screen. How things had changed. There was a time when little Shelley would have yelped with excitement at Brooke calling her. Now she would not pick up. On the first day, Brooke had left a message: "Shells. Your mother is going to be transferred to inpatient treatment at a mental health facility just outside of Boston, McLean Hospital. It's the highest-quality care. Can you get on the two o'clock train and come right here? Call me back. Ciao-ciao."

Shelley listened to the message four times, until she'd memorized the name of the hospital and Brooke's precise inflection when she said "come right here." Then she deleted the recording. She wouldn't entertain the idea of going to Boston. Every time she did, her face swelled with impending tears. This episode was clearly more severe than the others had been, and her mother wasn't coming back anytime soon. This fact was, among other things, dangerously disappointing.

Sitting up in bed, Shelley pictured Mr. Kamal's light touch on her face. If she had only stayed still in his Rhode Island office and not opened her mouth, she might be with him at this very moment. If she had only hung up the phone in the diner and controlled herself, and not thrown her apron over the counter. If she had only let Ollie and her roommate, Aleisha, explain themselves. Oh, the other places she could be, if she weren't always herself.

But because she was, she had spent the past week sitting around with

Nick, talking about Roger and discovering that time could fog over, multiple days seeping into one long swath of hours. Channel twenty-four almost exclusively aired the hour-long crime drama *The Good Life*, which she watched with half-open eyes for the whole day, half listening to Nick ramble on, as they drank screwdrivers. The show was about a law firm investigator named Good who was also a prostitute and used sexual-service jobs to gather classified information for her firm. Good was skilled, and she always—always—found the DNA evidence or the IP address of the hacker. Unfortunately, there were four infuriating hours in the late afternoon when the station played reruns of *Friends*.

Nick didn't seem to mind their daily pattern; he was on a break from regular life as well. On the night he'd arrived, by the time they were stationed on the floral couch with a box of crackers in front of each of them, Nick was fiercely shaking his head. He looked too thin and didn't smell good at all. "I am *not* in a good way," he had said, shoveling a fistful of Wheat Thins into his mouth. "You have no idea what's been happening. The world is actually fucking me right now." He spoke as if someone could overhear them.

There was Nick, being himself: the drama he exuded tickled her. She couldn't help smiling. She was aware that every time he showed up, she became a bumbling goofy teenager, dumb and happy.

"Where's your mother?" he'd asked, looking around the messy room.

"Vineyard." Shelley shrugged, unsure of exactly why she was lying. "She'll be there all summer. Selling the house."

He nodded sagely. "Cleaner on the conscience, owning fewer things." Then his already protruding eyes seemed to bug out farther. "Can I sleep here tonight? Or for a few days?"

"Where the hell have you been staying?" Shelley asked.

He shook his head again. Whatever the severity of what was going on with him, he believed that it was bad. He was like that though, simultaneously naive and exaggerated.

"And they didn't have laundry there? Your sweatshirt is rank."

"I can't tell you where I've been. Trust me, you don't want to know."

He rubbed his cheeks, an expression of true exhaustion. "It's okay if I sleep on the couch? I can leave tomorrow if you need me to."

"Don't be an idiot. You can stay as long as you want." Nick shifted himself so that his head rested on the yellow throw pillow, and his legs stretched out over Shelley's knees, making her smile. Her little weirdo.

As he closed his eyes he muttered, "You cannot tell anyone I'm here. I'm life-and-death serious. Okay?"

She shook his two knees, trying to jostle him awake, but he just waved his hands, eyes still closed. She'd assumed that he'd shown up like that because he'd heard about Roger and the will. But maybe he didn't actually know. What would happen when she told him? A flurry of action: Ms. Scribner would fly in, there would be meetings with Armond. A legal battle, most likely. She didn't want any of it, but the words wouldn't stay inside of her. She pushed on his knees again, more gently this time. "Nick, do you know about Dad?"

"Hmmm?"

"Roger. Dad. He's— Nick, he died. In April. That's why your mother has been looking for you so frantically. Did you know?"

Nick's eyes were wide-open now, but he didn't sit up. His body was completely still.

"You didn't know?" Shelley asked.

Then he let out an odd laugh, something that sounded close to a seagull's squawk. "No," he said. His expression was shocked but not sad. "No. That's not right."

She pushed his legs off of her lap and bundled her knees underneath her. He sat up too. "It is."

"No. I know he's been sick, but he's Roger. He'd always get the best doctor and figure out some way to beat the system."

"He had a stroke, in April. He was in California when he died."

"Ha!" Nick let out another bizarre squawk of a laugh, although he wasn't smiling. The news seemed to settle silently upon him. It seemed he truly hadn't known. And if he didn't know about Roger's death, then he didn't know about the will either.

"I wasn't even invited to the funeral," Shelley said.

Nick shook his head in disbelief. His hands went to his temples.

"Are you going to call your mother now? She was there, at the funeral."

Nick crunched into a fetal position on the sofa. The word *no* came out muffled, from his knees.

Shelley peeked down to see his face. He stayed in a ball, vibrating for a very long time. She didn't try to hug him or tell him it would be okay. How many times had Nick told her, while on the phone for hours or beside her as she smoked a bowl on the dock in the Vineyard, that he hated Roger? He had said that if Roger hadn't come into his life, everything would have been different: he would never have moved to California; he wouldn't have spent his childhood weekends in a sterile hotel room entirely alone; his mother could have met someone else or simply been happy alone; he might have had another sibling or a dog. And yet here was Nick, wailing into his knees about Shelley's dead father. But perhaps that was the normal response. Maybe that's what Shelley should have done in the Magic Mule the moment that Armond called her.

Finally, Nick looked up and said, "I can't call my mother. I can't tell anyone that I'm here."

Then he was still. He appeared to have cried himself to sleep, looking like an overgrown baby bird, with his two hands cupping his own bony shoulders. His right sweatshirt sleeve was shoved up, and a scaly red scar was visible underneath. What had happened to his arm? The dried-sweat odor of him was overwhelming, but rather than revolting her, it reminded Shelley of his innocence. She touched his cheek with the back of her fingers; the fine blond stubble was only slightly rough, the skin underneath it stretchy and soft. Her angry, beautiful, fake half brother. He could be so dumb and so small.

He was the first person she had told about Roger's death. She wondered if her words had rendered it real and made it part of her identity now. A stranger could point to her from across a crowded party, leaning in to describe her to a friend: "The long-legged one, with light brown hair?

That's Shelley Whitby, daughter of a dead father." That's who she was now. *Shelley Whitby: fatherless. Shelley Whitby: tied to no one.*

Maybe that was fine. Nick would find out soon enough about the will, but if she didn't tell him now she'd have a few more days of peace until everyone swooped in, causing a commotion. Before she had gone upstairs for bed that night, she had lightly draped her fingers over Nick's, which still cupped his shoulders. His hands had been curiously rough.

Now, a week later, she sighed in Biddy's bed, listening to the hum of some machine Nick was using. Could he be cleaning? Life was slowly getting back in order. She would wait to tell him about the will just a little while longer. She listened to what had to be a vacuum and felt, at that moment, wildly grateful.

As Brooke drove up the hill on the far edge of Belmont, Massachusetts, McLean Hospital came into view. She snickered to herself, "Looks like St. Paul's." The stone buildings of the hospital were much more reminiscent of a campus than of a medical institution. This would be Brooke's second trip there since Elizabeth had been admitted. Elizabeth's doctor had requested a meeting with Brooke to discuss a plan of care, and although Brooke was a nurse—or perhaps because she was a nurse—she wished she had someone else to bring along for support.

The week had been tumultuous and entirely strange, but also blissful. Brooke was simultaneously heartbroken over her interaction with Allie and in crisis mode trying to manage Elizabeth while tracking down Shelley. She was also elated about her resolute decision to become a mother. The decision felt not only private but also clandestine, as if she were doing something that was not allowed. Having a baby alone was, of course, not something that Whitbys did. But she came to understand that this was an opportunity offered to her, and she needed to grab it. And if there was anything she had learned in the past few weeks, it was that she was her own person. Plus, things were different now than they used to be.

Almost every Whitby who would have judged her was dead. Now she could have a new family, one of her own creation.

There was so much practical planning to do, and although she'd taken herself and her credit card to the baby book section of Trident Booksellers, she couldn't bring herself to begin looking at new rental apartments. She had the unrealistic fantasy of staying at the Joy Street house and converting the old maid's room behind the kitchen into a nursery. She found herself standing in the space alone nearly every day when she returned from work. She imagined the walls a peach color: happy and appropriate, even if the baby was a boy. She couldn't help wanting to call up Allie and ask her what she thought about peach walls. Brooke wouldn't let herself believe that Allie was gone. What would life be like right now, if they were together? At least, Brooke figured as she pulled her Jeep into a parking space at the hospital, the Elizabeth Saltman Whitby problem was a valid distraction.

After Brooke's initial phone call with Shelley, where she'd reported the news of what happened, Shelley had stopped answering her phone. Thus commenced two days of Brooke believing something bad had happened to her half sister, before her concern mutated into sheer anger. What was wrong with this child, leaving all of her responsibility to other people? Brooke had called her own mother to complain (Corney's response: "Elizabeth has always been out of her ever-loving mind, Birdie, I wouldn't be surprised if her daughter followed suit . . ."). Next she tried LJ to ask if he would help getting Shelley involved. ("Which one is Shelley? I got a lot of fires brewing for this new start-up. I don't have time for this shit.")

The meeting with Elizabeth's doctor, a short and unsmiling woman around her own age, took place in the oak-paneled hallway outside of Elizabeth's suite. Dr. Anne Huang was brusque, as Brooke knew doctors usually were. She said, "We're concerned about Elizabeth's progress. She's still having intermittent positive add-ons. She occasionally falls into what people think of as a catatonic state, and when she's alert, she's also jumpy and very distracted. She refuses to engage in any of the recreational activities, which is really impeding her progress. And last night she had an episode where she screamed for two and a half hours about keeping curses away from her. We need to get her into family therapy, ASAP."

"That's fine," Brooke said, "but I'm not the one who should be doing that. I'm not her family."

Dr. Huang, who wore a cashmere sweater under her open white lab coat, looked perplexed. "If you're not her family, who are you?"

"I'm her daughter's sister. From another marriage. Elizabeth is not really my stepmother though, because she was married to my father long after—" Brooke grimaced and dreamed of having someone else there, anyone, really, who would simply assure her with a sympathetic nod.

The doctor interrupted. "Is there the possibility of her daughter coming?"

"Yes. I'm trying to get her daughter to come."

"But you're here."

"I am for now—"

"Well, somebody needs to be here consistently. Elizabeth keeps telling us that she's waiting for someone."

The meeting concluded in an agreement that Brooke would keep searching for another person to be involved in family therapy, and she and Dr. Huang left each other with matching glares of frustration.

When Brooke opened the door to Elizabeth's room, she was presented with a large picture window framing a rolling hill of freshly cut grass, with a stone path weaving through it. The scene was idyllic. And then she wondered who would pay for this. What money did Shelley's part of the family still have? As far as she could tell, Elizabeth, who had become a mother at such an early age, had never had a job.

Elizabeth sat upright in her single bed, which was adorned with multiple pillows and a folded quilt at her feet. The place could have passed for a room at a quaint bed-and-breakfast.

"How are you, Elizabeth?" Brooke asked.

Although Elizabeth stared at her visitor, she didn't say a word of acknowledgment. As plush as the room was, with a Persian rug and a gray leather armchair atop it, Brooke began to notice the discreet details that medicalized it: a narrow armoire behind the bed, where the nurse kept her standing IV pole; the loops on each bedpost that were actually patient restraints for the hands and the feet.

Brooke went to the bedside. She looked into Elizabeth's eyes and said in her calm but firm nurse voice, "We need to talk about your daughter, Elizabeth."

Elizabeth gave no response.

"The doctor told us that you've been waiting for someone. Is it Shelley?"

After a few minutes of silence, Brooke left the room to refill the water pitcher and ice chips. When she returned, she sat at the end of the bed and smoothed out the gold-patterned comforter, accidentally hitting against Elizabeth's knee. It was so bony. The woman couldn't have weighed more than one hundred pounds. Brooke tried again, but in a softer, kinder voice this time, "Are you waiting for Shelley? Or are you waiting for someone else?"

Perhaps it was the closeness of Brooke's body or the harmlessness of her tone, but Elizabeth spoke up now, although she was looking toward a wall. "I'm waiting to be picked up. I am always picked up."

Nine largely silent minutes later, Brooke decided it was time to go. As she walked out of the room, Elizabeth said under her breath, "Roger has left us. Roger has left us for the boy, not for that woman. Do you think the boy is really his? It's impossible. But he loves the boy more than he loved your small brother. But why? Why did he leave us for the boy?"

Brooke froze in the doorway. No one had told Elizabeth about the will. No one had told her Roger was dead. It was more than unnerving. It was uncanny. "Mother will know," Elizabeth continued nonsensically. "She'll tell me when she picks me up. She always does."

2

Grace Kamal donned her kitten-heeled squish-toed shoes to go to her summer internship in the editorial department at the publishing house FSG. She shuffled into her own kitchen, grumpily, where she encountered a strange man hunching over the counter and reading the newspaper. The clock on the oven said 7:16 a.m.

"Hello?"

The stranger was tall, with dark curls that hung around his jaw and at the back of his neck. Objectively, he was quite handsome. "Hello." He smiled, dimples gouging both cheeks. He went right back to reading the paper as if he had more right to be there than she did.

"I'm Grace," she said, meaning to insinuate: *Who the hell are you and why are you making yourself comfortable in my home?*

She was already in a wretched mood. They had all come home from Rhode Island early, and she'd spent the past two days filing like a whirlwind. She hated the internship. The reason she was doing it was because she was, honestly, a first-class parent pleaser, and Yousef and Jillian deemed the summer position acceptable.

Now, the man in her own kitchen gave her the once-over. "I'm Hasan." She appeared to be putting *him* out. "Your mother is Dr. Kamal? She's my, uh, mentor. At the museum."

His eyes went to the paper again as Grace stared, incredulous.

Her mother waltzed into the kitchen as if nothing strange was going on. She opened the fridge and, pouring herself a glass of grapefruit juice, scanned Grace up and down, examining her daughter's work outfit.

Grace was horrified at the man's presence and disgusted at her mother. But this wasn't the first time she'd suspected her parents of affairs. She matched her mother in silence, until Jillian leaned across the breakfast bar and said, "You know, sweetie, your father needs an assistant terribly at the moment, what with all the work for his book. Perhaps we acted a *tad rash* getting rid of the Whitby girl. But I called her yesterday to try to bring her back, and no one answered."

Grace was mortified by how spectacularly she had embarrassed herself in front of Shelley in Little Compton. From her childish fight with her father about her haircut, to when he went American-animal-psycho on the beach, it was a catastrophe. And on top of it, they treated the goddess of Demming seniors like a servant. Her family had made a mess of her golden Whitby opportunity. Grace should have cut her losses, and if she happened to walk by Shelley on the street, now or in fifteen years, she could simply dash away while hiding her face in shame. But instead, she was under the spell of an elemental need embedded in her twenty-year-old psyche. She was dedicated to completing a singular goal that summer: to make friends.

"I could go by her house," Grace offered, aiming to sound nonchalant. "I can do it on the way home from work."

Jillian took a sip of juice. "No, dear. We want to offer her money, you know, as an incentive to return to work."

"I'll do it," Grace said again, her voice peaking. This was her second chance.

Jillian nodded at her daughter, although quizzically, and went to retrieve Shelley's address from the Rolodex in the library. Even if Jillian sensed Grace's ulterior motive, she would never outright ask. Although he didn't look up from his reading, and although she was actually thrilled at the prospect of seeing Shelley again, Grace glared at Hasan from across the counter. Glaring was the least she could do, for her father's sake.

That evening around six, the doorbell to the Whitby apartment rang. Shelley was upstairs in the bathtub, smoking a cigarette. With each sounding of the bell, she winced. As it rang through the rooms of her apartment, she had the irrational fear that Brooke was outside. Of course that was ridiculous. Brooke would be in Boston, helping Shelley's mother just as she promised. But what if she'd sent someone else over? Shelley's right foot hung outside of the claw-foot tub, which was jammed under the pedestal sink, which was itself below a white bookcase holding a decade's worth of half-used bath gels and miniature wrapped soaps. Cigarette ash fell onto the black-and-white-tiled floor, and with one arm held high, she sunk her face under the water.

Grace walked down Columbus Avenue while half-heartedly people-watching tourists and window-shopping in sporting goods stores. Perhaps Shelley was out of town again. At work that morning, as she had aimlessly copyedited, Grace had tried to plan out what she would say to her. As she rode the elevator holding coffee for six senior editors, she was reminded of the genius of Dale Carnegie and his well-researched adage: if you want someone to like you, become genuinely interested in the thing that they like. But what was it that Shelley liked? Around four, still disturbed by the handsome man's hovering in her kitchen that morning, she remembered Shelley's inquiries about the other girls who worked for her father and realized something that Shelley could very possibly be interested in: her parents. She didn't want to think too hard about why Shelley might be so interested, but she had a guilty inkling that this topic might be an entry into friendship.

Grace wandered for the better part of an hour, then for good measure, returned to the narrow alley and rang the Whitbys' bell in double time. She heard shuffling inside and then a pause, which could only mean she was being peered at through the peephole. After a moment, the door swung open and there she was: her Disheveled Equestrian, swathed in a maroon bathrobe and pink hair towel. Shelley held a box of saltine crackers and wore a peculiar smile. "Grace? Why are you here?" She did not appear surprised to see Grace. It seemed that was one of Shelley's many gifts: to be so self-possessed that she gave nothing, intentional or otherwise, to others.

"Hellllllo!" Grace swiped one hand over the top of her newly sheared hair. Fake it till you make it; pretend to be friends and then you will be. "My mom called a few times but there was no answer, so I thought I'd . . . *pop* by."

"Okay. Uh, what's up?" Shelley said.

Perhaps this plan was ill-conceived. "I'm wondering if I could talk to you," Grace said, her voice wavering. "I know you were working for my dad while I was still at school, and it's just, I—" She took a deep breath. "My parents have been acting weird around me. Like weirder than they usually are, which is, like, pretty hard." She searched Shelley's face for some softness. Nothing. "Well. There was a guy in my parents' kitchen this morning. A man. Do you think—" It seemed ridiculous to be bringing this up to a veritable stranger, but she was already in the middle of it. "Do you think my mother is having an affair?"

Stone-cold Shelley broke into a smile now. One that was edging toward goofy, even. She giggled. "You think your mother has a boyfriend?"

"Well, I wouldn't go that far. The guy said he was her, like, colleague." Heat spread across Grace's face, a rash of embarrassment she was sure was visible. It had been a mistake to come here.

Shelley stepped backward.

"Sorry—" *Humiliation* was not a bitter enough word to describe Grace's state at that moment.

Shelley grabbed her shoulders, and pulled Grace into her body. She was hugging her. A melodic and delicate laugh arose, an English bird with a rainbow plume. "Come in. You smell so good. Is that your shampoo?"

Shelley was not only asking about her, she was being kind. Stunned, Grace looked around the Whitby kitchen and said, "You live here?" Then she instantly regretted how judgmental she sounded. But the kitchen resembled the scene from *Home Alone* after Kevin booby-trapped his own house for the Wet Bandits: jumbles of dishes and saucepans peeked out of the peeling enamel sink; the fertile scent of rotting trash pervaded the room; junk mail splayed across the countertop. "I mean, sorry. Um. Who do you live with?"

"This is my parents' house," Shelley said, shrugging toward her bare toes. "My mother's been away for a while."

Grace scanned the room again. The adult Whitbys lived here? "I didn't even tell you why I'm really here," she said, afraid her impending lie was making her face blush. "Jillian, my mom, sent me over. She wanted me to come over in person and make sure that you're still going to be working for Yousef."

"Your *mother* wants me to come back?" Shelley unraveled the towel from her head, then combed out wet streaks of hair with her fingers.

"Yeah, that's the real reason I came over. Despite whatever else is going on with her, she said you're doing a great job. And—" Grace tried to think of something a motherly, overkind woman would say. "She's sorry about what happened in Rhode Island."

Shelley looked horrified.

Grace picked up a plastic liquor bottle that sat on the counter, in order to have a place to focus her gaze. "It's really embarrassing when my father does stuff like that." She swallowed. "It's, like—it's not the first time. I think he wants to feel manly or something."

Shelley was totally silent for a few beats, before letting out a burst of laughter.

Grace continued. "Really, it's exhausting trying to deal with the two of them. Anyway, I'm supposed to tell you that they want you to come over to our apartment at three on Monday." She pulled the envelope her mother had given her out of her purse. It was heavy and turgid. "And Jillian forgot to pay you." Grace had no idea how much cash was in there.

Shelley turned it over in her hands. After shoving it into her robe pocket, she walked away from Grace and into the living room, where she picked up the television remote and stood absently.

Grace followed her, stepping around two discarded sweatshirts and one crumpled pair of jeans.

Shelley, settling herself on a small floral couch, took a cigarette out of the same pocket of her robe. "Listen," she said, as if they'd still been talking about it, "I don't know who was at your house this morning. But the guy probably just works for your mother. Brilliant people have odd schedules. Want a cigarette?"

Grace shook her head but sat down. She was amazed. Her plot appeared to be working. Shelley looked at her and smiled. "Guess how many times my own father was married?"

"How many?" Grace asked. Shelley was talking about herself. This is how people become friends.

"Four. I shit you not. My mom was the third." It was clear these were lines she had said before. Now Grace needed to keep her talking.

"Really? How was that? Do you like your, uh, dad's other wives?"

Oh dear. That was too intrusive of a question. Dale would not approve. She was trying to determine the line between interest and intrusion, when, plodding down the stairs in navy basketball shorts and a bare chest, came a walking Adonis. This beautiful man carried under his arm a giant, clothbound book, underneath a stack of pencil drawings on computer paper.

"I'm starving, Shells—" He froze halfway down the stairs. "Who—?" He dropped the giant blue book and it bumped down each stair, falling open on the landing. The drawings scattered in front of him, a few flying through the oak balusters and landing on the carpet below. "Sorry." He turned and ran back up the stairs.

"Don't be such a freak, Nick," Shelley yelled from her seat.

He was the most attractive man, the most alluring person, Grace had ever seen. She jumped up and, without hesitation, went over and scooped up the giant blue book. It was *The Historical Atlas of New York City*; some of the stitched binding was coming out. "You dropped your drawings," she yelled up the stairs.

Shelley, from the couch, gave her an inquiring look. Grace picked up a few of the sheets of paper. The drawings were maps, perfect and intricate measured replicas of Manhattan streets. One sheet was downtown: William, Whitehall, and Broad all turning with the twenty-degree angle of the island. Another sheet was the east side of Central Park, around Terrace Drive and Seventy-Second. Grace trotted up the stairs with them. The door to a room at the end of the hall swung slightly, and when Grace walked in, there he was, shirtless, on his back on the floor. His neck awkwardly leaned against the side of the twin bed, as if he had fallen there with a splat.

"You dropped these." She handed him the book and the drawings.

"Who are you?" His eyes bulged out of his thin face.

She couldn't help grinning. His features were carved and sharp, his hair both angelic and boppy. He had a large red scar on his left arm. His chest was taut, lean. He was full of so much angular, American beauty.

Surprisingly, she was unable to speak loudly. "Grace," she whispered. And then something clicked. She knew this guy, or she'd known him, as a kid. She remembered him.

"What are you doing here?" he said.

Then she was back to her old self, a fountain with no cork. "I think I actually know you from somewhere? I mean, did you go to science camp at Bank Street when you were a kid? 'Cause you look just like this kid I remember from there—"

"Who are you?" he repeated.

"I'm the daughter of the person Shelley works—"

"She's my friend, you freak," Shelley growled. She had come up behind Grace and was standing in the doorway. "Put some clothes on, Nick. Come on, Grace."

Downstairs on the couch, Grace's mind buzzed. This was probably what it felt like to take speed. Shelley briefly apologized. ("Sorry. I think my brother's losing his mind.") Then she clicked on the television and began smoking again. Grace sat beside her, grinning like a moron. Shelley had called her her *friend*. On the news a tall white man with bleached teeth reported, "One hundred and ten dead in a ground attack in Fallujah, and three Americans reported missing."

Grace needed to focus, to say something cool. But she could not stop herself from imagining a whole life for the shirtless boy upstairs. She pictured the very same reporter holding his microphone, cheesing his smile: *Nick Whitby, age twenty-one, was very good at many things. He was once a high school track star. Or maybe a varsity swimmer, a champion of the 100 meter butterfly. Math and science made clear and perfect sense to him, and his ability to draw accurate and precise depictions of hockey players, school principals, and popular girls had shocked friends and teachers throughout his life. In fact, he was used to shocking teachers of all kinds with his abilities. Yes, he knew he was good at many things, but there was one thing he was terribly bad at: girls. That is, until he met Grace Kamal.*

Shelley clicked the television to a new station. "Do you like the show *The Good Life*?"

Grace had never seen it. "Love it," she said, grinning, and settled herself into the cushions. Summer could go quickly if one didn't grab it by the reins and attempt to wrangle it into a valuable shape. But it was June, and her prospects were looking up.

3

| 1997 |

When Nick arrived in Martha's Vineyard that first summer, he brought with him the sinking feeling of having made an atrocious decision. With a manatee-sized camping pack on his back, fifteen-year-old Nick, who had reached six feet but still carried with him the pudgy edges of childhood, boarded a bus at the tiny airport that proceeded to take him through the sinuous roads of the island. Mist dropped from the gray sky and green leaves burst over the sandy banks of the roads, hovering above heaps of tangled branches. Biddy's gray-shingled house was at the end of a brick path that cut through an overgrown front yard. He rang the bell four times, and after no one answered, he let himself in. "Hello?" he called. The old, damp house appeared to be empty. He wondered how much it would cost to go right back to the airport and book a flight home.

It had been Shelley's idea that he spend the summer on the Vineyard with her. ("It's paradise. Just rambling around the island.") His mother and Roger's marriage was quickly disintegrating. Although Roger had taken Nick on an extravagant trip to South America that spring, as far as he knew, his parents hadn't spoken in months. Nick's mother, who now seemed to spend her hours staring out at the lemon trees in their Newport

Beach backyard, spacey and distraught, was initially resistant to the idea of Nick's leaving for the summer. He had explained to her that Shelley's mother wouldn't be there, and it would be just her grandmother there, although he knew Biddy was far too ill and fragile now to spend more than a week or two there all summer. "And I'll be making money working at this clam shack place. And, ah, it's by the beach, so I can train for the swim team every day." Things had been bad for him at school that year. He had one real friend, Jake, the only other nerd who swam. His mother knew about his social struggles, but she still didn't want anything to do with Roger's ex-wife. So when she gave in too quickly, Nick wondered if his mother actually wanted him out of the house, if she somehow blamed him for the sourness of her relationship with Roger, as if he had stolen the small amount of affection Roger had to bestow.

That first day on the New England island, Nick camped out alone for hours in the basement. White panels rose halfway up the walls, which were adorned with frames containing shells and maps. The rooms themselves were redolent of his half sister: beachy and rumpled yet stinking of beauty. When seventeen-year-old Shelley finally ticked down the stairs with a cigarette sticking out of her mouth, she hollered, "Whooooooop! You made it!" and threw her arms around his shoulders. Nick didn't return the embrace; he was struck with an awkwardness he hadn't foreseen. It was going to be the two of them in this big house, alone, all summer?

That night Shelley had several friends "roll by," people she'd met years ago at family clambakes with her grandmother and the other skateboarders and tie-dye-wearers they'd picked up in the streets of Oak Bluffs. Five teenagers sat around the rope-covered coffee table, listening to some horrendous jam band, rolling joints and passing them. Nick consistently refused the drugs. He'd told Shelley that he was self-proclaimed "straight-edge," meaning he didn't drink or smoke. He never told her that his real reason for avoiding these vices was not that he was a part of the hard-core-punk, straight-edge subculture, but rather that his mother had warned him his whole life that he was biologically predisposed to alcoholism. But then,

Shelley hadn't ever asked about it, not before or then. That first Vineyard night, he didn't say more than two words out loud the whole time.

At six the next morning, Shelley, unwashed and sleep-creased, shook him awake from his slumber on the couch. "Come on, man."

"Huh?" The light coming in from the edges of the wooden shade was dim. It was barely morning.

"We gotta get to work! Calamity Shack doesn't sleep in."

Quahogs, apparently, are a kind of clam. And they were the only kind served from the one-room building on the cliffs of Gay Head, a fifteen-minute walk from Biddy's house. The Calamity Shack restaurant served two other foods: french fries and onion rings. All of this could be bought through three small service windows. It was the only establishment on the cliffs, and therefore the only clientele were people coming to see the sights: Asian tourists streaming out of small vans, and hordes of senior citizens lowering themselves from large buses behind fluorescent vest–wearing guides.

The owner of the quahog shack, Marnie, was a year-rounder on the island who had defected from Boston in the early nineties. She liked to make puns and then not laugh at them ("Calamity Shack: a shell of a good time"). She also thought that Nick was cute and told him so as she tousled his mop of hair, catching strands of it in her silver rings. When Marnie wasn't there though, it was Shelley who was unofficially in charge.

A week after Nick arrived, Shelley announced to the shack staff, "Marnie accidentally ordered all caffeinated coffee this month, folks, so we're pretending half of it is decaf. Capisce?"

Everyone shrugged, and one of the other servers, an older guy named Ronnie, kicked open the back screen door with one foot and flung a glass bottle onto a heap of garbage bags. "We'll tell 'em it's decaf, just like we tell 'em: *Of course we recycle.*"

Three weeks later, Nick's unbearable awkwardness had sustained itself. In those weeks, he went to parties with Shelley and didn't say a word to anyone; if she didn't bring him out with her, he ate bread and cheese and bowls of cereal for every meal, alone in the kitchen, often leaning over the sink. But that afternoon, Shelley came back to the house from an early shift at Calamity Shack, utterly distraught. It became clear that she wasn't just getting fired from her beloved shack but that she might be prosecuted. "It's not my fault!" She stomped down to the basement, explaining the whole thing. "An old woman had a heart attack after drinking our coffee and Marnie is blaming *me* for serving her caffeinated. But *she's the one* who told me to lie to the customers! You won't even believe what Marnie said to me, Nick: 'Better you than me. A legal fee must be nothing for a Whitby.'"

Shelley sobbed into Nick's tense arms for half an hour, but in typical fashion, gathered herself together by nightfall and decided to have one last party at the shack while she still had the keys. By midnight, all the jam-banders/basement-hangers were there, drinking silver cans of Natural Ice beer next to the fry-o-lator, passing around a bottle of Malibu rum, rolling joints, and listening to some guitar-and-bongo crap. As usual, Nick refused all libations and cigarettes, tobacco or otherwise.

The idea to walk through the field and climb down the cliffs to the bonfire on the beach came from one of the girls Shelley said was "tripping balls." Yet off went the band of idiots, making their way through chest-high brambles and bushes.

Nick didn't want to follow them, but he didn't want to be left out any further either. As the group hacked their way through the vegetation of the vast field, thorns from unseen plants smacking their legs, exclamations echoed through the darkness. *Ow! Shit. Dammit!* Nick was in the back of the line, directly behind Shelley. When they reached the cliffs they saw the beach below them, and the orange glow of their other friends' bonfire blurring in the muggy air. Cheers issued out and floated above them. They began to climb, one by one, down the steep drop of rock.

"Here, hold this for me," Shelley said, handing Nick the bottle of rum as she turned to climb down. He looked over the cliff. How the hell was he going to get down there? Then he looked back at the field of brambles they'd just crossed. He was stuck. He couldn't go either way. Shelley disappeared before him. He sniffed the top of the bottle: suntan oil, laden with something sweet. He held the bottle to his mouth and watched as all the rest of the people clung to the side of the cliff. It had to have been forty-five minutes later when Nick finally appeared down by the bonfire.

"Nicky! Better late than never. Good work climbing down, bro!" Shelley said, her knees knocking into his shins, and her arms wrapping around his hips. He beamed back at her and admitted to all that he'd finished off the bottle of Malibu. His insides were warmed and he was wide-awake. It was like he'd been flicked on with a switch: he spoke to everyone, laughing at their jokes. If this was what being drunk was, he was crazy to have never done it before. He announced to Shelley, "You don't even know what a world-class swimmer I am! I have, like, a special gift. I'm going to swim to Menemsha right now."

Nick dropped his pants and went running, ass bare as a baby's, into the ocean. He swam out one hundred meters, then two hundred. All of the kids on the beach, all of Shelley's friends onshore, jumped up, yelling at him to come in. The small peaks of the water glimmered in the dark and appeared sharp, almost icelike. Nick was plastered. He popped up and raised his arms above his head. Although no one heard it, he yelled, "Meet you at the fish market!" Then his white moonlit back curved and arched into the sea. The crowd laughed and cursed, and returned to their fire. But Nick's head didn't pop back up.

Shelley was still watching. "Shit, shit, shit! Someone needs to go and get him. Fuck! Who's a good swimmer?" When no one answered, she roared at the crowd, "Come on!"

The Paley twins looked at each other ruefully. They had eighteen years of expertise at boating and swimming behind them. They stripped down to their boxers and trotted into the ocean, then their darkened figures cut through the water precisely. In what appeared to be seconds, they were back—Tommy Paley led the way, with Nick hanging over one of his shoulders. Eben Paley was behind the two of them, corralling them in.

Soon all three boys had settled down on the beach again, catching their breath, the Paley brothers patting Nick on the shoulders while lighting cigarettes and telling him he was one "insane mo-fo." One of the tripping girls, Tracy, squealed, and pointed up. Over the shadowy outlines of brambles on the cliff above, orange flames rose from the quahog shack. The flames were high, licking and shooting up into the air in unreal motions. Shouts then spread through the circle of teenagers: *"The shack's on fire!" "Call 911!"*

The eleven teenagers stood in awe on the beach, as the shack became nothing but a black frame amid the bleeding, orange light. Clouds of smoke multiplied at a slant, roaring and whipping into the night sky. Nick stood beside Shelley stone-faced, shoulder to shoulder. Maybe he was terrified, or maybe the water had wrung him out, but he appeared totally sober now. Neither Whitby looked at each other. By the time Engine 5 arrived from Chilmark, the shack and all the receipts and order records in the office had burned to the ground.

Months later, the cause of the fire was determined to be electrical. The legal case against the shack, and against Shelley, was dropped too, and the kids assumed that it was because of the fire. Marnie never confirmed it, but Nick and Shelley decided that because the receipts of the heart attack victim's coffee order had turned to cinders, there must have been no evidence to proceed with.

It was fall by the time the case was dropped, but the story of that night made much faster rounds throughout the island. Starting the following day, wherever Nick went—to buy a soda at the A&P or to the movie theater in Oak Bluffs—people knew him.

"You're Shelley's brother? The strong swimmer?"

"You were there the night the shack burned down, right, man?"

"The Whitby hero! Don't go out night-swimming."

The primary outcome of that night was that it identified him as a Whitby, as though it were the most regular thing in the world, as though he had a real family that he just fit into and was a natural part of. This recognition was strange at first, but ultimately, it was miraculous. And it continued to be miraculous for the next three summers that Nick spent with Shelley at Biddy's house. For what felt like the first time in his whole life, Nick had been offered something redemptive: an opportunity to be Shelley's brother, which also meant being a part of something joyful, something fun. This opportunity had presented itself, and just as Roger would have wanted, Nick held on tight.

4

———

| 2003 |

As the town car pulled to a stop on Thirty-Third Street, just off of Fifth Avenue, Mr. Kamal announced to Shelley, "We will start with a lesser house." He cleared his throat and continued. "We will begin research at the bottom of the island. Past Fiftieth Street is what was once called the Gold Coast. That is where the houses of the Astors and the Vanderbilts, the—" Shelley waited to see if he would continue the sentence with "the Whitbys." She knew that at one point her family had owned a triplicate of mansions on Sixty-Eighth Street, one for each of her three great-aunts on the Ethan side, taking up the entire city block. But Mr. Kamal changed the direction of the conversation. "The house we will enter imminently was owned by a British entrepreneur named Worth. This is the oldest and the smallest manse we'll cover in our research."

At precisely three that afternoon, Shelley had stepped out of the Grisham's elevator into the penthouse foyer. "Mr. Kamal?" Her voice came out in a near whisper. When she got to the study, she saw that the door had been left open. Behind his broad desk, he looked remarkably small; his head tilted toward the ceiling, but the white slivers of his eyes were still visible. She was once again taken aback by the absence of pupils.

"Yes, Shelley. Sit and we shall discuss our work." The last time she had seen him was on the beach in Rhode Island. Was he not surprised in the least that she was there, that she had returned to him?

She braced herself for an explanation of why she was kicked out of the vacation house and why she'd been given all that cash. Touching her own mouth, she remembered the weight of his fingers there.

He said, "I have worked out my plans for this book, and I need you to act as my full assistant now. I ask that you keep this work confidential though, to ensure that no one steals my ideas."

So they were getting right into it? She found herself sitting down, straightening her long paisley skirt over her thighs. She didn't even pause. "Should I write this down?"

"That's why I've left the laptop for you."

She opened up the computer and then a new document. No explanation or apology was offered to her. Just like that, she was back to work.

"This book will be centered on the most intriguing and worthy subject, which is, of course, the pursuit of excellence. It shall be at once a historical document and a reenactment. This part needs to be verbatim."

"Yes."

"I will focus on the most impressive city in the world and the men who made it that way. I will be writing about New York City in the Gilded Age. Do you know what the Gilded Age is, Shelley?" He didn't wait for a response.

"The project will take much first-person research to investigate relics of the history of excellence. I will need you to accompany me on these trips. The resultant book shall be the crowning accomplishment of my writing career, for I'm at the age when I'm finally ready to embark upon this."

As he said this his hand went to his forehead, perhaps in some kind of distress. She had the odd desire to go around the desk and put her hands on his temples. The past week of her life—talking to Nick incessantly about her father, barely going out of the house, even avoiding Brooke's harassing phone calls—melted away and disappeared from her concerns. It was as if the fog she had fallen into had never happened. "I'm ready," she said.

Mr. Kamal asked her to write down notes concerning the locations of the remaining Gilded Age houses they would begin by visiting. "Once there were seven hundred houses. Now we are only permitted to visit the remaining forty."

When he had finished his dictations, he commanded her to follow him out of his office. "We are beginning our research this afternoon. But there's one more thing I must tell you about our project, Shelley. This is the part I do not want you to record."

"Okay," she said, hustling after him.

"On our several research outings I need you to pretend that I am not in fact visually impaired, in any way."

She sucked in a breath. Mr. Kamal didn't know what he looked like. There was no way anyone would believe that he wasn't blind.

Now, she was exiting the town car on Thirty-Third Street as the sky rumbled. Multiple gold plaques were mounted beside the front door of the town house. She clicked on the voice recorder he'd given her and put it in the chest pocket of her shirt. Mr. Kamal announced, "Great architects have always looked to the past for rules, for discipline. If you pay attention in these houses, you may learn valuable lessons." Then he whispered, "Shelley, you must remember what we discussed. For the next hour, I am a sighted person."

Inside the house, a middle-aged woman with a bowl cut of brown hair, dressed in all black, introduced herself as a docent. The unsmiling woman began her guided tour with the ground-floor kitchens. After describing the mechanical functioning of the white enamel stove, she revealed a stutter. "I *under-under*-understand you're writing a book about our old place here?"

"No. The book shall be about the men of the Gilded Age and the creations they made. It is only about the houses in relation to how they made them; how the actions of these men changed the physical blueprint of American history," Mr. Kamal answered. "This is a beautiful kitchen. I love the layout here."

The docent was taken aback and looked from Mr. Kamal to Shelley, waiting for an explanation of how a man with no visible pupils could see the beauty of the room. No one offered it to her. She continued. "This pantry was held *enti-enti*-entirely for the silver service, which one of the butlers polished every morning. . . ."

As the tour moved upstairs, Shelley realized that the house did not seem very grand. The rooms were small wood boxes from which emanated centuries of must; the beds were short and looked hard and uncomfortable. It wasn't all that different from her family's own duplex. At the top of the stairs the guard spoke of the wallpaper. "It was special ordered from *Guh-guh-guh*-Gstaad. So much of the furnishing here were imported from Europe. The Worths had something to prove, as they were not included in Mrs. Astor's 'four hundred,' the *fa-fa-fa*-four hundred most elite families of New York who could fit into Mrs. Astor's ballroom uptown."

Although she was recording the session, Mr. Kamal had also implored Shelley to take handwritten notes, which she scribbled down furiously as the docent spoke. He appeared to be paying no attention whatsoever to the tour. He did occasionally run his hand over a banister or down a curtain though, and mutter, "Gorgeous pattern. Exquisite."

When they had reached the third floor and the docent expounded facts about the Worths' children's playroom, Mr. Kamal began whispering things to Shelley. His nose touched the back of her ear, and his breath came in humid bursts. "There is a line between work and pleasure. My work is terribly important. A great many people will be inspired by the writing of this book." It was shocking—did he know what he was doing? In the playroom were archaic-looking toys: a small bear made of smooth oak blocks and hinges, a rocking horse made of pine. The warmth from Mr. Kamal's breath was on her neck; she couldn't concentrate, and her notes were growing sparser. Panic mounted. What if she screwed up the very first trip? At least the tape recorder was on.

The group moved back into the narrow hallway, and the docent descended the wooden staircase first.

He whispered, "I know what you have always been in want of: a teacher. You are still a little girl because you never had the right teacher. . . ."

Her whole body flushed with heat. He knew just what he was doing. She'd never needed or wanted a teacher in her whole life. In fact, she'd terrorized the ones she'd had. And yet, a thrill rang up in her at the words *little girl*. Her breath caught and the docent looked inquiringly at her two-person tour as if to ask if they needed a moment to themselves. Shelley wondered this also. She was simultaneously enraged and intoxicated by the sentiments Mr. Kamal was whispering into her ear. And she was also vindicated. He had never really wanted to fire her: he wanted her. A grin overtook her face.

He motioned for her to go ahead of him and as she stepped down the first step, she felt his hands lightly patting her back, in the same flattening-out manner that he used to determine what objects were placed on a tabletop. Was he confused about the space? She held her breath, frozen. Surely he'd figure out his mistake in a moment. But soon he breathed noisily into the back of her neck again and moved his hands around the circumference of her rib cage until his fingertips hit the under-curve of her breasts. Should she speak? Scream? He grabbed her, one breast in each hand, and held her there for just a moment. Then he squeezed his hands in unison, hard and fast.

"What?" she screeched. It hurt. He dropped his hands. She didn't turn around though—the memory of the office in Rhode Island, the lips, the teeth, it stopped her. She had given him the impression that this was what she wanted. Her back was still toward him. She whispered, "Why did you do that?"

He scoffed.

She remained perfectly still. "Mr. Kamal, why did you do that?"

He scoffed again. "Women these days. So uptight. I feel badly for you." His face was stern.

As Shelley began to make her way down the stairs, her whole body was vibrating at a low frequency, right below the skin. She was simultaneously compelled to run out of the old wooden mansion, and turn and throw her arms around his slumping shoulders.

When they'd been through all the bedrooms, bathrooms, dressing rooms, parlors, and libraries, they arrived back at the front door. "And *thi-thi*-this is where our tour ends," the docent said, taking a breath filled with relief. "The dish built into this entryway credenza was used for calling cards. If a *biz-biz-biz*-businessman or a neighbor came to call and the proprietors were not home, they would simply *le-le*-leave their card in this dish—"

"No!" Mr. Kamal interrupted. "The tour is not over. We did not see the servants' quarters."

"I'm *sor-sor*-sorry," said the docent. "The servants' quarters were actually in the adjoining building, which the Worth family trust no longer owns. And those quarters were demolished when that building was *ren-ren-ren*-renovated—"

"No!" Mr. Kamal's two fists clenched by his hips. "I needed to see those rooms. Describe to me what the rooms looked like."

"I assume they were just plain and small."

"How did the servants enter the house? How close to Mr. Worth's bedroom were their quarters?" He demanded information of the docent that she simply did not know, until he reached out and swatted at the air. Shelley produced her arm for him to grab.

As she and Mr. Kamal walked outside into the wet June air he asked, "Did you take down all the notes about the servants? Those facts are vitally important. What a disappointment to not see those rooms."

She had not, in fact, written down a word of that information. "Yes, of course."

It was raining in heavy sheets and neither of them had brought a proper coat or an umbrella. The driver was due back exactly an hour after he'd dropped them off.

"Do we have six minutes to wait?" Mr. Kamal asked.

Her watch read 5:54. His abilities were uncanny. "Six minutes exactly." Her chest burned from where he had grabbed her. She felt no obligation to speak. When she stepped outside, she thought of her mother and pictured her in a hospital bed, alone. This was the first time she'd pictured her that day. And the other daily guilt she was now used to fighting, the voice of reason telling her that she was obligated to tell Nick about the will, had been silent for hours as well. By standing next to Mr. Kamal, by working beside him, he gave her a gift: she was unable to think about anything else.

Thirty-Third Street was underpopulated for a summer evening, just a few people quickening their pace down the sidewalks, holding their umbrellas high above their heads. Thunder sounded directly above them, and Mr. Kamal stepped out from under the awning of the Worth house, pulling Shelley until she was close to his side. The drops were cold pelts, and Shelley, wearing a sleeveless top, began to shiver.

"June is a beautiful month," he said. His head bent into the crook of her neck. "I can see things in the rain. Sounds echo against the raindrops and take a shape that I can see. Your body is visible to me now. Shelley-kins, I can see all of its innocence." His arm wound over her back and he gripped her waist.

It was confusing. The nickname, under any other circumstances, would have been laugh-inducing. But heat bloomed in her chest; she felt honored. His pink oxford was going see-through, plastered against his skin. He was so solid, so permanent. Although Ollie was the only one who'd come close to being a boyfriend, the number of boys Shelley had slept with in her life was probably upwards of sixty. She felt grateful for Mr. Kamal's off-base assumption: her, *innocent*. What must they look like to the people passing by? Quickly, she decided she didn't care, and wondered if what she actually wanted was to kiss him. The fact that he had never once mentioned her physical appearance, that he had never so much as muttered that she must be pretty, was thrilling to her. Enticing even. All she had to do was turn her head. She closed her eyes. What was stopping her from first the kiss, then getting into the car and shedding her clothing? She could be naked and slippery in the back seat with Mr. Kamal, letting him do whatever he wanted.

Soon they were being driven across town in the back of a black town car. The rain had picked up, and the fake-leather odor of the car's interior, the stops and starts of early rush hour, lulled her into a nearly meditative state. Mr. Kamal sat by the other window perfectly still.

The car pulled to a stop in front of a restaurant door covered in ivy. As Shelley got out, a drag queen in a white mesh top skipped broadly down the sidewalk. She belted, "'Oh, what a night! Late December, back in 'sixty-three . . .'" As Shelley led Mr. Kamal down the steps, he said in a soft voice, "There is nothing I love to see as much as the rain." She smiled. They were a pair, walking into the dark and narrow restaurant together.

A squat maître d' led them to the back garden. "Your party insisted on being outside in this weather! Thankfully we've already set up our umbrellas for the season." The garden had a brick-laid patio floor and was lined in blooming crepe myrtles. It was not yet dusk, but small glass string lights had been turned on, illuminating the opened purple buds. At a back table was Dr. Jillian, legs crossed, laughing with a younger man.

"*Yoo-hoo!*" she called out. "Yousef, we're back here." Shelley continued to hold Mr. Kamal's arm as Dr. Jillian hopped up from her seat. Her hair was down and silver triangles swung from each ear. "Hell-o, darling!"

Shelley, unsure who the woman was addressing, turned to look behind her, only to slam a cheekbone directly into Dr. Jillian's puckered lips.

"Oh," she muttered, then guided her husband to his seat.

When they were at the table, Dr. Jillian exclaimed, "How nice! How nice that we could all be here!" The man beside her wore an expensive-looking sports coat. He had a black curling mop on his head.

"So this is Shelley *Whitby*," Dr. Jillian said to the man, letting one arm flop against the table in her direction.

"Hasan," he said. Immediately Shelley wondered if this was the man Grace had been so worried about. "Quite the pleasure." His voice had a tone Shelley knew well, cultivated to carefully insinuate *I'm de rigueur with all intellectual trends; I view myself with extraordinary respect, tinged with a specific note of irony.*

Hasan, Dr. Jillian explained, was her mentee at the museum and just today he learned that he got a book deal for an investigative project. This book would be about jihadists in Iraq and Syria, and the motivation to destroy ancient art and historical artifacts. "So that's why we're all here, to celebrate!" She raised an empty glass that had once contained white wine.

Mr. Kamal said nothing about his own book but mumbled, "You are Saudi?"

"I'm sorry, sir, I couldn't hear your question." Hasan grinned, perhaps for Shelley's benefit. "But I've read so much of your work that I'm guessing it was an utterly brilliant one."

"Are you from Saudi Arabia?"

"Indeed. I was born in Riyadh, then moved to Chicago as a child. My parents are heart surgeons."

Dr. Jillian cooed about how fascinating that move must have been. Shelley wondered if she and Mr. Kamal were on Dr. Jillian's date?

Dr. Jillian flagged down the waiter. "Bring us some olives, and more of that yummy bread."

"That's all?" The waiter had the dead eyes of a man who'd been to one too many Blue Man Group auditions.

"Oh, oysters? Should we do it? A dozen bluepoints, if you have them."

"Two negroni spritzers," Mr. Kamal grunted. He was still and unemotional, and yet he was ordering for Shelley. A bloom of warmth spread through her chest.

Hasan explained his research trips to Damascus and what his publication season would be. They were all on their second drink with the sun setting around them, when Hasan put one arm around the bony middle-aged shoulder of Dr. Jillian, who in turn leaned into the younger man.

Now it was confirmed: this was certainly the man Grace had seen in her own kitchen. Hasan kept his arm there, and Shelley crunched ice. Did the Kamals have a marital arrangement? The rain had let up, and the patio was remarkably quiet. Mr. Kamal, who had been nearly silent for over an hour, couldn't see what was happening. What did Mr. Kamal know of his wife's relationship? "I'm going to find the bathroom," Shelley announced.

The patio was almost totally dark when she returned, but the two other tables had filled up. "Now, why don't you think there are jihadist movements like that, in the United States?" Dr. Jillian was asking Hasan.

"We don't know that there aren't."

Mr. Kamal snorted.

"You know the Columbine killers? There's research being done now to investigate if they were, in fact, part of a larger network," Hasan said.

"Well, I suppose you wouldn't have any insider knowledge, as the youngest among us, now would you, Shelley?" Dr. Jillian's cheeks shone with alcohol, and her hand played with the fabric of her mentee's sleeve.

"I'm not sure what kind of knowledge—"

"Well, *of course* a Whitby wouldn't know about those things!" Dr. Jillian blurted. Then, turning to Hasan, she continued, "Did you know that my husband's attaché is a bona fide Whitby?" But without waiting for an answer, the woman dug right into another engrossing question about modern-day comparisons to Tiananmen Square.

As Hasan spoke, Mr. Kamal's hand slid under the table and touched the top of Shelley's skirt-covered thigh. This movement was gentler than the earlier one in the Worth house. His hand stayed there on top of her leg in a proprietary manner, as if he just wanted to touch the thing that he owned. She had been distracted, nearly drifting off at the table, but now her pulse made her heart bang; she could hear it. Dr. Jillian and Hasan were fully engrossed in each other. There was a smile on Mr. Kamal's face, but so faint one could have argued it wasn't there.

One hour and five oysters later, Shelley was fully inebriated, at least partially employed, and felt, at that moment, awakened to the world again. She'd taken a taxi home and was swinging her keys around her thumb as she walked up Strong Place in a zigzag fashion. She loved her tiny, dignified street. She would walk into the only home she'd ever known, and Nick would be waiting for her inside. She had a job again; Mr. Kamal wanted her back. To him, she was Shelley-kins. People were there for her, and they needed her. The problems with her mother and with her father's will were not something she should concern herself with now. She smiled. For the time being, she was going to be fine.

5

Nick was wasting his life. He never left Shelley's apartment—well, almost never. There was a great big, fucked-up, needy world out there that he was totally ignoring, while mooching off his sister. He was not meant for this existence. During the day, while Shelley was out at work, he tried to keep up a rigid schedule. Roger always said a daily routine was the key to achievement, and this was one of the old man's adages that Nick took to heart. Nick did his calisthenics, crunches and power squats and at least one hundred push-ups, every morning. Then he cleaned the apartment, read, drew, ate, cleaned some more, and then it was still early afternoon. By the time Shelley returned from her bizarre job, he was desperate for another person to interact with. Most nights, Shelley's friend Grace would come over as well, and the three of them would sit around, ordering take-out food on Shelley's dime, chatting and watching old movies or *The Good Life* on TV. Grace was becoming a fixture of the Whitbys' evenings, and occasionally those nights felt almost like the old Vineyard summers, when Nick had very little to care about and accepted friendship and sprawling days. But then he'd recall: those easy days, in both his life and in the world, were over. Now everything was fucked.

It was a mid-June night when Nick was upstairs drawing in the room that he'd now claimed as his own, and Shelley screamed up, as she often did, "*Niiiiiick, Grace is here.*"

He clomped down the stairs to see the two girls in a typical position, backs leaning up against the still-broken blue settee, having one of their typical conversations about Grace's family. They seemed to always talk about that, yet in front of Grace, he and Shelley never discussed Roger or the rest of their screwed-up Whitbys at all. A nice reprieve, Nick had to admit.

"So how goes the research with Yousef?" Grace was asking.

Shelley shrugged. "So many houses of the *graaaand* old days, *dah-ling*." She made two little air-kisses, for effect, and shoved both of her hands into Grace's hair. Shelley was like that, always touching people. It wasn't that she was overly affectionate—no, it was more that she was tactile. She seemed to like to touch others the way that some people like to dig their hands into dirt while gardening. Shelley and Grace's friendship seemed slightly peculiar, as Grace was unlike the other wastoid girls Shelley usually hung around with. But that was an admirable thing about Shelley: she was, at her core, undiscriminating. One could even call her slyly kind.

"And the *assailant*? Any recon on her moves?" Shelley asked Grace.

That was what the girls had begun calling Grace's mother, who they both seemed overly interested in talking about—"the assailant."

Shelley continued, "I saw not one clue of her at the Grisham today. Is she out of town on a trip? If not, we can assume what her absence means. . . ."

"Heyo," Nick said, settling himself on the floral couch. Grace was wearing a white blouse with puffy fabric on each shoulder. "You look ready to go into a business meeting."

She blushed. It was his nightly entertainment now, making Grace blush. What else did he have to do?

He continued, "I saw the best minds of my generation destroyed by summer internships! Starving, hysterical, wearing blouses . . ."

"*Hilarious*, Nick." Her face burned while she rolled her eyes. It turned out Grace was as well-read as he was, almost, and the two of them had entered into a sort of game together, a pastime for book nerds: Nick would quote the books he'd read and see if Grace could catch the reference. He waited now, eyebrows raised.

"Who said that? Nick Ginsburg," she said with a mock shrug.

"Now you're the funny one," he said. She was all that he had, in terms of entertainment. But she was pretty good.

That night, after the three of them had finished off a large pepperoni pizza and two orders of mozzarella sticks, Shelley went upstairs to do whatever she did when she disappeared. (Nick was no longer a vegetarian since coming to Shelley's. It was too difficult, really, with Shelley buying all his food.) He went into the kitchen to do the dishes, and Grace followed him in there, which she seemed to like doing. She was always looking at him, somehow, or sitting or standing beside him.

She asked him the question she'd asked repeatedly, for the past couple of weeks she'd been hanging around. "Can you please, like, admit that you went to the Number Wizards camp when you were younger? I know it was you there."

He grinned but shook his head. He remembered her from there too. There had been a handful of girls, and she was certainly the only chubby brown one. But not only did he not want her to know about his nerdy past, he also wasn't ready to let her in on any more identifying details about his life than he had to.

"Grace, I've actually been meaning to ask you something. Do you know this guy named David Kippling? He went to Demming but graduated a few years ago. He's, uh . . . He's involved in some cool political stuff I think you might like."

"David? I don't know him . . . ," she said. "Should I?"

He nodded slowly. For the past week, he'd been wondering if maybe Grace could help him, if maybe she was an opportunity. "Yeah, David's group, they have these activist meetings downtown. They're called GAG—stands for Gentrifiers Against Gentrification. It was a bunch of Demming kids at first, but now their little group is expanding into a real movement. Ever heard of them?" He picked up the last plate in the sink and rinsed a thin yellow film off of it.

"Sounds familiar," Grace said with a dubious smile. "What do they, um, work toward?"

"They're badass. They've been doing sit-ins in front of that old museum, the Doss—the one that is being taken over by ExxonMobil—I heard a while ago that David and the rest of the Gaggers wanted to turn their sit-ins into sleep-ins—like, they want to pitch tents and sleep out there. Make it a real occupation. Use their bodies to stop global corporate takeover."

Grace was silent, and Nick was fully turned to her now, trying to investigate if any ounce of her cared about what he had just said. Her mouth twitched and her shoulders scrunched up.

"Yeah, that's cool," she said. Then continued, "Have you been reading about this crazy thing that's happening with the eco-activist group called the Family?"

Nick flinched as if she'd punched him. He turned away, toward the running faucet.

"I mean, if you haven't read about it, you totally have to. They're crazy. But it *is* screwed up, what's happening to these people. They're being called terrorists even though they've never hurt even one person. And now they could be in jail for the rest of their lives. The case has the gleam of fascism all over it. I mean, remember the Red Scare?"

Nick couldn't help it. His hands covered his mouth and he was breathing heavily into his palms.

"Are you okay?" Grace asked.

With the faucet still running, he turned and began taking measured steps across the kitchen, nodding his head slightly with each step. He matched one step with one deep breath. For some reason, this action always calmed him.

Grace broke into an awkward laughter. Why was she bringing that up to him? What did she know? Maybe he'd made a mistake by bringing up anything political to her. He pivoted by the kitchen door and began pacing back toward her.

"Is something wrong?" she asked.

At this, he whipped his head up and growled, "The world is reaching a tipping point. The center cannot hold. And what am I doing about it? Wasting my life, living off my sister like a bourgeois leech."

She took a step backward. Shame filled him. It wasn't smart, the bite in his tone; Grace could be a resource for him, but she would never help him if she was afraid of him. Then he had an idea. He moved next to her and placed two hands on her upper arms. "Grace." He tried to make his voice softer. "Want to go running with me? I need to get out of the house."

"A run? Like, outside?" She lurched away, shaking her head. "I'm not a runner." One of the kitchen's two windows was open, letting in the deep blue night air. "Plus, you don't leave the house, right? For whatever grave reason?"

"I don't leave, except for at night sometimes. It's hard to be cooped up in here all day. Come with me. A quick jog through the park." He ran two hands through his curls. "I really need some company right now." She was smiling; he knew she'd come.

Ten minutes later, Nick stood beside Grace on the cobblestones of Strong Place. His sweatshirt hood covered his head and he jumped sideways down the street. The air was humid and not too hot, a perfect night to be outside. He was doing the right thing even if it was risky; he only had one life. He'd found Grace a pair of Shelley's Nikes, which he could see were at least a size too big, and he'd given her a pair of yellow Umbro shorts from the dresser in Shelley's room, which were certainly a size too small. She looked uncomfortable. But it was cute how she was trying to hide it.

"Ready?" he asked, and she let out a squeak of approval.

As they turned onto Columbus Avenue, Nick began jogging. Grace was keeping right up with him, although quickly she began breathing heavily. Normal evening traffic filled the avenue—couples walking, taxis and SUVs honking—and Nick, with his hood up, told himself the same thing he'd told himself the other three times he'd gone running: it was okay to be relaxed. If the cops were watching Shelley's apartment he would have been arrested already. If he was going to take the risk of going outside, he might as well take full advantage and enjoy it.

"You know, Grace," he said, "I'm alone in that house all day, thinking about how the world is fuckin' destroying itself: September Eleventh, globalization, gentrification, global warming. It's bursting at the seams. And I haven't even graduated from college!" He knew he was now talking too fast, jogging too fast. But it felt good, talking to someone, airing his mind. So he didn't stop. "I mean, there's a chance the economy will really crash soon, and then if capitalism falls, I guess going to college won't mean shit, huh?"

She offered a *mm-hmm* of acknowledgment. Her breaths were truly strained now as they turned, a pair moving in unison through the stone gate of Central Park, at Seventy-Ninth Street.

He continued, "I hate to admit it, but you know, it's my *duty* to admit it: as a kid, I'd always assumed that adulthood would simply come to me, arriving like a care package on my doorstep. Like, one day I'd open the door and instantly be a lawyer or an international aid worker. Did you ever feel that way? That life would settle itself out of its own accord and everything would be profitable and prosperous, even . . . peaceful? That's what *privilege* is. Growing up thinking like that. I know it's hard to admit, but you have to."

Grace let out another brief *mmm* noise, then huffed and coughed afterward. She was smiling though, with a shy kind of wonder in her face. He knew she was happy to be running next to him. But she really wasn't athletic. Nick slowed down a bit and watched her chest to see how much she was heaving. It was, he decided, a very nice chest.

They headed up the hill toward Sheep Meadow, and he suggested that they run on the grass beside the path. "Better on your knees. And makes you feel the earth beneath you. That's what I do most nights, when I'm alone."

Then they were silent and moving together. The park was fairly populated, but he didn't see a police officer anywhere: not on foot, or bike, or horseback.

"I'm glad I could tell you this secret, about my running," he piped up. "This animal activity, it's the one thing I've been looking forward to for the past few weeks. I don't even think Shelley knows I do it."

Her black T-shirt puffed up and down in rapid motion. She couldn't respond, the poor girl.

"Want to rest?"

She slowed to a stop, bending to catch her breath. "Whatever, we don't have to."

He smiled. Without thinking too hard about it, he grabbed her arm and pulled her down to the grass. "Don't you wish there were stars here? Where I grew up—well, where I went to high school—was by the beach in California. There's a riot of stars there. A fucking *riot* of 'em!"

As they sat side by side, he arched his chest out and gave a wolflike "Whooooo!" toward the sky. A few people passing on the path in front of them turned and frowned.

"So much for your paranoia," Grace huffed, her bare knees sticking out in front of her.

He poked her in the ribs. "I resent that word."

The whole city took on a peculiar calm from their perch in the park. All the usual noises warped into one ambient whir. Nick could feel the mud he'd kicked up splattered on the back of his legs. He had an idea. "Let's lay down and see if we can see even one star."

She sort of mewed again, still breathing hard, but lay down beside him. Nick, on his back, felt water seep into his T-shirt. Grace could be on his side. Her showing up at Shelley's house, and her evident interest in him—she could be the answer to his dilemma of not knowing what to do.

"What's it like to be you, Nick Whitby?" she asked.

He rolled his eyes but humored her. "Being Nick Whitby has more baggage than you can understand."

She erupted in giggles. "Well, being Grace Kamal is very straightforward."

They were silent for a few moments. But then it was a few moments too long. He had to go ahead and ask her.

"Listen, you know this thing at the Doss Museum, with that guy David and the group called GAG? I'm wondering if maybe you could go to the meetings for me, and just, like, figure out what's going on over there."

"Sure!" she said too quickly. "I'll call and tell you when we can go. But you know, I don't have your phone number."

Nick was quiet now. Opening up to her was a risk. But every day, he was wasting more time. He couldn't help but think of Roger and his corny sayings about opportunity, that it was something you created yourself. "I don't have a cell phone. I'm, uh, an aspiring luddite. . . . And I really can't go to a meeting, with all those people. What if you just came back to Shelley's place after the meetings, to, like, report back to me?"

"What's the real reason you can't go yourself?" she asked him.

Nick turned, with one arm propping up his head. Grace appeared to be investigating his face for signs of something—fear, or falseness. She seemed hesitant, and of course she would be.

"I can't tell you that. I'm sorry, I just can't. But it makes me happy that I can tell you about my secret runs. Can I tell you another secret, Grace?"

"Yes."

He moved his hand away and faced toward the sky again. "I don't know what to do . . . with my life. And every day, I obsess about that phrase, again and again. My mom used to say it when she was really upset. My adopted dad, Roger, he left us when I was in high school. He moved us all to California and then left us there, alone. At night I'd hear my mother crying through the walls. We were really alone out there, 'cause she doesn't speak to her own family—my grandparents and my aunts. She's bonkers, but she's, well, she's my mother. I'd go in there and sit at the bottom of her bed, holding on to the outline of her ankle under the blanket. Her body would vibrate, and she would repeat that phrase: 'I don't know what to do.'"

Grace was speechless. Maybe she'd never encountered that kind of desperation. Maybe she'd always been the child in her house, and it was run by real adults. It was during those awful teenage years that Nick vowed to never be like his mother. As angry as he was at Roger for leaving, Roger had continued to pick him up on weekends and take him on fishing trips out of Newport and to Dodgers games and sometimes lavish restaurants up in LA, and to heap gifts and advice onto Nick when he did. While his mother was destroyed by the separation, although he was occasionally in a wheelchair, Roger was still himself, as fine as he always was. It was mortifying, really, to both Nick and his mother, what she'd allowed to happen to her. She had always thought she had great things coming to her. If Nick had to aspire to be like one of them, he was determined it be Roger.

"I'm so sorry," Grace said. Her shoulder was very nearly touching his.

Yes—the sharing of these personal details usually worked for him. He scooted in closer. "Just trust me that I'm in a bad situation right now."

"Of course I do. I want to help," she replied.

The top of his left bare knee now touched the top of her right one. The heat of her breath bellowed against his chin. Now he had a plan. He moved a finger down the side of her unbelievably soft and cool cheek.

"I just don't know if those activist meetings are the kind of thing I'm into, Nick. I'm sorry."

His eyes closed, and when he opened them again they were glassy. She was his only recourse. He had to push. "You know that our father died? Roger. That's part of why I'm staying at Shelley's house. Did she tell you?"

"What?" Grace gasped. "I didn't know."

It seemed like tears were about to fall from her eyes. When he was this close to her, he could see that each of her features was dramatically large. Her eyes, her eyelashes. Her lips.

She said, "Shelley never said a word. When did that happen?"

He shook his head. "It was recent. It's part of why everything's all screwed up."

He put his palm on her cheek. She was staring at him with hyper-focus. "So will you go? Will you start going to these meetings and sit-ins for me, because I can't?"

"Of course I will," she whispered.

Before she'd finished her statement, he pressed his lips into hers. They were thicker than he would have expected, with more padding. It felt almost miraculous to be kissing someone again—as if his life was opening back up. He moved his hands down to her shoulders and pulled her into him, kissing her more, tilting his head and not coming up for air. He was still alive; he was still himself. From the grass of Central Park, Nick thought meeting Grace was a sign. In the midst of all the fucked-up events swirling around him, she was sent to him as a genuine opportunity. Nick's right leg moved over both of hers and he pressed her into the sopping ground, then pulled his face back.

"I met you for a reason," he said.

She giggled, and he laughed back, and then thought: *Fuck it*. Letting his sweatshirt hood fall back, he raised his exposed face to the now dark sky and he howled like a wolf again, loudly, uncontrollably, until both he and Grace fell back together on the grass grinning and quivering, and for one split second, he was happier than he'd ever been.

6

As Brooke lay on the plush white bed at the Whitby-Grand, she wondered if she would even like New York if she wasn't able to stay at this hotel when she visited. The hotel was her ultimate ideal of luxury, of comfort. If only she could come more often. If only, she thought, she wasn't there alone. But was she alone? What was pregnancy, if not a doubling of the self? She put a hand on her lower stomach; there was a bump now, a small but firm dome. "I can talk to you, but you can't talk to me, poor thing," she said aloud. There's something exquisitely lonely about speaking into a void. This is why one is meant to share this strange doubling experience with a partner. Brooke had been in New York for almost twenty-four hours. She was treating herself to a mini vacation before diving into the sibling problem. She'd gone to the Met that morning and had dinner at her favorite Midtown restaurant the previous night. All the while, through her steak frites and with each new painting she absorbed, the thing on her mind was Allie. She felt almost as if she wanted to pause her actions, to not experience anything new, without Allie by her side. It was totally unrealistic. Maybe it was a chemical thing, the fetus and the increased estrogen ramping up her desperation.

When she was checking into the hotel the previous afternoon, Brooke told the man at the front desk that she used to know lots of the employees. "Richard, the chef—does he still work here? Or Annemarie, the head of events?" The young desk clerk just shook his head. He didn't even ask why or how she'd known these people. As the man gave her an electronic key card, Brooke added, "I remember when there were actual keys for each of the rooms! Like old-fashioned metal keys."

"Huh," he said. "Wild."

Allie was always one to speak up for Brooke, to explain the things that would have been crude for Brooke to explain herself. But alas, she was by herself now. "My family used to own the hotel," she said bluntly. "I'm Brooke Whitby. When I used to stay here with the metal keys, that was back when my family owned the whole place."

"Ah. Cool, cool," the guy said, with a shy smile. And that had been it. She went shrugging into the elevator. Really, what else was she expecting? But later, when she returned from dinner, an ice bucket with a bottle of Dom Pérignon sticking out of it rested on a silver tray at the end of her perfectly turned-down bed. The general manger had left a note, written in looping script on an ivory card embossed with the Whitby-Grand logo, that read: *So happy to have you here, Brooke! Welcome home!*

She had to admit she was pleased, made giddy even, by the gesture. Classy, just the acknowledgment. She thought of pouring herself a small glass of champagne and drinking it slowly as she stared out at the bustling metropolis in the early sweep of summer. But no. She'd bring the bottle to Shelley the next day, it could be a graduation present. She didn't deserve it, not with what she was doing to her own mother, but Brooke couldn't help her empathy for Shelley. What she'd been through was so similar to what Brooke herself had been through, and it was nothing either of them had asked for. And perhaps if she came bearing a gift, Shelley would have an easier time accepting Brooke in, totally uninvited.

"Dinnnnner," Shelley called as she jumped up to answer the door. It was Thai food night. She and Nick and Grace had been having dinner delivered nearly every day: Chinese, Italian hoagies, anchovy pizza. Shelley would always pay for it with crumpled-up bills pulled from her crocheted satchel. She paid for Grace and Nick without ever asking them to pitch in.

It wasn't that Mr. Kamal paid her well, it was just that she had the cash and didn't think once of saving it. Plus Nick was family, and Grace had sort of folded herself in, feeling fully part of the team now too.

Shelley returned to the parlor carrying two plastic I ♥ NY bags, brown liquid pooling at the bottom of both.

After placing the Styrofoam containers on the floor and sticking a fork into each, she called out, "Oodles of noodles! A different kind for each!" then toasted her fork against Grace's, who was standing directly above her. It was an odd realization Shelley was coming to, that she was settling into a pleasant routine. She was not just content anymore but also, with her life filled up by the two Kamals, quite possibly happy. There were the problems, of course. But it was summer. She wanted a little more time. She hadn't known she was ever going to get back to days like this.

"Ooh, pad thai! I am *starved*!" Grace said, dropping to the floor and picking up a clump of noodles with her thumb and forefinger.

Grace had been going on again about her dumb job—"I swear this internship is making me lose brain cells. I'm not learning how to be an editor. I'm learning how to become a professional filer. Does boredom cause stupidity?"

Shelley poked her friend with one bare toe, changing the topic. "What does the assailant do for fun? I mean, do you think she's ever even had fun, or she just reads books about China all day long?"

Grace shrugged. "Jillian likes yoga."

"I bet her boyfriends like her yoga too—know what I mean?" Shelley bounced her shoulders up and down, in time with her eyebrows.

Nick chuckled a little as he took his place in the circle on the floor. He leaned over and picked up the beat-up guitar that had been resting against the now-repaired blue settee, and began plucking. In a faux deep voice he announced, "This is a little tune I call, 'Our Mothers' Boyfriends.'" Then, in falsetto, he sang: "Mysterious, it's true / Poppin' up left and right / Always news to you."

A burst of heavy laughter came out of Grace.

"Again!" Shelley shouted, clapping. Then she and Nick sang the chorus together, with Shelley adding an additional bridge at the end: "I wish mine would get one!"

Grace was laughing so hard it seemed a noodle went down the wrong pipe. She curled forward in a coughing fit.

It was relaxed yet highly intimate, as if all of them had been hanging out on that floor for years. So very like their old Vineyard summers. Shelley found herself staring at Nick, wondering how long this peaceful arrangement could last.

"What are you looking at, weirdo?" he mumbled through a mouthful of food. It had been sixty-one days since Shelley had found out about her father's death and what Roger had left to Nick in the will. The temporary utopia they had constructed there—their joyful, phoneless, mess of a household—would come falling down as soon as he knew. She still didn't have a plan of when to tell him. She surveyed Nick's angular, naive face. She remembered the quahog shack on fire. He did love her. Maybe he would let her keep the house. Maybe he could be trusted.

"Tell me, Nick Scribner Whitby, when are you going to stay here until?"

"When are you going to let me stay until?"

"I'm not kicking you out, obviously, but I'm just wondering how long Grace's father's salary is going to keep us knee-deep in pad thai."

Grace's face simmered into a deep red. Apparently she was embarrassed by the fact that their dinner money actually came from her father.

Nick shoved a forkful of noodles into his mouth, letting the bottom half of them hang down his chin. He said, "Thank you for feeding me, Shelley-kins!"

"What did you just say?"

Chewing his dinner, Nick chuckled again, "I said thanks for the grub."

"No, what did you call me?"

"It was a joke."

Shelley stood up. She yelled, "Grace, what do you know about my job with your father?"

Grace gasped. She whispered, "Nothing."

"What are you talking about?" Nick asked from below her on the floor. "What is there to tell?"

Shocks of rage ran through Shelley's limbs: this was her call to impulsiveness, this was how her truth-telling always began. She crossed her arms. "Since when do you even care what I do at work, Nick?"

Simultaneously, Nick took on his morally indignant jaw jut. He yelled, "What is there to tell, Shelley? Your boss is a creep. Is there more to know?"

And just like that he showed himself to be the same disturbed child. Everyone was a little bit crazy—Shelley knew this—but Nick, he was an extremist. He was vicious. She remembered their fight last winter over nothing, when he'd poured her coffee out on the street. Maybe it *was* time to just tell him about the will.

"Why are you even here? What stupid thing did you do? You're overreacting just like you always do. It's so typical. You need to call your home-wrecking mommy. She's looking for you."

"Don't get pissed at me for nothing." He jumped to his feet now too. His face was taut with anger.

"You're eating up all my money," Shelley said. From the evidence he left in the house, it seemed all Nick did while she was at work was draw and eat. She'd come home to the kitchen cleaned but stacked with empty cereal boxes, macaroni and cheese containers, and cardboard from the bottom of frozen pizzas.

"I was just asking about your job. Is this really about money? It's not like you to be such an insecure . . . *brat.*"

The two Whitbys froze in a sculptural position. Silence filled up the room. Nick opened his mouth and closed it, twice, as if holding himself back from speaking. He finally broke the silence. "You don't have any idea about the shit I've been doing or the reason I have to live here. And as for your little self-righteous attitude: you're a personal assistant to a rich asshole. You're just sucking the dick of the rich, just like everyone else. You are a whore for the goddamn system."

Then Shelley said the thing that constantly lurked under her daily thoughts. "Our parents have abandoned us, and we're fucking broke. If I am sucking any dicks, I'm doing it for you."

Nick spun around and muttered, "You know nothing about my mother," and punched the coffee table, hard, with his right arm.

"Nice job," Shelley spat.

When he whimpered and cradled the baby bird of his right fist, Shelley threw down the fork she'd been holding; it clanged against the hardwood on the edge of the room. She continued, "Grace, tell your boyfriend he can call his mommy whenever he—"

That was when the doorbell rang. The three of them looked at one another.

"Who is that?" Grace squeaked. Her face was wide with alarm; she hadn't moved a muscle during the whole fight.

"I didn't invite anyone."

"Me neither."

"Don't answer it?" Shelley suggested.

Grace was standing up. "I'll get it."

"Wait!" Nick screeched, still clutching his hand. "Don't."

"Just go upstairs, Nick," Shelley said, suddenly calm.

Grace looked from one Whitby to the other.

"I'm not here." He ran up the stairs.

Shelley put her fingers to her lips as she walked through the kitchen and peered through the peephole. "Shit," she said. Of course this was happening now, just when Nick was throwing a massive fit. The knock came again. All Shelley wanted was some peace. She wanted a few weeks, a month, when no one died, no one fought, and everything was stable. She could feel Grace right behind her back.

A low-pitched, infuriatingly assured voice came through the door. "Shelley, are you there? You need to let me in."

"What's going on?" Grace whispered. Her constant questions. She could really be aggravating.

Brooke, standing out on the street, said loudly, "I have news about your mother. Let me in so we can talk about it." Shelley's stomach dropped. She considered not letting Brooke in at all; if she didn't hear the bad news, then it wouldn't exist. But even she didn't have that kind of willpower. She turned to Grace and said in a stern whisper, "The person coming in is my half sister. She doesn't know Nick is here. And you cannot, under any circumstances, tell her that he is. Understand?"

Grace nodded, her jaw slung wide in confusion. Shelley opened the door.

"Hey." Brooke, in ugly sneakers with a pastel sweater tied around her neck, shouldered her way inside.

She stood in the kitchen, and Shelley just looked at her. They were silent.

Grace stuck her hand out. "I'm Grace."

"Oh, sorry." Brooke gave an awkward laugh and shook Grace's hand. "I'm Brooke. Shelley's, uh, sister."

Shelley felt stunned. And anxious. "So?" she said.

"So what?" Brooke gave Grace a knowing glance, as if to say, *Isn't this typical Shelley behavior?*

It was too much. Shelley said, "What's going on with my mother, Brooke? You can't just say something dramatic like that and then not follow up." Her tone was sharp, and she noticed Grace flinch.

"No, no. Your mother's fine, sweetie. Well, she's in the hospital still, but she's stable. We just need to talk about a plan for the future. You haven't been calling me back, at all, Shelley. What else could I do but come to see you?"

Shelley sighed and only realized then that she'd been barely breathing. "Jesus. Fine, come on."

When the three women were settled on the couches in the parlor, Shelley realized that there were traces of Nick everywhere. On the floor lay three Styrofoam containers with three forks. His sneakers had been kicked into a corner by a bookshelf. Stacks of his drawings were on the coffee table right in front of them, precisely drawn maps of various New York City neighborhoods, a profile view of Grace with one exposed shoulder. Yes, there were telltale signs of him everywhere, but this woman, this near-stranger, could never know that.

Brooke and Grace were making small talk.

"A friend of Shelley's?" Brooke asked.

"Yes! I mean. She works for my father—"

"I didn't know you had a job, Shelley."

"You'd be surprised what I can do," Shelley grumbled.

Brooke clucked her tongue. "No, I wouldn't! I think you can do any-thing you put your mind to!" She pulled the champagne out of her leather tote bag. "And, I am so proud of you for graduating. My smarty-pants little sister, a college grad. Here, this is a little gift for you."

Grace piped up, "But didn't you graduate this—"

"Thanks!" Shelley cut her off. "Thanks, Brooke." For once, Grace seemed to take a hint. She looked at the floor.

Brooke smiled and said, "So . . . still no word about Nick?"

"I thought you were here to talk about my mom."

"I am, yes. But we need to discuss the other thing as well."

Grace leaned in, as if she were part of the discussion. As if she had any imaginable right to be there.

Brooke reached her hand out to touch Shelley's. "I know this is hard to deal with, but your mother needs help. I have the doctor's information."

Shelley yanked her hand back. Brooke had been a distant yet stable presence in her life for so many years, always taking her aside on the Vineyard and at family gatherings to tell her harsh news in a gentle manner. Logically, Shelley was grateful. But at this moment, she just wanted Brooke to leave.

Brooke continued, "What we need to do is to figure out a way for her to be transferred to a hospital in New York."

"What happened to your mother?" Grace said. "My parents know lots of good doctors here. What can we—"

"This is a private matter!" Shelley barked. She quickly regretted it. But who knew what Grace might pass on to Mr. Kamal, in her steady stream of unhampered verbal blather. She said, "Can you, like, let us have a family discussion in here?"

Grace didn't move at first, then said, "Right. I'll just go into the kitchen."

As soon as Brooke and Shelley were alone, Brooke tried again to get her to set a date to pick up her mother, or at least have her transferred by ambulance to New York. But Shelley kept shaking her head. She couldn't find the words to describe how impossibly difficult the whole process seemed. So she simply didn't say anything. After a long ten minutes of this, Brooke hissed, "I'm sick of this! This is your mother and not mine. This is not my responsibility. I am going to give you the doctor's card and then you're going to call and arrange for the transfer." And with that, she stood up and slammed the tiny card down on the coffee table.

"Wait." Shelley's word came out as a sigh. "Wait. You say that this is the best hospital for her to be in? Then keep her there. I'll come visit. I'll come in a few weekends, when I don't have to work."

Brooke's tiny body seemed to wilt with relief. "Thank you. I'll buy the ticket right now," she said, fishing into her tote bag for her cell phone. "What weekend can you come?"

As Brooke was on hold with Amtrak, Shelley said, "Grace and I were just about to leave when you arrived. 'Cause we have, like, plans and lives." She got up and led Brooke by the shoulder into the kitchen, where Grace was sitting, head hung, on a stool by the counter.

"But when can you come to Boston?"

"Soon. Two weekends?"

Brooke pointed to the phone and mouthed, "Finally got an Amtrak person. Yes, hello?"

"We need to leave," Shelley screeched. "Brooke, you can make this phone call later." She opened the front door.

Brooke was shaking her head while she pointed to the phone. Then she put a hand on Grace's shoulder and said, "I'm staying at the Whitby-Grand until tomorrow. If you guys find out anything about Nick, or think of any place he might be, please let me know right away."

Grace, baffled, nodded. Brooke kissed Shelley on the cheek while still on the phone. "Good to see you, Shells. And happy graduation! I'm so proud of you. I know your mother is too. I'll call you with the train ticket information later." As she walked out, she yelled over her shoulder, "Ciao-ciao, babe!"

"Ciao-ciao," Shelley said in a soft, exhausted voice.

As Brooke made her way back to Columbus, she rolled her neck left and then right. She had the sinking feeling that Shelley was not going to make it to Boston as she'd promised. She wondered if this was really her problem anymore, any of this extended family. In the darkening air, she raised her arm to hail a cab back to the hotel and realized that her father's problems, and thus her father's judgment, were gone now. They disappeared with him. What could she do now that she couldn't have let herself do before?

It had been a full six years since that morning when Roger had shown up on her Beacon Hill doorstep at six. Brooke had answered the door in her summer-weight tartan pajamas, but she had already been awake for a while. As the door swung open, Roger gruffly muttered, "Why didn't my key work?" As Brooke registered the fact that the man standing in front of her was her father, she simultaneously felt panicked: Allie had slept over and was probably plodding her way to the kitchen at that very moment, in her own set of matching pajamas.

"Dad?" Brooke managed to say. "What are you doing here?"

"I'm here to go fishing." He forced a chuckle, and let himself be hugged by her. He had done this a few times in the previous decade, showing up at the house unexpectedly. It seemed he was aware that although he was not a resident, the house definitively belonged to him and he could claim use of it whenever he pleased. But every time he'd shown up had also corresponded with a minor breakdown in his daily life.

As she stepped back to look at him, Brooke was overcome by a feeling of desperation. Perhaps adult children who saw their parents all the time didn't notice the aging process so starkly. But she hadn't seen her father in more than a year, and as he shuffled and hauled himself into the house, his brown leather monogrammed suitcase dragging behind him, he looked fragile, weak, and very old. Roger's khakis and checkered button-down shirt were rumpled, and a growing hump protruded from his back. What was left of his hair was matted down, and Brooke noticed that his arm was trembling more than it used to as he braced himself against the mahogany console in the entryway. He had been diagnosed with Parkinson's disease a few years before, but Brooke was under the impression the disease was still in stage one. Now she wasn't sure.

Once they were sitting at the white aluminum table in the kitchen, a stovetop espresso pot whistling, Brooke asked him again, "Why are you here, Dad? Was this a planned trip?" And then, more quietly, she said, "Is everything okay with your wife?"

Roger sighed. "Oh, little chicken," he said, using a pet name he'd used for both her and Kiki when they were small. "I'm here to regroup. I need to think about new business prospects, and I've always thought best out on a boat on the Boston Harbor. Come fishing with me this afternoon."

Brooke shook her head, acknowledging that her father was simply not going to answer her direct questioning. "I have to go to work today . . ." She trailed off. His arm continued to shake as it rested on the tabletop. "When was the last time you went to the doctor?" she asked. When he didn't answer that, she tried again, "Does Susan know that you're here?" At that moment, Allie entered the kitchen in her pajamas, her hair large and fuzzy from sleep and her eyes still narrowed.

"Oh!" she exclaimed, shocked by the unexpected body in the room.

"Allie, this is my father. Roger."

Roger looked Allie up and down, and then, without giving his daughter a skeptical look or skipping a beat in his Roger-has-an-audience act, he simply stuck out his hand. "Nice to meet you, m'dear."

Brooke looked from her girlfriend to her father and tried her hardest to keep any expression at all from unwillingly invading her face. Maybe her father was simply too old to question why Allie would be there so early in the morning. Maybe in his generation, a friendly sleepover on a weekday between two thirtysomething women was commonplace.

"So nice to finally meet you!" Allie gushed, and Brooke withered in her chair. After rushing through the rest of the coffee drinking, and shooing Allie out of the house, Brooke—dressed in scrubs and Reebok sneakers—pleaded with her father to not go fishing by himself while she was at work at the hospital.

"I'll have a captain with me, Birdie, I'll be fine. It's what I came here to do."

Hours later, after Brooke had spent the day practicing yogic calming breathing while sitting behind the nurses' station, after she had called her home phone repeatedly without anyone answering, she couldn't take it any longer. It would be dark soon, and she had no idea what he was capable of getting himself into. He was in sincere denial about his age, health, and abilities. She could have called his current wife and asked her what the hell was going on. But instead, she called Allie.

"Als, I'm at work for another two hours. Can you drive down to the Navy Yard in Charlestown and see if anyone there has taken my father out on a bass-fishing excursion today? I can't get in touch with him, and, I just don't trust him to keep himself safe."

By nine thirty, Brooke was rushing back into her own house, convincing herself over and over not to lose it, when she heard friendly voices arising from the kitchen. Her shoulders fell with sincere relief. Allie and her father were chatting jovially. As she tiptoed down the narrow front hallway, she heard the occasional clink and pouring sound that made it clear they were drinking together.

"A business venture got unalterably screwed," Roger huffed. "There was a faulty ceiling put into every building that I built, in all these damn freeway-side mini malls, from Bakersfield to San Diego. And my wife, Susan, she didn't understand the kind of blow this was. She thought it was my fault. That all that money lost was my fault. But what do I know about ceilings! I kept telling her, 'Susan, my time left on this earth is limited. I can't spend it fighting with you about a shitty ceiling.'"

Brooke held her breath and sunk down to the floor in the darkened hallway. She would listen as long as she possibly could. She heard more pouring and wondered if it was her father or Allie who was doing the honors. Allie knew that her father should not be drinking.

"That's an enlightened attitude, Roger," Allie said thoughtfully. "But do you think she deserves a chance to calm down about it?"

"That woman was never calm," he grunted. "I used to like that she was ambitious, or, that she supported my ambition. But now it's clear that she's a pusher. I still want to do big things. I haven't yet made my grand mark on the world, the one that the later generations will be talking about. But there's no way I can do it with her breathing down my neck. I'm too old for that charade."

"Hmmmm," Allie responded, in the most neutral way possible. Brooke carefully got to her feet again. She would save her girlfriend from this typical Roger drama.

Then her father spoke, more quietly. "Lemme ask you something," he said. "What are you to my daughter? It's clear that you sleep in this house. In my house."

Allie paused. "On occasion, I do sleep in this house," she said matter-of-factly.

"So you sleep here. And . . . you do everything that goes along with that?" Roger asked.

There was a silence that Brooke could only imagine consisted of Allie nodding.

"Listen, kid," Roger said, "I appreciate happiness. I sure do." There was another pause, some more ice crunching. "But have you ever considered that Birdie is fragile? That her little brother's death, and everything that happened with me and her mother, that those are the reasons why she's decided to . . . to act out with you? It's not in her nature. It's not in her blood."

Brooke would have screamed if she had the capacity for breathing. It was a horrible thing to say. And after what Allie had done for him already, on that very day? She was spending her precious time sitting there drinking with an old, sick man. Allie said nothing, but Brooke heard a screech from a chair. She was getting up.

"Things have changed, these days," Allie said firmly, yet also respectfully.

"I didn't mean to offend you. You seem like a nice girl. It's just that this kind of life, or lifestyle, is so damn hard. And our Birdie wasn't made for that."

"She *was* made for it, Roger," Allie said.

And with those words she might as well have harpooned Brooke in the gut. Brooke sunk to the floor again, her whole attitude radically shifting. How dare Allie say that to her own father, without her permission.

A glass clinked. Allie putting hers in the sink? And then footsteps. Brooke stayed exactly where she was. She would stay there for another hour, listen to her father slowly rise and shakily walk, with the pace of an invalid, to the old maid's room in the back where they had a guest bed. When Brooke finally went back to her own room, Allie, in bed already with a book and a blank face, asked her how work was. Brooke simply mumbled that it was fine.

The next morning while Brooke was making a smoothie for breakfast, Roger hobbled out of the maid's room with his back stooped and his leather suitcase dragging behind him.

"Are you headed back to California, Dad? Such a quick trip?" Brooke asked, standing next to her blender.

"No, no," he grumbled, head down, not looking her in the eye. "I'm going to stay at the hotel—going to the Copley. You're busy here. Don't want to bother you." She watched as he slowly shuffled across the old tile floor. Her stomach dropped, and her heart began to fall beside it. She didn't have the wherewithal at that moment to even protest. Her father was disappointed. Or disgusted. Brooke decided then that she would never tell Allie she had heard the conversation from the night before, but she would, she told herself, never fully forgive her either.

Now, six years later, Brooke exited a taxi in front of the Whitby-Grand and realized that she could change her mind. Since that morning when her father left, Allie had moved into her home and out of it. Both of their careers had taken off. Brooke was having a baby. As a doorman in a navy-and-gold suit offered her a "Good evening, ma'am," she stepped into the hotel lobby and considered that maybe, with her father's death, all the pain he caused could be forgiven. Maybe Brooke could not only absolve Allie but absolve herself of her shame. Perhaps, amid all her sadness, this turn of events offered a new kind of hope.

7

———————

"It is a true disgrace that so many of the stately mansions are gone," Mr. Kamal said as he and Shelley walked arm in arm down Sixty-First Street. He had yet to kiss her on the mouth, but there had been other things. They were a pair now, and content within it. The June rains were slowing down, and it had only been drizzling on and off in the afternoons. "Many of the larger mansions were destroyed in the 1960s, directly before the historical protection laws were passed. What this city would be like if those buildings had been preserved. Imagine the greater stead of Americans . . ."

"Why were the buildings destroyed?" Shelley asked.

"Simply too expensive to maintain. It took extensive resources to run them. Coal would be shipped into the basements via special railway lines. Tons of it was needed to heat every room of the mansions, and to run the lights and the newfangled elevators."

They walked up to the building they were researching that day, the Weld mansion. It had construction scaffolding around the entryway. "Couldn't they have converted them into apartments? Split them up?"

"Rehabilitation was not valued in those days. The base stock of architects wanted to level the buildings and then begin again, in the ever-popular, vulgar, modernist style. And please, Shelley, there is no grand *they*. Be more precise in your spoken language."

She nodded and unlinked her arm from his as they ascended the steps. They had been steadily visiting houses for weeks. Since Nick had insisted that the Strong Place apartment remain without a landline, she would wait every morning for Mr. Kamal's call on her cell phone. For a while she had been very careful to not silence his calls, as she was so used to silencing Brooke's, but ever since her surprise arrival, Brooke's calls had been less and less frequent. So Shelley now answered her phone on the first ring. Mr. Kamal would pronounce the exact time they would meet at the Grisham, then they would proceed to the assigned house of the day. He continued to treat her with an air of disdain for the length of their day's work at each house. But once they were finished with their research, his attitude would shift. Since the grabbing incident at their first house visit, he had never so much as grazed her body during their research outings. In fact, he was quite brusque with her until they returned to the Grisham. This was part of their game: always the sting, then the soft touch. The mansion they approached on Sixty-First Street was, like many of the awe-inspiring buildings they'd visited, designed in the beaux arts style: wide stone buildings with flat roofs. But this monstrous house had an odd ornamental addition of a tower rising from the back of it, baroque and overblown, with gargoyles and angels adorning the rim. The juxtaposition of the architectural styles made the whole house look bric-a-brac, a garish palace that was inexpertly put together.

Many of the houses they visited had been turned into museums, but there were a few houses, such as the one they were banging the knocker of, that had been preserved for no apparent purpose. The furnishings were all there and in place, but the buildings themselves were vacant of people. Shelley hadn't known that places like that existed within her own city.

A strikingly wrinkled man opened the door, the groundskeeper or building manager. "You the architect?" he asked Shelley.

Mr. Kamal extended his hand. "Yousef Abdel Kamal, here to conduct research." Shelley watched the groundskeeper grab the top of Mr. Kamal's hand and hold it awkwardly, before noticing the location where Mr. Kamal's eyeballs would have been. A gulp traveled down the man's neck.

"You can walk around for three hours," he grunted, then clomped away in his work boots.

A grand foyer spread out before them. This house, like nearly every house they'd visited, had a staircase that curved around itself until it spilled out onto the ground floor, as if the stairs themselves were engaged in a deep bow.

Mr. Kamal cleared his throat. "Every time you enter a house, Shelley, consider the threshold and its relation to the street. All of the houses I built abide by the maxim: the more private the entry, the more proper the home." He paused. "A spiral staircase here?"

"Yes."

A strange thing had been occurring since they began conducting their "research." Mr. Kamal seemed able to sense the way the spaces looked. Of course she'd noticed it before, his peculiar ability to know what was around him. But now it was much more pronounced. In the first few houses, when he'd guessed how large the windows were or what colors the ornate drapery was, Shelley had gasped and asked him how he could tell. "I have very strong facial vision," he'd answered, and explained to her that his nerves were able to sense the shapes of things in front of them. But she found herself inspecting his eyes as they walked through the houses, searching for a sign that he could actually see, that the whole life he'd created was a ruse. Implausible, she knew, but she couldn't stop herself.

Now that Shelley had entrenched herself with the Kamals, both her days and her nights were activity filled. At dinnertime, Grace would lie on the floor of the Whitby parlor, eating takeout and talking incessantly to Nick about whatever party or meeting she'd been to recently. Grace's endless presence had allowed Shelley the opportunity to entirely avoid the thing she needed to tell Nick. Grace allowed her to stave off the catastrophe for a little longer.

Now, in the Weld mansion morning room, Mr. Kamal commanded sternly: "Speak to me." Shelley began to play her part, describing the details of her surroundings as efficiently as possible. This was quick and hard work, for if she paused for a moment to decide which part of the room to recount first—the small breakfast table or the mahogany sideboard holding the grapevine-patterned drink dispenser—Mr. Kamal would yell "Speak!" and then berate her for wasting his time. She had, at this point, depicted countless rooms to him. There were petit salons that were entirely mono-chromatic, with peach-painted walls, peach panels of art, windows dressed in sumptuous peach drapes. These rooms were beside grand salons, ar-ranged similarly with the accoutrements dressed in one color: sky blue or emerald green or burgundy. These salons had a few pieces of art displayed on the walls but were next to designated gallery rooms, some boasting lesser-known Rembrandts and Monets and Manets. Porcelain urns were everywhere: large ones stood on their own in corners, smaller ones sat atop bureaus and side tables beside golden clocks with swinging pendulums. The rooms, she had begun to believe, were hidden treasures in the midst of the metropolis. She cherished the act of simply standing in the middle of them.

The pair had visited seven mansions so far. During each visit, Mr. Kamal would yell at her, insisting that she wasn't working fast enough and that he wasn't getting as far into his research as he needed. His cheeks flared, and occasionally he would break into a sweat. His frustration was honest, visceral. Rather than indignant rage, her typical old reaction, Shelley felt concern for him. She was humbled by her desire to do better.

"What am I missing?" she had asked squeakily, while standing in the Johnson house on West Forty-Sixth. She was doing what she was told to the best of her abilities.

"I want to know the lines of the room, the angles of the corners. The pitch of the vaulted ceilings! You simply are not educated enough to de-scribe these things to me."

He was right. She wasn't an architect; she wasn't even an artist. What he needed was to be able to feel the outline of a room, to have a three-dimensional archetype of these spaces. What he needed was a sculptor or a model maker. He must have had assistants who could do things in the past. And perhaps Shelley would have been able to describe what he wanted more accurately if she were clearer on the goal of this project. She didn't entirely understand the objective of the "research." He often re-peated that he wanted to write the "seminal book on the Gilded Age in New York City," but it was unclear what he was gaining from walking through the rooms in these old houses. His frustration was also amplified, Shelley suspected, from the fact that he was inside houses that were, for all modern intents, art galleries, and he couldn't see the art.

Throughout all of his growling and pushing as they crossed through the rooms of the Weld mansion, Shelley reminded herself that he was an orderly, consistent man. While they were in a house, she was his worker. But after the research was done, he would come to her.

Two days earlier they had been in the back of the black car, returning from the Eaton mansion. He sat beside her with one hand on her right hip, and she beamed. His torso twisted so that he could rub the smooth surface of her stomach with his other hand. He did this to her often, after work, and Shelley had come to think of it as an animal gesture of affection. Two days ago though, he'd asked her a new question. "Have you ever been pregnant?"

For the amount of sloppy sexual encounters she'd had, for all the times she had not protected herself, Shelley had, in fact, never been pregnant. And she told him so. His questions were inappropriate, yet she was honored that he cared enough to ask.

"Hmm." He'd appeared satisfied with the answer. She felt drawn into his body by a brutish, earthly force.

After two hours of work in the Weld mansion, she was exhausted. The dining room, which was the size of a regular New York City apartment, had a too-small table in the center of it, set for only four, which gave off a lackluster effect. This kind of gaffe had begun to offend Shelley—it wasted the grandeur of the space. Mr. Kamal rested his hand on the tabletop and said sternly, apropos of nothing, "I am doing something original with this book! This is a feat that no one has accomplished before, and it will be acknowledged in the future." He spoke as if he thought someone doubted him.

"Yes," she said.

He moved one hand across the back of a carved wooden dining chair. "History has shown that if I struggle to collect my research—the harder it is to get to the bottom of a subject—then the better the final project will be. Which may render the meager research you've been able to do for me beneficial." Then he growled, "Walk to the tower."

They made their way to the third floor, then began wandering through the back of the house and slowly climbed up the tower stairs. Soon she stood in a sparse apartment, with all the furniture covered in clear plastic sheets.

"This was the quarantine ward," Mr. Kamal explained. "In years before antibiotics, this room was used to quarantine the sick. Of course, it would have been available to only one of the four people in the immediate Weld family and no one else. But this room would have been a lifesaver to one of them."

She entered the unused kitchen. All the counters were covered with a thick layer of brown dust, as was the old-fashioned farmhouse sink. Did the plumbing still work? Mr. Kamal walked behind her, and she was careful not to pause for him. He followed her into what was meant to be a bedroom. The oddly small bed was high off the floor, but instead of being covered in plastic, it had white sheets draping off the sides of it. "Do you think the room was ever used?"

"Speculation like that is not necessary," he said. "This certainly would have been in use when tuberculosis was a killer." She saw that his body was angled toward the bed and she waited for his command to describe it. But instead of his usual order to speak, he sat down and placed his two hands beneath him, like an expectant little boy. After a moment, in a tone less gruff than usual, he said, "Strip."

"Excuse me?"

"Take off your clothes, Shelley. Begin by removing your pants."

What was he doing? What about the separation between work and play? Anger ran through her. He shouldn't be allowed to break his own rules.

"Do it now."

Adrenaline shot through her blood. She was trembling. This was the kind of bold thing that made her who she was. She couldn't shy away now. She unbuttoned her jean shorts and let them drop to the floor. She wore pink cotton underwear with a small bow at the front. As she stood there, half-naked, she recalled the groundskeeper's heavy boots. She would certainly be able to hear if the man was coming up the stairs.

"Take everything off but your shoes," Mr. Kamal said.

So it was happening, finally. And yet, in the moment, it was nowhere near as enticing as she'd pictured it would be. Was she about to have sex with this aging man? She would begin the motions and then it would be fine, just as she'd done with those Choate boys in high school and dozens upon dozens of times since then. She kicked off her underpants and removed her soft-gray T-shirt to reveal a lavender bra, unattractive in its supportive structures. But, then, he would never know. She stood in front of the one rectangular window and dust streamed around her in the afternoon light. Naked save her leather sandals, her figure made a stark shadow on the floor: the droop of her breasts and the curve of her waist outlined in black. She longed for coolness against her stomach and the tops of her shoulders, but the staid air in the attic room offered only heat and moisture. "I'm—" She was unsure of how to alert him that she'd followed his request. "I've done it."

"Now speak," he ordered. "Describe the room to me."

He faced her from the bed as if he were watching, and again she looked around the apartment. Why wasn't he coming over? She was naked and waiting—ready.

Perhaps she needed to insert herself, ever so slightly. "Can I come over to you?"

"Speak from there!"

She described the dull room: the folding wooden bedside table, the trunk at the foot of the bed. The sheets of plastic over the bureaus obscured all structural details though, and she had to scrape the bottom of her imagination to keep speaking. "The floorboards are striated and look as though they're made of oak." It was a tiring game, but soon, she hoped, it could have a happy ending.

He said, then, in an unwavering voice, "Shelley, tell me. What's the most shameful moment of your life?"

Even though she should have known better by that point, she was taken aback. The direct questioning. It was unrelentingly intrusive. Yet a part of her wanted to be asked these questions. She nearly responded, *You. In the office in Rhode Island, when you pushed away my advances. On the stairs in the Worth house, when you grabbed me.* Those moments had been humiliating. But if that was shameful, what was her explanation for standing where she was standing, naked and exposed? No one was forcing her to be there. She closed her eyes and tried to remember any other moment of true shame. Bodily noises escaping in a classroom. Throwing up in a closet from drinking vodka. That childhood night waiting for her father in her purple crushed-velvet dress. That night was the shame, her greatest one.

"I don't get embarrassed," she said.

He seemed to be considering her claim silently.

"And you?" she ventured.

He chuckled then and, rather than answering, gave her a soft command that sounded more like a suggestion. "Turn around. Face the window."

She turned obediently and heard the bed creak. "What do you see outside? Describe it to me."

The crosshatched window was large, but the glass was so old and dirt-covered it had become totally fogged. She couldn't see a thing out of it.

"Speak," he barked.

"I can see all of Central Park. The sun is brilliant, lighting up Strawberry Fields and glinting off the water of the lake."

Then, as fast as a bull, he charged against her from behind. She heard the crescendo of his shoes and felt his weight thrust into her. The coolness of the glass smashed into her clavicle and breasts. His body consumed hers from behind, and with his arms underneath her armpits, he hoisted her up like a child as his crotch pressed against her ass. She held her breath. His forehead burrowed into her neck and he began a slight jerking motion. She could now feel his hands at the small of her back, as they worked to undo his belt.

Shelley moved her head, aiming to turn around and kiss him, but as she did that Mr. Kamal simultaneously flung his head toward her. His forehead cracked into the edge of the white wooden shutter. The noise was loud: bone against wood. He dropped her body, and stumbled backward. There was an open gash above his right eyebrow.

She shrieked at the sight of the blood.

"Shut up!" he growled, steadying himself.

"Are you okay?"

Blood formed a wide rivulet on the side of his face, running down with the force of pressure behind it. There was so much of it coming from such a small wound.

"I think you need a doctor."

The back of Mr. Kamal's hand pressed against his head and he hissed, "Abide by our agreement. Treat me as if I am a sighted person."

Shelley did not know what to do. The two of them stood, paused in inaction, her naked and him clothed, while the blood trickled off his chin and dripped to the floor. She wanted to say, *I don't think any less of you.* He remained totally silent. Soon they heard a soft banging: footsteps of the groundskeeper headed toward them. Shelley walked away from the window and calmly found first her underwear, then her shorts.

The groundskeeper entered the back of the quarantine apartment, shouting hello. Mr. Kamal came to her and grabbed her hand. He spoke quietly, apparently feeling the need to reassure her, as well. "You are seemingly like many of the girls I have had before. But, Shelley, I know you are different. Nature gave you precious seeds but the world has let them rot inside of you." The groundskeeper was approaching the room now. "I will help you, Shelley Whitby. I will find your seeds and I will make you flower."

8

Grace sat in her FSG intern cubicle like a prisoner, watching the clock on her computer. When it read 4:59, she nearly ran to the elevators. Downstairs, she busted through the glass revolving doors and headed up Sixth Avenue, weaving at quite a clip through the after-work Midtown crush. She had spent the entire previous night at an activist meeting downtown, at Judson Memorial Church, and was now headed uptown to tell Nick about it. As she pushed through bodies of sidewalk traffic, she focused not on her bleeding heels (work shoes, blisters) but rather on the most exhilarating, piercing type of ache she had ever felt. This ache stemmed directly from her knowledge of one thing: Nick Whitby was perfect. His physical being touched her in a way she had never felt before. His broad shoulders and narrow hips, his once-blond hair, his junky New Balance sneakers, and his unsmiling deportment; every part of him in-duced pain in her. The way that he kept popping up—how it had to have been him at that summer camp years ago, and then there he was, Shelley's brother—had convinced her that their meeting was mystical, something destined to be. Since the day she had walked in on him lying shirtless on the bedroom floor at Shelley's house, her thoughts had been possessed by him. She was still shocked to be Shelley's friend, but that shock was over-ridden by her feelings for Nick. When still in bed in the morning or sitting at her miserable intern desk, she'd close her eyes and picture doing the simplest activities with him: sitting beside him on the subway with his arm around her shoulder, passing high school classmates on Broadway while holding his hand, breathing in the scent of his pale skin. If she had sketched out her ideal boyfriend on a sheet of paper, then cut it out like a paper doll and watched it take on human form, she would have seen Nick, entirely. Of course, he was not her boyfriend, exactly. Not yet anyway.

By Fifty-Eighth Street she was walking away from the imposing glass buildings of Midtown toward the lower, stone edifices of the Upper West Side, the type of historic buildings her father approved of. The street was slick from earlier rain, but several people squinted in the sun by Columbus Circle, their hands raised for taxis. The city bustled around her and she felt grateful for the cars honking and the buses braking, the traffic lines painted in the roads, even for her shoes filling up with blood and the sweat collecting in her armpits. Every bit of New York had worked together to bring Nick into her life, a fact that was unimaginably lucky.

In a few short weeks, she'd fallen into a habit: in the evenings she attended activist meetings and, if they got out early enough, went to Strong Place and reported the meeting directly to Nick, while she simultaneously dug herself, daily, into a deeper trench of friendship with Shelley. She was becoming a fixture in the Whitbys' lives and her summer employment receded to a mere appointment she endured during the day. Every night with them felt like a holiday. Grace kept expecting that the next day she would return to her dull, lonely existence, but the holiday kept going.

By the time she was stationed in her usual spot on the floor of the Whitby parlor, Grace announced to Nick, who was sitting behind her: "I went to that meeting last night. The action-group meeting at Judson church."

"*Shhhh* . . . Wait for the commercial!" Shelley commanded.

The first two activist meetings Grace had gone to were in Art Park on East Seventy-Second Street, in the grassy area in front of the Doss Museum, where twenty people in their early twenties sat around in a circle. The guy Nick had mentioned, David from Demming, was there, seeming to be one of the leaders.

"People's mic!" David called as Grace walked up. The rest of the crowd repeated after him, *"People's mic!"* He continued yelling out basic sentences and the circle of people continued to repeat him:

"The purpose of this meeting . . ." (*"The purpose of this meeting . . ."*)

"Is to determine a list of demands . . ." (*"Is to determine a list of demands . . ."*)

"For this anti-globalization GAG movement!" (*"For this anti-globalization GAG movement!"*)

After the meeting, David filled her in on the background of their cause. The anti-globalization movement started with a Zapatista uprising in southern Mexico, was fomented in a rail workers' strike in France, and took hold on US soil in the shape of a chain of human bodies surrounding the opening ceremonies of the World Trade Organization meeting in Seattle, preventing the greed-fueled, neoliberal warmongers from entering the building. Now their GAG group was planning a giant march at the end of the summer, to protest the fact that the Doss Museum was closing down and the newly merged gas company, ExxonMobil, was moving their world headquarters in and building a glass tower on top of the historically protected building.

Although Grace didn't say it to Nick, the first few activist meetings she attended had been drawn out, and, honestly, boring. It felt like hours before anything of substance was discussed. She had knelt in the circle among the blond dreadlocks and amid the small girls with facial piercings, and witnessed everyone checking one another out. They all knew one another, but Grace couldn't figure out how, just as she couldn't understand the hand symbols that they made. A person would hold a triangle shape in the air and holler out, "Process point!"—which allowed that person to interrupt whomever was speaking. Other times someone would start wiggling her fingers, and then more people would do it—a form of approval or a silent applause. Every time anyone mentioned 9/11, the whole group fell silent, as if in tribute to those killed in the attack.

Now, she sat in the Whitbys' parlor, watching the television screen. Nick was in his basketball shorts, with his two calves crossed over Shelley's lap. Just like Shelley, Nick was a frequent toucher, but only with his sister. On the floor, on the couches, on the stairs; they reclined, they lay, they draped. How could people look so luxurious while horizontal? The weather was heating up, and often they wore minimal cotton clothing. She couldn't be jealous: they were siblings.

When the TV cut to a Reebok commercial, Grace announced to Nick, "So, when I walked into the meeting last night—" Now he turned toward her. "When I walked into the special meeting I was invited to at Judson church, a bunch of people sitting in folding chairs gave me the impression they were *super-duper* skeptical of me. Like, ice-cold stares."

"Ice-cold!" Shelley said in a cartoonish voice.

Nick poked his sister's ankle with his bare foot. "Go on, Grace."

"Then David from Demming said that he would 'vouch' for me. And he said something about needing 'diversity of voices,' and I was all, *Um, I go to the same college as you did, so how diverse is that, man?*"

"Show's back on," Shelley announced. Grace stared straight ahead for another twelve minutes of television, unable to focus on the action or dialogue, just aware of Nick's breathing beside her.

As soon as the show went to commercial, he asked, "So, why was this meeting special?"

"I think I got an invitation to be involved in their inner-circle thing. They want to be more radical than the rest of the protestors. But I don't think I'm hard-core enough for it anyways." She snorted.

When the show was over, Shelley clicked off the television and totally absorbed herself in a *Rolling Stone* magazine. She did that sometimes: just shut off in front of other people, signaling that she didn't care if you or anyone else stuck around.

Nick jabbed an elbow into Grace's side and whispered, "Come upstairs to my room." It was more of a command than an invitation. The words sounded miraculous, coming out of his mouth. She was on her feet in seconds.

On the table beside the twin bed that Nick had now claimed as his own lay a stack of his perfect pencil drawings of maps. They were intricate, controlled, shaded, and labeled. Nick, she thought, was undoubtedly a genius. On top was a map of Art Park, the park by the Doss.

The Doss Museum had started out as a private home and art collection of Henry Gray Doss, a steel-industry magnate who was also an art lover. In 1919, Doss died and his wife, Isabella, followed through with his wishes for their home to be turned into a museum, one that would include not only their personal European art collection but also reserve wings for exhibits centering on the varied and contrasting groups of people who populated their great American city. For more than eighty years, the museum had displayed artifacts, from eighteenth-century oyster shuckers and photographs from Lower East Side tenements, beside jewelry and designer gowns created on Seventh Avenue, next to silent films shot by Warhol and friends in the Factory.

Henry and Isabella famously desired that their museum let its "doors be open to all the people." In the early 1990s, the museum board followed through on the founders' wishes and began letting their patrons in free of charge. Then art programs for low-income youth were put in place, with classes taught in Spanish and Mandarin and Russian. The museum was a celebration of the city, and an inspiration—right up until it was forty million dollars in debt. Mobil, the New York half of the newly formed gas company, convinced the Texans at Exxon that setting up shop close to Wall Street was a smart move, and snapped up the Doss building as soon as it went on the market. The cost was chump change, to them.

Nick sat right beside her on the thin mattress, his hands tucked under his thighs. He leaned in, his chin resting on her shoulder, and Grace felt a rush of energy that made her mind go blank.

"The thing I was talking about before, about what they told me at the meeting last night, I'm not really supposed to tell anyone else. These kids take themselves so seriously—" An uncontrolled nervous giggle came out. "But they're, like, declaring themselves to be their own special hard-core group called the Family-Support Network, because they're, like, super committed to helping that group of eco-activists who are being accused of terrorism."

Nick nodded, his face stern. "How do they want to help them?"

"Well, David and the group want to turn the sit-ins that have been taking place in front of the Doss into sleep-ins. We want to pitch tents, and sleep out there. Make it a real occupation. We think that can have even more impact with ExxonMobil that way, but also raise awareness about the Family. We'll make freeing them one of our demands and use our bodies to stop this global corporate takeover."

Nick leaned back on the blue-swirl-patterned bedspread. He smirked. "You said 'our bodies.' *You* are going to participate in this?"

She hadn't even realized she'd said that. "I guess—" The words were coming out of her mouth before she really thought about it. Although something *had* broken inside of her at the meeting the previous night, she had been careful to not commit to anything. In the attic of Judson church, the dust was thick in the darkened air among a small circle of people, and as soon as David said the words *We've all discussed it, and we want you to join us, Grace,* she felt revulsion for the other clubs of her life: for the debate team, her schools, her family. Everyone else nodded, eyes focused on her, expressions earnest. They wanted her to join them. Everything she'd been doing with her life up to that point seemed like a silly, mindless contribution to doing what she'd been told. Nothing would ever change from within her idiotic campus Democrats, the Demming debaters, her other milquetoast organizations. The world was splitting at the seams, and American capitalism was the central destructive force. And these people, her friends, wanted to fight against it.

As she lay on her back beside Nick, on the second floor of the Whitby apartment, she found herself saying, "I'm part of it now, the Family-Support Network." With her words, it became true. "I'm going to do it." A honk of a nervous laugh escaped her throat again. She clapped a hand over her mouth.

Nick moved closer. He appeared to be investigating her face for signs of something—fear, or falseness.

She continued. "The dream is to get all kinds of groups involved in the sleep-in in Art Park: labor unions, and even, like, Democrats for Peace, or whatever. When they're all involved in the movement, then the march itself will have to make an impact."

He moved a finger down her cheek again, and she held her breath. Then his mouth was on hers. His fingers entwined with hers; he kissed her neck. She fingered the red scar on his arm. Maybe now he would tell her its origin story. He helped her out of her white work blouse. Grace was in her bra, in Nick's bed. It was clear that they were going to have sex. This was what she had wanted; this was her goal. And yet, she felt more shy than she ever had in her life.

Nick turned the knob on the table lamp and then Grace shed the rest of her clothing in the dark. Her hand, her adult hand, was on this man's chest and then he slid over her, turning himself into a warm, dim light. Her body moved in an automatic way it never had before, and she moved her mouth down the trail of soft hair on his abdomen. Then he was behind her, giving her pleasure, slowly. This happiness was so new to her. It was overwhelming, all of it, and she wondered if she might break out sobbing, right then. Nick moved his face to the back of her hair and breathed in. Grace didn't cry. Then three days passed.

9

| 1979 |

The repeated, echoing bangs of the shutters during Hurricane Mattias, that violent, threatening racket, was the sound that heralded in the end of Brooke's parents' marriage. Outside, the Caribbean wind shrieked through the macaw palms and slammed into parked cars. Brooke was thirteen and had been living on the island of Barbados for three months. She had moved there with her family, of course, but it didn't feel like it: in Boston she had lived in the middle of so much noise and excitement. Being the third of four children, she was overcome by daily chaos, and she loved it. But Peter had died in May of last year, and after Peter's death—after the service at King's Chapel, the burial in Brookline, and the reception at the Harvard Club, where Brooke felt herself watching the whole scene from above the crowd—the volume in her young life turned down. Afterward, her older brother, LJ, disappeared into his last year at boarding school and Kiki to her college a few hours north of New York City. And their formerly rowdy, joyous parents stopped speaking. Now in Barbados, they didn't say a word, either to each other or to her.

In August, after Brooke and her mother had gone to see her mother's parents on the North Shore of Massachusetts, just as the old Mercedes was turning onto Storrow Drive, Corney had announced to Brooke, "It looks like your father got the ambassador job. We'll move to Barbados in two weeks." And that was it. That was all the information Brooke was given. Her possessions were packed for her by a moving company. She was taken out of the school she'd gone to since she was five years old and told she'd do eighth grade at the International School of Barbados. Brooke had two weeks of sleepovers at her friends' houses, crying to them underneath shared sleeping bags as she admitted that she was terrified to live in a place she had never been before. Her friends had cried too, and their parents had come in with cookies and brownies and promises to buy plane tickets so the girls could visit one another. But Brooke never cried in front of her own parents. She knew, even at thirteen, that it was her responsibility to maintain a semblance of normalcy. At one of those final sleepovers, while Brooke was walking up the stairs from Amanda's basement, she had heard Amanda's parents talking in their kitchen. Her father said, "Carter's been looking for a way to pay back the Whitbys for years. And with the death of the boy, I'm sure it seemed that now was the time to offer Roger the ambassadorship." Amanda's mother responded, "And after that gubernatorial disaster, everyone knew they were in need."

Brooke's family had moved in the middle of hurricane season. The US ambassador's residence in the Caribbean was a big house with yellow shingles, four stories tall, with salmon-pink shutters that the staff closed every time a storm was coming. The shutters were giant, made for creatures larger than humans, and Brooke never knew how the staff was actually able to close them. Did they have poles they used from the outside, or hooks that caught the shutters from the inside? When the charcoal plumes of storm clouds rolled in over the ocean, the shutters would be instantly shut, as if by magic.

The first two months in Barbados were terrifying. The island's dirt roads and strange desert cacti; its fields of craters. She felt as if she had landed in a haunted dream, and that soon her imagination would dissolve this hallucination and return her to the stable, joyful bubble she had always known. But as the weeks added up, along with the number of tropical storms they weathered, her fear grew. It seemed that this off-kilter world was now her reality. The safety of her former life was gone forever.

Her father had to host dinners most nights when he was in town, with visiting dignitaries or minor celebrities who happened to have grown up on other Caribbean islands. "The residence," as they referred to it, was always bustling: not only with the family and the eleven staff members who worked there, but also with local politicians and business owners from Barbados and the other islands. When these people were around, Roger would cheese his toothy smile and hum even, as he organized papers and poured iced tea and snapped on his State Department poncho. When the staff or company was there, it was as if he had been inflated with life again. But as soon as other people left, as soon as the last of the staff members turned around, he would deflate. He wouldn't even look at Brooke, and Corney also appeared to be trying her hardest to just stop existing. She had her own bedroom now, where no one else was welcome. She never attended dinners with her family or the important visitors. Corney had become silent, thin, and blank. She had not asked Brooke once how she was faring in school.

Brooke was miserable. Mosquitoes loved her, and giant welts popped up all over her body, sometimes growing to the size of quarters. Although she'd gotten her period twice that previous spring, it had mysteriously stopped coming after Peter's death. By the fall, she'd withered down to eighty pounds. Although there were four other American girls in her school, they instantly decided that Brooke was stuck-up and they banded against her. She had already read all the books assigned in English class, and the math was geometry she'd learned two years prior. An embassy staff member named Derelin drove her to school every morning, and she was supposed to take the bus home after sports practice. But usually Brooke would skip soccer—the only sport offered there—and spend an hour walking home alone. She took her time as she walked along the road banks, darkening her white Keds with the sand turned to silt from the nightly rains. It was on those walks that she sometimes spoke out loud to Peter. "This is just temporary, Pete. In our family we go to boarding school, so we won't have to do a walk like this many more times at all."

By the end of November though, Brooke was beginning to make one friend, a girl named Kaylia whose parents were from Senegal by way of London. Kaylia had lived in Barbados for three years, which made her a veteran at the international school. She had heard Brooke playing "Greased Lightning" on the recorder during music class and shrieked in excitement. And so the girls began to spend time together after school, usually at Kaylia's house, which was smaller but altogether less somber than Brooke's.

The day that Brooke finally invited Kaylia over to watch her video of *West Side Story* in the embassy screening room was also the day that Hurricane Mattias struck. It had been raining for twenty-four hours, but the news reported that Mattias had been downgraded to a tropical storm.

The girls were watching Maria look down on Tony from the fire escape, when the lights flickered twice and then all the electricity in the residence went out.

"Eeee!" Kaylia screeched, hugging Brooke closely. "A blackout!" Brooke hugged her friend in return, giggling. Even she was used to the power outages, by that point. There were kerosene lamps fixed to the walls for just that reason, and as soon as the rooms turned dark, footsteps would patter down every hallway, the staff scurrying around to light the wicks. But the day Mattias struck, Brooke also heard a loud bang from outside, one that she'd never heard before. Then she heard it again: banging once, then twice.

Derelin poked into the screening room, holding a long-handled lighter. "Ready to camp out in the dark, girls?" He was a kind soul, with a constant smile. He said he'd just been speaking to Chef Cara, who reported that all the ice cream in the freezer was going to melt. "Cara says we *have* to find something to do with it."

"Have you ever had waffles with ice cream? We had those the last time I was in Amsterdam," Kaylia announced.

Derelin gave the girls a thumbs-up, but just as he was turning to deliver the order to Cara and her kerosene cooktop, Brooke stopped him. "Derelin, what's that strange banging? I've never heard it before."

"The shutters." He nodded. "*Very* odd: the fasteners on them all snapped off today. Must have been wind. No worries though. This is just a little storm. It will pass quick."

But by the time the girls were at the end of the long dining table, waffle crusts and humps of melted spumoni ice cream on large plates in front of them, the storm had been upgraded, and most of the staff, even Derelin, had run through the hard and fast raindrops to their nearby homes.

The two girls were in the dining room alone when they heard Roger yell from upstairs. "It's not fair, Corney!" It was a gravelly yell, with one word slipping into the next: a sure sign that he had been drinking.

Brooke gripped the side of the table. Her father could not do this in front of her one friend.

"I think you should call your parents," Brooke whispered. "Who knows how long our lights will be out. If you call them now they could probably still come and get you."

Kaylia looked hurt. "No way, my parents would never drive in this weather. And my lights are probably out too. You know what, while the lights are out, we could put on a play! We could practice *West Side Story*."

Brooke shook her head as she walked into the kitchen. Roger's voice from upstairs echoed through the house again. "You let it happen!" he screamed. Panic spread through Brooke's limbs.

"What's your phone number?" Brooke called through the open kitchen door, picking up the receiver of the wall-mounted rotary telephone. But before Kaylia could answer, Brooke heard that there was no dial tone whatsoever. The line was dead.

Something upstairs crashed to the floor.

"What was that?" Kaylia asked.

Brooke shook her head and grabbed her friend's hand. "Let's go to my room." But by the time they made it to the front hallway, Brooke's mother was running down the stairs in front of them, wearing a long cotton nightgown with a brown stain down the front of it. Roger stood on the landing above, leaning over the wrought iron rail. The entire entryway flickered from the kerosene lamps.

"You let your child die!" he screamed down to Corney. Brooke flinched. She wanted to cover Kaylia's eyes and ears at the same time. Instead, she simply stood in front of her friend, as if she could shield her from the scene.

Roger continued yelling. "You are his mother! You were supposed to prevent that. You let him die."

Corney was by the front door now, her hand on the handle. She displayed no emotion at all. She could have been in a trance. The shutters banged loudly, and rain seemed to be not falling from the sky but rather throwing itself in reckless waves against the windows on either side of the door. Brooke saw the palm trees by the driveway curving all the way over themselves, bending as if they were animate beings, taking a low bow. Corney, keeping her hand on the handle, turned around, and with a nearly comatose expression said, "You ignored him because you wanted to be governor. You left our baby all alone when he was dying. You are a goddamn monster."

Roger must have run down the stairs then, but it happened so quickly that Brooke didn't see him moving. When her father was next to her mother, he punched one arm forward and through the long glass window beside the door. A smack sounded, then glass shattered to the ground. Brooke found her own arms around Kaylia, embracing the torso of her new friend who was stunned into absolute silence.

Roger crouched over her mother and she screamed, prompting Brooke to drop her friend and run toward her parents, embarrassment be damned. Corney, on the ground now, was being throttled around the neck by Roger's left hand. He had a large shard of glass in the other hand, which he held to his wife's chin. Roger huffed, "That boy was my one hope. He was going to do the great things that I can't do. And I can't un-see him. He is everywhere I go. He pops up in the trees and on the beaches of this terrible island. Our son is everywhere but here. And it's your fault. You were supposed to be his mother." Roger was crying.

Brooke's mother didn't move at all. She was a stunned fish, unblinking. It appeared, for a moment, that she wanted to be speared and eaten.

"Stop it!" Brooke yelled. Then she grabbed her father's arm and pulled it away from her mother's neck.

Roger turned, apparently in shock that anyone else was in the room. Roger looked at his daughter and dropped the glass in his hand, letting it break into smaller pieces on the floor. Then he opened the front door. Wind ripped through the opening. The clattering and banging was deafeningly loud. Roger walked outside with one blood-covered arm and continued walking down the front path, through the middle of the hurricane.

"Stop!" Brooke cried. "Where are you going?" She began to follow him, but her mother, from her huddle on the floor, grabbed Brooke by the ankle.

"Don't even think about it," Corney said. "Let him go wherever he wants."

A palm frond blew into the house just as Roger disappeared from sight down the hill. As Brooke closed the door, she couldn't help herself from thinking she was cursed because her father had loved Peter more than he loved her. He had always been more animated, more excited and enlivened when Peter was around. He had loved his son—the one who was supposed to grow up to be better than him—so much that the fact of losing him had pushed him to potentially killing himself at that very moment.

A voice from the second-floor balcony of the ambassador's residence asked, "Will he be okay?" It was Kaylia.

Brooke hadn't even noticed her go upstairs. She looked up at her friend and experienced sincere humiliation for the first time in her life.

Corney, without picking herself up off the floor, said in the clearest, loudest voice she had used in months, "No, girls. That man is beyond help. He's hexed. It does not matter if he's okay."

10

| 2003 |

On the last Thursday in June, Shelley had been standing in her up-stairs hallway for ten minutes listening to the revolting sounds from behind her old bedroom door—Grace's lower giggles and Nick's high-pitched ones—when her cell phone rang. The thing that Grace had so clearly wanted to happen finally had: Nick and Grace were having sex. Expected, of course, but repulsive nonetheless. The number on Shelley's phone screen reported that the call came from the Grisham. The time read 8:41; later than he usually phoned, these days.

His even voice rose from the speaker. "Meet me tomorrow. Four in the afternoon, 301 Park Avenue. That's at Forty-Ninth Street."

"Nothing in the morning, then?"

"I said four."

Shelley was scheduled to go to Boston to see her mother on Saturday; she'd finally settled the plan with Brooke. For the week before her trip, she had been able to basically ignore the upcoming inevitable upset. Every day with Mr. Kamal had been exquisite torture. She scarcely breathed as she walked beside him in the Schneider mansion in the Bronx, or sat in the car that drove them back to the Upper East Side. He had told her that this was the week he was going to give her what she "deserved." She waited for her grand surprise to arrive, but with each added day their routine passed without any change.

Perhaps Mr. Kamal was actually more malicious than she had imagined, and what she deserved was punishment. Maybe he would blindfold her, cut off her vision just as his was cut off. And then, perhaps, he'd hurt her: hitting, slapping, spanking. But just enough for it to ache, not enough for it to disable her. The thought of it made the hairs on her arms stand on end with excitement. Surely, this *was* what she deserved. But every morning that week he had simply called her and outlined his typical orders. Until Thursday night.

When he had given her the address of where to meet, she'd had the sinking feeling she knew what building stood there, and on Friday afternoon she discovered she was correct. The street was loud and hot, and crowded with summer tourists squinting at maps and photographing the concrete and steel of Midtown Manhattan.

"May I help you, ma'am?" a red-capped bellman asked.

She was in front of the automatic glass doors to the hotel, blocking foot traffic.

"Is the address here 301 Park Avenue?"

"It is indeed."

Her shoulders crumpled. Shelley made her way into the opulent space of the lobby: soaring arched ceilings and marble-tiled floors, clusters of cocktail tables and plush upholstered chairs. This was not just any hotel, this was the Whitby-Grand, what had once been the property of her family. Maybe Mr. Kamal had simply set up a tour of the space, as research for the book. It was only so long, she realized, until the work they were doing would hit upon the Whitby name. Of course, her family had no claim to this hotel space anymore, and hadn't for years. The Davidsons had bought the last of the shares ten years prior.

Inside the fragrant lobby—lilies?—she passed beneath a massive chandelier and took a seat at a circular booth, which was also a base for a grandfather clock. Coming from the bustling street, the lobby appeared hushed, even on this afternoon at the height of tourist season. She crossed her ankles and waited for him to come through: her boss, her almost lover. In many ways he actually felt like her ward. Although he made all the decisions, it was her job to care for him.

The previous night, Shelley had barely slept, but when she had, she'd fallen into a dream where she was in a helicopter with her father. In the dream, the sliding helicopter door was open and the chopping sound of the propeller was deafening. Her father was laughing, his broad face cast in sunlight. He was younger, and she must have been too. They sat side by side in the jump seats, content, until suddenly his hands were on her bony shoulders and he was pushing her out the open door. "Stop!" her dream self had yelled. But Roger kept laughing, pushing her with all his strength into the air. The bottom half of her body went over the ledge, then she saw nothing: open sky, whitish-blue air. She had jerked herself awake.

The dream returned to her now as she watched a gray-haired woman play a baby grand piano from the balcony above her. Yes, the scent in the air was certainly lilies; the honeyed fragrance reminded her of her extended family and the hotels just like this that she stayed at during family weddings and funerals. The woman crooned, "'Should auld acquaintance be forgot and never brought to mind.'" Shelley had always thought the song was about keeping friends, but perhaps it was about the opposite. At ten after four, her earlier suspicions were becoming confirmed: Mr. Kamal had not asked her there to work. He was never late for a research trip. His voice echoed through her head, and the image of herself blindfolded could not be kept at bay. *I want to find out just what it is that you are deprived of. . . . I will give you what you deserve. . . .*

She tried to calm herself, to breathe slowly, as she pictured the most sensitive parts of her body and whether they had been properly trimmed and shaved. She was sniffing the inside of her wrist in an attempt to understand what he would be able to register, when Mr. Kamal walked through the glass doors all by himself, wearing dark sunglasses. He headed straight for her in his plodding, definitive steps, and something akin to panic jolted through her limbs. She stood up, confused. Why would she want to run from the one thing she'd been wanting, the very thing she had been working toward?

Mr. Kamal stopped directly underneath the chandelier, obstructing the flow of people. Frustrated hotel guests clucked their tongues in a particularly European manner—Danish? If they had been confronted by his absence of eyes, their audible gripes would have been sucked back with the swiftness of guilt.

Shelley steadied herself and, although timid, made the move to him. "Mr. Kamal, hello." She was surprised by the suaveness of her own voice. She was a woman, and a grown one, with the capability to follow through on her plans.

"Shelley-kins," he said with a smirk. It was confirmed then. This trip would involve no observation, no note-taking whatsoever. He held no bags. She felt suddenly, surprisingly upset. What was she, a child with spoiled expectations?

Mr. Kamal leaned in. "Have you ever been here before, dear Shelley-kins?"

"Yes," she answered curtly. It was her family's hotel, after all. But she couldn't remember the exact times she'd been there. She had a vague recollection of attending a dinner there when she was small, sitting beside her father in a bow-encrusted dress, falling asleep at the table beside a dish of crème brûlée. That was when her father's older sister, Aunt Julia, still lived there. She'd been ill and elderly and had taken a suite out in the hotel rather than stay confined to the hospital. Rumor was she never left the hotel room. She'd had around-the-clock staff that catered to her, nurses and aides and personal assistants. Supposedly Julia didn't usually even venture into the hallway, and not once in all the years that she lived there did she ever go outside into the fresh air. Shelley couldn't recall if she had ever died.

Mr. Kamal's expression fell. It seemed he desired to bring her into an unknown space.

"I went to a dinner here only once, with my father. I was—"

He frowned still, so she stopped speaking. "I presume you have never, in fact, stayed in a room in this establishment," he said, and then continued, "so I have taken the liberty of providing you with this experience. My Shelley-kins. My *treat*," he said quietly. "Lead me to the front desk." He brought his hands to the tops of her shoulders. "Then you and I can be alone, together, above the whole of this marvelous city. And then I can give you what you've been wanting." He touched her stomach.

She was scheduled to get on a train the next morning at eight. Brooke had promised to be waiting for her at Back Bay station in Boston at noon, and they would go directly to the hospital where her mother was. As Shelley stood by the front desk, she calculated that she had sixteen hours until her train. Plenty of time to go up to the hotel room, then return home to collect her bags.

Mr. Kamal announced to the blue-blazer-wearing attendant, "We have a room reservation. Under the name Whitby. Shelley Whitby."

Why had he made the reservation in her name? Surely he had done this in order to discuss her family with her. Or to point out that although she was a Whitby, she was working for him now. The man behind the front desk appeared confused for a moment, but upon finding the reservation in his computer system and being given a credit card, he ceased to care about the coincidence of names.

An attendant asked if they needed help with their bags, and Mr. Kamal shook his head. "Not yet." The way he casually lied made Shelley wonder if he'd done this before. With his assistants, or with prostitutes? Certainly he wasn't getting affection from his cold stick of a wife. He had special needs that other men didn't have; he couldn't be judged by the same standards as other men. If he had done this before, even if he did this often, nothing was so wrong about that.

The elevator was filled with Japanese tourists, and everyone rode up in silence. At the eighteenth floor, Shelley led Mr. Kamal to a two-room suite, dressed in all ivory tones. He felt the top of various pieces of furniture while making his way on his own into the inner bedroom, where he sat pertly on the edge of the bed with his knees pressed into each other. Was there a smirk upon his lips? He was proud of himself, Shelley could see, for arranging this situation. And in return Shelley was filled with gratitude, and something deeper: pride that she had the ability to instill such satisfaction in him.

Delicate molecules of silence floated in the air. She was proud, but, also, she was unsure of herself. In the study of his apartment, Clova or Dr. Jillian could have swung open a door at any moment. Even in the quarantine turret of the Weld mansion they had been at risk of being walked in on by the groundskeeper. But here they had a key card to the door, and it was locked behind them. It was just her, Shelley Whitby, and he, Yousef Kamal, alone together.

Her body thrummed. He had touched her everywhere, and her hands were familiar with the outer shape of his body as well. But this implication that sex was about to happen was rendering Shelley speechless. Sex: what a dumb, animal mystery. Clearing her throat, she signaled to where she was standing without having to be the one to speak first. Yet Mr. Kamal sat in silence. What she wanted, badly, was to run her hand along the top of the beautifully made bed. Something she had always loved about high-end hotels were the beds: she loved the cleanliness of them, how they contained no human trace. The cool, taut sheets, the softness into which one's body could sink; how beautiful it would be to throw herself onto the sheets alone, locked in this safe compartment. But in front of her sat this man, aging yet semifamous, expectant and upright. The collection of hours that Shelley had spent envisioning this was astounding, and now that she was there, she felt wholly uninterested in fucking her dear Mr. Kamal.

"Should I take off my clothes?"

Heavy gold drapes hung open around the large windows. Sunlight broke through, entering the room from the small slit between them, and Shelley stood in the middle of a shard of it. If she mined herself for honesty, she knew she didn't desire him. But she wanted to crack him, to understand him totally. She wanted to make him desire her so that she was the one on top.

Mr. Kamal had an oddly serene air. "I'm not sure," he said, with more warmth than she was used to. "If you take off your clothes . . . then you would be a naked woman, *ahem* . . . naked girl. A vulnerable girl, standing right in front of me."

"Yes."

"Do you want to be a naked girl in front of me?"

She unzipped her pants and pushed them over her hips, letting them fall to the floor. She continued to take off all her clothes, grateful that the rustling and unzipping filled the silence. After disrobing, she went over to him and sat behind him on the impeccable bed, which was just as smooth and luxurious on her bare thighs as she had envisioned.

"Hmm" was the only noise he made. Behind him, wrapping her two nude legs around his waist, Shelley put her hands on his shoulders and began to massage lightly. He was fully dressed and wearing too much to begin with, considering the summer weather.

"Do you want to take your clothes off now?" As she spoke, her old friend, the anvil of disappointment, fell from her heart to her bowels. Why was she suddenly in charge? This wasn't the unspoken agreement they had.

"Yes—yes," he answered. Could he be nervous? Standing, he methodically unbuttoned his oxford and precisely folded the garment on the bed. He did this with all articles of clothing, even turning the top of one black sock over the other. When naked, he looked shorter. His body protruded with bags and sags. She averted her eyes before they fell below his waist; she didn't want to look there. A full and dapper outfit lay precariously on the edge of the bed. Apparently Mr. Kamal did not have plans to be very energetic. Even a little exuberance and that whole pile of clothes would be on the floor.

She took his hand. "I want to get under the covers." That was what they needed. Skin against skin and everything changes: the brute urge takes over, the unpretty gripping and clawing. He crawled over the sheets and then into the opening. Shelley did the same, and soon her breasts and pelvis and two arms pressed into him, her lower leg crossing his.

He asked, "Do you have the desire to have a child?"

"What?"

"If I impregnated you, would you keep it?"

She was physically repulsed by the idea. She had never once desired to have a child; that hadn't occurred to her as a possibility.

"Um." She tried to think of the question as simply a practical one. "I'm twenty-three" was the only answer she could muster. Of course, that meant nothing. Her own mother was younger than that when Shelley was born.

He grunted in response, not a grunt of pleasure but of something else. She pushed into him harder now, put a hand on his stomach. His skin was warmer than she would have guessed, with coarse, wiry hairs. She began to rub her hand up and down, above the region of his crotch. "Tell me what to do," she whispered.

He let her keep rubbing but did not respond. She heard some wheels going down the hallway, a room service table or a rolling suitcase. "Is this good?"

It was as if he was stuck in this corpse-like position.

"Recite to me some lines of Shelley, my Shelley."

"What?"

"'I met a traveler from an antique land . . .' 'Ozymandias'? No? What about 'Love's Philosophy'?"

She was silent.

"You have no Shelley?" He sighed. He began to slowly orate the words: "'Nothing in the world is single; all things by a law divine, in another's being mingle . . .'" At the end of the poem he moved his right hand in between her legs.

He pressed his palm against her, which she took as a sign that she could act further, and she straddled either side of his hips. He began reciting a new poem, announcing the title as "Goodnight." "'How can I call the lone night good, though thy sweet wishes wing its flight?'" When he paused his lines of poetry, she bent down and kissed him, openmouthed, keeping her tongue still. There it was: their first kiss. He didn't pull away, but he certainly didn't reciprocate as she might have expected. Then she boldly placed her hand against his crotch. She fully expected to feel blood-stiffened, hardened flesh. But instead she was greeted by a soft and pliant nest.

"Is there something wrong?"

"No," he answered defiantly. His tone evoked a slideshow of images in her mind: the fight with Grace about her haircut, him on the ground of the beach in Rhode Island, his temple gushing blood in the tower of the Weld mansion. All she could see of him was weakness, need. With these memories a deep sadness filled her, although she wasn't sure if it was for him or for herself.

Skin on skin, she rolled with him, their knees pedaling slowly. *This is going to be an important moment,* she found herself thinking. This would be a time she would think back to often. He let his hand slide down her limp brown hair. As they were engaged in these movements, Shelley couldn't help but think of Dr. Jillian. How long had it been since she had tumbled with her husband in this manner? Had it, at one point, become so routine that Jill lost interest in the act altogether? And how much did she know about where Shelley's body was right now, the parts of her husband that Shelley was tugging? Shelley imagined Dr. Jillian standing beside the bed with reading glasses on, observing the scene like a social scientist. And then a scowling vision of Grace appeared beside her mother as well, mortified, but watching through splayed fingers. With Mr. Kamal's hologram family members present, Shelley kissed him harder. She would force this, she would make this work.

Soon, it felt as if it had gone on for too long. He had tried to enter her several times, but his loins wouldn't commence. He sighed and touched her elsewhere: a hand on her thigh, and then the back of her neck. Yet he didn't seem devastated. This sexual issue had only happened once before to Shelley, two years prior with a drunk Demming frat boy, who had then promptly thrown up onto his wall-to-wall carpeting.

Now, as the couple failed to have sex, the hotel room was too quiet. If only Shelley had thought to turn on the radio. Maybe she wasn't emitting the appropriate hormones or feline scents. It became clear to her this encounter was not going to come to fruition for either party, so she stopped any kind of reciprocation, hoping he would come to the same conclusion. After interminable minutes of her lying still, he finally turned and lay on his back as well. She sat up and took a breath. It crossed her mind that if he could see her, if he could view her naked stomach and bare breasts, then he would have no problem being turned on. Again the disappointment threatened to sink her: he would never, ever, know what she looked like.

He shuffled himself up against the headboard. "Are you hungry now?"

She could have cried. Where were the gifts she was promised? It was time for her to put on her clothes and return home, to get ready to go to Boston in the morning. She had to face the consequences of her real life. Tomorrow she would hold her mother's hand, feel the woman's arms around her. They would make a plan for the future.

But she could have dinner first. "Yes, I'm hungry," Shelley said.

Mr. Kamal pushed away the covers and stood up. With his back to her, she saw that his ass, flat and barely jutting out from his legs, had extra, wrinkled chicken skin hanging from each cheek. She didn't even know how old he was.

For dinner they ordered steaks from room service, and afterward Shelley, determined in a way that surprised even her, made sure that at least one of them had an orgasm. When they had finished the tres leches cake, while he was sitting in a chair in a white terry robe, she put herself back into the opening of the beautifully smooth sheets. In the bed alone, in only a pair of lilac-colored underwear and a T-shirt, Shelley shoved a hand into her underwear and began rubbing herself. She was not silent: her breath panted as she worked herself up. As she watched Mr. Kamal across the room, she imagined him at an important dinner after a reading performance in a crowded auditorium. At this dinner, he would sit across from businessmen and she would crawl underneath the table, unzipping his pants and taking him fully into her mouth, in public, in a restaurant. In the hotel bed, she moved her fingers faster, up and down, letting out small moans. She pictured Mr. Kamal's hands underneath the restaurant table, taking one-hundred-dollar bills out of his pockets and shoving them down her shirt, he hard in her mouth, her breasts bobbing lightly on his thighs as she worked away. The money would be freshly printed, the paper cool against her skin; she would work harder and faster when she felt the coolness. Mr. Kamal would begin to come, and above the table he would cough slightly, a hand moving to his mouth—that was it. When Shelley hit a precipice in her imagining, she let out a blunted moan. Light returned to the room. Mr. Kamal did not move a muscle in his chair, but she was sure he had a serene grin on his face.

Shelley got out of bed and finished the bottle of room service wine quickly. She needed to go home. Her train for Boston left from Penn Station in less than eleven hours. But Mr. Kamal seemed strangely pleased then, as if he had overeaten. He asked her to read to him in bed, and she assented. Beside his solid, distinguished body, she read several pages from the book of Exodus, from the bible they'd found in the nightstand. He closed his eyes, and Shelley felt content; she felt protected there, propped up beside him. She considered the fact that if she slept there, she could go directly to the train station in the morning and still make her trip.

They both woke before seven, and although they lay tenderly beside each other for several bleary minutes, neither party was interested in attempting sex again. Mr. Kamal dressed quickly and left the hotel, stating that he had important work to do. On the way out he did not kiss her but rather touched her stomach sensually, proprietarily. Shelley had half an hour to make her train. She lay alone on the hotel bed and decided she would not go. There were more important things happening in her life right now. Her mother and Brooke would just have to wait. She stretched out her arms and felt the smoothness of the taut cotton sheets beneath her. Despite the night's surprises, despite the failed intercourse with Mr. Kamal, she was making progress. She had reached the next step of their game. He wanted her. Perhaps he needed her. She was succeeding in her goals.

11

As Nick sat in the circle of activists on the parlor floor, David Kipling, with his goatee and a newsboy hat, said: "In order for us to make any impact at all, we need the mass mobilization march to be huge. If we can really start an occupation in the park—if we can get all the media out there, watching people pitch tents and sleep in them, then we'll get exposure. If we can build this sleep-in occupation, we can build a movement."

Nick and Grace had invited all these people, who were now nodding profusely, over to Shelley's apartment. It was a reckless thing to do, inviting people into the place that was now his home. Although he hadn't told Grace the details of what happened in Maine, she understood that he was in serious trouble. But she had convinced him it would be fine; these were his compadres, his compatriots, his brothers in the struggle. They weren't going to out him to the authorities. And it was the Fourth of July, a holiday, a time to do new and unexpected things. Plus, he was using a fake name.

Including Nick and Grace, there were thirteen unwashed people sitting on the parlor floor, stinking up the place with BO and patchouli oil. Some seemed to be around Nick's age, but one woman had a wickedly wrinkled face between two long braids. And there was another, heavyset guy with wire-framed glasses, who had to be at least forty. A few were thick, but some were bony, and most were white. Many of them had bandannas tied around their necks, and many also wore cutoff versions of Carhartt cargos, the same brand as Nick's only pair of pants. Reusable water bottles dotted the floor. Backpacks were scattered about, and a few bedrolls and sleeping bags were stacked into a pile in the corner of the parlor. Everyone was grimly serious.

The big guy with small glasses, John, broke in, "There are five tents set up right now. Quentin, Grace, you are the only two who haven't promised to sleep there. Bodies are what we need. Can you come tonight? Do you have a tent?"

Quentin was the fake name that Nick had taken on. It was the name of Roger's brother, the one who had committed suicide when the men were in their early twenties. It seemed to Nick a good time to become Quentin.

In the meeting, from across the circle, a small Latina girl in a studded belt, Esmerelda, said to John, "Don't be so defeatist, man. Five tents doesn't seem like a lot, but it's a start. We've got to start somewhere."

The larger collective, which had been holding meetings in Art Park outside the Doss Museum every afternoon, was referring to itself not just as the GAG movement, not just as the now anti-ExxonMobil movement, but also as the "anti-gas" movement. The anti-gas movement had set plans for the Global Day of Protest at the end of the summer. There would be a major march, spearheaded in New York and echoed in cities across the globe. The WTO protests in Seattle and the International Monetary Fund protest in Washington had been proof that people power existed. The Doss Museum was a figurehead for democratic values. Everyone needed to see that replacing it with ExxonMobil was a symbol of the disastrous direction the neoliberals were leading the world.

As Nick sat in the meeting, he had a type of epiphany. All the windows in the brownstone were open, and as his eyes adjusted to the darkness brought in by the setting sun, he saw only the shaded outlines of the twelve faces around him: the swoop of their noses, the curve of their foreheads. For days, he had been petrified about the idea of essentially rejoining society by hosting this meeting. He had woken up beside Grace several times a night, sure that the cops were knocking on the apartment door. But after the two of them had invited all their comrades over for the meeting—after the ideas and voices of others like him shot around the house, growing on the energy of one another—he felt strangely at peace. He was back into the world and planning something worthwhile. Maybe all this trouble from the Maine action would simply blow over and he could be himself again: a person with friends, a community, a girl who wanted to go upstairs and roll around together. Maybe he could even call his poor mother, who—he occasionally considered—was probably losing her mind with worry. If someone was going to arrest him, if his life was going to take a miserable turn, so be it. Happiness, he realized, could be within his control. But then he remembered Roger, who had died with the knowledge that Nick hadn't accomplished anything at all.

Grace had given full reports to Nick about the protests around the takeover of the Doss. Although rather thin in numbers, daily meetings were taking place on the concrete plaza of Art Park, ending with a few people holding signs and chanting, "This is what democracy looks like!" and "ExxonMobil's not our boss! Come on, people, save the Doss!" While the liberals who showed up for the daytime rallies might care about history or art or small businesses, the group of people in the Whitby parlor, the Family-Support Network, had unanimously committed to do *something*, to plan and work together—to fight together—and not only stop the destruction of the museum but also to take a true stand against corporate rule and consumer capitalism. And yet, Nick felt that their sleep-in occupation plans still weren't enough.

The next part of the meeting was filled with writing political-prisoner letters of support to the Family members. Fliers and the other scraps of paper covered the rug, and Nick picked one up and began absentmindedly drawing on it in black pen.

On the back of one of them, Nick drew the Strong Place brownstone with sunflowers and wild lilies growing out of the sides, and small, smiling figures popping out of the windows. On the roof perched the figure of a dancer, one leg in the air, holding a flag that read: OCCUPY THE MANSION. When most people were licking the envelopes in the darkened room, Nick dropped his black-and-white drawing on the rug, then instructed the room, "Let's stack all the finished letters in a pile by the door."

He wasn't the leader. If anyone was a leader it was David, but there was an obvious control that Nick held. It was, in effect, his apartment, and everyone responded to him with reverence.

After they'd been sitting there for more than two hours, David announced to the crowd: "I want everyone to break into subgroups now. And I'm gonna ask each of you to come up with answers to three questions: *Why are you frustrated? What change do you want to see in the world?* And finally, *What are you willing to do to create that change?"*

Everyone nodded gravely. Nick and David and a guy named Roiphe decided to form their own subgroup, and Nick led them up the stairs to what was now his bedroom so they could talk privately.

He was sitting on the floor of that cramped bedroom when Shelley's voice, from downstairs, called up, "Nick! Where are you, you little bastard?"

Soon she burst into the room, almost hitting the slumped-over Roiphe.

"Shells—hey!" he said. "This is a meeting. For the, uh, the GAG sit-in. I thought you were still at work . . ." He looked at his feet. "And I know you don't like to be disturbed there."

Footsteps made their way up the stairs and soon Grace's voice was behind Shelley's head. "We're all really psyched that we're able to meet here, Shelley. It's so nice of you. We needed our own space, away from, like . . ." Grace sighed. "The diluted liberals who are hanging around the other meetings."

The word *liberals* rolled out of Grace's throat as if it were something repulsive. Nick smiled. She was really joining the cause, and with speed. It was adorable.

Shelley rolled her eyes. She said over her shoulder, "Grace? I expected better from you."

Grace's shoulders dropped.

"Who the hell are these people, Nick? We need to talk," Shelley hissed. "In the hall, right now."

David, who was sitting on the floor, pointed to her. "Quentin, can you vouch that this individual is cool?"

Shelley huffed in exasperation. Nick told David, "She lives here. Let's just leave her out of our planning; she doesn't want to be involved."

"What do I not want to be involved in?"

Grace pushed by Shelley and into the room, making space for more people who had begun clumping up in the hall. As she walked, Nick snuck his arm out and grabbed her ankle. Squealing, she fell to the floor. The side of her breast was poking out of her black tank top. He couldn't help it; he began crawling on top of her, and she pushed him back, playfully; she bit him gently on the ear and he bit her shoulder.

David climbed around the two of them and hollered into the hallway, "Are we ready for the working groups to reconvene?" Grumbles of assent reverberated, and the floorboards began squeaking under the weight of everyone going downstairs. Soon Shelley retreated to Biddy's old bedroom. Then there was a *pop pop* from above. At the first *pop*, Nick, who had been talking quietly to David, raised his arms to his forehead, flinching. He was so on edge. Then Cate, the older woman with braids, hollered, "Fireworks!" It was, after all, the Fourth of July.

Shelley, intending to flip through *Rolling Stone* in front of the air conditioner, while imagining Mr. Kamal's hands on her face and her ass, went to her room trying to forget about Nick and his party of idiots. Falling in love is a form of insanity that blurs one's surroundings—trees and cars and speech and time—rendering the individual's own distinct actions and emotions impossible to pin down. The phrase *I love you* threatened to burst from her larynx. She came close to saying it aloud. But more than she wanted to say those words, she craved to hear Mr. Kamal say them to her. Before the night at the Whitby-Grand, she thought what was happening between them wasn't exactly love. But now she was engulfed by a tunnel from which she could see only the voluptuous, delicious darkness of that very moment. But she couldn't help herself from wondering: How many other girls had he touched before? She thought of the *Gawker* article again, about Kamal's seeing-eye girl. How many of his assistants had made it through to this final round? She had a hunch that it was only her, at least in the past many years. She didn't think she was special, but she had, for once in her life, dedicated herself to achieving something. She had dug in her heels at the Grisham, worked hard for Mr. Kamal, and she had succeeded. She let her mind flash to who his other assistants may have been: the girl with the crooked teeth from *Gawker*, a twenty-five-years-younger Dr. Jillian. She recalled her initial interest in Grace, on the beach in Rhode Island. Shelley would ask Grace about the others.

A loud *pop pop pop* sounded from above. "Christ!" Shelley shrieked, before she remembered: fireworks. Independence Day. The inane fascination with explosives was something she had zero interest in. She sat on her bed but was distracted again by a clanging outside her window. Nick's torso moved quickly by the glass, then his legs, then his sneakers. Another similarly dressed man followed. They were moving up the fire escape. She watched the bodies climb by her window, up to the roof; with each new body she scoffed at the sheer audacity of her entitled brother. One of the climbers had some kind of speaker, and the Ramones' "Beat on the Brat" rose in a crescendo as the body holding it passed by the glass, then the *Oh yeahs* grew softer as the body climbed away. How was she supposed to plan her course of action with Mr. Kamal in the midst of this clattering? And, technically there were neighbors on the top two floors of the building, an elderly couple who actually lived in Sag Harbor and were never in the city. But still. This was not Nick's house. At that thought, a shard of fear jabbed her stomach; if she didn't do something to stop it, soon enough, it could be his.

After the climbing bodies disappeared, laughter ricocheted off the roof and into the concrete gully between the buildings. The sky boomed and popped at full tilt. Shelley got up, ready to go up there and announce to Nick that his party was over, but at that moment the air conditioner abruptly stopped and her lamp went out. "Shit," she whispered. She went to the hallway fuse box and flipped the switch to the left. Nothing happened. She found the switch for her old bedroom. Again, nothing. All the rooms were totally dark. She went to try the lights in the bathroom next, as a small seed of realization floated into her head: since she'd come home nearly three months ago, she hadn't paid any bills. It wasn't just the electricity bill, it was all of them. She simply hadn't focused on it. The truth was she had never paid any bills before. Although she slipped Mr. Kamal's checks into the mouth of an ATM every week, she had no idea where her actual checkbook was. And never once did Shelley open the official-looking mail that had come from Con Edison or Metro New York Gas. It was all addressed to her mother.

Standing in the bathroom in the dark, letting the reality of the circumstance fall upon her, Shelley was on the verge of laughter. How horrendous! With the meager money that Mr. Kamal paid her, she'd bought plentiful groceries, most of which Nick consumed. And last week alone she purchased a new scarf and two necklaces from a street stand by the park, a new pair of flip-flops, and the Grateful Dead's *Steal Your Face* record on clear vinyl. She hadn't thought to save any of the cash.

On the corner of the roof, Nick sat and pulled Grace down beside him. He was addicted to her body now and needed to always be touching her soft brown arms and legs and stomach and breasts. At the start of the summer he had been headed down a tunnel of gloom, and she had, in effect, saved him.

That morning, while lying in bed, Grace had asked him, "What exactly happened to you? You can trust me with the real story." When he didn't respond, she tried another angle. "I'm letting you change my whole life here!" she squealed. "At least you could let me in on your secrets." She was referring to the fact that after four days of not going to her internship at the publishing house, she'd had Nick call her boss and quit for her. He hadn't said his name or even provided a reason, just reported in a monotone voice from Grace's cell phone: "Grace Kamal needs to quit her internship. She's discovered that she doesn't have time for it this summer."

She had made sacrifices for him, or for the work they were going to do together. But he couldn't tell her the facts about what he'd done in Maine; it was for her own good that she didn't know. In bed, she threw a sheet off her naked body and asked, "Do you know the Family?" Honestly, Nick was surprised she hadn't asked him earlier.

Still, he'd clammed up. "Do *you* know the Family?" was his only response.

"No!" She giggled. "Obviously, they've been in jail since before I got involved."

Nick had pulled the sheet above their heads, took a deep breath, and began to kiss her again right below her belly button. That was the end of their conversation.

On the roof, the night wind chilled his arms and he pulled her in closer, whispering, "Come here, you miracle woman." That was when Nick saw Shelley hoisting herself up on the fire-escape ladder. In high school she'd brought Nick up there a couple of times, when he was visiting and she was partying with some asshole private school boys. They'd smoked out of bongs they'd passed carefully up a ladder of hands, and smashed glass bottles down on the pavement, eliciting terrified screams from pedestrians. But Nick hadn't been up there in years, and he wasn't sure she had either.

Shelley was kneeling on the tar-covered roof, her hair whipping around her face and eyes, and Nick was struck for a moment by his stunning sister. Then he shook his head violently and squeezed Grace in closer. All the other people—were they now his friends?—were in clusters of two or three, looking up in awe at the fireworks display. Something less melodic than the Ramones played, something Nick couldn't place, with a man screeching over fast drums. He kissed Grace's shoulder, and she turned into him, finding his mouth with hers.

Someone kicked his side lightly. "Nick—"

He looked up to see Shelley.

"Call him *Quentin*!" Grace hissed.

"Something strange happened," Shelley whispered.

Nick murmured, "Listen, sorry about all the people. I didn't think it was the kind of thing you would care about. Old Vineyard Shelley never would have cared—"

"Will you listen!" She sat down beside them on the black tar. "We need to talk about money, and a . . . legal thing."

Nick pushed himself into a sitting position. "Can I have a cigarette?"

Shelley scoffed. So what if he had never been a smoker before? So what if on the Vineyard he used to take the cigarettes out of her mouth and fling them off the dock? Everything was different now. This was an urgent time. Shelley dug a Virginia Slim out of the pack in her pocket and handed it over to him, while Grace wrinkled her nose in cute mock disgust.

Shelley lit her own cigarette and closed her eyes. "I have to tell you something—"

It occurred to Nick that she might know about what happened in Maine. Maybe someone had gotten through to her on her cell phone—a cop, an investigator. Maybe his mother had found out and was on her way to New York right then, to get him, to punish him. He jumped to his feet. "Stop!" he yelled to Shelley. "Let's go downstairs. It's too loud up here. And too hot. Let's sit in front of your air conditioner." He grabbed her hand. With the other hand he inhaled from the cigarette in hyper little puffs.

Shelley cracked up. "Listen to me, you freak!" She seemed to have lightened up since earlier. "We can't use the air conditioner. Jesus, that's what I'm trying to tell you. The electricity just went out."

"Huh?"

"It's totally dark down there." She stubbed the cigarette out on the roof.

"What?" he said. "It's not even raining."

"The electricity just went out because I didn't pay the bill."

"You didn't pay the bill?"

"Didn't know I had to." Shelley shrugged.

"Didn't know you had to?" Nick was confused, but only briefly. Then relief flooded his bloodstream. "You didn't know you had to pay the fucking bills, Shells?" He found himself cracking up. He dropped to his knees and folded himself into Grace's body. "Shelley didn't know she had to pay the bills!" he said, his voice muffled by Grace's chest.

Grace giggled now too, but softly. "Can we fix this?" she asked. "Can we call the company right now and turn them back on?"

Green and pink bursts in the sky began to pop at faster rates, leading into the grand finale. Shelley took the pack out of her pocket again and through her cigarette-clenched mouth said, "Nope. We're broke. No money left, 'cause Nick eats it all, in the form of boxed mac and cheese."

Nick was in stitches. He sat up straight. "We have no money?"

Shelley giggled then, too. "None at all!"

In the sky, golden tadpoles shot upward before falling back with shimmering tails dissolving behind them. He stared at his sister in amazement. How had they gotten themselves into this?

Grace offered, "I've been telling Nick that my dad will hire him to draw. All you'd have to do is ask."

Shelley said, "Yeah. Clearly you are done hiding from the world, Nick." She gestured to the group of people on the roof. "It's time to get a job."

His laughter cut off, and he felt his jaw jutting out. This is how it happened with him: he was always aware when his anger was about to take over. He was aware of it but still couldn't stop it. "No. I can't just go out into the world and get a job. I can't explain it, but trust me, it's not safe. It's something I cannot do."

"You have to," Shelley said bluntly.

"I thought you were going to help me," Nick said in a bitter whisper. "I'm in trouble, Roger is dead, and things are entirely fucked."

Above them a flourish of bigger fireworks burst, then a pause, before a line of fuzzy red dots appeared on the surface of the Hudson River. The line soared into the sky and was followed by another line of white dots. Nick saw his sister, face up, take several deep breaths. Finally she said, "Fine. I'll help you, little Nicky, if you can't take care of yourself. But that doesn't change anything about the frigging electricity."

He didn't thank her and didn't let his shoulders fall from where they were hunched around his ears. But he was grateful. He didn't want to get into another blowout with her, not on that night, when he'd just broken through his barrier of fear and rejoined the world.

Shelley said, "Guess we're camping in the dark tonight!"

Thank God for her, his laissez-faire sister. In the sky, the lines of fuzzy red and white dots alternated, until blue appeared in one corner. The final firework display was supposed to be an American flag. But a mistake had occurred. The flag that exploded before them was upside down.

"Whooo-whoo-whooo!" a mohawked girl behind them howled. Then the whole roof joined in on the cheering. Soon enough, everyone was cheering, thrilled and awed by the firework malfunction. Roiphe hopped over and presented Nick with a bottle of Jack Daniel's, which he swigged from before handing it over to Shelley. After the howls, a few members of the group broke out into a song that seemed to be a relic of the 1960s. They sang, "'Solidarity forever, soli-darity for-ever.'"

Nick sang too. It was goofy. Grace smiled so large her cheeks pulsated in the wind. Even Shelley had half a cynical smile on her face. Nick thought: this is hokey enough to be summer camp. And yet. He was happy. So they didn't have lights in the house. So they were low on cash. So their father had passed away. Shitty things had happened, but weren't those things out of his control? Nick took the whiskey bottle back from Shelley and, leaning back on the cool tar of the rooftop, joined in on the chorus. It was good to be back in his life.

12

Brooke was aware of the fact that what she was about to do was dumb. Her plan was dumb in that it was silly, but also dumb insomuch as there was a good chance that it would not work out. It was certainly the most un-Brooke-like plan she'd ever concocted. But she needed to show Allie that she could change, that she had changed. She would show her that she was no longer afraid of other people's judgment. Yes, that was actually true, Brooke thought, as she walked under the beating sun down Revere Street, toward the Charles River. If she proved this to Allie, maybe Allie would show that she could change too. Maybe she would embrace the soon-to-be baby. Brooke sweated in her jeans and peach polo shirt as she carried all the large black poster board signs, and she had to catch her breath as she waited to cross over to the footbridge to the river path. She had wondered if she should dress up for the occasion but figured that kneeling on a dock would be better in casual clothes.

It had been weeks since Shelley had promised to come see poor Elizabeth Saltman Whitby, but not only had Shelley not shown up in Boston, not only had Brooke waited for her for three hours in the sparse municipal lobby of Back Bay station, but now Shelley had returned to sheer avoidance: she never answered her phone. How could someone act like that toward her own mother? It was chilling. But if the events of that summer had taught Brooke anything, it was that, sometimes, the only person to depend on was oneself. This determination, this lesson, was precisely why half of

Brooke's apartment was in boxes already and why she was walking down—pregnant, backache, and all—to where Allie would be finishing up her workday, in order to publicly admit the one thing she had not been able to get out of her mind for months: she loved Allie and could not live without her. Brooke had recruited several nurses to join in her plan, as well as eight of the sailing students Allie was working with that summer. The proposal would be a grand and uncouth gesture. It was, Brooke thought, her only recourse.

Allie's students were the most excited about it. Brooke had gone into the Dorchester offices of Urban Adventurers one afternoon when the secretary had assured her that Allie was going to be in a board meeting. She'd told a group of fifteen-year-old girls, fighting back a shy smile, "I want to propose marriage to Allie to the Michael Jackson song 'The Way You Make Me Feel.'"

One of the more outgoing girls, Thea, clapped her hands, saying, "Ohhhh, we got this!" and making the other girls giggle. "We got all the choreography, all the dance moves. We're going to practice with your nurse friends. Ms. Allie is going to freak the hell out!"

Brooke, laughing, had left a CD with the girls, as well as several phone numbers and explicit instructions about the date and time.

Once the plan was set into motion, Brooke, terrified but committed, did an even more out-of-character thing: she'd called up her Beacon Hill friends and told them about the whole spectacle. Although she didn't ask them to learn the dance moves or leap across the dock-slash-stage, she did ask them if they would come and bear witness. So, the Pickney sisters and Waloffs and Ben Carlson and his wife would all be there, they said. If she had never officially come out before, she was doing it now. There would be no turning back after this, no denying anything. Even more terrifying than inviting her friends to this spectacle, almost as terrifying as the prospect of what Allie would say to her, was the fact that she had called up Armond and told him of her plan. On the phone she had said, "I know you're often busy in the afternoon, Armond, but I'm planning on proposing to Allie Wainwright . . . Yes, that same Allie. The proposal itself will be a bit of a, um, show, and therefore I'm inviting people to come and watch and be part of the whole thing. And, well, I'm wondering if you'd like to join?"

Armond had not expressed surprise at her announcement of romantic interest with a woman. Had he known beforehand? Instead, he had responded with several *hmm* and *huh* noises, before muttering, "Of course, dear. What's the hour?"

Now, the day had arrived. The surface of the Charles River glistened with beams of sun across it. White triangular sailboat sails dotted the water, floating peacefully, and the clouds above reflected their pillowy softness. Sometimes, the center of Boston could be more breathtaking than anywhere else. Brooke hadn't seen Allie since that night outside of Mass General, when she had rebuffed her and her honesty about the pregnancy. But, when you've known someone so long and so well, one passing fight can be absorbed by a little time. The amount that Brooke had been missing Allie in the past month was verging on obsession: she thought of her when she awoke in the morning, as she sipped her coffee at the nurses' station, and on the long and lonely drives out to visit Elizabeth Saltman Whitby in the hospital. Brooke simply had to believe that Allie was focused on her too. A love this strong could not be one-sided. As she walked past the Hatch Shell with a few picnicking college kids on the lawn, beside some nannies freeing children from overpriced strollers, the gray stone building of Community Boating came into view. She recalled her father's favorite book, which she had read time after time after he left, trying to decipher what it was about the story that spoke so strongly to her father. That terribly tense moment when Gatsby is finally going to see Daisy again, at the arranged tea inside Nick Carraway's house; how Gatsby arrives early, bringing in florists to decorate Nick's rooms and a man to cut his grass, the whole time Gatsby's face gray and sickly with worry—that was how Brooke felt right now. But she wasn't going to make the same mistakes as Gatsby. No, she was determined to have a happy ending.

A state supreme court case had been going on since 2001, to determine the legality of same-sex marriage, and of course Brooke had been following it closely. She was convinced that within the next year, Massachusetts would be the first state in the nation to legalize gay marriage. And she was, surprisingly, filled with pride now, at the prospect of being one of the first couples to use the law. It wasn't something her family had done before, but then again, it wasn't something anyone's family had done before. She would even invite her mother and siblings and her stepsiblings to the wedding party, she thought. If they didn't understand it at first, they would get to understand it with time. The chance of losing her childhood home, the reality of losing her father and all that came with him, had set something free inside of her. She could do it: live a life that was unexpected. And in a way, she would be embarking upon that rare boldness that Whitbys were known for, just in a different context.

She was almost at the boathouse. Although it was a public boathouse, it was just as stately and dignified as the private ones on both sides of the river, and perhaps more so. The large wooden deck that rolled into the water, the gray blocks of stone; it felt so reassuring in its build. In the past few weeks Brooke had come to the realization that, with a child growing inside of her and the better part of four decades lived, the choices she made now were her permanent ones. She wondered, briefly, if her father had ever thought of his choices like that. When he was thirty-seven years old he was still married to her mother, still living in their house and convincing everyone that's where he would always be. But some part of him had to know that he had the capacity to drop everything, to leave them all behind. How could he not have understood that his actions would have lasting, heartbreaking consequences? Or maybe he did know but was too weak to do anything about it. As Brooke walked toward Allie's place of work with Grandmother Whitby's diamond ring burning a hole in her front pocket, she was proud that she was going to willingly embarrass herself in front of loved ones and strangers. It would be mortifying, and moreover terrifying. But she would do it for Allie.

Clara Pickney stood thirty yards ahead of Brooke, on the paved path leading up to the boathouse, waving exaggeratedly. She skipped up in her striped tank top and big sunglasses and, giving Brooke a surprisingly tight hug, whispered, "The rest of the crew is right up there!" Brooke turned to see about ten people, including Caroline Pickney with her front-facing baby carrier on, waving from the path on the far side of the boathouse, blowing kisses and giving her two thumbs-ups. She was touched. They had all shown up.

In the distance, Caroline touched her pointer finger to her watch, miming the question, *Is it time yet?* Brooke nodded, motioning everyone down from the upper path. She could see that the training sailboats, with their navy-printed numbers on their thicker white sails, were coming in for the afternoon. Allie would surely be on one of them.

"Hey, lady," a loud voice said from beside her. It was Betta, a nurse she'd been working with for years. She was in her light yellow scrubs. "We're all here and we all know our moves," she said with a wink.

"Shhhh!" Brooke couldn't help smiling. "And thank you for coming!"

Betta gave a smile. "The music is all queued up. As soon as you give me the nod, it'll play loud and clear through the boathouse speakers."

"Thank you!" Brooke said again, although she realized she was shaking. All four of the other nurses were in a huddle by the open garage door of the boathouse, heads tilted in, rapt in gossip or planning. Allie's student Thea walked with purpose into the middle of the group of nurses. Soon they all turned to Brooke with tentative thumbs in the air. Brooke nodded back to them. It was time.

Brooke had, in fact, always envisioned being part of a grand proposal. She just didn't know she'd be the one putting it on. Her parents' proposal occurred in the mid-1950s, at the Orpheum Theatre in Boston. Roger and Corney went to see Frank Sinatra perform, and thanks to Roger's connections, they had front-row seats. Roger was not yet divorced, technically, from the New York Vanderbilt girl. But he no longer lived in New York, and he and his current Boston sweetheart were smitten with each other. It was the dead of winter, but Corney still wore a sleeveless dark green scoopneck dress, with a full skirt. Brooke knew this because she had the photograph from the aftermath, as her parents beamed in the light of their decision. But before that photograph was snapped, up on the stage Ol'

Blue Eyes entered into his final song of the night. He smiled, winked, and climbed up on a chair as the orchestra picked up. Spreading out his arms, he pitched into his song. "'I've got the world on a string, sittin' on a rainbow . . .'"

As Sinatra leaped down, then swayed and snapped his way down the stage in his tall and thin, charmingly surprised manner, Roger got up from his seat and made for the exit door to the left of the stage.

"Roger?" Corney had gasped. Was he sick? Angry? "Roger!" she hissed again, but the man didn't turn back, and so she giggled nervously and glanced to the people sitting beside her in a type of embarrassed apology for disturbing their show.

But not more than one minute later—how could he have gotten there so quickly?—Roger appeared on stage right, walking confidently toward the center. An intake of breath resounded from every member of the audience. Who was this crazy man; what was this disruption? But soon Sinatra announced to the crowd as the orchestra played a bridge, "Roger Whitby, everyone! My old friend!"

Everyone in the audience clapped, and Sinatra patted Roger on the shoulder, nodding in time with the music. That was when the two men in their matching tuxedos, both with a bow tie adorning their necks, launched—together—into the final lines of the song. They sang, "'This here is life, and I'mmmmmm in lo-ve!'" Their hands flew to the ceiling at the final note, and the crowd went wild. Corney, from her seat, had covered her mouth with two hands. Her beau on the stage with Sinatra? But what happened next surprised her even more: once the clapping died down, a woman in a white evening gown walked out onto the stage and handed Roger a wired-in microphone. Taking it, he bent down on one knee and said, in front of the entire theater, "Cornelia Wesner, it's taken me most of my life, but I've found you." He shook his head, looking down in exaggerated wistfulness. "I've finally found you, and I am more than in love. Won't you become Cornelia Whitby?"

The crowd exploded again, with even more applause than when Sinatra finished his tune, and Corney shot up straight out of her red velvet seat in sheer surprise. She genuinely loved him too. She nodded profusely, her two white-glove-covered arms pinned to her sides, and said, "Yes, yes. I will marry you!" Sinatra pounded the kneeling Roger on the back again and flashed a grin more alluring, more hopeful than the twinkle of the lights on the Rockefeller Center Christmas tree.

A black-and-white photograph was taken of Roger and Corney just afterward, in front of the ornate brass-engraved doors in the Orpheum's lobby. They looked ecstatic, unbelievably young and fit, as they stood beside each other in their evening wear. Their faces radiated a joy that is rare in this world, as their bodies posed awkwardly: tense with excitement, imbued with the knowledge that in a few brief moments they would be out in the sparse snowfall, entwined in the other's exquisite limbs. Brooke cherished this old photograph and kept it in a sterling silver frame on her bureau, in the same home where her parents had acted out that very love. She wondered if today, someone would take a similar photograph of her and Allie. The circumstances were different: their photograph would be in full color, they'd be in casual clothes, and more wizened than her parents had been. But love like that couldn't be hidden from a camera, or a crowd. She stomped toward the boathouse, patting the pocket with Grandmother Whitby's ring, assuring herself that the photograph of her parents was magical because of the feeling it captured. And that was something she and Allie had.

There she was: Allie trudged through the shallow edge of the river, her calves covered in water, as she towed in the teacher's instructional boat. She looked both strong and compact in her Adidas shorts and protective visor. Her body movements portrayed how concentrated she was on wrangling the boat, showing a student beside her how to swing the boom around and batten it down with a cleat hitch. As Brooke watched, she thought to herself that Allie was a living embodiment of home. The sun shone hard on the striated gray expanse of wooden dock, and Brooke stepped back into the darkness of the boat garage to hide until the moment was right. Thea now led three other girls, Allie's students, to the middle of the dock, all in slightly wet T-shirts from having recently shed their life vests. The girls grinned, and Thea nodded to Brooke to indicate that they were ready. They formed a straight line in the middle of the wooden platform, with their heads down. Someone turned on the PA system, and Michael Jackson's song blasted out. The students' fists were clutched, elbows out, as the synthesizer began over a man's voice going, *Ohhhh, that is fo-xy!* They raised their heads and arms in unison. They had been practicing! These girls adored Allie and were doing this silly thing totally for her.

Soon the girls shimmied backward on their sandal-covered toes, threw their arms high in the air, and with jazz hands fluttering, kicked a right leg up, cheerleader-style. As they ran forward to their initial starting line, all four of the women who were nurses with Brooke—Sue, Betta, Matilda, and Deb—ran in to join the dance, in their matching scrubs. Brooke was overcome with the kindness of these people. All the dancing women, young and older, repeated the initial elbows-out dance move, as Michael Jackson's lyrics sang out: "The way you make me fe-eeel! You really turn me on." By the next round the group had pulled a bewildered, openmouthed Allie into the center of the dock and were circling around her, clapping, while four more of her students shimmied into the mix in their sports shorts and T-shirts.

Allie looked from left to right in sheer confusion. All the Beacon Hill friends had moved to the edge of the dock now, everyone knee bopping and head nodding; everyone was smiling. It was happening. In fact, it was going according to plan, which meant that Brooke was actually about to publicly expose her most personal desires. It seemed that the only person she'd invited who had not shown up was Armond. His slim, serious figure was nowhere to be seen. Her heart sank for a moment. Well, so what if he didn't approve. She'd told him her intentions, she'd been honest with him, and that was all she needed to do.

It was time. Soon it would be a fact that she, Brooke Whitby, had publicly proposed to a woman. She imagined that some people had been through this sort of anointment as children: owning up to themselves and their desires, then crying through the knowledge that they were different from the herd. Then again, some people's honest desires fit right into their family's standards. And others, still, had families with no rigid standards at all, those rare and blessed individuals who were simply accepted by their parents with open arms. But Brooke was, for the first real time, coming out as herself. It turned out that at any age, this was a nausea-inducing, shaky process. All the dancers, the students and the nurses, God bless them, were in three straight lines now, doing a leg-crossed-over-leg spin. The song was winding down. Allie finally noticed Brooke and exclaimed, "What the hell?" She whipped her visor off her head and put her other hand over her eyes to shade them. "What is going on here, B?" Allie yelled.

Brooke tried to smile; she would portray confidence, lightheartedness. She would pretend that she was the type of person who liked to be the center of attention. She felt as if she were stepping off a cliff. The instrumentals ceased and Michael Jackson muttered the final words: "You knock me off of my feet, my baby." The dancers froze in the middle of the dock, in their final dramatic position, beaming, then took a bow to the great applause of the little crowd.

The next song queued up, the one Brooke had spent a long time deciding on. This song, Queen's "You're My Best Friend," played at a lower volume. Brooke walked toward Allie and, holding the giant signs in one hand, put her sunglasses to rest on the top of her head. She took a deep breath and belted out as loud as she could, "I love you, Allie Wainwright." Then she knelt down in the middle of the dock. She looked quickly from left to right. Her friends were smiling with what appeared to be genuine delight. They still loved her. She scanned the crowd again. This was a whole new Brooke Whitby. With the poster boards in her hands, she displayed the first one. Allie, her arms clamped to her sides and her mouth still agape in shock, was fifteen feet in front of her. Brooke let the first sign sink in before discarding it to the side and moving on to the next.

The signs read:

Allie, you are an amazing woman

And a gift to the world

Allie's lips moved as she read them. Her two hands went to her mouth. Queen's lyrics played: "When things turn out bad, you know I'll never be lonely . . ." Brooke unveiled the rest of the signs.

No one has ever loved anyone

More than I love you

As soon as we are legally able to . . .

Will you marry me?

With her hands still covering her mouth, Allie surveyed the crowd, which had now gathered more tourists and a cluster of spandex-covered onlookers holding their bicycles. Without uttering a word, she marched toward Brooke, who was still kneeling while holding the last sign. She pulled her to her feet.

"I am in shock, Brooke Whitby," Allie whispered, smiling. Close-up, Brooke could see that a few tears had escaped out of the corners of Allie's eyes. Brooke put her arms around Allie's damp red City Sports T-shirt. She smiled.

"I would do anything for you. Even this." Brooke motioned to the gathered crowd, and that's when she saw him: arms crossed in his rolled-up checkered shirtsleeves, wearing a navy Red Sox hat. Armond stood on the side of the dock next to the Pickneys. He made eye contact with Brooke, with the hint of a slight smile. He was there, watching, and in his own way, approving. It was, Brooke thought, one of the kindest things that had ever happened to her. Her chest burst with gratitude. She thought to herself: this was all worth it.

Allie giggled and grabbed Brooke by the upper arms. "I cannot believe you just did that," she said, then moved in for a kiss. Her mouth touched Brooke's. Allie's kiss was warm and plush and perfectly comforting. Brooke could hear the crowd cheering again.

Then Allie pulled her face back. Brooke just wanted to keep kissing her, but instead she said, "Allie, I'm doing the thing I should have done a very long time ago. I want to tell the whole world that I love you. I'm sorry that it took me so long to understand that I can't live without you."

Allie took a breath. She mumbled, "And I love you. You know that." She took another breath then, and continued. "Brooke, I'm going to keep smiling so as to not make this any more awkward than it already is, but . . ." She was whispering very quietly. "Are you having the baby?"

"Yes. I am. But it's only my child." Her stomach was now a small perfect dome, but after hours spent poking it in the mirror, Brooke determined she was still the only one who would notice it.

"And it's not mine," Allie said matter-of-factly. "You can't undo your past actions. I'm sorry, but that's just a fact. Actions have consequences."

"But I love you." Brooke was aware that her voice was taking on a whine. She tried to quiet herself to a lower volume. "And I know . . . I know that you share this love. We can move on to a new chapter."

"That is unrealistic," Allie said. There was a bite in her tone now.

Brooke took a step backward and felt her expression falling into one of despair. The Queen song had ended. The crowd around them was totally silent. "Are you saying no?" she asked.

"I can't say yes," Allie whispered. Brooke was sure that their body language would reveal to anyone around exactly what was happening.

Allie looked around and gave an apologetic grimace to the crowd, then patted Brooke's shoulder as if they were teammates after a failed play. She walked off the dock to the left side of the boathouse, crossing over to the paved path. Surely she had a bag to retrieve, or duties to complete at the end of the day—sails to furl or life vests to stack. But she must have figured she needed to exit the situation as soon as possible. Soon Brooke stood completely alone, discarded poster board signs strewn around her feet.

She wondered if she should cry. Or, potentially, she should laugh, wave to the crowd, and then trot away. She wondered if she could quit her job and move to a new town, never see Armond or anyone she worked with, anyone she was friends with, again. Perhaps that was the only move she could make now. She hadn't given herself an exit strategy for this eventuality. What kind of delusional thinking had prevented her from planning for this? She was mortified. And yet. A small tickle of excitement lurked in her chest, underneath the embarrassment. Even though the spectacle hadn't gone as planned, she'd done what she'd wanted to do; she had shown the people around her who she really was. She pulled her sunglasses back over her eyes, yet remained standing there, totally still, in the middle of the dock. She couldn't move.

Soon someone pulled on her arm. It was her neighborhood friend Caroline Pickney. The baby cooed in the carrier on her chest as Caroline said softly, "Come on, sweetie, it's all going to be fine," and led Brooke away from the dock.

This friend she had known her whole life, this saint of a human, walked with Brooke toward the grass. Her nurse colleagues and Allie's students had dispersed, or disappeared really. There were just a few lingering people around. As they walked to the right, Caroline rubbing her back, another hand touched Brooke's shoulder lightly.

Armond. She couldn't remember if he had ever touched her once, in all the years that she had known him. He nodded rather gravely, but then managed another weak smile. "Don't worry, Birdie," he said, and then cleared his throat. "You did an admirable thing, dear, and, well. It will all work out for the best, in the end. That's a bet I'd take." Then he winked. A wink, from Armond! With that, he nodded again and turned, crossing the dock in the other direction.

Brooke thought: she loved that man. Although she still couldn't speak a word, she was entirely grateful for him, and Caroline, and her friends, and her home. Once she could speak again, she would pull herself together, pack up the rest of her apartment, and find a new, close place to live. Despite everything, she was at that moment veraciously proud to be in the middle of the beastly process of becoming herself.

13

Two weeks later, Shelley sat in the back of a chauffeured town car beside Mr. Kamal, while Nick sat in the front passenger's seat. They were on their way to their research site of the day, the Doss Museum, which happened to be the same place where Nick's protests were going down. As they drove, Shelley's heart thrummed with some combination of elation and fear. There was a thrill to it, being in a shared space with her family and her lover, surrounded by the people she held most dear and yet who could not truly know about each other. Nick was entirely unaware of the nature of her relationship with Mr. Kamal. And Mr. Kamal thought her brother's name was Quentin.

The driver and the three passengers were silent as the air-conditioning blew cold and chemical onto their bodies. Before Shelley could even see the crowds in the park, she heard drumming from down the block. In the past two weeks, two major things had happened: Nick's little anti-ExxonMobil movement had taken off, and he had become another one of Mr. Kamal's employees. He was an "artist assistant" now, and had come to four different houses where he had made drawings of various rooms and angles and ancient furniture, at the blind man's seemingly random commands. For this work, Nick had been furnished with a set of 4H chisel-head pencils, a T square, and a ream of high-quality chlorine-free watercolor paper. Shelley was there when the materials were gifted to him. "These are all the tools you'll need," Mr. Kamal had grunted. "At least, it was all that the multitudes of professional artists I have worked with needed."

At the end of each day's work, Shelley felt sick with anticipation as Nick stood in the foyer of whatever grand house they were in, ripping his drawings out of the sketchbook. Mr. Kamal would quickly finger each of the surfaces of the drawings, reading the etchings as if they were braille, before nodding to assert that Nick's work was sufficient. Never once did Mr. Kamal offer a compliment, never once did he even mutter an approval. Then Nick would be dismissed, free to pull his hood over his head and make his way home. He would scurry back to their apartment, which had, in the past few weeks, without Shelley's explicit permission, become a weirdo-activist flop-house, filled with the runoff from the people sleeping in Art Park. The electricity was still off, and it was wildly chaotic inside, but Shelley couldn't bring herself to care about it, really. After every workday when Nick left, her tense body would deflate as she calmly helped Mr. Kamal into the waiting car. Then, after they traveled up the elevator and into the private space of his study, she would be at his command for whatever pain or pleasure he desired. She wouldn't return home to Strong Place for several hours.

Since the night at the hotel, Mr. Kamal had continued to call her cell phone as usual, barking out the time she should arrive the next morning. She would show up at the Grisham smirking, then proceed to follow his orders to read aloud and later, sometimes with Nick, trail him through mansions. She and Mr. Kamal's actions were basically the same as they had been on previous weeks, but now he touched her whenever he was alone with her, now her sly smile was met with his; they were a part of each other. They still hadn't actually engaged in sex, but there was groping and thrusting—she thought to the point of his completion—and quite often, spanking. Earlier that day, as she'd typed her notes alone in his dim study, she inhaled the scent of furniture polish while waiting to hear the creak of the floorboards and the shuffle of his steps. Finally, he entered the room. After fifteen minutes of her reading back her notes, he had cried out, "No!" Then elaborated, "I am still not getting what I need here. *Why, why, why* can you not access the appropriate details?" But once he calmed down, he dictated some more thoughts on the Irving mansion, then went over to her chair and pulled her out of it. He sat down and spread her over his lap, muttering into her neck, "Shelley-kins. My Shelley-kins. I own every part of you. You are mine now." He began spanking her on the outside of her shorts. She closed her eyes and imagined that the words were on the tip of his tongue; he spanked once, twice, getting harder with each hit, and Shelley knew that he was oh so close to whispering, "I love you."

For that afternoon though, Mr. Kamal had received special viewing privileges at the Doss House and Museum, as well as for the following three Mondays, as it was the only day of the week the place was not open to the public. He was thrilled to be one of the final researchers allowed in the museum before it was dismantled. As the town car pulled around East Seventieth Street, Shelley was able to clearly see inside the wrought iron fence of Art Park: the music came from a small circle of people, centered on a few hippies with oblong drums slung around their necks. There were many, many more people there though, standing alone or in small groups, most of them just watching the scene around them.

From the front seat Nick mumbled, "Holy shit." Through the sliver of the passenger's seat, she saw him lower his Yankees cap over his face and let his shoulders sink below the window. He whispered, "I had no idea it would look like this."

No one in the car responded. Shelley inspected Mr. Kamal's face. Was he insulted by her coarse brother? Rather than being grateful that Shelley had gotten him a paying job, Nick seemed bitter: a spoiled child who believed he was being forced to work. In fact, early that morning he'd resisted coming on this research trip, dramatically proclaiming in the unelectrified Whitby kitchen, "Going into the heart of the movement, into the headquarters of the Art Park and not participating—do you get that that's my idea of torture?"

Shelley poured herself a bowl of cereal and, filling up the bowl with tap water, as there was no working fridge to keep milk in, said, "If you want this job, and if you want this house to ever have lights again, you're coming."

"The park will be crawling with police, Shelley. Don't you care about me? Do you seriously hate me that much now?"

She had shaken her head. What she didn't tell Nick was that she knew that Mr. Kamal was, in his own withholding manner, appreciative of the work Nick was doing. And as he was Shelley's brother, she was partially credited for this assistance. Plus Nick had been all over upper Manhattan already, going in and out of the various houses on their research list. It couldn't be that different.

From the car, through the spaces in the Art Park fence, she could see an older homeless woman dancing beside the drummers. There were at least a hundred people packed into the concrete-bedded park, and card tables set up with various items—food, books, pamphlets. Tourists and commuters stopped to lean over the fence and take photographs, and navy-uniformed cops stood at the periphery, with bored thumbs hooked into their belt loops. Nick's forehead was pasted to the window now. He was probably looking for his dirt-crusted pals.

What was happening at her own apartment was getting out of control. Every evening there were more people there than the night before, lighting candles, whispering in groups on the floor. How Nick had changed since their early teenage summers on the Vineyard: he was, apparently, a highly social person now. A social person who was using her apartment as a kind of base camp for an unwashed group of entitled activists. Shelley was aware that part of the cachet of the apartment was that, although the electricity was still off, the place had couches and rugs, running water and two bathrooms with doors that closed: utilities all of these "hard-core" activists were missing in the public park. She had been reading daily with Mr. Kamal about the movement, mostly short articles in the *Times*, but she still didn't totally understand the motivations of these people. But then, she couldn't really be bothered to focus on it. In fact, she couldn't be bothered to focus on much except Mr. Kamal's hands. She was, she knew, in a full-fledged obsession. Brooke's calls were less frequent now, and Armond's had basically ceased. Not telling Nick about the will had been the right move: it seemed to her that the issue was all but over. She'd probably just be able to keep living in her house. Whenever Shelley was not working, she would come home and float upstairs, then lie on her back in bed and remember the musky smell of the man who made her feel unique, as if she deserved his attention. He wanted to mold her into a better version of herself. And she wanted so much more of him.

The town car driver addressed Mr. Kamal: "We're headed to the back entrance of the museum, sir, on Seventy-First Street?" His voice slid through his nose, straight out of Brooklyn.

"I was informed we'd be greeted at the freight entrance."

"Very good."

The car rounded Fifth Avenue, away from carnivalesque action of the park, away from the crowds and drums and Nick's friends. They pulled into a small driveway off Seventy-First Street, which led up to a steel-covered loading dock. A pantsuited young woman, probably not much older than Shelley, was waiting.

After introductions and the museum aide gushing over Mr. Kamal, as they often did, the aide led Mr. Kamal and the Whitby children inside, through the loading dock. "This protest is pretty crazy," the aide said. "We want to save the museum too, of course. But it's a total circus getting to work every day, and all of us here at the Doss just keep asking each other: 'Why us?' Why did these crazies make an example of our museum of all places, ya know?"

All eight feet clacked down a narrow hallway and through a rolling oak door. Mr. Kamal moved cautiously, his two hands flexed, fingers straight, and Shelley forced herself to avert her eyes; he didn't want to be helped.

Soon the group stood in the museum's grand courtyard: pristine and glass-roofed, with a kidney-shaped pond decorated with artfully placed boulders and small islands out of which pygmy palm trees angled. The walls of the courtyard were carved stone, with semicircular inlets highlighting sculptural busts and headless Grecian torsos. An older, grand, and immaculately preserved world was instantly around them. They were transported.

Mr. Kamal grunted and said, "This structure inspires the most powerful feeling an architect ever has: envy. How I wish I had built it." A faint chant from outside could be heard—"Hey-hey, ho-ho, this classist system has got to go. Say wha?"—but mixed with the tinkling of water running up and over the small fountain at the midpoint of the pond, even the chant took on the nature of soothing background music. This place had five times the grandeur of the other mansions they'd been researching all summer.

"It's really something, isn't it?" the museum aide said. "This space was part of the original home. This glass ceiling went in around 1930. Before that, the courtyard was paved and cars could drive right in here. . . ." She sighed, in love with the story. "The temporary exhibitions we have right now are the early-twentieth-century Yiddish theater retrospective in the south wing, and the hip-hop revolution photography exhibition—"

"We are only interested in the Dosses' original collection, in the European masters," Mr. Kamal interrupted.

"Right, that's fine. All researchers get three hours, so just come knock on the glass at five and I'll let you out the back," she said, and clacked away.

The Whitbys and Mr. Kamal stood silently, taking in the cool, verdant space. Finally, Mr. Kamal barked, "We'll start in the central foyer," and then they heard the scratch of the oak rolling door opening again.

"Yoo-hoo, Kamal?" The museum aide waved her clipboard in the air. "I forgot about the forms to sign! I need the signature and information of the primary researcher, please."

"She wants us to go to her," Shelley whispered. Mr. Kamal took off walking.

Back in the industrial hallway Mr. Kamal grunted, "Shelley, sign the forms." She moved as fast as possible to sign and flip the pages.

After the signing, after the woman and her dress shoes walked away, Nick silently nudged Shelley with his elbow and pointed to two gray doors in the museum's hallway that had a metal ring of keys hanging off the lock. His eyes were sparking with mischief in their old Nick way, but Shelley raised her two hands as if to say, *Who cares about that?* He gave her an exaggerated thumbs-down. She didn't care if she wasn't fun anymore.

Soon Mr. Kamal commanded them all, yet again, to go to the main foyer. As they passed the side doors though, Shelley reached out and grabbed the forgotten keys, holding them with two hands to prevent them from jangling. She didn't have a reason to take them, other than the fact that Nick was right: she used to be fun. From behind her, he silently squeezed her two shoulders. He'd seen her do it. She shrugged him off but couldn't help her sneaky smile. They were still, sometimes, a good team.

The Doss Museum's many public galleries were downstairs, but the upstairs, although blocked off, was still preserved in the style with which the Doss family had lived. Mr. Kamal and the Whitbys stood in the foyer, beneath the curving, grand staircase. A gold runner ran up the center of the marble steps, and the pipes of a bronze organ were built into the wall behind them.

Mr. Kamal turned to Nick. "Quentin, we will end up with you doing drawings of the masterfully restored bowling alley that the Dosses had built for entertaining purposes, in the basement. But first, I need you to spend several hours upstairs. I want precise drawings of the furnishings of the master bedroom and bathrooms, the ones that would have belonged to the lord and lady of the house, Henry and his sickly wife, Isabella. Then move on to the servants' quarters. I need to know the differences in size and scale between the two types of rooms. I must have all the details of the furniture. Nothing sloppy, Quentin."

"Sure," Nick said then, looking at the red velvet rope at the bottom of the stairs. "But I don't think we're supposed to go up there."

"Do you always do what you're supposed to do?" Mr. Kamal shot back. His eyes would have rolled if they could have. Nick's certainly did.

As Nick stepped over the velvet rope at the top of the second floor of the Doss, he wondered if the elite of previous generations—art collectors and diplomats, Roger's father, Roger Sr.—were able to bypass the rope, too. Wasn't it hypocritical, the supposedly progressive bent of the museum? The Robin Hood–esque mission was dependent on the preservation of the über rich: the upstairs had to exist in order for it to give to the downstairs.

As he moved in and out of several second-floor bedrooms, the silence around him enabled him to think clearly about the past months. He still hadn't told Grace the details of the fire in Maine and the screaming that had happened on the roof of the biotech site, how he had limped behind as Big D carried a moaning Kever through the woods. But he had a partner now. He and Grace were in this mess together. He wasn't sure if it was because of *her*, or because of the time she showed up in his life, but now he wanted her beside him always. But along with his desire for Grace, he had an odd competitive edge. She was able to go into the park and actually participate in this growing anti-gas movement. And she was rising up within it, sitting center stage at the greater movement's spokes council meetings, not worried in the slightest about being photographed. It wasn't fair.

He walked into the final bedroom at the end of the upstairs hallway of the Doss, which was the largest as well as the most frilly, and decided this must be the one that belonged to the "lady of the house," Isabella.

The bed was pushed lengthwise against the wall, and above it an upholstered awning hung from the ceiling, with canopy curtains falling to either side. The wall's molding had four layers of looping designs, like strips of a wedding cake. The ceiling itself was painted with swirls of gold, green vines growing out of them and faded pink blossoms reaching toward the center of the room. Three identical chandeliers hung from the midline of the ceiling, built with strands of crystals and shrunken ivory lampshades. Nick lay in several different positions on the floor in order to catch all the details of the room above him, and after he'd been sketching for God knows how long, his hand began to ache.

He moved on to the adjoining bathroom and was about to sit on the edge of the claw-foot tub to get the best view of the porcelain toilet and bidet, when he again heard faint sounds coming from outside. Cheering rose as if a celebrity had taken the stage. Drums started up, and someone on a megaphone began chanting: "We won't take another loss! We are here to save the Doss!"

Nick opened the bathroom window and stuck his torso out. He couldn't tell exactly what was happening in the park, as it was at least two hundred yards away, but he did see people clumping together, clapping.

This commotion had been happening for the past several hours, while he had been sitting in a darkened room, sketching an old, fancy bed, laboring for an old rich man. Nick asked himself: *What the hell am I doing with my life?* He was standing quite literally on the wrong side of history.

He left the window open and sank to the cool black-and-white tile of the bathroom floor. His head ached from what he guessed was a hangover. What he needed to do was to smoke and think. Why had he been so against this meditative habit for years? In his pocket he had a pack of cigarettes that he'd swiped off the coffee table at Strong Place. He lit one while searching the distant Art Park crowd for the short dark hair that belonged to Grace. Although he couldn't find her in the crowd, bolts of jealousy ran through his chest.

He was fairly sure that the figure standing on top of a mailbox at the other end of the park was David. Nick needed to leave the museum, before he did something stupid. He had told Shelley it would be too much for him, being this close to the park and not joining his comrades. Nick knew himself; he could feel it when his irrational impulses were coming on. He could sense the heat growing in his bloodstream, the first warning sign. He should go find Mr. Kamal and tell him he was feeling sick and had to go home. Stubbing out the cigarette on the window sash, he got up from the floor of the bathroom and left Isabella's room. He stomped over the carpets, thinking that nothing, especially not eight dollars an hour, was worth having what he craved dangled right in front of him.

Downstairs, he found himself in a maze of gallery rooms holding the newer art. The hip-hop exhibit had Adidas sneakers and LL Cool J's bucket hat on display, beside a huge gold portable boom box. After he'd been downstairs for more than ten minutes, he tried simply calling out, "Hello? Shelley?"

No one answered. He realized he'd walked in a circle. Had he walked it twice? He found an archway and turned down a hallway he was fairly sure he hadn't been down before. This was a long corridor that held the Robert Moses exhibit. Wall-mounted cases displayed miniature three-dimensional models of highways and bridges. White stands held brochures and photographs propped up in glass boxes, in front of a blown-up photo-graph of Moses himself wearing an old-fashioned hard hat, in front of a half-built Triborough Bridge. Halfway down the corridor, Nick heard the dull din of his half sister's voice.

He followed the sound. His line was prepared: *Mr. Kamal, I am having a personal issue I'd rather not explain.* Hopefully the old man would assume a physical problem and send him home, no questions asked. And then Nick would never return to this awful job.

Shelley's voice was audible now, and Nick made out a few words: *master, excitement, learning.* He moved toward the open doorway, and then he saw something truly shocking. His feet stopped, and he stood in the middle of the hall, struck with confusion. He looked behind himself, fool-ishly checking if anyone else was there to witness this too.

In a gallery room, Shelley, although speaking fairly calmly, was lying on the gleaming wood floor on her stomach. On the high walls above her hung golden frames, inside of which was heavy black paint around bloated and pale faces. On the floor, Shelley's two arms were stretched behind her back as if tied together, but as far as Nick could tell there was no rope. Her face and neck were lifted to the wall before her, and her two legs made one tail-like line. Mr. Kamal was above her, the weak slope of his shoulders falling into his arms, hands shoved into his pockets. Although Nick couldn't make out the old man's words, he could hear that occa-sionally he spoke and Shelley answered him, almost shouting from her awkward position on the floor.

For a moment Nick wondered: was Shelley trying to turn this old blind man into a buffoon? Evil in her utter disregard, that would be his old Shelley. But no, there was something in her strained voice, her breathless answers to the old man, that made him think Mr. Kamal knew Shelley was lying there.

He must have been close to Art Park now, because the chant from outside was clearly audible: "Corporate rule, you're gonna fail! New York City is not for sale!" But Nick could hear both of the voices on the other side of the wall more clearly now as well.

"And the Vermeer on the right. Describe it," Mr. Kamal ordered.

Shelley said, "The plaque says the painting is titled *Girl Interrupted at Her Music*. A man stands above a younger woman—a girl. He's teaching and guiding her, handing her sheets of paper." She took a deep breath. "There is no malice in her stare. And the man does not even look up. One wonders how many times he has practiced just like this, with a young woman. Worked to make her learned and cultured. It is new for her, but certainly not for him."

She stopped speaking, and Mr. Kamal didn't say a word. Nick peeked around the corner, afraid that the old man could be hurting Shelley. Both Shelley and Mr. Kamal were faced toward the paintings still, but now his foot was on the small of her back. He was stepping on her. Hot anger roiled in Nick's stomach.

"Describe the Vermeer on the left. Speak!" Mr. Kamal barked.

Shelley spoke more fluidly now. Perhaps she had been planning in the silence. "The painting on the left is nearly the same setup: a young woman and an older man, at a table, below a window ushering light into the room and into the painting. But the location of the woman and man are flipped. In this painting we can only see the back of the man's red coat, but we get to see the woman's face. It's broad and excited. The window is open in this painting, and the light and air from the outside seem to inhabit the room."

"And which of the paintings do you enjoy more, Shelley Whitby?" After a silent beat, Mr. Kamal roared again, "Speak!"

Her voice lowered. "I like the painting on the right better. The master and his pupil. But not for the reason that you think."

What the hell was going on? Nick was faced with a decision: he could burst in, effectively catching the two of them in whatever sordid activity this was, or he could run away and pretend that he had never witnessed this bizarre interaction at all. Shelley wasn't being hurt. She appeared, as far as he could tell, to be a willing participant. But the foot. No one, especially not Shelley, deserved to be treated like that. And then Nick remembered: this pervert was Grace's father.

Shelley continued. "The painting on the right with the interrupted girl, it's private. You can tell that this time with her teacher is sacred. This one moment is going to make an indelible mark on that girl's life."

Shelley looked down, her nose touching the floor.

"What the hell is happening?" Nick's voice preceded him as he tore into the gallery room. Mr. Kamal appeared to lose his balance for a moment, and he stumbled sideways. Shelley jumped up so quickly it was as if she were never on the ground. "Are you okay, Shelley?"

"I just—" She was flustered.

Mr. Kamal, steadied on his two feet, crossed his arms. "Every artist has a particular way to work, young man, and you've just seriously disrupted mine."

"Artist? What kind of fucking art is that?" Nick's words cut through the room in a high register. He marched over to Shelley and grabbed her upper arm. "Was he hurting you?"

"Get the hell off of me!" She pushed him away. In a growl she said, "I got you this job, and this is how you repay me?"

Although Mr. Kamal's arms remained crossed, his body and his face now displayed very little anger, and even less embarrassment. It was absurd: the man looked smug. Nick's blood raced in his veins as he looked from the aging man to Shelley and back. The three of them stood in the middle of the empty gallery.

Nick asked Mr. Kamal again, "Why the hell were you doing that to my sister? What kind of bullshit art do you think you're creating?"

"The book is about America when there was a ruling class."

"Ha!" Nick's hands flew up in front of his face. "*When* there was a ruling class?"

Mr. Kamal, cool and even, articulated, "Shelley, it appears your brother is not interested in working on this project with us."

"Half brother," Nick grumbled. "We have different mothers."

"And Ni—*Quentin*—is adopted," Shelley added. She looked out the side of her eye at Nick. "Not that it matters."

Nick shook his head, trying with all his might to let that comment bounce off him. Who the hell knew if he was a blood-related Whitby? Shelley certainly didn't. And even if his mother denied it, she cared too much about appearances to be trusted. Adrenaline spiked through his limbs. "I just need to ask you, Mr. Kamal, *sir*: What are we even doing here? What do you think you're going to learn from these houses? People were rich then, and they're rich now."

Mr. Kamal shoved his hands into his pockets. "These houses and the greatness that brought them into being, the seemingly impossible dreams that were made possible—these are bold feats that great men accomplished. And they need to be paid attention to, studied, and observed. These men made things! These are the men who tell the beautiful, surprising story of America."

"It's men like that who make their daughters want to die."

"Excuse me?"

There was a long silence where no one said anything. Shelley shook her head rapidly at Nick. While pointing out the window, she mouthed the words, *Leave, asshole.*

"Quentin, I would like you to repeat what you just said," Mr. Kamal commanded. "May I add that you are currently in my employ."

Nick shifted his weight. "All I said was that ruling-class men like the ones you're interested in, they're the same exact men who make their daughters want to die."

Mr. Kamal snorted. Shelley was totally silent. After a few moments, mostly for the sake of something to do, Nick took off the Yankees cap he was wearing and turned it around to examine the label.

"What on earth do you know about the men of the ruling class?" Mr. Kamal asked.

"More than I want to," Nick shot back.

Shelley put one hand over her eyes. "Stop it, Nick."

Mr. Kamal said, "Quentin, do you know my daughter?"

When Nick awoke that morning, Grace's warm, naked side touched his, her bare breast pointing to the corner of the ceiling. He'd rolled over and buried his nose in the scent of her hair. At that moment, in the museum, other smells of her were still on his chin, his elbows. "Yes, I do know Grace, sir. In fact, sir, I love Grace."

Mr. Kamal spun around to Shelley. He had become the apex of the triangle, the Whitby children two lesser points he alternated between. He wasted no time now. He hollered, "As my amanuensis and assistant I would have expected you to let me know that your family was intruding on mine."

"They're just friends." Shelley's voice became a whine. "Like Grace and I. Why would you want to know a bland detail like that?"

Mr. Kamal's nostrils flared. "Like Grace and *me*." He stomped once on the ground. "This is entirely inappropriate." He stomped again, twice. "My daughter has better things to focus on. I do not approve of some tramp boy, born of a tramp mother, defiling the most precious—the most invested in—project of my life." His fists were clenched by his sides. This was an impending tantrum.

"Defiling? What the hell were you just doing to my sister you piece of sh—"

"Stop! Let's leave!" Shelley interrupted.

"I will leave. And I'm never working for you again, *Yousef*," Nick said.

"Trash" was all Mr. Kamal muttered in response.

Nick screamed in anguish. His scream sounded childish, he knew, like a little boy being ordered into the corner for a time-out. He thought about Roger then, about how much he simultaneously hated the man and everything he represented, and yet felt desolate at the idea that he had let him down. Or was letting him down every single day. Nick's familiar friend, outrage, rushed through his arms. He could still hear the chanting outside, now echoing the old standard of "This is what democracy looks like. This is what democracy looks—"

Nick turned and yelled over his shoulder, "I'll send you a bill, you sadistic psychopath." Then he began to jog away, retracing his path into the Robert Moses hallway. Once in the hallway he broke into an actual run. How the hell did someone get out of this museum? His pulse pumped rapidly, he was seething. Nick took a few wrong turns but then found the bright and dazzling courtyard and the rolling doors leading to the back exit of the Doss. Outside, the anti-gassers wanted to save the place. But they didn't get the complexity of it all. The founders of the museum were the very people who created the capitalist system that was currently destroying the world. As he moved down the long industrial hallway, he fantasized about seeing the whole museum go up in flames. He needed to grow a pair and rejoin the world. At that moment, he could hear no chants or songs coming from Art Park, only some faint drumming. He pushed through the back door and the direct sun struck his eyes, making, for a second, his whole world go dark.

The traffic on Seventy-First Street zoomed by, and he heard a voice from Art Park call out, "Mic check!" Then many voices, in a higher-pitched unison, respond, "Mic check!" One trickle of sweat ran from his right temple down his cheek, and more ran from his armpits over his rib cage. Shelley didn't understand him, and never would. She was just like the rest of her screwed-up, catastrophe-causing, cursed, money-worshipping family. Maybe he should feel lucky that they'd never considered him a real part of them. He never should have shown up at her house in the first place. He only had one life. What if this was the only summer he would ever have again? What if this was his only time to be young and wild and make a difference in this toxic, self-destructing, non-sensical world? He stretched both hands over his head, fingers entwined, then cracked his neck to the left and the right. He was done with hiding, done with living inside the cramped apartment like a fugitive. He would go by Quentin Scribner; he would keep his secrets close to him. But this was his goddamn movement, his goddamn life, and he was going to be a goddamn part of it.

The silence around Shelley and Mr. Kamal echoed from the pitched ceiling to the decorative art objects propped on their white stands, then bounced off the marble floors. Nick had done the exact thing she had expected him to: let his psychotic anger loose at Mr. Kamal, humiliating her. But she wasn't concerned with Nick at that moment. Standing an arm's-length distance was the man she felt she certainly did love, his face contorted in confusion. Should she go over and rub his shoulders? Would he let her press her body against his, let himself feel all the parts of her that made her a woman?

"I'm sorry about my brother," she offered. "He's always had a temper."

Mr. Kamal grunted. She recalled the little moans he made nearly every weekday evening when he groped, spanked, or kissed her. She was making him happy.

"When it comes down to it he's actually a good guy, Quentin," she tried. "He's a little extreme at times. . . ."

Mr. Kamal's pale shirt had two half-moons of sweat growing toward his chest. She had given him so much trust. She'd just let him stand above her with a foot on her back, completely at his will and control. He owed it to her, to trust her now.

She placed one hand at his collar. The tang of garlic came off his breath. "It's really nothing to worry about." He let her kiss him, but as she pressed harder, standing on her toes, he pushed her away.

"This arrangement is over," he announced.

"Excuse me?"

"You need to leave the museum at once. Our work together is done."

"What?"

One hand went to his brow. He growled, "You heard me."

Shelley didn't move. Was he joking?

"Leave here at once!"

Shelley began, out of shock, to walk backward. She still had her notepad in her hand. The tape recorder was still on, sitting in her shorts pocket.

"Walk faster!" he yelled. "Out of my sight!"

She turned. She didn't know how to get out of the maze of museum rooms but kept moving, sandals hitting against the tiles rapidly: *flip-flip, flip-flip, flip-flip.* Why was he doing this? It was just another outburst. He could not want to be rid of her permanently. He had threatened this before, but he'd always been bluffing. She'd been banished from Rhode Island and then asked to return. He needed her.

She finally found the front exit of the museum and pushed herself out into the blindingly bright afternoon. She walked west through the Manhattan streets, now with the stunted pace of sheer confusion. Mr. Kamal couldn't really fire her, because if he did, she would be alone. She pictured her mother. Was a penchant for repulsing people genetic? As Shelley wove through the tourists and joggers in Central Park, she felt as if she were falling without any sort of parachute. Somewhere along the way, it seemed she had fucked up her whole life. But no one single decision had seemed so out of line. Maybe another person would not have left college. Perhaps someone else would have told Nick about Roger and the money from the start. But choosing each of those actions would have been more work than an average person should be asked to do. Why couldn't she ever just be average?

When she entered her apartment, sweaty and sunstruck, a few of the anti-gas activists were lounging on the floor of the parlor. They nodded but didn't say a proper hello. Somehow the lack of light made everything quieter inside as well. "Quentin!" Shelley hollered up the stairs, now accustomed to using his fake name even in their house.

"He's not here," a girl with an affectless voice said. "I got a text that he and Grace are down at the park."

Shelley guffawed. "He's decided to go out into the park now?" The pair of activists on the floor didn't respond. Maybe they were stoned.

Shelley spent the next hour in an old aluminum chair at the lacquered kitchen table, watching Nick's bozos come in and go out: David, Esmerelda, four or five others she knew by sight but not name. They dropped their bags on the floor, a few waved hello. They were used to walking right in, as the Whitbys had stopped locking the door.

"How's life, Shells?" David asked. One of the nameless ones went upstairs and took a shower. Shelley kept her small black cell phone resting on her knee, but Nick didn't come into the apartment and Mr. Kamal didn't call her. Eventually she retreated back to Biddy's room but came down to check for Nick every forty-five minutes. He didn't come back all night.

The next morning, Shelley lay in her sweat-damp underwear on Biddy's bed, clutching her barely charged cell phone. She had been charging it at the Grisham every day, but it had been too many hours since she'd been there. All the windows were open in her apartment, yet the place was still like the inside of a steam shower. By a quarter after ten she'd received no instructing phone call from Mr. Kamal. She got up and checked her old bedroom: no sleeping Nick. No Grace either.

As the hours of being ignored stacked up, her initial confusion at the situation transformed into anger. Everything had been perfect: her relationship with Mr. Kamal was building steadily, rapturously; the house was lively with all these people, stinking or not. But Nick and his temper, Nick and his inability to understand the nuances of a situation, fucked it all up.

By one in the afternoon Shelley was entirely pissed off. She borrowed one of the activist's phones and called Mr. Kamal herself. Clova answered and reported that the boss was "indisposed" but assured her she would pass on the message. Just like that, Shelley had been abandoned again. It was inevitable; it was her curse.

14

_____

Susan Scribner counted to ten, slowly, then turned her rented Ford Focus onto Trapelo Road in Belmont, Massachusetts, when the *waa-ah, waa-ah* of a police cruiser's siren went off behind her.

"Crap!" she said aloud. She slowed the car and watched the back of Brooke's wood-paneled Jeep reach the peak of a hill and then disappear behind it. The cop who showed up at Susan's window was a young and fit man, or boy rather. He looked just out of high school.

He asked, "Are you aware that you ran a red back there, ma'am?"

"My son is sick!" she found herself yelping through the open window, and then, as if she believed it, her face began to quiver. "I'm sorry, but I'm on my way to see my son. And he's very sick." She took a deep breath, and the police officer, as young as he was, appeared unimpressed. "I'm sure you have a mother. A mother who cares about you more than life itself. I'm just so worried. My baby— Don't you have a mother who loves you?"

The kid was blushing now. He took the aviator sunglasses off his forehead and muttered, "Well, I'd hate for something to happen to you when your son needs you." She wrung her hands together as he wrote her out a warning, not out of worry for Nick but rather out of the knowledge that she'd certainly lost track of Brooke's car, and was now in an inconsequential suburb of Boston for no reason whatsoever.

Susan had arrived at Logan airport eight hours earlier. The previous morning, in her kitchen in California, she'd read an article in the *New York Times* that reported that a recent graduate of New York University, a girl named Devorah Jacobson, had been arrested as part of a violent political protest against a military recruitment center in New York City. As Susan read this, sitting at her round butcher-block table, her heart dropped into her Teva sandals. She had heard this girl's name from Nick's mouth, and if she knew her son (and she did, she knew the location of every nerve in his body, could predict every thought he would ever think), she knew that he could be taken in by an abominable person like this girl. And if this girl was committing crimes in the name of liberal politics, who was to say what Nick was doing. This article, in conjunction with that haunted postcard she'd received two months ago, was too much. Within twenty minutes, Susan had booked a flight out of John Wayne Airport and made an appointment to talk with the family lawyer, Steven Armond, in person. She arrived in Boston and checked into the Copley Plaza—the only hotel in the city where Whitbys ever stayed—before seven in the morning, which meant that she had nearly thirty hours free before her meeting with Armond.

The car stalking, or investigating, wasn't exactly premeditated. Susan had simply spent the early afternoon lingering outside Brooke's family's home, the Beacon Hill stone manse that would soon be the property of Nick. Or her own property, if they still couldn't find Nick. During the two hours of sitting in the car, coffee drinking and radio flipping and smoking two cigarettes she guiltily puffed through a crack in the window, Susan was consumed by the notion that this wasn't how her life should have panned out. She was meant for something greater. She was meant for the glory, acknowledgment, and excitement that she'd almost received when she moved to California as the new Mrs. Whitby. But Roger had fully baited her, then fully switched on her. Instead of thrilling, her full-time life with him, her life as his wife, had been painful and depressing. And the most depressing part, for Susan, was the missed opportunity. That was what she had told Roger a few months before he died, as she sat across from him on his elderly, sick man's porch in Pasadena. She'd clearly stated: "You missed the chance to accomplish great things, Rog, and I am on my way to missing that as well. But our son doesn't have to. Don't you want one son of yours to fulfill the dreams you have for him? He's your youngest child, and he's still alive. Give him this chance." Roger had remained expressionless, turning his tongue over in his open mouth. But when she'd put a pen and the amended will in his lap, he'd signed it. He had done it himself, with his own shaky right hand.

In the car in Boston, Susan was so distracted that she'd almost missed Brooke. It had to be her: a petite blonde walked out of the house's front door and took prissy little steps into a Jeep that was parked across the street. It wasn't as if Susan wanted to follow her. She had been intending, of course, to hail the girl down to chat. But Brooke moved too fast—there simply wasn't time to jump out and flag her down.

And now here Susan was on this empty stretch of Massachusetts road, surrounded on all sides by lush elms, as the baby police officer pulled his car out from behind hers and gave her a friendly wave as he sped away. She cursed under her breath. She had no idea why Brooke would be out there in the suburbs. She was probably walking into the front door of a boring boyfriend's house by now, a dentist or a life insurance broker, just another nobody who would marry into the Whitby family, dragging it further down.

As Susan drove up and over the hill, looking from side to side for a sign of the Jeep, she realized she'd barely slept and hadn't drank any water in hours. The houses on the sides of the road were becoming depressing one-level ranch houses, a step above trailers with their wheels off. She felt old. These past few months had aged her indecorously. In her purse she had the postcard she looked at every night, the physical item that convinced her that her baby was certainly alive. It wasn't even a real postcard but rather a ragged, rectangular piece of cardboard with a pen drawing on it, of a younger version of herself. The woman in the drawing had her old flipped hair, wide cheeks, and freckles, and stood in front of 1970s retro brick buildings with a water tower in the distance. Her son had certainly drawn this picture of her in old New York. The back had no note, only an X drawn on it. The postmark was from Maine. Maine! Why Nick would be in Maine perplexed her. But after talking herself out of the fear that he had been kidnapped, she had settled on the idea that her son did not want to be found. The truth was that even before she had received the postcard, she'd been suspicious. Nick might have gotten himself involved in something that was over his head, that he wasn't equipped to handle. But she'd also begun to be suspicious of the other members of the Whitby family. That rotten girl in New York, Shelley, for one. And Susan knew almost nothing about the daughter who lived in Roger's house in Boston. What would Brooke, no longer a young woman at all, be able to convince her child to do? Susan just didn't know.

That was why she had sat outside the house on Beacon Hill. It was the only smart move, to collect all the information that she could before going in to see Armond the next morning. She hadn't yet decided if she would show Armond the postcard. But she was planning to mention to him the story about the NYU girl, just to pass it by his ears under attorney-client privilege and hear what he had to say.

She had been driving for miles now, without a sign of Brooke's Jeep. There were no malls, no movie theaters, no nothing. Soon she entered a new town, Waltham, and pulled into the sparsely populated parking lot of a Bickford's Restaurant. By the time she had a tall stack of pancakes in front of her and was pouring maple syrup over her whole plate— prediabetes be damned—she was distraught. Her waitress had sprayed-up bangs and the pancakes were not very good.

In the booth behind her a mother was talking to her teenage daughter, hands pressed against the table. "I know it's tough to see your dad in there, lovie, but this is the best facility on the Eastern Seaboard, and he needs to remain there until he's stable enough to come home. We're doing the right thing by keeping him in the hospital."

The daughter looked nearly catatonic and didn't touch the sandwich or french fries on her plate. The mother continued talking. "Mental illness is just like any other illness, and he needs to heal." The daughter continued giving zero response. Some people really only thought of themselves. By the time Susan's plate was empty, it was clear the woman's husband was in a psych hospital, and Susan's anxiety was winding up by the minute.

Susan put an arm over the back of the booth, swiveling around. "I'm sorry—the hospital you're discussing. Is it near here?"

The woman's mouth dropped open, and now the teenage girl moved: her hands covered her eyes and her face dropped down.

"We're having a private conversation!" the woman huffed.

Susan pushed on. "Is the hospital near here?"

"Well, McLean," the woman said as if she were conveying a secret. "It's just a mile up the road."

"On Trapelo? Back toward Belmont?"

The confused woman nodded hesitantly, but Susan was already rummaging through her purse for her wallet. She didn't even bother to ask for the bill, just threw a twenty down on the table and bolted out the door.

At the traffic light outside Bickford's, she rolled down her window and screamed to a car beside her, "Where's McLean Hospital?" And a man with a wretched Boston accent informed her to simply go straight and take a left at a "big yellah house."

Sure enough, right before the yellow clapboard house was a stone sign almost entirely obscured by a bush, announcing the name of the hospital, McLean. Susan was a woman possessed, convinced by the notion that somehow, Brooke could be at this hospital visiting Nick. Her poor baby. No doctor had ever diagnosed him, but she was his mother and she knew him so intimately, so much better than anyone else ever could, and therefore she knew that he was prone to doing peculiar things. Impulsiveness, that was his problem. But also anger. Could his anger have landed him in a psych ward? Her heart sped faster than the car. At the end of a long and winding driveway was a parking lot, and there it was: Brooke's wood-paneled Jeep. Susan actually ran inside.

The main hallway appeared as if it belonged in a museum, but at the end of it a nurse sat behind bulletproof glass. The nurse peered over the top of her glasses, giving Susan a practiced, perhaps permanent, pissed-off glare. "ID," she demanded.

"I'm here because I'm supposed to be visiting someone. My sister, Brooke Whitby, she just came in?"

"I need an ID." This woman was not friendly.

After checking out Susan Scribner Whitby's license, the nurse consulted a clipboard. "You can visit Ms. Whitby until eight, if you'd like."

"Right, but my sister—she's visiting someone else. What room is she visiting?"

"Ms. Whitby is in 103."

Susan asked, "Did my sister just check in?" But even as she spoke the words, the realization dawned on her.

"No. She's visiting Ms. Whitby. Aren't you doing the same damn thing?" The nurse looked ready to fight.

Susan paused, her mouth falling open. Then she tried something. "Uh, what time am I allowed to see *Elizabeth* until?" Susan said, planting the name.

"Visiting hours go until eight. Did I not just say that?"

Susan shook her head, turned, and scuttled down the hallway back toward the front door.

"Excuse me? Ma'am, where the hell are you going?"

"I'll come back!" Susan hollered as her footfalls quickened on the hardwood floor. The last thing she wanted to do was see Elizabeth Saltman Whitby. She was simultaneously entirely relieved that Nick was not a patient in this place, and sorely disappointed that she wasn't going to see him, but her suspicions were confirmed: Brooke and Shelley, Roger's spoiled children, were colluding somehow. Why else would Brooke be visiting Shelley's mother? They were certainly working together to try to take down her son and steal what was lawfully his.

The next day, Brooke, in salmon-colored shorts and a very loose-fitting T-shirt, held up a persimmon fruit in her right hand as she stood like a surprised child in the doorway of Armond's home office, and her stomach dropped to her knees. Susan Scribner sat on the leather couch, and

Armond sat across from her in one of his black, carved wood Harvard chairs, the same chairs that everyone in the Back Bay seemed to have. It had been a very hard few weeks since the botched proposal. Brooke had packed up the rest of her home and found herself a rental off of Cambridge Street, in a squat elevator building with stained tan carpet in the hallway. All she wanted was to have a few moments alone with Armond, in order to tell him the baby news. Susan wasn't supposed to be there until later. "I thought we were meeting alone first," Brooke said.

"Mrs. Whitby, uh," Armond stuttered, motioning to Susan and looking more mortified than usual. "She arrived earlier than expected."

"Brooke. You're looking better than you did in April," Susan snickered.

What a ray of positivity that woman was. Earlier that morning, Brooke had gone to an appointment at Beth Israel's Women's Health Center, where an ultrasound tech had told her, with a weak-tea smile, that not only was the baby a boy, but "This week, he's the size of a passion fruit!" On her walk to Commonwealth Avenue, Brooke—who had no idea what a passion fruit was—had stopped at Savenor's market and asked the clerk if they had them there. As she stood over the outdoor crates overflowing with oranges and pummelos and jicamas, the clerk informed Brooke that a passion fruit was similar to a persimmon, and handed her a fruit that resembled an oversize orange lemon. She bought the thing, chuckling about how Armond would get a kick out of this visual aid when she told him. She hadn't even told her own mother yet, but to Corney, her child would just be another grandchild. Armond, Brooke believed, would consider this baby special. And he would be proud of Brooke and her decision to have it by herself. Now she raised the persimmon in the air. "I had something personal I needed to discuss with you, Armond."

The word *personal* made him blush again. "Well, come in, please, sit down, Bird—Brooke. Plenty of time to discuss other matters later."

Soon the three sat in silence. Armond's office, and his whole house, carried the air of a university library: ample dark brown wood and ample echoing silence. Finally, he cleared his throat. "As you both know, in the matter of locating Nick Whitby, I have been struggling. As the executor of

Roger's will, I'm legally bound to protect the interest of the deceased, and therefore contacting Nick is my primary—"

"You know where he is?" Brooke asked with a gasp.

"No, no." Susan shook her head. "That's not what he means." Her arms were crossed over her chest in her typical haughty way.

"Is there a chance that we need to be considering the idea that something happened to him? That's he's been hurt or . . ." Brooke trailed off.

Susan took a deep breath. "I have reason to believe that he is in fine condition, or at least he was as of two months ago." Off the coffee table, she picked up what appeared to be a postcard and leaned over, handing it to Armond.

Armond held the card by the very edges, as if it were part of a crime scene and he didn't want to implicate himself by putting his fingerprints on it. It was clear that this wasn't the first time he'd examined it, though. He said to Brooke, "This is a piece of mail we believe was sent by Nick, in May of this year."

"What?" Brooke nearly roared. "Why are we only hearing about this now?"

Armond asked Susan, "Is there any chance that Nick knows about the inheritance and just does not want to claim it?"

Susan said, "No. My baby would call me, unless there was some reason he was being prevented." She sighed and ran one stressed-out hand through her hair. "He may be twenty-one, but he's a very *young* twenty-one. He's got ideas. You know, in the past few years . . . he's gotten some political ideas about radicalism and money and all of that. It's something he's going to grow out of. It's something he should have grown out of already."

"Where do we think he is?"

"The postcard came from Maine. The private investigator was looking for him there but didn't turn up any leads."

Armond began, "But there was an attack—"

"No need to discuss that anymore! He's not in Maine. That chapter is closed." Susan abruptly cut him off.

"Then where the hell is he?"

"I believe he's back in New York, and I think that Roger's daughter Shelley knows exactly where he is," Susan announced.

This was absurd, Brooke contended. The whole situation. As usual, this Susan woman understood little to nothing about the Whitby family. "Shelley doesn't know where he is."

Susan snorted. "Liars, all of you. Brooke, what on earth have you been doing with her and Elizabeth Saltman?"

Brooke coughed in surprise. "What?"

"I know that you've been visiting Elizabeth in the mental hospital."

Armond, without letting one visible emotion inflect the composure of his face, stood up and asked in a calm voice, "Tea or coffee for anyone? Celia, my secretary—I'll go ask her for a cup of tea." He took long, measured strides across the room and closed the door gently, leaving Brooke and Susan alone in the dimly lit office.

"Susan, how do you know that Elizabeth Saltman is in the hospital?"

"Word travels. And what you probably don't know is that women in that family, the Saltmans, they're all like that: not right in the head. That Shelley girl is very troubled, and frankly she's a dangerous person to be involved with. I've been trying to get my Nick away from her for years."

The gall of this woman. Shelley had never done a thing to her. "I went to New York a few weeks ago, and I went over to Shelley's house. She knows nothing about where Nick is. What about the investigator? Hasn't he found *anything* that can help us?"

"Not a thing. And that's why I need to become the beneficiary of the inheritance until we can find my son. It's the only thing that makes sense. I'm his next of kin."

Brooke's whole body contracted. This woman was a bona fide thief. She'd stolen Roger from Elizabeth and Shelley, and now she was trying to steal Brooke's home. If the houses were put into Susan's name, even briefly, that was the end of them. Brooke surprised herself with the words she said next. "What did you do to my father to make him leave everything to Nick?"

Susan grunted and shook her head, as if she'd been expecting to hear those words. She clutched the top of her purse and began rooting around in it. "Oh no. No, no. I'm not getting into this with you. Roger did exactly what he wanted with the will, and nothing else."

Armond walked back into the room, followed by Celia, the kindly middle-aged woman who had been his secretary for more than twenty years. Celia carried a teapot and three porcelain cups and saucers.

Susan pulled a package of cigarettes out of her purse and began tapping it against the leather sofa arm. She told on Brooke. "Armond, this discussion is turning uncivil. I'm being accused of illegal acts, and I do not appreciate the accusations."

Armond made eye contact with Brooke and gave her a slight nod of acknowledgment, which Brooke knew was his sincerest indication that he was on her side.

Brooke said, "My father did a lot of careless things to us, but he didn't do cruel things. At least not purposefully. I just can't believe he would have given my home away."

Susan, still clutching the cigarette package, spat out, "You should be thankful that you've been freeloading off Roger for this long. You're a grown woman! You don't even need his house."

"I'm pregnant," Brooke said slowly. It didn't need to be a secret anymore. It was the first time she'd realized she could use the news to her own advantage. "I'm pregnant and I'm single. And soon I'll have nowhere to live, because of you, Susan."

Susan lurched backward on the couch. Apparently this was not the response she was expecting to hear.

"Birdie!" Armond exclaimed. He sounded genuinely shocked. "My goodness."

Brooke couldn't help herself from smiling. She took the persimmon off the coffee table. "That's what I wanted to come early to tell you, Armond. I went to the doctor this morning. She tells me it's a boy and this is his size."

Brooke could have sworn that Armond's eyes were damp. "Oh, dear. Birdie. That is terrifically wonderful news. Terrifically wonderful."

Susan cleared her throat and crossed her legs. Her head vibrated left to right, as if she were disagreeing with something vehemently. "I was a single mother of a boy once too. Soon you will know how I feel. I am obligated to fight for him, and to ensure that he gets every opportunity that is rightfully his. That is my job."

"My house isn't rightfully his."

"The law says otherwise."

"Armond?" Brooke asked.

Armond's fingers tented on both of his knees, and he avoided eye contact with either woman. "We have three different state laws to contend with here: Massachusetts, New York, and California. They're all slightly different. But basically, if we cannot locate the heir in the next few weeks, the houses will be transferred into my name, as the executor of the will. Everyone will have to vacate the houses, and they'll remain empty for yet another waiting period, varying from one to three years, according to each respective state."

"This is absurd," Brooke said. "In this day and age, how is it possible that we simply can't find him?"

Armond nodded ceremoniously. "The other circumstance to consider is that if there is a chance that Nick will be convicted of a crime, there is also a chance that he will have to pay restitution for his crimes. If he inherits money and assets, depending on the severity of the discretion and the financial loss of the victim, that money could go directly to the victim or the corporate interest acting as the victim."

"Enough!" Susan yelled.

At the same time, Brooke exclaimed, "A crime?" Then she asked Susan, "What do you think he did?"

"He did nothing wrong!" Susan said, standing up. She must have crushed all the cigarettes in the package by then, as she'd been gripping it so tightly her knuckles were blanching. As she swung her purse over her shoulder, she said, "Nick is very susceptible to influence. Brooke, you're not as old as Steven and I, but cults are a real thing. In the seventies, I knew plenty of people who were brainwashed by them and led right out of New York City and into abominable situations. They were brainwashed. They didn't want to do the things they did, but they'd been convinced."

"So you think Nick has been abducted by a cult?" Brooke asked. One hand went instinctively to her stomach, but she wasn't sure why. The idea was laughable, really. But no one was laughing.

"On top of my concern for the health and safety of my only child, I do not need your ridicule," Susan seethed. "I'm hiring my own lawyer." She pointed at Armond's face. "Nice to see that the corrupt old-boy runaround of the Whitbys is still going strong."

"I am the executor of the will, it's not my job to represent *you*—"

But Susan was already stomping out of the room and attempting to slam the oversize, heavy office door. A small thud sounded.

Brooke picked up the persimmon. She and Armond were alone. She was beginning to realize that any hope she still had wasn't just improbable, but preposterous. Allie was gone, and soon Brooke's physical home would be too.

"I'm trying my best to hold everything together. But I can't help but think . . . ," she said. "What am I going to do?" she asked in a whisper.

Armond shook his head, and Brooke had the distinct impression he knew more about the case now than he had before. He said, "If we can get these titles into probate court before anything else happens to the boy, we may be able to save the property."

"What does that mean?" Brooke asked.

"I'm sorry, I shouldn't have said that. As the executor, I'm legally bound to protect the interest of the boy. You need to talk to Shelley again. And soon."

15

"If you wanna start a revolution, you're gonna need coff-ee! If you wanna start a revolution, you're gonna need coff-ee." The crooning came from a small man in a multicolored Rasta hat, jamming away at an electric keyboard, at the edge of the concrete plaza of Art Park. Despite the somberness of what had happened at anti-gas Oakland the night before, it was a lively day at the anti-gas encampment in New York City. Perhaps some of the crowd didn't yet know about the police brutality that had occurred across the country, and about the Iraq War vet who had been shot outside his tent.

Grace stepped onto a milk crate, then hoisted herself, awkwardly, onto the top of the blue mailbox. The midday sun beat down on her as she bent her knees for balance. She looked out from the top of the mailbox, and to her great surprise, her eyes began to well up. She was overwhelmed by the beauty of the sight before her.

As she cupped her mouth, ready to do a mic check, she smelled herself. She and Nick had vacated Shelley's apartment after a mysterious fight between the two Whitbys, and now she didn't get to shower every day. Plus, it had been a week since she'd stopped wearing deodorant, after a physical health workshop in the medic tent taught her about all those chemicals seeping into her body, how name-brand deodorant was basically cancerous runoff of the capitalist system. But soon after she'd stopped applying it every morning, she realized just how well the stuff worked.

"Everyone, I'm standing up here to address what happened last night in Oakland. Can I get a mic check?"

A few people gathered in front of the mailbox and hollered back, "Mic check!" The activists in the park were still forbidden by the city to use a megaphone, thus the "human megaphone" had to suffice. As Grace continued the call-and-response, a few other stragglers abandoned their posts at the people's library and zine tables around the park. The unzipping of tent doors sounded off.

She had lost a real conception of time. It could have been one day or two years since she'd begun to be Nick's girlfriend, since *Grace and Quentin* was a phrase usually said together. Their tent had been gifted to them by another couple, Rita and Luke, who were now famous among the anti-gassers for "liberating" various items from camping-goods stores. And the tent had become Nick and Grace's private home, their own nylon temple where they prayed to each other's bodies and shared the secrets of their lives. Or, most of them. She had told Nick all the gritty details of the devastating fight she'd had with her parents the last time she'd gone home. They'd forced her to sit at the dining room table and announced they'd found out where she'd been sleeping. Her father, arms crossed, had bellowed: "We are concerned that you have been consorting with the wrong type of people. As the hackneyed saying goes, *The company one keeps is a sincere reflection of character*. Grace, we have done everything in the world to make you into the most extraordinary person that you are—"

After Grace's shrieking reaction, after she'd stood up in sheer rage, her mother—face pinched and reddened—slid a rectangular piece of paper across the table. It was a plane ticket. Her mother said, "We believe that you should use the rest of your free time this summer to engage in the act of enrichment. We've purchased you a round-trip ticket, flying direct from JFK to Cairo International. Uncle Abasi suggested an intensive course in Sufi mythologies, which appears to be captivating."

Grace had told them exactly where they could shove their plane ticket. As she stomped back to the elevator, her mother had called after her, "The trip would be such a treat. I'm tempted to put my research on hold and join you!"

This had prompted a curdling scream from Grace. She responded, "I can't live in this elitist hellhole anymore," while pumping the call button five times in succession.

Above their foam bedroll and unzipped single sleeping bag, Grace had relayed this story to Nick. Then she'd asked him why he refused to go back to the Strong Place apartment.

Nick, gritting his teeth, told her that things with his family were "more fucked up" than he was able to explain. "It might not seem like it, but Shelley has a lot of anger. You know, Roger was my biological father, too." He proceeded to outline a theory that his adopted father and his mother had been having an affair for years before they both admitted to it. As he spoke, Grace held his bare torso, and her heart cracked for him. The poor guy; anyone who had never known their father would resort to that type of fiction. But since that day, she had been noticing that Nick's features were similar to those that she'd seen in sepia photographs of Whitbys printed in her high school American history textbooks: the square jaw, the smile that was all teeth. Even his hair looked like it belonged on a poster for the Industrial Revolution. Oddly, Shelley did not display many of these traits. But there was something about Shelley that stunk of blue blood. Her family's past was visible in her particular confident-yet-wispy manner, how she entered a room as if everyone was lucky to behold her presence. That's what Grace imagined as the greatest benefit of being a Whitby: you were born knowing you had worth. This entitlement, randomly assigned by the universe, was simply not fair. And yet, even Grace had been taken in by it. She had been entranced by the smooth appeal of Shelley the moment she sat beside her in the car on the way to Rhode Island. But that unfairness was also part of the reason why she was up on her mailbox soapbox that day in August.

In the park, Grace launched into the heart of her speech. "Last night in Oakland the peaceful protesters were woken up to thugs. State-supported police thugs, wearing riot gear, carrying guns . . ."

The crowd was steadily growing, and there was her own gallant Whitby. Nick walked up to her makeshift pulpit, smoking a cigarette. Formerly straight-edge Nick had, it seemed, become a full-fledged smoker: he puffed sitting in the circle in their afternoon meetings and while leaning halfway out the tent at night. The few times she had snuck him back into Shelley's house to take a shower, he had slipped up onto the roof and smoked up there. But she didn't mind his stink. Despite the fetid conditions, when they were inside the tent, it seemed that everything that Nick and she did during the day—making plans for the march, painting banners, writing letters to prisoners, carrying donations from restaurants back to the park to feed the other anti-gassers—were just punctuations, brief obligations until they could get back into their tented bubble and fold into each other's limbs.

Just that morning, he had said to her, "I love how your pointed nose and these wild, unkempt eyebrows, how they act together in perfect unison."

"Jerk." She had giggled, focused on him.

He squirmed out from under her, then rolled on top of her, one knee straddling each of her hips. "I also love these very dark brown circles you have." He plucked at her shirt, directly above where each nipple was. "And I love the way they are cockeyed, pointing outward in two different directions."

"Je-erk!" she had squealed again, and understood that she had never in her life felt so entirely elated, so inebriated, by another person's actions.

Now, Nick walked toward her in a Dead Kennedys T-shirt with the sleeves cut off. His scar was visible for all to see. Even glancing at the sight of his lightly freckled, sinewy arms caused a frenzy inside of her, but she tried to keep her face lifted, alternating where she projected her voice as she spoke, employing her well-crafted debate-team public-speaking skills.

He reached the side of the mailbox and squeezed her ankle twice. In the past few weeks Grace had become, in many ways, a leader of the movement. She was all in, now. If there was anything her years of private school and extensive extracurriculars were good for, she was damn pleased it turned out to be this. She could have been nervous, speaking out against the government as a Middle Easterner. But instead she used the racism in

the news as fuel. And with every speech she made and meeting she facili-
tated, she became more enmeshed in the circle of activists; they were not
only her friends but her people—she was an integral part of the club. But
the thought occasionally crossed her mind that Nick was jealous of her
popularity and her place in the spotlight. He'd told her repeatedly that he
was still nervous to be photographed, and therefore couldn't make
speeches himself. But now as he stood below her, he tapped on her ankle.
He looked like he'd drunk too much caffeine.

Without wasting a moment, he grabbed her two hands and helped her
down. Before she knew it, she was standing on the concrete pavement and
Nick was on top of the mailbox, launching right into his own words,
without introducing himself. The transition was seamless.

He was a natural public speaker. The tenor of his voice was captivating. "We need a moment of silence. We need to all be peaceful for a
moment, and retreat to whatever space of reflection or God that you carry,
and thank our comrades in Oakland for the work that they're doing. . . ."

He looked around nervously, perhaps taking register of how many
cops were on the periphery of the park, the number of television crews and
photographers. Soon, the staccato rhythm of Nick's voice suggested he
was nearing an end point, and the crowd, which had grown substantially
since Grace had begun speaking, now preemptively cheered and *whooed*.
They loved him.

Nick said, "Capitalism used to be about making things and then selling
them. It was based on labor and compensation for that labor. But in the
information age, that labor is no longer happening. Yet the compensation
still is. And all that money, it is going not to laborers but directly back into
companies like ExxonMobil. These warmongers, these police, they're
fighting—they're killing—in order to protect goddamn corporations. We
need to act now to stop the corporate takeover of our nation. Corporations
are *not* people!"

When he was silent for several moments, voices from the crowd hollered, "Damn straight!" "Yes!"

Once Nick was back on the ground, Grace whispered into his ear, "I'm glad you're not hiding anymore." He turned to her, then jumped back with a gasp. A lanky white man stood right beside her. The guy had a voluminous beard and a Mets hat on, so that his exact features were hard to discern.

Nick looked petrified. "Dumpster," he said. "I didn't know you were here."

The guy stuck out a hand. Grace could have sworn there was a smirk on his beard-covered face. "You're Quentin, right? My name is Jamie."

Nick's mouth twisted in confusion. But he said, "Uh, right. Hey."

The guy scanned Grace up and down critically, then seemed to determine that she didn't matter. He held a new-looking paperback book in his hand, which he waved in the air. "I don't have time to stick around, but I came up to donate books to the people's library. Heard you're doing great work there. And this one's a gift for you."

It was a copy of *The Great Gatsby*. "Sure you've read it before. All about capitalist greed. But it's also"—he paused—"a grand story."

Nick took the book out of his hand. A paper sticking out of it fluttered to the concrete.

The guy, Jamie, lunged for it at the same time that Grace did. She swiped up the bookmark before he could reach it.

"Got it!" she exclaimed. "Oh, I'm Grace," she added, offering her hand.

Jamie didn't shake it. "The bookmark is for Quentin," he said in a monotone voice. Then he leaned toward Nick. "You know the deal: read it big to small." As he finished his last word he was already pivoting on his heels. He quickly slipped into the crowd.

The bookmark was just a strip of manila envelope cut into a rectangle. On the top, in small and controlled handwriting, was a list of numbers:

24-17-1

176-28-5

114-2-10

57-1-5

39-15-2

40-13-2

Nick looked around and then frantically flipped through the other pages in the book, as if there might be other things stuck between them.

"Who was that?" Grace asked.

Nick was visibly upset. "I need that sheet of paper. The bookmark. Give it to me."

"Why? Who was that guy?"

Another activist, an older man with a salt-and-pepper Afro, tapped Nick on the shoulder. As he talked to the man, Nick's hand slipped into Grace's and he grabbed the bookmark, which he stuck into the pocket of his Carhartt jeans without ever looking up.

16

Nine days and twenty-three unreturned phone calls to the Grisham's penthouse later, Shelley stood silently in her kitchen drinking a glass of gin with a splash of warm apple juice in it, staring at the counter, which overflowed with the appendages of Nick's "movement." Although his comrades still inhabited the unelectrified apartment at all hours of the day and night, Nick had still not returned to Strong Place. His friends reported he and Grace had been sleeping in Art Park every night. Shelley had considered locking the doors, kicking everyone else out of the apartment, and ending the party. But the thought of forcibly removing all of these people from the humid, underoxygenated rooms took more energy than she seemed to possess. Now a medic's station took up the kitchen island, with bandages of all shapes and sizes, disinfectant, and insulin shots. A dry-food storing station occupied all of the back counter, with dumpstered and donated food spilling out of paper bags: bagels, dozens of cans of black beans, miniature tins of peaches in syrup, twenty jars of Skippy peanut butter. Blankets and sneakers lay on the floor in piles, and old books were stacked in the parlor—the overflow from the park's People's Library. Grace came by the apartment every few days, meeting friends or picking up food or using the bathroom. Shelley was rendered silent with fear when Grace was in the room; she had to know, at that point, what Nick had seen in the museum. But Grace was always blithely herself, hugging Shelley absently, chewing on stale bagels.

Since the day of the fight at the Doss, it was as if Shelley had been cast out of her life. Aimlessly walking had become her primary occupation. That, and listening to music as she wandered, letting her Discman sink to the bottom of her batik shoulder bag and then knock against her thighs as she wandered through Central Park and tried her hardest not to think about her mother, who lay alone in a loony bin in some desolate Massachusetts suburb. The bands the Slip and Spoon were becoming the soundtrack to the gaping space of her days and nights. She would spend an hour in a Starbucks coffee shop in order to charge her phone, then begin to wander again. Sometimes she wanted to be unencumbered, and since the door to the apartment wasn't ever locked now, she wouldn't even take her keys: she'd just light out of the house in her long skirt and sandals, free of money and cell phone and responsibility. She often found herself on the East Side. Once she'd even lingered in front of Charlotte's parents' building for fifteen minutes, on the off chance that her friend was back in town from her sexual-orientation vacation. But Shelley hadn't seen Charlotte, or any member of Charlotte's family, for that matter.

It was the time of year when so many New Yorkers left town, and the streams of tourists ebbed as well, due to warnings in guidebooks that the pavement was too hot and the garbage too fragrant to enjoy the city in August. A handful of times Shelley strolled into the Met and offered the perturbed clerk a fifty-cent "suggested donation." She would cross through the Asian art wing, peering around for Dr. Jillian or her younger love interest, before heading to the decorative-arts portion of the American Wing. She would briefly investigate the details of rolltop desks and ornately carved frames for wall mirrors, and find herself considering how she would describe the pieces in a both concise and descriptive manner. Then she would rest on a red leather bench with her eyes closed, letting the air-conditioning slowly lower her body temperature.

That week, she had also found herself, often, standing beside the long green awning of the Grisham. With nothing else to do and nowhere else to be, she would linger there for twenty minutes or half an hour, waiting and watching to see if Mr. Kamal would come or go. Of course, she held a large advantage in this stakeout, for even if he did pass by, he would have no way of knowing she was there. Four afternoons in a row she found herself in front of his building, but standing there to no end. She didn't glimpse him or any of the Kamals.

Now, on that August afternoon, after three juice cups of gin, she went out for her daily walk. Soon she was once again standing outside the building on Sixty-Eighth Street, but on this day, she finally saw him. Only ten minutes after she had arrived at the building, Mr. Kamal exited a black car with Dr. Jillian, who took her husband's elbow as she checked her watch repeatedly. Had she been conducting research with him? It was a Monday. Could they have just left the Doss? Shelley nearly gagged, imagining what Dr. Jillian would have to say about the Vermeers: historical facts, well-known critiques. Nothing honest.

Shelley waited for another five minutes on the sticky sidewalk and then walked casually into the building. Tomás, one of her favorite doormen, was perched on a stool, twirling his hat in one hand, a folded magazine in the other. She smiled at him briefly, then pointed to the elevators, heading straight there.

"Whoa," he said, with his nasal twang. "Can I help you?"

"Just going up to the penthouse, as per usual." There was no way Tomás didn't remember her; she had seen him nearly every weekday for the past few months.

"Let me call up, ma'am." He picked up the phone at his small desk.

She raised both eyebrows. "It's Shelley."

He turned his back to her and spoke softly into the receiver. "A guest here to visit the penthouse. Shelley. . . . Uh-uh. No problem. . . . Thank you." He turned back to her. "Sorry, ma'am, the Kamals are not home right now and didn't leave a message that they were expecting anyone."

"What? I just saw them."

The doorman kept a steady blank face and didn't respond to her incredulous pointing. "Have to get in touch with them later. Can't let you in."

Now that she had time to really focus on him for once, she noticed

Tomás was shorter and younger than she had initially imagined. How funny it was, how sad, that almost everyone wants to do their inane, pointless job well.

"This is insane," she hissed. She turned and with short, quick steps, left the building, pulling her earphones up from around her neck and raising the volume.

She speed-walked up Madison Avenue. Her satchel bag hit against her thigh, but she didn't care; it felt good to move fast. If Nick hadn't shown up at her house in May, she would be hard at work, probably at this very moment, writing a book with Mr. Kamal. Nick came into her life and ruined everything once before, when she was thirteen. How could he be doing it again? Something had to change: she decided, right there on her walk from the Grisham, that it was time. She would tell him about the will and the money and the houses. Even if that meant everyone else was going to swoop in. Even if that meant finally going to her mother and dealing with the problem that she had been avoiding so fervently. Shelley would tell Nick the truth, and then he would have to deal with her. He would be forced to come back.

She turned onto Seventy-First and saw that Art Park was packed. As she approached the wrought iron fence, she passed a few cops standing by one of the gates, fanning themselves with papers. The scene wasn't that different from a country fair, but instead of party games and animal viewing, there were petitions to sign and large sheets of chaap paper where people drew with markers: peace signs and suns and moons and mountains. Where there would have been fried dough, there was vegan mush being scooped out of a giant pot.

One corner of the park had been cleared of tents and tables and replaced with several piles of junk: a clothes pile, a small-appliances pile, and a mound of children's toys, which included a paint-peeling kitchen set and several pairs of seventies-era roller skates. Propped up against each pile was a cardboard sign scrawled with the word *Free!* Beside one of these signs, stuck into the sparse grass, sat David of the goatee, leaning back in a lawn chair.

Shelley approached him. "Where's my brother?"

David, grinning, said, "So glad to see you here, Shells!" as if they were friends. He pointed across the park. "Quentin and Grace reside in an orange-and-black tent, middle of the encampment."

When she found the expensive-looking high-tech tent, adorned with excessive flaps and zippers, she also heard Grace's voice emanating from inside of it. Then Grace, pummeling out of the tent flap, nearly smacked right into her. "What!" she exclaimed. "I can't believe you're here—"

Shelley, imagining what Grace must know about her, couldn't make eye contact with the girl who had so recently been her friend. "Nick in there?"

"Yeah, but he's being difficult."

Shelley let herself in. There was Nick on his knees, illuminated by orange nylon. He looked dirty and thin, but most of all exhausted, with black pouches under his eyes.

"You okay?" she asked, surprising herself with her tenderness.

He rubbed his face with both hands. "What the hell? Why are you here?"

"We need to talk."

The inside of the tent reeked like a locker room that had just housed a frat party: beer and stale cigarettes, an underbelly of dirty socks.

"Obviously I don't want to talk to you."

She moved farther in and dropped into a squatting crouch. "Well, you have to. Why do you look like such shit?"

"Didn't sleep much. Listen, I don't want to judge you about what I saw in the museum," he said. Her head flinched backward. He rubbed two hands over his face again, as if trying hard to stay awake. "It's just—I think you're being taken advantage of. It's repulsive, that guy's fucked-up manipulations."

"Will you shut up! It's none of your business. And I know you've told Grace—"

"I haven't told her a thing."

Shelley rolled her eyes, but as soon as Nick said those words, she instantly felt relieved. His anger seemed to have totally dissolved, which was rapidly dampening hers down too. It was the kind of dial-down, from rage to regular within moments, that can only happen with one's family. Her thighs started to burn from the crouching, and she crawled over to Nick, adjusting her legs so they pretzeled under her. The two Whitby children looked at their laps.

"Mr. Kamal won't speak to me anymore. I've been fired."

Nick shrugged. He moved his Jansport backpack behind his head and lay down. "Good. You don't need that shit. You're so much better than him."

She took a deep breath and tried to remind herself of her decision; things needed to change. "I do need the Kamals, because I need a job, Nick. I'm broke."

He was shaking his head now, as if she were lying.

"Listen," she said. "There's something I should have told you a long time ago. My dad—our dad—Roger. He left you something in his will. I mean, he left you everything in his will."

"What are you talking about?"

"When Dad died, he left his property and money to you. That includes my house."

"What?" Nick said.

"That's why your mother's been looking for you for months. I mean, I guess she'd like to know you're safe. But the lawyer's been looking for you too."

"What?" he said again. And after a silent half minute, Nick began hysterically laughing. "You're making this up, right?" His face was scrunched.

She shook her head. "It's true."

"I'm going to own your house? I can do whatever I want?"

"Don't you think it's unfair?" Shelley said, her voice cresting. "It's not fair that you would get everything from Dad, and the rest of us, we wouldn't get a thing. There are seven other kids. I know you care about fairness, Nick. And this isn't."

He was intermittently giggling in a strained, halting way, while running two hands through his curls. "This can't be true," he muttered.

Then he giggled again. "And, yeah. Of course it's not fair. Why would I deserve this?" He paused for a moment. Something else appeared to occur to him. "But then, why would anyone else deserve it either?"

"Well, he is my biological father," Shelley said quietly. Nick's neck snapped up as if he'd been hit. In that moment she knew it was a mistake, telling Nick altogether.

"What the *fuck* is that supposed to mean? You think you have some divine right or something? You're just as bad as the rest of these bourgeois soul-sucking bankers who are ruining the fucking world."

As soon as he began to yell, Shelley felt herself turning off. She was disconnecting from the situation. "No," she said.

Nick added, "And you know he's obviously my biological father too."

Shelley laughed. "Whatever, psycho. I'm sorry you believe that. Once you calm down, call your mother. She's going to try to convince you to keep my house and Brooke's house, but hopefully you're better than that—"

"Brooke's house?" Nick asked, confused.

Shelley walked on her knees toward the exit. "Your mother will explain everything."

"When did you talk to her?" he asked.

Halfway out of the tent, Shelley turned and, feeling nothing at all—no sadness, no anger, no fear of the future—told him, "I already told you. I talked to your mother in April. She's been looking for you."

The timeline seemed to clarify for Nick then. He spoke with purpose. "Have you lost your fucking mind, just like your mother?"

Shelley hovered in the unzipped door of the tent. "This isn't about me."

"You've known about this will since April? Since Roger died? Only a true sociopath would live with me every day and not tell me about it."

Soon both Whitbys were outside the tent, yelling at each other in the middle of the urban campground. Nick roared, "You've known about this for months, and I've been living in your house. And you didn't say a thing to me?"

He was out of control. Closing her eyes, Shelley remembered him in the Doss, his face lengthening with fury as he stood in front of the

Vermeers. She tried to remind herself: he was not a regular person. He would always do this, fly off the handle and bare his frighteningly angry, testosterone teeth, at any unlikely moment. She said, "I thought all you cared about was your make-believe revolution. I thought you didn't care about money. But look at you now, *Quentin*. Who's a capitalist now?"

"I don't need your evil fucking money. And I certainly don't want to be indebted to our monster of a father for the rest of my living days."

"Then give it all to me." Shelley crossed her arms over her chest. "I need to keep my house. I'm not like you. I don't have a mommy who still gives me everything. If you don't care about it, just give the house to me." A small crowd of anti-gassers was timidly but steadily forming a circle, as if they were at a cockfight and the Whitbys were the animal attractions.

Nick looked at the crowd and took a deep breath, clearly trying to calm himself and whatever rage-induced brain chemicals coursed through his veins.

"You've been lying to me for months, keeping secrets." He growled, then: "And now you're asking *me* for something? You owe me, Shelley Whitby. You owe me so, so much."

17

A few days later, as Esmerelda spoke from the other side of the circle on the bedroom floor at Strong Place, Nick found himself picturing what her two plum breasts looked like beneath her tank top; she probably had the kind of nipples that surprised you by their vast circumference. She was totally naked under there. They all were. He stared at Esmerelda's chest for too long, then realized what he was doing and flinched toward the ceiling. To recover, he fiddled with the book that rested in his lap, while silently berating himself.

As with most of their meetings, the group began by lamenting the fate of the Family. Esmerelda announced to the other activists gathered on Shelley's old bedroom floor, "We might be winning today, but I can't sleep at night thinking about our comrades in the Family, locked in jail with no self-determination. It's more than a crime to label them as terrorists; it's a goddamn sin. They were combating the destruction of our precious world."

All of Nick's friends nodded. The air was thick with unshaved armpits and Roiphe's patchouli oil. Nick was facing an awful decision. The purpose of this meeting was to figure out exactly what the group could do during the mass mobilization march that would be more radical, more hard-core, than the rest of the liberals, who would simply be carrying signs. Nick had to decide whether he would really participate in this direct action they were planning. If he got himself arrested, the cops could easily connect him to the Maine action.

He was no longer avoiding Shelley as he had been after the blowup at the Doss. Since she'd shown up in his tent, he didn't give a fuck. He would come and go from her place whenever he wanted. If she could lie to his face all summer, and lie about money, then they obviously didn't have the kind of bond he thought they had. For the past few days, Nick had been wired—buzzing and wide-awake—with the idea that Roger had left the entire inheritance to him for a reason. Nick was fully aware that Roger had always had a strange attachment to him, as if Nick carried a special kind of potential that his other children didn't. And now, leaving all his worldly possessions to him, simply giving him all that money: it was a coded message. Roger *wanted* Nick to do something big with it. It was unfair. No, it was cruel, to put that kind of pressure on only one of your children. Now he had another terrible Whitby albatross to bear. He hated Roger for it. And yet, although he wouldn't admit it to a soul, he was also honored.

It wasn't long after Esmerelda's proclamation that David began laying down the direct-action plans for everyone else in the group: at a coordinated time on the afternoon of the march, they would all lock their bodies to various politically significant locations around the city and refuse to move until the jailed Family members were absolved of the "terrorist" charge. David said, "If we lock our bodies down in pairs of two, then we'll all have a partner to be arrested with. We'll certainly be arrested, folks. Everyone needs to commit to that."

A large sheet of chaap paper had been pinned to the wall, with David's scrawled notations about where the locations would be:

—New York Stock Exchange: 11 Wall Street
—The ICE Detention Center: 201 Varick Street
—The New York Times Building: 229 W. 43rd Street
—The United Nations Headquarters: 405 E. 42nd Street
—The *MTV Total Request Live* stage in Times Square:
Broadway and 44th Street
—The Doss Museum: 1 E. 70th Street

Nick reread the list and again debated if he was really going to get arrested, purposefully, for such an inconsequential action. There was no mystery about what would happen in response to this: the cops would saw off the bike locks, even next to the Family Supporters' delicate necks, and the Family would remain in jail. He would be risking so much for so little. But if the cops were trying to find him, wouldn't they have done so already? Still, if he was going to risk it all, he needed to make a bigger impact. Roger would have wanted him to.

David said, "Grace, do you want to lockdown at the ICE detention center?"

Grace, who had been conspicuously silent since the meeting started, rolled her eyes. "Uh, no, thanks." Then, although she hadn't checked with Nick first, she told the group, "It would mean a lot to me and Quentin if the two of us could lock down together at the Doss."

She smiled at Nick from across the room. Everyone, especially Grace, was taking it as a given that he would be involved. A thought flickered briefly in the front of his brain: What if they could do more at the Doss? He'd been inside there before, he knew the entrances and exits. And those keys, the ones that Shelley had pocketed during their research outing. Shelley probably still had them. What rooms would they unlock?

Nick nodded in agreement with Grace's statement and shifted the copy of *Gatsby* he had in his lap. He had wrapped the book in a dust jacket of the same size, from another book he'd taken out of the people's library, *Lies My Teacher Told Me*. He didn't actually know what Big D's mumbled instructional message about the bookmark had meant, to "read it big to small." And after nearly two weeks of staring at the bookmark, he hadn't made much progress deciphering the meaning. He didn't want Grace to know that he was studying it though, as she seemed truly convinced that Nick actually knew what he was doing.

Recently, things had been changing with Grace. The previous day, the two of them decided it had been too long since they'd showered, and they walked across the park to bathe together at Strong Place. In the shower, he had soaped up Grace's whole naked body, then made shampoo sculptures in her hair, chuckling as she chattered on and on. "Maybe in September we should get an apartment in Brooklyn. I mean, if we, like, shared a room in a collective house, then we'd barely pay any rent at all. So we wouldn't have to work too much. The most valuable resource we have is our time, you know."

He put two hands on her shoulders and moved his cheek right next to hers, beneath her shower mohawk. He whispered, "I don't even know where I will be in September, babe. You know how risky it is for me to get arrested on the day of the march."

She pecked his mouth. "I still don't know what it is that you actually did, *Quentin*. But I'm pretty sure that if the cops had any of your finger-prints or DNA, you would be in prison already. I don't think there's any-thing to worry about."

Maybe she was right, and they could start planning for the future. Sometimes, in the evening in Art Park, when all items of the spokes-council meeting agenda had been covered, the smaller group of Family Supporters would congregate in a clump on the still-warm concrete. David and Esmerelda and Christopher and all the rest would joke about what would happen after the march. They could move to a farm, each person employing differing skills: cooking, construction, planting, teaching, music. When these conversations came up, Nick would nod, joining in. But there was always a corner of his mind that considered whether he had a future.

In the shower, soapy water ran down Grace's back. Her ass, like two cartoon teardrops, created a perfect ramp for the suds to go skimming off. She said over her shoulder, "Whatever happens now, I'm with you. I love you, *Nick-Quentin*. I'm not going back to school, and I can't go back to my parents' place. Whatever it is we do, we'll do it together."

It was like she'd pulled a plug. With those words, all the excitement of staring at her big, sexy ass drained away. Grace, his savior, was a woman Nick loved. But when it came down to it, the sad truth was that he didn't love her as much as she loved him. Perhaps it was because they spent nearly every waking hour together, side by side in a twenty-five-square-foot tent, but now he understood everything that she was, from her private school upbringing to her hokey college debate team. Her utter availability was disappointing. It appeared that his old disease was raring its pernicious head, yet again. He constantly envisioned screwing Grace, of course. But also envisioned the same thing with dozens of other women, especially other Family-Support women. (He pictured taking them from behind, over the edge of the velvet blue settee downstairs; he imagined bouncing them against the wall of the Starbucks by Art Park, while they all stood in the bathroom line; he thought of sneaky hands slipping under skimpy clothing, right in the middle of a meeting.) It was sick. But he couldn't help himself: he needed the promise of others, the hunt.

In Nick's better moments, he was assured that his sickness was merely a symptom of yearning for the perfect girl, the one who could finally cure him. He knew what she was like, just not where to find her. She was dark-haired and silently moody, prone to unexpected acts of both sex and art; the fair skin on her face and breasts and bare stomach were all violently, hauntingly beautiful. Where was the Anaïs to his Henry Miller? The Daisy to his Gatsby? Nick had so many deeply shitty years of childhood to make up for—he was owed so much. But doesn't every human being deserve that: wild, unimaginable love?

In the shower, Grace had gotten on her knees and smiled up at him as she took him into her mouth. The water ran over her cheeks and breasts in rivulets. The sight of her giving a blow job in the shower was touching, poetic even, because he knew this was the last time he would see it. Right after the march he'd tell her, in the most gentle terms possible, that their love was a miraculous thing, but it wasn't meant to last forever. Yes, that's just how he would put it.

The meeting at Strong Place was coming to an end now. "We'll reconvene the day before the march," David said in a faux whisper. He sounded like Batman declaring his plans. "Every team needs to check out their location, then we'll have a collective report back."

As the meeting broke up and all of the Family Supporters turned to chat with their neighbors, Nick took another moment to study the book in his lap. He tried to reorder the bookmark numbers from the largest to the smallest, and then turned to each of those pages of Fitzgerald's novel.

176-114-57-40-39-28-24-17-15-13-10-5-5-2-2-2-1-1

When put into order, the first word on each of those pages read:

identity-servant-time-little-I-I-evidently-where-you-idea-she's-from-from-intimate-intimate-intimate-in-in

Gibberish.
And the last words from each page read:

awkward-under-plane-and-a-announced-it-hand-metalic-Baker-me-Chicago-Chicago-men-men-men-the-the

Gibberish again.
He tried reading each of these lines backward. Nothing.

It was during his friends' show-and-tell that Nick figured out the code. The other Family Supporters bared their tattoos: Cate's upper arm had a faint outline of an anarchy A with a heart around it. (*"My very first one!"*) Christopher had an ailanthus tree on his shoulder. Esmerelda had a childish butterfly above one hip.

Nick realized that the groups of three numbers on the bookmark could correspond to page number, line number, word number. Each chain of numbers would be a direction to get to one simple word. As everyone else examined one another's tattooed appendages, Nick scribbled onto the title page of the book. After four frantic minutes he had written down these words:

24-17-1: Meet
176-28-5: East
114-2-10: Village
57-1-5: Restaurant
39-15-2: Friday
40-13-2: Seven-o'-clock

It was not only the first lucid collection of words he'd found, it was an actual message. He checked them all a second time, and again the code had corresponded with these clear instructions: Meet East Village Restaurant Friday Seven-o'-clock. Had he missed it last week? It was Friday again the next day. It had to mean Odessa, the Russian diner next to the squat. Big D wanted to meet him. Why would Big D want to meet him? His brain hummed with the possibilities.

As it turned out, Grace was the only tattooless body in the whole room. "How could I be the only one?" she said innocently, then erupted in an uncalled-for fit of giggles. She said, "Ebony, I want Quentin's drawing! The one that he made in our Fourth of July meeting, the one we've been using on the fliers. Could you do that, like, a big outline of the Occupy the Mansion picture?"

Nick was still staring at *Gatsby* in shock, when Grace stood over him and began kneading one of his shoulders. "Wouldn't it be cool if I got that tattooed on me?"

"Uh. Really?" he said. "You know once you get a tattoo, you can't just change your mind about it."

She frowned. "Of course."

Half an hour later, in the dim room, Ebony began to dip her needle into a glass ink pot, then jab Grace's naked back.

In his tent that night, as he lay beside Grace, Nick's thoughts began to speed up and build upon one another. The money wasn't his concern. Well, it made him truly angry that Roger would put this burden on him.

But the fact of it was also a sign. There were too many signs popping up at once: the money in the will, the direct action during the march, the secret meeting with Big D. Certainly, Big D wanted to plan another action with him. Nick knew about the SUV plant fires happening on the West Coast. He'd heard muttered talk about a movement to stop hotel development in New England, on Cape Cod and Martha's Vineyard. But Big D had to be interested in doing something at the anti-gas march itself. Yes, of course that's what he wanted. Maybe something at the Doss Museum. All of these signs were leading to the same conclusion: this moment was predestined. The universe was telling Nick he only had one life and he had to live it. This was his moment to do something that mattered, to do something big.

18

It had been weeks since Shelley had seen Mr. Kamal walking into his building, and in those weeks she'd fallen into a piteous routine. She woke up at an ungodly hour, after very little sleep, and wandered around the Upper West Side in the quiet of the neighborhood stretching its limbs. The pavement was slick from the street sweepers. A few men rolled up the metal gates of bodegas, and pigeons stood curious on subway grates, heads tilted in the morning light. As Shelley walked, she reasoned that something else, something other than Nick's involvement with Grace, must have happened to explain Mr. Kamal's radio silence. Maybe he had come clean to Dr. Jillian about all the details of their time together, about the eighteenth floor of the Whitby-Grand and the luxurious bedsheets. But even if that was the case, couldn't he so much as pick up the phone to explain it to her? She had imagined that as soon as she told Nick about the will, his mother would show up, and somehow Brooke and Shelley's own mother would show up, too, followed by all the other half siblings. She had assumed instant hubbub would descend upon her. But instead, everything remained quiet.

At ten on a Tuesday morning, Shelley walked back through her kitchen. She was planning to carry up beverages (whiskey, ginger ale) to Biddy's room, then lock the door and proceed to sweat through the bedsheets for the afternoon. As she entered the parlor that day though, she passed an odd gathering. A slight woman with a swirl of dreadlocks on her head hurled herself into a line of Nick's friends, who stood linked up by the arms. The woman screamed at them: "You spoiled pieces of protestor shit! You say you hate the police, but no one's shooting up your goddamn neighborhoods."

The dreadlocked woman threw her body into the line of people again, and they pushed her back, faces set like athletes at a face-off.

"What the hell is happening?" Shelley asked.

The woman stopped herself midhurl and smiled. "We're having police brutality training. I'm the facilitator. Are you here to join?"

"Jesus." Shelley shook her head. "No."

As she began to make her way upstairs, David jumped out of his locked-arm line and grabbed the crook of her elbow. "Isn't it awesome?" he said with a wide grin.

"What?" She was not in the mood to talk to this doofus.

"The lights!" He beamed. "Thank you guys so much for turning them back on."

Shelley realized the television was on. And all the lamps were glowing. She heard the rumble of the ancient air conditioner from Biddy's room upstairs. "What on earth? I didn't pay the bill."

"Oh. Quentin said he took care of it, so I figured it was, like, a family expense," said David.

"What?" Shelley said. "Where is he?"

"I guess he's at the park," David said with a shrug.

Shelley marched directly upstairs. Since learning about the will and the houses, Nick had been in and out of the house a few times, acting crazier than ever. He was so rabidly angry every time he spoke to her that the whole thing seemed like a put-on. She wanted him to knock it off and drop the front; he couldn't be that consistently vicious. But she didn't say anything. Instead, she just did everything he demanded of her, including giving him the set of keys that she'd snatched from the back hallway of the Doss Museum. Those were from a former life—her life with Mr. Kamal. She handed them over; she simply didn't have the energy to do anything else.

Soon Shelley was lying in her bed with the air conditioner on full blast, considering where he could have gotten the money to pay the bill. Of course, the logical answer was that he'd talked to his mother by that point and reactivated his bank card. But maybe Grace had just given some money to him, from whatever Kamal reserve of dough she had access to. It was just then that Shelley's cell phone rang. A 212 number that flashed on the small screen: the Grisham. She let out a loud sigh that she hadn't known she'd been holding in for weeks.

"Yes, hello?" She tried to sound nonchalant.

"Shelley, this is Yousef Abdel Kamal," he said in his overly formal, reassuring tone.

She closed her eyes. "Nice to hear from you, Mr. Kamal."

He was calling to invite her over and wanted her there by two. Their conversation was stunted, with terse sentences on both sides. It reminded her of her early days working for him, and she swelled with joy that the tension between them, the mystery, was still there.

How sad that all it took was one phone call to jolt her back to life. But just like that, she was awake again. She took her time bathing and dressing. Donning a long wrap skirt, she dabbed the insides of her wrists and the back of her neck with lavender oil, then wandered leisurely across the park in a round straw sun hat her mother had worn during Shelley's childhood summers. As she walked through the winding paths and the low-hanging oak braches, her back was very straight, her posture aligned. Rather than being nervous, Shelley was calm. She felt mature. She knew he would come back to her.

Drifting into the Grisham, she was greeted by a different doorman than Tomás. This man was old and expressionless, and when Shelley announced that she was expected in the penthouse he didn't so much as twitch an eye. The elevator grumbled up. She knew that most of the other floors would be empty and unlit, with so many of the building's residents swimming in lakes on summer holiday or crunching potato chips warmed from the sun at that very moment. The elevator doors opened with a *bing*, and Shelley prepared her brightened face. But the foyer was empty. She stepped into the hallway and slipped out of her sandals quietly, then peeked around the wall to the dining room. Dr. Jillian sat at the dining table, reading under the crystal chandelier. "Good afternoon," Shelley said, raising a palm in greeting.

Dr. Jillian, unruffled as always, scanned Shelley from head to toe, lingering on the broad-brimmed hat that Shelley quickly removed. Without a word, the older woman picked up her book and walked down the private hallway where the help was never permitted to enter.

Shelley began to make her way to the study when she heard his familiar shuffling. He was coming out of the back hallway. He looked diminutive, but his head was high, and he knew she was there. In one hand he carried a brown paper shopping bag that had the words *Big Brown Bag* printed on its side. Bloomingdale's.

She would not kiss him when she sat beside him and would not bring up their past weeks of silence. No. She would not even ask how the research was going, but rather simply offer her services, tell him that she was ready and willing to get back to work.

"Not the office, Shelley," his voice resounded through the living room. "To the library."

Soon she sat in the chinoiserie chair where she had sat so many times before, staring at the Enlightenment philosophy section of his bookshelves. Midday sun streamed through the crosshatched windows. Her straight hair was tucked behind her ears. Mr. Kamal, she thought, was almost smiling.

"I've missed our afternoons," she said lowly, then instantly regretted her words. She wasn't following her plan.

"I have gotten you a present." He held the shopping bag toward her.

She plumped with pride. But she was puzzled: she pictured him wandering through the variegated aisles of Bloomingdale's by himself, yet he would never be able to go there alone. Who would have gone with him?

"Thank you." She regretted her words yet again. The sound of his frustrated barking from months before echoed in her mind: *I do not want you to thank me!* She touched the handle of the paper bag, letting her knuckles graze against the side of his.

Upon opening the bag, a mass of fabric was visible, but Shelley had to pull the garment up to see what it was. As she raised it further she realized it was a coat. It was a deep plum Burberry coat made of cashmere and wool, long, and insulated for winter. Brown toggle closures made of horn had been stitched tightly to its breastplate. She held it in the air to see it fully.

"Do you like it?"

"You don't— Yes." Then she was silent.

"Of course it won't be useful in the summertime, but soon enough the chill will return to the air and then winter will be upon us. It is surely on its way."

She remembered her old coat with the safety-pin closure, then again inspected the heavyweight wool in her hands. How had he known she needed it?

Mr. Kamal's molded cheeks broke. His face looked burnished, loosened. He was smiling.

The two sat together noiselessly, and Shelley felt the heat of the late-summer sun. She considered stretching out her hand and grabbing his, which rested limply in his lap. She wanted to feel the softness, the thin spring of his skin. The heavy door to the study was closed. She imagined stripping off her clothes and putting the coat over her naked body, then gliding Mr. Kamal's hand under it and over her shoulders, her breasts, her ribs, her smooth stomach. She contemplated these actions but did nothing. She would wait for his commands.

There were minutes of silence—companionable, delicate silence. But the minutes went on and on. Shelley felt the sunrays pinking her cheeks and saw the newspaper untouched on the side table. She moved to pick it up.

Mr. Kamal's expression contracted. "Stop. I have something to tell you."

She waited.

"Obviously, I can no longer use you."

Without an answer from her, he continued. "Your research and descriptions have been very poor from the beginning and are still not good enough for me."

"What?" she said before catching herself.

"I could inch along with you, but that wouldn't be fair to myself. And certainly not to the book that I am producing. I will mail you the last check for your services, if there are outstanding fees. Please take your gift."

At that, he raised himself and appeared ready to leave the room. Shelley froze in her chair, dumbstruck. She thought of how he had slept in the hotel, his mouth agape and breath laboring, loudly. She considered reminding him of how he had touched her stomach, how she was young and fertile, how he'd given her his very own pet name. She thought of how when he thrashed her backside and her legs, his other steady hand resting on her upper back, she had never felt so safe. How could he do this? What had happened to Shelley-kins?

"I did excellent work for you," she managed to say.

He was shuffling his way out of the room by then but cleared his throat. "I suppose you shouldn't feel too disparaged." Then he stopped for a moment. "You're a very shy person, Shelley. Very shy." With that, Mr. Kamal scuffed away, leaving her alone in the library.

Her skin might have peeled from her boiling flesh. Who did he think he was? Didn't he know who *she* was? How dare he treat someone like her like that. She was liable to pull every book off the shelves, throw them to the ground, tearing out pages. She could have shrieked, turning over upholstered chairs and mahogany tea tables. The pain Mr. Kamal had just inflicted on her felt physical. Her old self, the brash and shining girl she'd always been, would have ransacked the place, then gone screaming into Dr. Jillian's room and told the woman every single detail of what her husband had done.

But now Shelley, standing in the rectangle of fading sun, said nothing.

Nausea overtook her. She picked up the handles of the paper bag and walked to the elevator quietly. When she reached the lobby, her brain flooded with questions. How could he be done with her? Hot air rushed her face from someone pushing through the glass door of the building. A dark-haired girl about her age entered the lobby. She was tall, thin, and freckled, in an awkwardly fitting blue suit. As she passed Shelley, the girl raised her upper lip in anxious acknowledgment. Shelley stopped and leaned against the beige wallpaper without pretending to be doing anything but watching. The girl waved to the doorman and waited for the elevator to open. The doors locked shut with her inside. The numbers above the elevator lit up one by one, until the final light: of course, she was headed to the penthouse.

Shelley knew what would happen upstairs. Her replacement would cautiously enter the darkened study, where God knows how many had been before her. The girl would read to Mr. Kamal behind closed doors, and he would growl at her, disparage her abilities. He would vary his speech slightly, tailoring his questioning for each candidate before landing on his final one, the one that Shelley considered now, as she walked out into the heat and the noise of Madison Avenue. He would ask in his deep bellow, his sincere tone, the question she could never answer honestly: *Just what is it that you are deprived of?*

A week after she watched Mr. Kamal's new girl go up to the penthouse, Shelley was ill. It was as if she'd been floating in and out of sleep for days. She wasn't sure if she was having regular dreams or amplified daydreams, but when she closed her eyes her imagination wandered the city by itself. Objects and places that had once been comforting now roared behind her eyelids, unnerving her: the 2 train screaming violently into the station at Seventy-Second Street; near misses of taxicab collisions on Central Park West; window washers hanging forty stories up on a fraying rope that threatened to plunge them through the air, shattering their bodies on the pavement below into a mess of blood and crowds and terror. Shelley opened her eyes to stop seeing shards of glass and concrete piled up, to stop smelling burning gasoline.

Three nights before the protest march, all the Family Supporters were in the Strong Place parlor building props for their direct-action protest. The whole group was downstairs, save for Nick, who had been disappearing from the group quite a bit. The Family Supporters had acquired twice the amount of PVC pipes they needed and had watched internet videos to learn how to construct confetti cannons. On the floor, they arranged all the necessary materials: the wide gray pipes, a metal saw, drills with metal drill bits, a pressure gauge, a bicycle pump. David and Cate and Esmerelda and all the rest sat in a circle, stuffing the pipes with photocopied notes, using tissue and tape to cover the top of them, the pump to get them pressurized. They were all gleeful, energized. Grace was making one for Nick. The cannons were joyous, ridiculous props that they would shoot off at the march, in unison, right before four o'clock, at their various lockdown locations throughout the city. As the sounds distracted the police and the onlookers, the Family Supporters would shove their arms into the other empty pipes, then chain their necks to fences and street signs, as small scraps of white paper flew up and out over the city streets. The scraps would float to the pavement, spreading their messages in blocky hand:

ExxonMobil Is a Terrorist
Bush and Cheney are Terrorists
People Over Profits; No War for Oil
GAG Forever! Free the Family!

Shelley knew this was happening downstairs, just as she knew that something was going on with Brooke; she'd received five missed calls from her that day alone. And yet Shelley didn't care about anyone else. Despair will do that to a person. At midnight on August 21, she stood barefoot on the hardwood floor of the tiny upstairs office, flipping the light switch up and down, watching the room flash from bright to brighter. Her mother was sick, and showing up in Boston wouldn't do a damn thing to change that. Shelley had no money and nothing to do; it was time to go on the internet and get herself another job. *Flick*. Maybe things would get better. *Flick*. Maybe everyone would come back to her.

She sat down in front of the ancient gray Macintosh and began looking for moneymaking opportunities. A job, a new start, another Mr. Kamal. She went onto Craigslist, back to the Etc. jobs section where she had originally found her ex-employer's ad. There was nothing of interest there, so she went to *Casual Encounters* and she clicked on the *Men Seeking Women*, recalling the email responses she'd received months before. Now there were the usual eye-rollers:

INTERESTED IN ASSES OF ALL SIZES.
PUSSY EATING: NO GAMES—JUST LICK AND LEAVE.
NEED A GIRL WHO CAN HANDLE MY ENDOWMENT.

She responded to a few ads but chose the simpler ones. A MARRIED & LOOKING FOR MORE headline, with the inside message reading: "Want a nonstressful encounter, into 'rock climbing.' Have connections." Another headline, SUCCESSFUL LAWYER SEEKS FUN WITH STUDENT, with the message: "43-year-old self-made man prepared to help out the right girl with living in this expensive city. Interested in YOUNGER, submissive, up for anything girls."

Within forty-five minutes Shelley had two responses, one asking if she was available immediately and one asking for tomorrow at noon. A change, a new job; it was that easy. Shelley responded with the affirmative for the noon meeting the next day, allowing her sufficient time to mull it over. The man said his name was Hall. She chose a random yet reasonable-sounding rate of two hundred dollars for full penetration. In any case, the rate wouldn't matter if she didn't show up. She thought of her friend's mother's silk teddy crumpled at the back of her closet.

Shelley tossed fitfully all night in a vivid dreamscape. She dreamed of her older self, who had become rather sophisticated; slimmer and more upright and elegant than she was in the years of her early twenties. In her dream, thirty-nine-year-old Shelley told her clients her real name. She was at the end of a long day of work and was slipping one leg into her trousers in the bathroom, where she always re-dressed, when a client she'd had three sessions with called through the door, "I've been meaning to ask. Are you *related*?"

Back in the well-appointed hotel room, she snickered, "Of course."

She did most of her work at the Lucerne Hotel now, on Seventy-Ninth, just west of the park, a block away from where her father had his shop. Her regulars, the Manhattanites, often asked: "Shelley Whitby like Shelley *Whitby*, or like the old Whitby Shades and Blinds?" She always smiled, said "Yes and yes," and they chuckled and winked and pulled her clumsily toward their bodies, usually hard, fat, mole-pricked, and fuzz covered, but occasionally atrophied-soft and clammy cold. The men believed she was lying about who she was. As her limbs entwined their aging hips, her mind blanked white. They'd paw and slap in embarrassed bursts, and her skin buzzed with the warm satisfaction that she was helping, helping, healing these famished souls. When other people—deli men, shopgirls, guys at bars—asked her what she did for a living she said she was a social worker, because for the many things she had done in her thirty-nine years, she'd never been a liar.

Downstairs, nodding to the bellboy with his perpetual smirk, Shelley tied her black anorak around her waist and walked out into a late summer Saturday afternoon. Spandexed joggers on Amsterdam, mothers with nylon carriage battering rams, Europeans in popped-collar polos strolled toward the park. To Shelley, leaving the hotel in the afternoon was like coming out of a movie matinee at Lincoln Center while skipping school: you walk outside to discover the lights still on, the world still honking and braking, and you *still* have three more hours to be entirely your own person.

It was with that sense of freedom that twenty-three-year-old Shelley opened her eyes. It was nine in the morning. Perhaps she could, in fact, go meet this Craigslist man, Hall, at the Days Inn at noon. She pictured herself walking through the outlawish seaport, among the slick, abandoned streets. It always felt a few degrees cooler down there than anywhere else in Manhattan. Then she wondered where Mr. Kamal was at that moment. Was his new amanuensis girl draping her hair over his face, as she had? Was the girl, at this very moment, crawling on her hands and spindly knees across the floor of Mr. Kamal's office?

Two hours later, she walked out her front door in a type of haze. She wasn't scared. In fact, she felt no emotion whatsoever. She told herself she was simply going to work. And yet, the incantation *Mom, Mom, Mom* ran through her mind. She was, in fact, totally alone.

Shelley, with her satchel slung over her shoulder, walked down Strong Place in the steaming, end-of-summer air. *Mom, Mom, Mom,* her brain chanted, as if she was trying to conjure up the woman. After she completed this Craigslist job, she would simply flip-flop out onto cobblestone and stink of the underpopulated fish market. She wouldn't be any different, except that her pockets would be stuffed with cash. A person has only one life, and limited time within it. She thought about walking through the snow alone to Bergdorf's as a child, then walking home again with her new dress. Life was simply a series of actions; the consequences exist only if you let them.

As she rounded the corner a voice called out. "Shelley? Shelley—hey!"

The sound was coming from a car window. It was a Jeep, with wooden siding.

"Shells! I was just about to call you." The driver's door was opening, and Brooke was stepping down onto the sidewalk. She wore an orange tank top, from which a small but distinct pregnant belly protruded.

Shelley gasped. "What the hell?"

"I'm so happy to see you," Brooke said as her arms spread open to take Shelley into an embrace. "Are you going somewhere? Get in, and I can give you a ride."

The chanting in Shelley's head stopped abruptly. The hot pressure of relief made her sigh. She was being enveloped in two prim yet warm arms. "No," Shelley said. "No, I'm not going anywhere."

"Good, then let's go out to lunch." Brooke beamed. Despite the belly, she seemed lighter than usual, brighter even. "I'm going to convince you to go on a trip with me."

19

The surprising thing that happened on the ferry to the island was that Nick showed up. This wasn't a total surprise for Brooke, of course—after he'd called her the week before, she'd planned the trip and sent him a check that he had presumably cashed to buy his ticket there. His call had come at the conspicuous time when she was packing her final box in the house on Joy Street. He'd reported that he was fine and healthy and in New York, and that he had a proposal for her about how she could keep her home. "Anything!" Brooke had huffed into the phone, before thinking it through. His proposal involved going to the Vineyard. But although it was his idea, Nick had not proved himself to be very reliable, and she still hadn't been convinced he would come. And Shelley was caught completely unaware. Brooke and Shelley were sitting at a booth inside the ferry when it blew its deep horn and began to back out of the Woods Hole port. Shelley ordered a watery Bloody Mary, tomato juice and vodka with a dusting of black pepper really, so Brooke ordered a virgin one. They sipped and told each other how nice it would be to while away a few days on the island, relaxing. They had spent the previous day at the hospital outside Boston visiting with Shelley's mother, an event that had been both as banal and as productive as one could have hoped for. Elizabeth's doctor had arranged to do phone therapy with Shelley and her mother in the coming weeks, and Shelley had gone as far as signing a written form committing herself to this act. Since seeing her mother, Shelley seemed softened and relaxed—happier, maybe. Now Brooke had talked her into a few days' vacation on the Vineyard, where they would visit the beaches and cafés and fish markets that they had spent respective formative years frequenting. She hadn't mentioned Nick because she didn't want to over-complicate the situation. And convincing Shelley to go to the island hadn't been a hard sell.

The rocking of the ferry subsided as it picked up speed. The cabin was crowded with couples of all ages wearing fleece jackets and windbreakers; parents of small children shoved diapers and wipes into monogramed L.L. Bean tote bags; a black poodle yapped, and a yellow Lab lay down, placidly. It was just when Brooke was missing her dog, Phoebe, and regretting leaving her at the kennel on Cambridge Street, that Shelley let out a muted cough of surprise and jumped up from her reclining position on the booth's bench.

"Nick?" she called across the middle rows of seats.

The two kids moved toward each other, meeting in the back of the cabin. They seemed to share some unfriendly words, interspersed with threatening looks back toward Brooke. Brooke waved from her seat each time they turned toward her. She was shocked to see him; it had been years. But there he stood, almost a real adult. Which also meant every-thing was out in the open now. Brooke exhaled as her two half siblings marched back toward the table with indignation displayed on their faces. Her relief was tempered by a tightening of her nerves. Finally, all three of them were together. They could talk about the houses. She was so very close to getting what she wanted.

Shelley exclaimed, arms crossed over her chest, "It is very bizarre that you would not tell me Nick was coming with us on this trip."

Brooke nodded slowly as Nick flung himself onto the booth bench across from her. He looked terrible: exhausted and unwashed, and rigid with anger. Was this his usual state? He didn't smile or acknowledge Brooke at all. That was the moment she should have done something. She should have asked him directly what was going on. His very appearance was a warning sign. Many boys, at twenty-one, are prone to doing ill-conceived things. The rich are no different from the rest; different only, perhaps, in the inclination to be more outrageous.

"You're right," Brooke said very calmly, trying to lower the tension. "I just wasn't sure that Nick would make it. And I didn't want to . . . I didn't want to confuse the situation. But I'm so very pleased that we're all here now." It really was a thrilling relief to finally be sitting at a table with these two kids who she had been trying to reach for months. "We need to discuss what's happening. I know it's what Dad would have wanted."

Nick snorted from across the booth. He pulled the hood of his sweatshirt over his head and hunched his two shoulders up.

Shelley sat beside Brooke. "Are you bringing us to the Vineyard to have a two-day family meeting? 'Cause I really am not in the mood for that. Nick knows about the deal with the will. I'm sure he'll make a decision about what he wants to do, just like he always does. He's not dependent on anyone else's schedule. Aren't I right, Nick?"

He snorted.

Something surprising seemed to occur to Shelley, and she shook her head while saying, "Poor Grace. Of course you would let her go to that silly protest alone."

Nick's jaw jutted out, and he gave Shelley a deathly glare.

"Have you told Shelley what you told me?" Brooke asked Nick.

He didn't respond. All around them on the ferry, people were involved in the activities of pleasantly preoccupying themselves. Eleven people read the *Boston Globe*, six people read the *New York Times*. Two older men, at opposite sides of the boat, read the same article in the *Economist* at a nearly identical pace. A thirteen-year-old boy masturbated in the second-floor bathroom. Outside at the center of the bow, a couple kissed as the wind whipped through their hair and the cold spray of the ocean flecked their cheeks; they both considered leaving the unhappy marriages they occupied on the mainland.

Nick's total silence, it was strange. A seed of fear began to foment in Brooke's brain: Why did this kid want to go to the island so badly? Why did he not care about giving up the property that would have been so easy for him to keep? She assessed his disheveled, irate figure in front of her: anyone would think that he was capable of creating serious harm, to others or to himself. Something was wrong.

She touched his sweatshirt-covered arm. "Nick and I made a verbal arrangement about my house. He's promised to let me keep it."

He shirked away from her hand.

"What? Why?" Shelley asked.

Nick didn't speak up, so Brooke reported their deal. "He said if I took him to the Vineyard for this trip, then he'd simply sign the Boston house over to me and it would become legally mine. All he wanted in return for the house was this trip."

When Nick had called her, speaking in a low voice from Shelley's cell phone, he'd said he would come to an agreement about her property. But it wasn't until the second phone call that he articulated just what he wanted that to be. "I need to stay at your Vineyard house, the one by Menemsha Pond. I need to be there alone on the night of August twentieth." Brooke explained to him that he was confused. It wasn't her house, she'd only stayed there in the summer because it belonged to the parents of a friend of hers. Then he asked if he could stay at their house—also alone.

When she asked him why, he had responded, "This is my offer. I'll give you what you want if you give me what I want." And in light of his declaration, she had sucked in all her apprehension about what had happened between her and Allie, and called the Wainwrights. She expected them to say something about the proposal, at least a word of acknowledgment. But they didn't bring it up, so neither did she. Brooke couldn't ask them to leave their own house, but she could invite herself and two of her siblings to come stay with them. And of course, being the Wainwrights, they enthusiastically accepted.

So there the Whitby children were, all together on the high-speed ferry. Nick continued to not move a muscle. Shelley's eyes narrowed to slits. She seemed to be investigating her half brother's appearance.

"Why would you make that deal, Nick?" she said in a stern whisper.

When he continued to remain mute, Shelley lunged over the vinyl tabletop and shook him by both shoulders. "Dude! Come back to earth! If you don't actually care about the houses at all, then give me mine too. Just call the lawyer and sign them over. Why are you even here? What about your big protest march tomorrow?"

Nick looked as if he'd been burned by Shelley's final words. He managed to whisper, "I do care about the houses. But I don't want to fucking talk about it now! I'll talk about it tomorrow. Can't you both just give me until tomorrow?"

Brooke shrugged. Later she would regret that, that all she did then was shrug. Shelley frowned and went back to the snack bar counter to order another Bloody Mary, as Nick put his head down on the table and covered it up with his two arms. It must have been a strange sight; Brooke was sure that she'd run into a friend at any moment but honestly couldn't bring herself to care about appearances right then. Anxiety swelled within her. She envisioned—miraculously—unpacking her entire kitchen of boxes. She had already scheduled the movers, but she could call and cancel. Her son would have the home and the life she wanted for him. Maybe it was this odd new energy that had emerged in the past few weeks of her pregnancy, but she was so ecstatic at that moment she could have burst out into song.

An hour later, the crowd lined up by the exit as the giant boat bobbed and rocked into the Oak Bluffs port. What a beautiful sight, pulling into the summer afternoon island world. From the deck one could see lines of cars crowding the parking lot, but Brooke couldn't find the Wainwrights' old beat-up Volvo anywhere. Perhaps they were running late. It wasn't until the three Whitbys were making their way down the ramp in the middle of the crowd of anxious travelers that Brooke noticed Nick's giant bags. He rolled behind him a huge, fraying, navy suitcase and carried on his shoulder a large black duffel bag.

"What the hell is in there?" Shelley asked.

"Stuff for a friend," he grumbled.

"What friend?" she questioned. "When was the last time you were even back here?"

Brooke's stomach dropped. What did Nick have with him? The early-afternoon sun glinted against the docks and the houses beyond it; seagulls squawked as they circled through the salty New England air. Brooke stepped onto the ground in her favorite place on earth and sighed. She would simply watch Nick vigilantly for the next few days. What else could she do?

The Whitbys found the Wainwrights in the back of the parking lot, both of them reading in the front seat of a new silver SUV with its doors open. "*Hello?*" Brooke said dubiously. She had never seen them in such a shiny, flashy vehicle.

"Oh!" Paula shouted. She threw her book down and jumped from the passenger's seat with the agility of a woman half her age. Her hair, parted in the middle, was pulled back tightly, and her shirt was tucked neatly into her khaki shorts. It had been several years since Brooke had seen her, but Paula looked just as she always did, filled with elegance and warmth at the same time. "Oh, my precious Brooke!" she exclaimed, throwing her arms around Brooke's shoulders. Brooke was grateful for the baggy top she'd chosen to wear, as she wasn't yet ready to discuss the baby.

After a similar reception from Thomas, then handshake introductions to the other Whitbys and quizzical looks about the amount of luggage the kids were piling into the trunk, they were all strapped into the car and rolling down State Road on the way to Chilmark. Thomas said resolutely, "We are very sorry to hear about your father's passing," and Paula put one hand behind her seat, finding Brooke's wrist and giving it a squeeze. Brooke felt like a small child and was content to feel that way. How nice to be taken care of. The Wainwrights didn't mention a word about the proposal, nor a word about Allie. Was it possible they didn't know? Outside the windows, the sandy banks of the road and green bursts of island flora and gray shingles of the old houses were all reminiscent of the happiest days of Brooke's life. Shelley, glaze-eyed and mellow, looked similarly at peace. Nick didn't utter a peep.

By the time the Whitbys were settled into their rooms—Charlie's room had recently been converted into an office, so Nick and Shelley would each take a twin bed in the guest room, and Brooke would sleep in Allie's old bedroom—no one had mentioned the status of Brooke and Allie's relationship. Allie was one of those adult children who told everything to her parents, but it seemed they truly didn't know. Before dinner, as Brooke stood by the kitchen island telling the Wainwrights about the latest nursing news on the oncology floor, Paula said to Brooke for a third time, "Sangria, sweetie? Have a glass." Brooke knew she should have told her about the pregnancy then, but instead she accepted the drink and pretended to sip it.

Thomas was chopping up a massive pile of grapefruits on the counter, far too many for one pitcher of sangria. He looked up at Brooke and, she could have sworn, let his eyes rest on her stomach. Then he began to quarter another grapefruit. Perhaps the Wainwrights were on edge too. Their avoidance of their daughter's name was conspicuous. "Sam will be here soon enough. Did we tell you that our neighbor, Samoset, he's coming for dinner? Sorry for us to not get your full attention." He winked. "But this dinner has been planned for weeks."

"Paula told me. And I remember Samoset." Sam was a frequent visitor around the Wainwright house. A conservative-looking guy, save for his short ponytail. He was a member of the Wampanoag Indian tribe, and had grown up and still lived in the tribal lands on Aquinnah, right across Menemsha Pond from Chilmark. He was also a member of the Democratic State Committee, and Brooke remembered that he, like most politically minded people, could not help himself from talking about politics constantly.

When they were all seated at the long wood table, tea candles glowing in the middle of it and Billie Holiday playing on the old record player, Brooke finally inquired about Allie. "I haven't heard if Allie's been out here to visit lately." Paula and Thomas gave each other a brief knowing glance.

Shelley handed Brooke a ceramic bowl with homemade tartar sauce in it. They were having crab cakes.

Thomas offered, "Hmmm, she should be coming out next weekend, if her schedule stays stable," then consumed himself in heaping salad onto his plate.

Paula asked Shelley, "So what do you do, dear? Are you still in school?"

"I've been working as a personal assistant," Shelley said with a shrug. "Helping a blind architect who decided to write a book."

"Fascinating!" Thomas said, clearly relieved to be off the subject of his daughter. "Would I know any of his buildings? What's his book about?"

After a short explanation of Shelley's investigations of old houses, Sam piped right up. "Well, protected land. Protecting our history. That's the name of the game this summer!" He asked the Whitby children if they knew what had been happening with the Wampanoag reservation on the island. They all shook their heads. "My tribe has lived on this island for centuries, but since we were officially granted parcels of land in 1987, there have been a host of lawsuits about the land rights surrounding Lobsterville Beach in Aquinnah. For years, corporations have been frothing at the mouth to develop it, because it is of course prime landscape to turn into a hotel. But you couldn't get to the beach without cutting through the land held privately by tribe members. And last year one of the members of our tribe took the buyout—he sold his giant parcel of land to the Davidson Corporation. You know, they're the ones putting hotels and mini malls all over the Cape? And they're moving out to the islands next."

Brooke sucked in a surprised breath. "They're here too? I know the local Boston guys who the Davidsons work with, Costa Construction. They're awful. Well, not all. I mean. One of them is the father," Brooke said, putting a hand on her stomach. The words had popped out of her mouth. But then, the news had to come out sooner or later.

Everyone was totally silent. Shelley gave Brooke a cocked eyebrow, meant to imply, *Smooth move.*

"The father of what?" Thomas finally asked.

Brooke coughed. "I'm due in December. It's a boy."

For a split second Paula and Thomas caught each other's eye again. But soon they were both on their feet, cheering, and Sam was raising his glass of sangria with a "Hear-hear! What news!"

Arms enveloped Brooke, and the two Wainwrights kissed her cheeks, spouting indiscriminate exclamations of excitement. It was, Brooke understood, the nicest reception to the news that she had received yet.

When they were all seated back at the table, Sam led a toast and Paula jumped up again saying, "Don't you drink that sangria! Let me get you another drink."

As Paula, giggling, retrieved a glass bottle of sparkling water from the kitchen's island, Thomas said, "So tell us about the sperm donor. He's a developer?"

"Oh . . ." Brooke's voice trailed off. There was no choice but to be honest. That's the thing about pregnancy: the facts will come out eventually. "I was dating the man for a while. But I'm not any longer."

Everyone at the table joined in a collective pause. The two Wainwrights appeared perplexed. "I was unaware of your status," Thomas said solidly then. He was a psychiatrist, and practiced verbalizing clear statements in emotionally heightened moments.

Paula jumped in, saying hurriedly, "It's just that Allie doesn't, you know, date men. She came out so long ago and that was it. So we just assumed, that because of you and Allie, you know, you wouldn't see men either."

Shelley's sangria sprayed out of her mouth, landing on her placemat and the tabletop. "You're gay?" she asked.

Even Nick looked alert now.

Brooke's lips pursed. This was exactly the kind of attention she did not like to call to herself. "Well, I'm not entirely gay. Obviously," she said as she gestured toward her stomach. Shelley threw her head back and let out one long *Hoooo*, before raising her glass into the air again.

Thomas Wainwright put a hand on his forehead wearily. Sam cleared his throat and leaned over the table toward Nick. "As I was saying . . ." He continued, in the wonky tone of a politician, to explain the land-use dispute.

"It's going to ruin the island as we know it," Thomas said, joining his friend in the slow head shake. "It'll be the biggest hotel this place has ever seen, but it's not just the hotel. The corporation has a ten-year plan to expand the development. If they can buy more land, soon enough there will be parking lots and a Starbucks coffee shop and a Target out there."

"A true tragedy," Paula agreed.

"We know about the Davidsons," Nick said, surprising everyone with the sound of his voice. "They bought our family's hotel, too, a couple decades ago."

"Where's that hotel?" Sam asked.

"In Manhattan, the Whitby-Grand. That used to belong to us."

Shelley and Brooke locked eyes. Nick was very easily saying the words *us* and *our*. Brooke hadn't spent much time with the kid, but from what she knew of him, he had never included himself in the family so easily. Perhaps, even in a run-down, bitter state, a person can't help but feel empowered by a legal document. It seemed that with this will, Nick had become a real Whitby.

Sam gave each of the Whitby children an amused look and finished his last bite of crab cake. "Then maybe you three know what I'm talking about. The Davidsons have no humanity. They don't care about the history of a place or how this development is going to destroy the culture of my tribe. I was in the courtroom this summer when our lawyer explained the foundational story of our tribe, and the Davidson business guys—they weren't even listening."

Sam dived into a well-practiced speech, explaining how the Wampanoag people believe that an ancient giant named Moshup carved out the land around Aquinnah himself. Moshup was from the mainland but would come out to this island to fish. He fed himself well and then would leave the rest of the bounty for the Wampanoag people to feast on. The giant would catch whales with his bare hands, then hurl them against the rocks before broiling them over his constantly burning fire on the shore.

The blood of the thrashed whales, that's what turned the cliffs of Aquinnah red. Sam explained that the tribe believes Moshup is still sleeping right there, in an underwater cave.

Then he chuckled. "My people want to try to wake him, to disturb the seas when the construction of the road begins."

Nick pounded the table with his two fists, and Brooke nearly jumped out of her skin. "It's all coming together," he said. "We can wake Moshup up. We have to."

Sam chuckled nervously. "Yes. If only we could."

Shelley looked nothing short of tickled. Her face was flushed. Maybe she was drunk. Brooke mouthed to her, *Is he okay?*

Shelley shrugged. That was another moment Brooke should have paid more attention to. But she was just so afraid of spooking him. If she pushed too hard, he could take back his offer about her house. There was so much riding on this one unlikely, angry kid.

After apricot upside-down cake, after Shelley drank about seven more glasses of sangria, when Sam had shaken Brooke's hand and wished her the greatest success with the new baby, she was settled into bed. It was strange to be lying in the same location that Allie had laid on so many nights of her life. Brooke thought she could smell Allie's particular scent: coconut and laundry detergent. Just as she was drifting off, a light knock sounded at the door. Thomas, in navy pajamas, and Paula, in a lavender robe, came in and sat together at the end of her bed. Such a unified parental gesture. Brooke was touched by the very act of their sitting.

"We are so sorry about discussing your, uh, dating preferences earlier," Thomas said. "We just—we were so surprised by the baby news, and it came out. Does Allie know about the baby?"

"She knows," Brooke said quietly.

The two parents nodded.

Paula asked then, "Brooke, dear . . . we're wondering something else. Is there a reason you and your siblings came to see us this weekend? Are you here to ask us something?"

"We just wanted to visit the island."

Both Wainwrights seemed to deflate with relief. Thomas said, "This thing with the Davidson hotel has gotten us crazy. And we thought, with your father passing, you might have the opportunity to buy a house up here. And maybe you were going to ask us about ours!" Both Wainwrights let out breathy laughs. It was strange to see them embarrassed.

"Buy the house? That is the opposite of the position I'm in right now." She paused, wondering if she should feel bad about their assumption but brushed it off. They were so generous about everything else. She considered telling them the whole story then, about the will and Nick and how she couldn't find him all summer. But it was late. And she had surprised them enough already that day.

Thomas tapped her blanket-covered foot. "Well, I'm glad we've got that cleared away. We should all go to the beach in the morning." Paula kissed her forehead and asked if she'd like the light turned off. Thirty-seven-year-old Brooke said she would indeed, and fell into the grateful slumber of being granted a few hours, or even days, of pretending that she was not, in fact, a fully grown, responsibility-laden adult.

At three thirty in the morning, Shelley stood over Brooke in the dark, shaking her awake. She whispered, "Nick just left the house. He woke me up when he left our room and then went out the back door."

"Shit," Brooke said. She was very quickly very alert. Her one thought was: *This kid is going to kill himself.* She sat up. "Obviously he was planning something. Where do you think he's going?"

"I don't know," Shelley screeched. "Get up!"

As Brooke threw the covers off her body, she asked, "Do you think he's planning to hurt himself?"

Shelley was silent for a few beats too long. "I don't know."

Soon Brooke was trailing behind Shelley across the Wainwrights' field-like backyard, with Allie's Middlebury sweatshirt thrown on over her pajamas. She should have acted earlier; it was out of pure selfishness that she hadn't. There was a collective beach at the base of the yard, on the shores of Menemsha Pond. By the time they reached the beach they saw Nick's back in the darkness, just a charcoal outline of shoulders and arms rowing in a small white rusted rowboat, moving at a rapid pace away from the shore of the sandy boat launch. The air was windless, the island stars extremely clear. An evening bird on the other side of the saltwater pond hooted.

"Nick!" Shelley yelled from the beach. Brooke joined in. His name echoed off water before them. He didn't turn around.

"Nick, we need to talk to you!" Brooke tried. Shelley had gone down to the water's edge and was now a shadow climbing around the small boats turned on their bellies on the grass. She flipped over a canoe and began dragging it onto the sand.

"Are you getting in here with me?" she hollered in Brooke's general direction.

"That's not our boat," Brooke said.

"That's your concern right now?"

Soon Brooke was in the stern of the green canoe, with Shelley at the bow, steering. Brooke heaved the paddles back. She was certainly doing the bulk of the work. This couldn't be good for the baby. But of course, Shelley would never consider that; she was too young and self-absorbed. As Brooke pulled her paddles back again, beginning to sweat, she kept her eyes trained on Nick's swaying back in the boat fifty yards in front of them. She feared that at any moment his outlined figure could drop off into the water.

"Is he going to stop?" Brooke asked through her huffs and pulls.

"How am I supposed to know?" Shelley spat over her shoulder.

Nick's little white boat had turned now, and his sisters could see that he had his suitcase and duffel bag stacked up in front of it. It didn't make sense. Why would he have brought the luggage with him?

The water beside the boat was a swirling black mirror: there was no way to tell how deep it was. Nick was now close to the other shore and got out of the boat in the shallow water, not even bothering to pull up the bottom of his jeans. Once they were close enough, Shelley jumped out and let her paddles slip over the side and float on the top of the salt water.

Nick stood on the sand with the duffel bag slung over his shoulder and two hands pulling at the handle of the giant suitcase. Shelley ran toward him, sloshing through the ankle-deep water. Brooke, bobbing alone in the canoe, took a moment to catch her breath and realized the madness of the situation. It was the middle of the night. Why had she let these kids pull her into all of this? The whole thing was absurd, and she felt, at that moment, incredibly duped by her father. She had once again let him dictate her actions. By the time she had rolled up the bottom of her pajama pants and was dragging the canoe onto the sand, Nick was growling at both women. "Neither of you should be here," he said. "You weren't supposed to follow me."

Brooke could see that his eyes were just angry slits. He was on the edge. She felt herself shift into professional nursing mode: there was an adrenaline that came with taking on a challenging patient and a life-threatening emergency. Energy kicked into her veins, and she said in an authoritative tone, "Everyone needs to take a deep breath. We're all going to take a deep breath and remember that no matter how bad the situation might seem at the moment, Nick, life has the possibility of getting better. Roger's death and his will threw us all for a loop. But none of this has to affect you forever." As she said these words aloud, she also began to believe them herself.

The three Whitbys stood in a triangle on the beach. The moon illuminated Nick's frustrated grimace. He dropped the duffel bag and let out a curdled cry. "You don't get it! All the signs came together. The houses, the inheritance coming to me, they were signs. And Big D meeting with me last week, and the march in New York happening on the same day as the construction here on the island. And Samoset! The story tonight about his tribe. There are so many signals. All of them telling me that I have to act."

Shelley spoke up now, her voice wavering. "Nick, you cannot leave me alone. You're the only person who comes close to understanding the bizarre circumstances of my life. I—I love you." She was pleading.

"What do you think I'm about to do?" he said.

Both women silently turned toward each other in the darkness. Brooke's training taught her that when a patient is having a psychotic episode, you should never utter the word *suicide*. It was too dangerous. Words are also ideas.

Nick ran his hands through his hair and then dropped to the sand. "I only have one life, and this is what I'm choosing to do with it." He began unzipping the large suitcase and revealed a peculiar sight: the side of a red aluminum box. He unzipped it farther and took out a two-gallon can that read *Eagle Gasoline* on the side of it. "All my friends in New York, they're about to get arrested in a giant march tomorrow. But I'm going to do something that actually makes an impact."

What was going on? What was he pulling out of his bag? Brooke wondered if it was part of a weapon. She tried to get Shelley's attention, but she was moving toward her brother.

"What are you going to do with that?" Shelley whispered to Nick as she sank into the sand beside him.

"I'm going to hit these developer motherfuckers in the only place that actually hurts them: their bank account. I'm going to make the Davidson Corporation hemorrhage money, by burning down their fucking construction site for the hotel's road cut," he said.

Brooke covered her face with her hands. All she could think of were the words *spoiled brat*. Nick wasn't planning to kill himself, or ruin his own life. He was going to ruin all their lives. Now his bizarre behavior actually made sense. He was going to get himself needlessly arrested, and then lose all the money from her father, buying himself out of jail and paying back a development company. And he had asked *her* to take him to the Vineyard. He had implicated her in this idiocy! Overcome with anger, she dropped to her knees on the wet sand too, exasperated. "You cannot do this," she said.

Brooke looked to Shelley for reassurance—reassurance, she supposed, that this ludicrous situation was actually happening. But, although Brooke couldn't see the details of her half sister's expression clearly in the darkness, she could understand that Shelley was not mad.

Shelley said softly, "Did you do something like this before you came to my house at the beginning of the summer?"

Nick nodded. "But I was a coward after the first action, and I'm never going to be again. You know, this inheritance from Roger, it's a test. The universe is testing me. It's *him* testing me. Roger believed in me, and I'm going to do things in the world. I don't give a shit if the fascist police want to arrest me."

Brooke considered the options she had that could stop this kid. They were alone on the beach, at what had to be four in the morning. Should she tackle him? She was small and pregnant. He had at least a foot on her. She tried to calm herself with deep breaths. With one hand on her stomach she said, "Please don't do this to our family, Nick. Don't do this to the nephew you haven't met yet."

When Nick didn't respond, Shelley asked in an almost sweet voice, "Are you doing this for Roger? Do you think this will piss him off, or make him proud? Neither thing will happen, Nick. He will never know about this. Dad is gone."

"I know he's fucking gone!" Nick yelled. His two clenched fists hit the wet sand beside him. Now Brooke understood Shelley's calmness; she knew how her brother would react.

Nick continued, "Don't you two remember how unhappy Roger was? He was tortured. He spent his life trying to get out from behind his own name, trying to do something big to prove himself. It was manipulative and mean of him to give me this money. Didn't he understand the kind of pressure that comes with that? But I'm going to do my own big things— big things that matter."

As Nick yelled, Shelley dug her fingers into the sand, letting a wall of her brown hair cover her face. She was eerily calm. Brooke couldn't take this. Her calculated nurse voice had entirely disappeared now. "Our own biological father left both Shelley and me when we were kids. He disappeared on us. And now, after he's dead, he gives away our actual homes to you. And *you* are the one complaining? He gave you everything he had. Literally."

"You don't get it," Nick barked, standing up and brushing the sand off his jeans. "Roger, Dad, he never knew what to do. That's why he left you both, and me. He left us because he had the Whitby Curse of *not knowing what to do*. So I'm going to do something with my life. I'm going to stop this corporation from destroying the one place in the world I've ever been happy. And I'm going to get arrested"—his voice wavered as he looked down at the girls—"and if I go to prison, at least I will be fucking proud of myself."

It occurred to Brooke then that Nick was too young, really, to understand the value of the property. What did he know about paying for himself? His home, his food, it had probably always just arrived for him, as if by magic. If the government took all the inheritance, it wouldn't change his life one bit. None of this was about money for him, at all.

"No," Brooke said firmly. She stood up too. "You want this to be sensational. You want to do this so the news will report that you're not what people think you are just because you're a Whitby. You can't fool us, Nick."

"I get it," Shelley said softly. She stood up as well and put two arms on Nick's shoulders. Surprisingly, he let himself be touched. "This island is the only place I've ever been happy, too." The two kids faced each other in the dark and just stood there, shoulders squared to each other.

It was very clear that Shelley and Nick loved each other. This clarity made an uncharacteristic knot spring into Brooke's throat. She wondered, briefly, if she and Peter would have had a relationship like that. A deep, emptying sadness threatened her. Then she thought of Allie. The only other times Brooke had even been on that beach, she'd been there with Allie. They had lain on striped towels and drank cold sodas and thought of nothing and felt at peace. What a privilege, to have someone to love like that.

That was when Brooke had a bizarre idea. It was so not like her, but then, she wasn't sure exactly what she was like, anymore. She said, "This place is important to me too, guys." Shelley's clutch loosened on Nick's shoulders, and they both turned to her. "What if we help you to do something else, Nick? We can't let you set a fire. But we could, you know, protest this with you."

As surprised as Brooke was to hear herself make the suggestion, she was more surprised at how easily Nick acquiesced to it. Perhaps he'd been waiting for that kind of out. All three Whitbys and the suitcase and the duffel bag loaded into the canoe again. Brooke sat in the middle and didn't row—they were down a set of paddles because Shelley's original ones had floated away—as Nick was in the back, using the liberated rowboat oars to power them all. When they reached the middle of the saltwater pond they stopped, and Brooke pushed Nick's bags over the edge of the boat. The moment took on the sincerity of a funeral at sea. The suitcase containing all the gasoline sunk immediately, but the duffel floated for a few minutes until Shelley batted it down with the tip of an oar. The moon was still bright in the sky, and all three of them were silent for a few minutes.

As they made their way back toward the Wainwrights' beach, Nick told his sisters everything, from the action in Maine to how Big D had met him at a diner and tried to arrange a larger group action on the Vineyard, but Nick had insisted that he carry it out alone. The girls received the information quietly. Brooke tried to remember what it was like to be his age. When she was twenty-one, every day had felt much more urgent than it did now, as if the future was not necessarily ever going to happen. There was no way Nick would be able to understand that this feeling too shall pass. By the time the three Whitbys stepped into the cold concrete of the Wainwrights' garage, Brooke was rubbing her stomach and thinking about how it would be decades before her own son understood the art of acceptance and patience that comes with age. And that was just the way it should be.

In the garage they found all the supplies they needed: four rolls of extra-strength duct tape, a curly wire bicycle lock with a mini padlock and key, and a few bottles of water. Before getting back into the boat,

Nick wrote a three-line note on the back of a manila envelope that signed the houses over to one beneficiary: Michelle Whitby. He dated it August 22, 2003. None of them was sure if it was a legal document or not, but it was the best they could do at that moment. Shelley verbally promised to gift Brooke's house to her, and Brooke had no other recourse than to believe her. Brooke paused in the garage, holding the makeshift contract. This paper envelope might just be the thing that would bring her happiness for years to come. She was grateful to have it in her hand. And yet at that moment, she cared so much less about it than she did about taking care of these troubled, lovable kids who had somehow ended up her family.

After two granola bars and another largely silent canoe ride, Brooke marched behind her half siblings on a dirt path cutting through the marshy land that rightfully belonged to the Wampanoag tribe. They stopped twice for her to pee in the brush, and by the time they reached the large yellow excavator, the sun was rising over the water in the distance. Shelley went first, putting her arms around the front silver tube of the excavator, each of her hands gripping the opposite elbow. Nick wound the duct tape around Shelley's forearms, making a thick seal. "Usually it's better if there's a PVC pipe here, and then, like, a plaster cast around it, sealing your arms in. I'm not sure how the cops are gonna cut this off without sawing your arm in half."

Shelley giggled. The whole thing felt like a joke. Perhaps Brooke should have taken it more seriously, but she certainly did not feel she was in any type of actual danger. She peed one last time in the tall reeds. They all decided it was best if Brooke was tied to the machine with just one arm, so that she could pour water into her own mouth or pull her pants down in an emergency situation. "Concessions for pregnant activists," she said with a chuckle. Then added, "Oh, the things I never thought I'd say." But she'd done so many things that summer that she'd never imagined doing. And there was very little to worry about, legally. She was a grown-up, an esteemed employee in a helping profession. And she had to admit that it went through her head: the police wouldn't hurt three Whitbys.

Nick was the final body to be tied to the excavator, but no one was left to tie him, which is why they had brought the bicycle lock. He doubled the curly wire around his neck and looped it around the same metal pipe his sisters' arms were tied to, but higher up. The girls were able to sit on the back of the metal shovel, but Nick had to stand behind them. "What should I do with the key?" he asked.

"Throw it?"

"Bury it?"

"What would Dad do?" Shelley asked.

"Eat it," Brooke said. They all laughed.

"Give it to me," Brooke ordered. She was, after all, the oldest. She shoved the key into the side of her underwear, by her hip.

The sun had risen and warblers had begun their morning songs. The cold, wet current was fading from the air. "How long do you think we'll be here, Nick?"

"Can't be later than nine, right?"

The three kids were quiet for a while, until Nick asked, "Do you think Roger would be proud of us? All of us standing up for something we believe in, together?"

"How much did he care about that kind of thing, really?" Shelley said.

Brooke shook her head. "My mom always said she thought Dad—Roger—would have been a really simple and straightforward man, if he hadn't been born a Whitby."

"My mother said the same thing," Shelley said.

"And mine too," Nick said with a sigh. "You know our mothers, they weren't born into this like you two, or forced into it like me. They didn't have to walk into every new environment in their lives and wonder if people were judging them, wonder what kind of assumptions people had about them, false praise or ill will. None of the rest of us asked for this. Roger certainly didn't."

Shelley said, "You don't think Dad *wanted* us to fight about the will, do you?"

"Maybe he actually wanted to spare you and me, Shelley, and the rest of my family and his older kids," Brooke said. "Keep the money drama away from us. He knew how this kind of money question goes, in families like ours."

"Or maybe he just felt guilty about everything that happened in my life," Nick said.

Shelley snickered. "What happened in your life is the same thing that happened in all our lives. Just with a different set of actors."

"True," Nick said. "But it really sucked at the time."

They all giggled softly.

Brooke was strangely at peace there with her half siblings, with the cool metal of the construction machine pressing through her sweatshirt. She wondered what LJ and Kiki would think if they could see her now. They might go into physical anaphylactic shock from surprise. She wished she had the ability to take a photograph. From the path where the machine sat, Brooke, Shelley, and Nick couldn't see the ocean, but they could still smell it.

Nick said, "Once, Roger took me on a helicopter trip from New York to Connecticut. And right before we got in, he said to me in his deep echoey voice, 'How do you like adventure, son?' . . . I think about that all the time."

Brooke smiled. "That's what he wanted, for himself and for us. Adventure, excitement. All the rest of you—Kiki and LJ, and the kids from the first family—every single one of you seems to have inherited that from Roger. But I never got the appeal."

"Oh yeah: the rest of them," Shelley said, as if she'd completely forgotten that Roger had several other children. "There's five more of us! They're going to absolutely love what we're doing right now."

As they laughed, Brooke felt the pressure of pregnancy pressing dangerously on her bladder. There was a chance, now, that she could live at home, where she wanted to be, with her son. But even if that didn't work out, she was proud of herself for trying. She was proud of Nick, and even of Shelley, for doing what they thought was right and for caring about each other, even if it wasn't what they'd been taught to do. She had faith now that her other siblings might do the same. "Let me take care of the rest of them," she said with a grin. Each Whitby kid, at that moment, felt grateful for the others. As the morning sun heated up their skin and the growing racket of birds broke into song, Shelley, Nick, and Brooke breathed in the salty air and felt distinctly lucky that they had grown up with the same name pinned to them, occasionally been kissed good night by the same distracted lips, and disappointed by the absence of the same man. It was complicated and imperfect—and usually it was painful. But right now, there was joy in their numbers.

That's when the blue pickup truck drove up. A man in a hard hat and a Bruins sweatshirt stepped out of the driver's seat. "Jesus H. Christ," he said. Then he quickly reached down to the radio clipped to his belt. "Ross, we got a problem here by the site at Lobsterville. Some lunatics have tied themselves to the machinery."

All three Whitbys cracked up. They were lunatics together.

20

On the day of the march Grace rose alone in the gray post-dawn hours, to friendly laughter outside of her tent in Art Park. She hadn't seen Nick since the previous morning. He had told her he needed some time alone before the action and was going to stay at Shelley's apartment. He'd been pulling back from her, acting strange, really, for the past few weeks. He was just scared, she reminded herself. He would meet her later, downtown at the start of the march, just as he promised. She would reassure him then. She would make him brave.

All the other Family Supporters had slept in their tents in the park that night, and they convened in a circle on the grass in the morning just as the heavy clouds were burning off. The group had conducted assorted rituals in preparation for the Day of Action. Cate and Zac and Roiphe did a cleanse where all they ate for two days was instant oatmeal and leafy greens; they wanted their bodies and minds to be as pure and alert as possible. For those days, Ebony led everyone in morning and evening meditation sessions. Christopher and Nick and Esmerelda went for three-mile runs each afternoon, did burpees on the grass in the center of the park, then mixed protein powder with water in their Nalgene bottles and downed the whole thing.

By midmorning on the day of the march they were all together—save for Nick—and they took the 1 train downtown. Their PVC-pipe confetti cannons had already been stored at various locations: office buildings and apartment buildings with sympathetic doormen, or behind the counter at stores where their friends worked. The pipes were far too heavy to be carried around all day. But what the Family Supporters did have with them was not light. They carried a rolled-up banner staple-gunned to two sticks of plywood, reading: PACIFISM = TERRORISM? HAS THE WORLD GONE MAD? Six of them had their own individual signs as well, two of them had small timpani drums with slings, two others carried woks they had attached guitar straps to—homemade percussion instruments. Most of them wore backpacks filled with water, granola, napkins, and apple cider vinegar to flush out the tear gas. Those who planned to be on the front lines had goggles attached to their belts, in order to withstand a direct tear gas attack. Christopher carried an entire medic's kit in his backpack. They were moving toward an event that was one-half celebration and one-half battle. They were prepared.

Washington Square Park, the starting point for the march, was a raucous festival. The scent of sunscreen and marijuana, the sound of drums, the scorch of the sun; it overwhelmed all their senses. Toddlers sat on their parents' shoulders wearing brightly colored sunglasses. Colleagues and acquaintances clustered together: union members in orange T-shirts; college kids with banners stating, NEW SCHOOL STUDENTS AGAINST CORPORATE TAKEOVER; Grandmothers for Peace in pink; the Gay Men's Equality Organization holding rainbow flags. And the puppets: a larger-than-life George Bush head, a papier-mâché long-haired goddess with blood dripping down her cheek and a sign that read, RIP MOTHER EARTH. Grace was thrilled: the scene was better than she could have ever imagined. And she'd been integral in creating it.

Someone was doing a mic check in front of a crowd by the fountain. It was an older voice Grace knew, a former Students for Democratic Society leader named Colin. He shouted, "To paraphrase Dr. King, 'When machines and computers, profit motives and property rights are considered more important than people . . . ,' that's when exploitation is incapable of being conquered. And so I ask you to repeat after me: This movement is a true revolution of our values!"

The crowd responded, *"This movement is a true revolution of our values!"*

"Today is about writing new stories, ones with happier endings!"

"Today is about writing new stories, ones with happier endings!"

The Family-Support Network took their place under the grand arch at the base of Fifth Avenue, at the very front of the crowd, in order to lead the march. Grace was thrilled to have these people around her, her people, her real friends. Nick was nowhere to be seen. She asked David and Ebony and Christopher, "Have you run into Quentin yet?" But no one had. Despite the utter pride her surroundings were bringing—the movement, her movement, really showing up and taking action—a hole of sadness and abandonment steadily grew inside of her. *Please don't do this, Nick,* she silently wished. *Please don't let me down like this.*

At noon they began to move slowly north down the wide street, everyone chanting, "Globalization is a crime, from New York to Palestine!"

Although a hollowness was forming inside of Grace—where the hell was he?—she felt the exterior of her body melting into joy, into other people's bodies and voices.

Behind Grace were thousands of people, maybe tens of thousands, marching together. All the groups the Family Supporters were in touch with were there, their comrades in the struggle.

"Ours is my favorite sign!" she yelled in the general direction of David's ear.

"What?"

The crowd started singing "We Shall Overcome," led by a priest in a white cassock, just behind them. He alternated verses in Spanish, English, and something that sounded like Gaelic, but most people seemed to be following along.

"The sign that I made with Quentin, it's my favorite!" Grace grinned.

She and Nick had made their sign together that past Saturday and agreed to pass it back and forth throughout the day. It was made of white paint on black poster board, and Grace's even, looping cursive spelled out: THE FUTURE IS UNWRITTEN.

When he caught up with the rest of them, she would let Nick hold it high above his head. She couldn't help thinking that the two of them were more than just some young idiots in love; their union felt miraculous. She would tell him that, too, when he showed up. They had done this, they had been a major part of making this march and movement happen. If they could do this together, what couldn't they do? She recalled her childish dream of being the president of the United States. Perhaps, perhaps, if another world was possible—perhaps that could still happen.

At noon, Susan Scribner, sweating in her blazer with a large pocketbook hanging to her hip, banged her hand against the blue door of Elizabeth Saltman Whitby's apartment in New York City and bellowed, "Shelley? Michelle Whitby? Are you there?"

She wondered what Shelley would think of her when she opened the door. Although it had only been three years since she'd last seen her, Susan was acutely aware that she had gained nearly twenty pounds in the interim. And with the combination of the weight and her orange bob striped with gray, she was sure she would now look like an old person.

No one was answering the door. No one appeared to be home. It was excruciatingly hot. Susan wished she did not have to be in this awful city at all. She hadn't slept a wink on the red-eye flight, and all this back-and-forth across the country had given her what appeared to be a permanent cough. But she was convinced now that Nick was in New York, that he was certain to be involved in the antiestablishment activist march taking place that day. She was nearly sick with the anticipation of seeing her baby. And she knew that if he were in the city, this wayward daughter of Roger would certainly have spoken to him.

She tried the knocker on the apartment door one more time, then rested her weary body against the brick wall beside it. She could use a nap. She was staying at the old hotel and had gotten two rooms, that's how hopeful she was that she would find Nick. As Susan wondered if it was worth it to wait there for Shelley, she was driven back into a memory of a semicircle of desks in her third-grade classroom at Spence, where her small students were sharing their Thanksgiving-themed art projects. Little Shelley's sculpture was a fortune-telling turkey: a Styrofoam ball with feathers stuck in it, some googly eyes, and a bandanna tied around the head. Shelley had announced to the class, "This is my psychic turkey! She knows the future. She can tell that I'm going to be a famous actress and Dan is going to be a basketball star. She also knows that Ms. Scribner is so mean because she doesn't have a husband." The third graders, confused but willing to laugh at anything the class bully said, had doubled over their baby fat. Susan had the clear memory of swishing over and confiscating the turkey and then sending the girl to the headmaster's office. Shelley had been mean then, and surely the girl continued to be vicious today. Those attributes do not leave a person. How could her son consort with someone of that ilk? It wasn't fair, she reasoned, what her brilliant son had endured in his short life. That was the first thing she would tell him when she finally found him.

Nick and Grace had promised each other days before that if they got separated during the march, they would meet up by three forty-five in Art Park. And by 3:40, Grace was standing in the concrete plaza outside the Doss, holding a heavy pipe under each arm. She scanned the crowd left to right, then right to left. No Nick. Somewhere in the fracas on Fortieth Street she had lost the sign that they made together. The clash began when three whistle blows sounded near the police line, and the cops, wearing riot gear and helmets with plexiglass face masks, started to march forward. They had blue-and-white NYC Police vans behind them. The horizontal line of cops had continued to descend, an unstoppable wave heading toward them. Around Grace other marchers screamed and broke apart—bodies fleeing toward the sidewalks. Then single policemen had detached from their perfect line and charged after single marchers, aiming to hit anything within their reach. The younger and more agile demonstrators had hopped over the still-hooked metal gates, while the men in body armor pulled the civilian bodies backward and down onto the cement, letting their nightsticks land hard on the demonstrators' shoulders and knees. You could hear the thwacks and thuds between the screams.

But Grace had made it out of that confrontation. And it didn't matter that she'd lost her sign; what mattered now was the action. In her bag she had a bicycle U-lock, PowerBars, and water. Her cell phone let out a mechanical beep, and the tiny screen on the front said she had a new text message, from a number she didn't recognize. The message read: *Stay safe! Almost at Art Park, meet you there.*

Who was that text from? It had to be Nick, borrowing someone's phone. She clicked hers shut and all her nerves collected in a balloon in her stomach. She would be with him soon; it was she and Nick, against the world. Despite it all, she smiled. She was in love—with the movement, and with Nick. He would be there soon. They were winning.

"Good thing you didn't want to go to the East Side," the taxi driver said to Susan Scribner through the partition window. "Whole city—total mess today. So much traffic. I sat on Thirty-Eighth Street for an hour, just still, not moving. People think they fightin' for the workingman, but here I am, no fare. Only traffic! After this I'm going home, givin' up on today."

She nodded absently. The Hudson River was wide and still, bluer than usual, with an iridescent shimmer on the surface. How dismal and polluted the river used to be, when she was young and lived in this godforsaken place. It was surprising, really, that the water got cleaned up and the weather got better. It would be so only briefly. The cabbie turned east on Sixty-Eighth. Traffic had stopped on the other side of the highway. Susan realized that strangely, even now while she could hear the whipping and beating of news and police helicopters overhead, the city seemed so much less menacing than it had all those years ago.

It occurred to Susan, in the lull of traffic beside the river, that she could give up this fight. For the first time since Roger's death, she imagined a life beyond her complications with the Whitbys. Roger was gone now, and things were different. If her son didn't get an inheritance, he would be fine. She would find him and he would be safe and they would both apologize and carry on together, the two of them together as they had once been, so long ago: a two-member team, a complete family.

Nick could have a different story than she'd had; she could understand and support his choices, mature with him and branch out herself. She could meet another boyfriend, a quieter man, someone who wanted to wake up at dawn and walk along the Orange County beaches with her, someone interested in keeping the creep of extra weight off, in having a daily routine and calm, early dinners al fresco by her lemon tree. She'd done her duty: she'd fought to help her son, to give him the best chances in the world. But if her fighting and pushing weren't working, she could, in fact, back down. The cab picked up again, darting forward two short blocks before slamming on the brakes. The driver leaned on the horn and screamed out the cracked window, "Learn how to drive in the city!"

It was as if the vehicle jostled her out of her daydream. She couldn't just give up on everything that she'd worked for. For all that Roger had done to them—for the ways in which he had hurt Nick's life—this was one way he could begin to pay them back. The modern world doesn't offer up many opportunities, and hers happened to have come through the vehicle of the Whitbys. Who's to say that she'd be offered anything at all in the future? She was being stupid: Susan would get her son what he deserved.

By three the cab had been in stand-still traffic for ten minutes, so Susan got out. The whole town was in a commotion, and she found herself with nothing to do but follow it. She walked through Central Park, then kept walking until she found herself at the tent-city plaza of Art Park next to the Doss Museum. It was mobbed with people: policemen, camera guys running around frantically. Susan's heart raced as she wove through them all. She was confident that she would find her son soon, take him into her arms and hold him there, protected. They had so much to look forward to. Around her were more people than she could have imagined would ever congregate in one place, but she was certain she would spot Nick's face in the crowd. She could feel his presence there. She hung by the periphery of

Art Park, nearer to the museum building than the center of the protest crowd, scanning the passing faces.

"Sorry." Susan tapped an older, sunburned man who had loped up beside her. "What exactly are you protesting here?"

In an overeager manner the man began, "I'm an anti-capitalist, generally, and I consider myself a democrat with a little *d*. What we're all protesting is not only ExxonMobil or the closing of the museum, not even globalization, but really basic economic inequality: the shrinking and disappearing act of the middle class, the rat race that everyone is stuck in, the eighty-hour workweek, the inability to enjoy life . . ."

He kept talking, but Susan's focus drifted. It was the same story it had always been. If there was one thing she had learned since she was a young woman on these very streets, it was that there was nothing to be surprised about in this world. The giant oil company buying the elegant old building was expected; the protesters and their meager demands were expected; every new story was just a repetition of one that had already been told. How many years would it take for her son to understand that?

Susan was vigilantly searching the crowd for the outline of Nick's broad shoulders and the bulk of his hair, when she heard the crashing noise. It took her a moment to register it. Everyone gasped: it sounded like a car crash, somewhere very close by. Police officers popped out of every corner. They looked left and right, pulled radios off their belts or whispered into microphones attached to their collars. It seemed no one knew where the noise had come from. A siren sounded from a few blocks away, growing louder. Then police officers, a few of them, began to walk quickly toward the opened section of the wrought iron gate around the Doss Museum.

Susan was struck with a bolt of panic. She rose onto her toes to watch the police across the narrow street, and then a few voices screamed. She tried to find the source of it but couldn't identify anyone, and when she looked back toward the museum, a stream of dark gray smoke rushed out of an arched doorway on the first floor. There were three identical glass doorways in a row, but the smoke only blew out of the one on the right.

Then cries shot up from the crowd like a trick fountain: a scream over there, now a scream over here. Epithets skimmed through them: "What the fuck?" "Shit, move!" "Go." Masses of people flooded away from the Doss and toward Susan, then past her. They yelled, "Terrorists," "Twin Towers." Two other jets of smoke began shooting out of the other two doorways. There was no sign of Nick. Susan was aware that she wasn't moving. She recalled that early morning, before Nick was born, when the fire jumped from one apartment roof to another in her West Village neighborhood. Her own thin, young body had lay nearly lifeless on the dirty mattress, watching the plumes of smoke billow through the window. That morning felt so distant it could have been in another lifetime. It could have happened to another person. But it had been her who watched that fire, and she hadn't moved then, either.

Now the smoke reached the street with a campfire swell, but it wasn't dense enough to sting her eyes. She began to walk slowly against the traffic of people running. Even cops were running away. An orange tongue of flames snapped itself out of the first door of the museum. She couldn't shake the feeling that her son was involved in this. Sirens came from all sides behind her. How had they gotten there that fast? What the police and Susan didn't yet know was that a communiqué had been hung inside the building in the form of a large black banner, with one line stenciled on it in stark white paint. It read: FROM THE ASHES OF THE OLD, A NEW WORLD IS POSSIBLE.

Susan continued to move toward the museum in a fog of calmness. She saw a small body running toward the fire and nearly screamed out for Nick. But she realized that wasn't her son's back; it was a girl, but with very short hair. And she had something white sticking up from the right side of her—a flag of some kind? The girl was young, and she lifted her knees high as she began to run, taking on the air of a guerrilla. She had only moved twenty feet when the banging went off. It came in a spurt, rapid and steady, like fireworks. Susan saw the girl run for a moment longer and then seem to trip over her own feet and fall forward, landing on her shoulder on the grass in front of the museum. When the girl was already on the ground a police officer's voice yelled: "Drop the weapon! Put your hands behind your head!"

For some reason, Susan ran across the street, trying to make it all the way to the body on the ground. But two policemen caught her by the upper arms.

Someone else, somewhere near, shrieked in a higher pitch than Susan had ever heard, "Jesus! Jesus! Jesus. Jesus. Jesus."

Susan only understood that she too was screaming when she was pushed back by the police officers. She crumpled at the sight in front of her, as the men held her up on either side. There was no blood on the girl's face or the grass around her, but the shape of her body on the ground wasn't right. Her chest peaked up and her head was back and to the side, neck exposed. Her leg moved on the ground, right foot twitching and crossing over the left foot, which was for some reason shoeless and bare.

Susan looked left and right for Nick. Behind her she heard voices shrieking, "Main organizer." "Grace Kamal." "They shot her."

Then there was a female police officer, a brown ponytail swinging in front of Susan. "Calm down, ma'am. Put your hands behind your head. Calm down."

"They shot the child," Susan said, stunned, as the three police officers began guiding her back across the street, occasionally having to drag her along before she stood up again and tried to walk. The officers stayed beside Susan as if she were a threat. By the time she was sitting on the curb, fire engines had driven into the gates of the Doss driveway and two cranes stretched up to the third story of the museum. Men in the crane's buckets guided surges of water down on the building. The dark smoke began to billow rather than stream. An ambulance pulled up to the other curb. A group of police stood and kneeled around the girl's body, which appeared to still be moving. They faced outward, forming a perimeter, and Susan, who could no longer see the body on the grass, crouched down, involuntarily repeating, "They shot that child. They shot someone's child."

21

A week later, Nick lingered on the edge of Washington Square Park, outside Judson church, where the benefit party for Grace was being held. He hunched over his knees, nauseous. Grace was still at Mount Sinai hospital and it looked like she was going to be fine, save for the permanent metal splint in her leg where the bullets had gone in. But Nick was sure that he would never be the same. What had happened to her had nothing to do with a curse; it had nothing to do with the universe acting against him. Grace had been shot because he wasn't there with her as he had told her he would be. For the past week, he had been so filled with guilt and stress that he'd constantly felt like he was going to vomit.

It was almost September. Perhaps his friends from NYU who hadn't yet graduated would walk by and see him in this position. Perhaps his former professors would pass, or even the NYPD, wondering why this young man was about to get sick on a street corner in the early evening. But he didn't care anymore. He would go out into any public space, anywhere in the world. If they were going to arrest him, so be it.

Nick's head was burning, and he was dizzy. He'd promised Shelley that he'd go with her to this benefit for Grace that the Family Supporters were throwing, but getting up the stairs to the large open event space of the church was proving much more difficult than he'd imagined. Everyone upstairs hated him now. As soon as it became clear that Grace had been waiting for Nick when she was shot, and it became public knowledge that he had never even shown up to the march at all, he became the archenemy of all those people who had been his close friends just the day before. Now they were all out to get him. Shelley reported that as soon as she'd returned from the Vineyard—as soon as she'd opened the door to her own home—all of the anti-gassers and Family Supporters squatting there had growled: "Quentin doesn't know anything about accountability." "Is he a narc? Are you really a narc?" When Shelley had defended him, all the squatters had cleared out themselves and their backpacks and their bedrolls, leaving behind a floor filled with stray bottles and cans, receipts and fliers and other little crumpled pieces of trash. The Whitbys were pariahs: not one of the anti-gassers wanted anything to do with Quentin or his sister. Nick, remembering this as he stood outside Judson church, turned to the bushes and threw up.

He shouldn't be there, but Shelley had been insistent that they go and that they go together. The evening after the march, he and Shelley and Brooke stood in the Wainwrights' kitchen on the Vineyard making dinner, when the small television tucked into a bookshelf reported that a protestor had been shot in New York. Nick grabbed Shelley's cell phone and ran out to the driveway. After Grace didn't answer, he'd called David and learned what had happened. They had been happy in the kitchen, the three Whitby children, chatting lightly as they helped to prepare the steak au poivre. After their action and subsequent arrest, they had been held for a few hours in clean cells at the Dukes County Jail, then bailed out by Mr. and Mrs. Wainwright, who had offered them proud smiles and warm embraces. But when Nick had heard the news that Grace had been hurt, while he knelt on the blacktop of the driveway, sobbing, he finally called his mother. He didn't think twice; he needed her beside him.

Susan had picked him up on the Vineyard, as if he were a small child, then driven him from Cape Cod to New York and taken him to the old hotel, the same Marriott where they had spent nearly every weekend when he was a kid. This time, Susan had rented them each separate but adjoining rooms. Nick spent each day of the past week lying in a queen-sized bed in his own room, in the dark. He didn't once consider going to the pool, engaging in his old routine. The amount that he had actually been crying filled him with shame. He'd told his mother everything: everything about the Family, about the action in Maine, about the silly jail time in Martha's Vineyard. His admissions pushed him over the edge of guilt. As he owned up to it all, he realized that every single action was a result of his own choices. He was responsible for it all.

On the first day at the hotel, the phone had rung and rung until he'd unplugged the receiver. Maybe it was his activist friends, perhaps it was Grace herself. That was why he didn't answer. When Grace ran toward the Doss, when her body had fallen onto the grass, she had to have been thinking of him, but Nick had not been thinking of her at all. And on top of everything, he had already been planning to break up with her. He could never bring himself to talk to her, ever again.

The morning before the Judson church benefit, Nick had sat on the edge of his hotel bed listening to a pitch about why he needed to travel back to California with his mother and wait for the cash part of the will to be transferred into his name. She had said, "We're going to prove that whatever chicken-scratch note you wrote in the Vineyard does not constitute a real contract; those houses are rightfully yours."

"I gave them away," he had groaned, and laid back on the bedspread, exasperated. His mother was very much herself.

Now, standing below the entryway to the church, Nick took a deep breath and a swig from the small bottle of Jim Beam he'd stuffed into his front pocket, in order to freshen his breath. As he ascended the church stairs and entered the large second-floor function room, he heard a cartoonish voice cry, "Amen, children. Amen!" At the front of the room, on a stage, a big man with a duckbill bouffant of white hair paced before the crowd who sat in folding chairs or on the floor. The man was wearing a black suit and clerical collar. This "preacher" was a New York City activist legend, Reverend Jebediah of the Church of Stop Shopping, who led faux-spiritual events in favor of myriad left-wing causes.

A guy about Nick's age—someone he had never seen before—sat on a stool by the door and silently shoved a donation bucket into Nick's chest. Nick dropped a crumpled ten-dollar bill into it, then slunk against the back wall.

The room was packed. Nick spotted David at the front, holding a home-made flag: a stick with a piece of canvas stapled to it, on which was stenciled a reproduction of Nick's own drawing, the ridiculous tattoo that Grace had gotten on her back of the Strong Place brownstone bursting with flowers, a dancer on top of the building, and the flag stating "Occupy the Mansion!" Throughout the crowd other people held up signs: STOP POLICE TERROR. And: JUSTICE FOR GRACE KAMAL. END POLICE BRUTALITY. WE WILL NOT BE SILENT. Nick would not go over and talk to David. He would try to never talk to him again, if possible. Instead, he scanned the room for Shelley.

On the stage, the reverend gestured toward the door that Nick hovered in. "Keep on comin' in. Everybody, the whole community, needs to be in here today together." His deep Southern twang, a mock-evangelical put-on, added absurd gravitas to everything he hollered. "We come to-gether to meditate on a tragedy. A tragedy that fell upon a Middle Eastern woman. Join hands, my children, join hands."

Nervous laughter issued out of the crowd, then arms stretched out toward other arms. Nick leaned against the wall and finished off the bottle of whiskey.

"On August twenty-two, in the year of our Lord two thousand and three, in the middle of all of these courageous people, people making a new culture from scratch, in the midst of beauty and the great American circus, a shooting and a tragedy occurred. But Grace Kamal, she was part of that beauty."

Some of the audience clapped, a few erupted in cheers. The atmo-sphere in this church was a festive one.

Jebediah continued, "Grace said to herself: 'I am doing the only thing I can do, because this life is corrupt. I am protesting warmongering glo-balization and this corrupt economy, because there is nothing else I can do.' Grace was a hero, but a hero acting out of sheer necessity."

This elicited cries of "Amen!" "Preach!"

At that a drum sounded, and Nick flinched. From each side of the stage, a ragtag choir descended on Reverend Jebediah. Two lines of men and women in wrinkled green choir robes walked in, swaying and clapping. Jebediah raised his arms to the ceiling and screamed out: *"Change-a-lleujah,* children! Change-a-lleujah!" The choir began to hum an up-tempo version of "Amazing Grace." "We need to celebrate Grace's work! Celebrate her sacrifice." Jebediah clapped along with his own chant.

Nick was confused. Grace was still alive. She was in a hospital suite, ninety-six blocks north of where they all stood. But this party did not seem to be about Grace at all. Nick wondered if she even knew it was going on.

That was when Nick spotted Shelley; she was in the front of the room, wearing a dark brown dress that hit the very top of her thighs. And she had some shiny leather shoes on, making her stand out even more starkly from the rest of the jeans-and-bandanna-clad crowd. She stood beside a folding chair, sharply focused on something directly across the room from her. Sure enough, leaning against the opposite wall, were Grace's parents, Mr. and Dr. Kamal. These two tight-lipped Upper East Siders somehow managed to blend into the wall in the middle of this insane environment. Who had invited them? They were certainly the only people in the whole room, save for the reverend himself, who were older than thirty. They faced toward the commotion on the stage, their bodies rigidly still, and Dr. Jillian gripped her purse flush against her thighs.

As Nick made his way toward Shelley, she began walking toward the Kamals. He followed her path and soon became aware that although there were dozens upon dozens of strangers in the room, the Family Supporters were all there and were all glaring at him: David and Ebony and Cate and Christopher and Esmerelda. They had ceased clapping and had instead crossed their arms over themselves in a threatening gesture.

"Shells!" Nick hollered, over the commotion. She turned her head but didn't respond to him. She was waving a hand in front of her.

"Mr. Kamal," she called. He didn't look up. "Yousef—"

He still didn't respond but Dr. Jillian did, crossing her arms over her chest in a similar manner to the Family Supporters. The woman whispered something into her husband's ear, and he nodded.

Just as the two Kamals turned, Dr. Jillian taking her husband by the elbow, Shelley began, "I need to—" But the couple was already walking back toward the entrance of the church.

"Stop!" Shelley cried out.

By the door to the hallway, Dr. Jillian's narrow face finally turned around. She dropped her husband's elbow, and he continued making his way to the stairs.

Shelley huffed, "I have to talk to him—Mr. Kam—Yousef. Please."

Dr. Jillian leaned against the doorway. She spoke in a precise and articulate manner. "Listen to me," she breathed. "You are nothing, Ms. Whitby. You are nothing in my husband's life and you are nothing in my daughter's life. In the great recorded history of the Kamals, you will not be written down as part of it. You are a ghost. A thing of the past." Now Dr. Jillian made eye contact with Nick. Her face was stern, pinched, and yet highly alert and composed. "My daughter is going to be fine. She will be successful and flourish. But my family will never, ever, have anything to do with you Whitbys ever again."

At that, Dr. Jillian snapped her head around, and her lithe body rushed to join her husband on the stairs. Shelley looked as if she were about to crumple onto the floor in devastation. Guilt threatened to floor Nick.

At that moment, a crash sounded in front of them, then the beating of a bass drum. Nick didn't flinch this time. Coming up the stairs, right where the Kamals had descended, was a marching band. From the stage, the preacher announced that the Wind-up Boor Orchestra was coming in. They carried drums attached to their chests and trumpets hanging from their mouths. Some had cymbals and tambourines, and all were dressed in green: short shorts and striped knee socks, fishnets, neon-green tutus, and funny pointed hats. Some had pink hair, some had no hair. The good reverend, and then the rest of the crowd, sang along with their happy tune. "Oh when the saints—" (*"Oh when the saints!"*) "Go marchin' in—" (*"Go marchin' in!"*)

People in the room who had been lounging, leaning on folding chairs or against walls, began to perk up, and many swirled out into the middle of the room, dancing and clapping. The benefit was unraveling into a wild party. Would Grace be pleased that this party was occurring because of her?

Shelley turned to Nick now, and he had the simultaneous impulse to embrace her and punch her. He wished she was to blame for what had happened on the Vineyard, and for his going there at all, and then he could also blame her for what had happened to Grace. He wanted to blame her for everything: for her father existing and for her father dying, for the will and the money he never asked for, for having to live in a hotel for half his childhood, for reaching out to him when they were children and for making him love her.

"Hey," she said sadly. He could see now that up close, she looked awful. Her hair was matted and unwashed, and her face was gray and gaunt. Just being close to her evaporated his rage. None of these circumstances were her fault.

Two kegs had been set up in front of the DJ table. A crowd of more than one hundred people danced in the middle of the room. The party had turned into a rager.

Shelley took him by the elbow, pulling him toward the wall. "How's your mother?" she asked, puffing out her cheeks and sliding down the floor with her knees in front of her.

As Nick slid down to his own knees, beside her, he mumbled, "As nuts as ever," before sucking in his breath. That wasn't a nice thing to say in front of Shelley, considering he knew now that her own mother was still in a mental hospital in another state.

She didn't seem to notice. She put a hand on his shoulder. "Who planned this party?"

"I thought you had."

She rolled her eyes. "I've been talking to Grace on the phone. She told me you haven't called her or seen her, not once since the incident."

He shook his head and felt the nausea roll up inside of him again. He couldn't respond.

"You want a beer?" Shelley finally asked.

Four beers later, Nick found himself unleashing everything to Shelley: "I left Grace alone. If I hadn't lied to her and said I would be there, she wouldn't have gotten shot. I'm scum, Shelley. I did this to her."

She shook her head vehemently. "It was an accident, Nick. This was not your fault."

His jaw jutted out in defiance. "If I hadn't gone to Martha's Vineyard, Grace would be fine. And the really, truly fucked-up part is that I didn't even do anything there. You and Brooke convinced me *not* to do the action that would have made an actual difference. And now, she was fucking shot for *nothing*." His hands were clenched into fists against the wall, which was vibrating from people dancing and jumping before them.

"That's not true, Nick," Shelley said. "If you had gone through with your plans Grace would still have been shot by that racist, psycho police officer. But you would also be in jail right now."

"I wish I was in jail right now," he whispered, although he didn't really mean it.

Next to the DJ table, a woman in a red overall dress took ahold of the microphone. "I want to take this opportunity," she slurred, "to sing a song that I think that Grace Kamal would love." The woman wore combat boots, and one strap of her dress had slipped off her bare shoulders.

Then this woman cleared her throat, and the DJ cut his music. She began to sing in an off-key pitch a song that began with the line, "'Baby, I'm an Anarchist, you're a spineless liberal . . .'"

"Have you talked to Armond?" Shelley asked. "Do you think our makeshift contract about the will and the houses will hold up?"

"My mother talked to him," Nick yelled over the singing. "Armond is going to come to the Vineyard next week when we have our court day and bring the paperwork to transfer the deeds of the properties. And my mother—*heh-heh*!" He let out a high-pitched laugh that he knew sounded crazy. "She is mad as hell. She's never going to forgive me!" He heard the sound coming out of his throat in an exaggerated, staccato pattern. It was automatic, as if he was no longer in control of his own actions. He was sure he looked too wired and too happy for the circumstances. Well—that was just more fodder for these activists to hate him with. They would whisper that he was *happy* at Grace's benefit party.

Nick threw his arms around Shelley's shoulders and whispered, "But giving back the houses is something good I can do. I have no idea why Roger left me everything—that was out of my own control. But I've been realizing, in the past few days, that I'm a grown person and there are things that are in my control, now." She stared at him without any visible response. He straightened his arms, gripping her biceps, and said, "Listen, I know Roger wasn't my biological father. I know he would have told me if he was. I want to own up to things. I'm ready to admit that."

After a beat, Shelley responded softly. "Yeah. But that doesn't mean you're any less a part of us."

Another woman had joined the first one at the microphone, and they launched into an old Green Day song. Two nasal voices: "'Do you have the time . . .'"

"Remember when I used to play this song for you on my guitar, over the phone?" Nick squealed.

"Ha, yeah," Shelley whispered. Then, seemingly out of nowhere, she asked, "Did you set the Calamity Shack on fire, when we were in high school?"

He nodded slowly. "I did it to help you."

"I know."

She wriggled out of his grasp, and he screamed the lyrics of the Green Day song with the crowd. He felt his face plumping a bit, life returning to his veins. He said, "Why are we standing here right now, Shelley, rather than in goddamn jail? Why am I not in prison with the rest of the Family activists? Is it because of who we are?"

"What we did on the Vineyard was peaceful. And legal," she said. "We didn't do anything wrong."

"But neither did Grace," he answered. "And look what happened."

"It's not fair," Shelley said. "It's not fair, and it's not right. But you didn't cause it."

Nick shook his head. Shelley pulled him toward her again. A faint whiff of cigarettes came off her dress, and that, mixed with her bodily perfume and the patchouli oil she'd put on that morning, smelled distinctly like childhood, like waking up early with a slight headache on an already-muggy morning at Biddy's old house. Nick let his cool, stubble-covered cheek rest against her smooth one.

He was grateful she was there. Something in his torso ached—for Grace, or another girl, or maybe for Roger. He stepped back, pushing himself away from Shelley and into the pit of dancing bodies. Then he began slamming into others' limbs and torsos mindlessly. Although he didn't want to be laughing, his odd laughter continued. In his peripheral vision, he saw his sister turn gracefully, moving away from him and the edge of the dancing pit, and toward the door. The gallant gait, the steady horse of her silhouette, moved away from the commotion of people.

Nick had tried to do something daring and as a result he'd hurt a person he loved. He had acted like Roger, in the worst possible way. As Shelley stepped alone into the almost-fall night, Nick was in the nexus of the pit of moving people. Nick wondered then, in the middle of the sweat and the limbs and the music, *What happens when the party's over?* He promised himself that whatever happened, he would fully consider who was affected by his actions. The Whitby Curse was a myth.

Fall

| 2019 |

Life starts all over again
when it gets crisp in the fall.

—F. SCOTT FITZGERALD

1

I t was a perfect day for an autumn wedding. The wind swept across the water, creating rows of gentle, blue-green waves. A few private yachts and commercial fishing boats tugged through the distance. Shelley sat on the dock, in the front row a multilayered semicircle of white chairs, which contained almost all the Whitbys fit to travel—so many, in fact, that their family spilled over onto the bride's side. They always came for weddings. How utterly ideal, how perfect this weather was for a big family affair. It had been years since they'd had one. The trees on the water's edge had turned gold with the season, and the sun blazed in its early October splendor.

Shelley adjusted her scarf on her bare shoulders and sighed. She was pleased to see so many of her generation were in attendance: cousins Theo Jr., Anna, and Eliot IV. Once-little Julia was now a grown woman. And, to her surprise, all of the half siblings had shown up, some with husbands and wives and children in tow. Andrew, Tobin, and Roger III were all pushing old age themselves, and Kiki and LJ and Brooke appeared to be reaching the upper thresholds of middle age as well. Although Shelley was thirty-nine, she still felt so young, in many ways. Maybe because she'd always thought of herself as a young person, as the youngest in her family, she'd aged without being conscious of it. Funny how that happens, years blurring as they pile up.

It was a pleasant feeling, to sit at a classic family affair, among people she had known her whole life. She sat with those who had loved her father and known her mother, and attended her parents' own beach wedding thirty-nine years prior; among others who were tall and slim in stature, pale and windblown and toothy when smiling; amid those who had been taught from their earliest years to revere Great-Grandfather Hildebrand and the little rowboat he had propelled into a dynasty, and to worship that dynasty as if it were their own familial God; she was in the middle of others like her who had eaten alone during childhood dinners, who had sped past all the teammates on lacrosse and field hockey fields, across rugby pitches, down ski slopes, and through sailing bays along the Eastern Seaboard; those who'd frequently been hauled into the headmaster's offices at their private schools, who'd drunk so much in their twenties they barely remembered them; in the midst of her kin who had been repeatedly asked the same irking question of *So are you related . . . ?*, and who now, as they eased their way into middle and advanced age, were slightly disturbed and entirely surprised by the banal course their lives had taken. Shelley, from the front row of the crowd, just where she'd been told to sit, took a sip out of the paper coffee cup she'd been handed on her walk into the venue, and smiled.

Well, a brunch wedding was perhaps not exactly classic, she reasoned, but the setting, looking out on the water in the crisp weather, was historic and just right. Classic. From the row behind her, her half brother LJ tapped her shoulder. "They couldn't give us a drink for the wait? What kind of Whitby shindig is this?" he said with a good-natured snicker. Shelley gave him a weak smile in return. Beside LJ, Brooke raised her own coffee cup up in the air, as if to cheers. Shelley hadn't had a sip of alcohol in six years and had been pleasantly relieved to not have to refuse a caterer trying to push a long-stemmed glass on her as she walked in.

With the view in front of her, the puffy white clouds and the sun shining on the water, the boats floating by, one could imagine that she was up at the family's estate at Idlehour, or at the very least on Menemsha Harbor on the Vineyard or somewhere like Northport or Little Compton. But when she turned her head, she saw behind her the restored nineteenth-century brick warehouse, where the wedding brunch would be served. The torn-up half cobblestone, half-paved streets on either side of the dock revealed that instead of on a country estate, they were in the once-industrial pocket of Brooklyn waterfront, known as Red Hook. On the way there from their hotels in the city, all the Whitbys had peered quizzically out taxi windows as they passed small row houses covered in shingles of chipping dark red and off-white. Old-fashioned iron street lamps, turned off in the morning light, sat in front of wood fences covered in yellow and black looping graffiti. The commercial strip, Van Brunt Street, had a few remaining old New York bodegas, yet beside those the street was spotted with new art galleries, coffee shops, and artisan bakeries.

When the taxis pulled to a stop in front of the wide brick warehouse dotted with iron star anchor plates added in the building's renovation, the Whitby family members, clacking out onto the cobblestone, gave one another raised-eyebrow shrugs, as if to say, *Who knows where the heck we are?* But by the time the family was mingling at the back of the dock with their little paper coffee cups, an unspoken agreement of positivity seemed to have taken place, and men's and women's voices shot out of the din, "What a funky location!" "How quaint this pocket of the city is!" Kiki, who had acquired a prominent British accent now that she'd been living in London for nearly three decades, leaned into Shelley and exclaimed, "This little neighborhood reminds me so of Howth—that sweet fishing village just north of Dublin? Have you been, dear? You must go next time you find yourself in Ireland. A whimsical place, like this area. What's it called again, around here?" Shelley had smiled, nodded, and actually tried to quash her judgment. Not only had they all shown up for the wedding, but they were trying now, in their own way. Making an effort to understand this foreign environment.

As both families milled around the warped wooden planks before the 11:00 a.m. start to the ceremony, the bride's family, the de la Vegas, all broad smiles and large, whooping embraces for one another, glanced sidelong at the Whitbys but also maintained polite smiles and the shine of forced warmth. Even though they'd traveled to this hip part of Brooklyn, the

Whitbys still wore what they wore: navy blazers and khakis, navy-and-white striped dresses, pearls, bow ties of all shades. They were markedly less dressed up than the de la Vegas, Esmerelda's family hailing from Corona, Queens. The de la Vega men all wore dark suits, and the women sported dresses of black and bright patterns, flowing silk scarves and gold-encrusted tiny purses, heels higher than anything a Whitby had ever tried on.

Finally, with all the guests seated and waiting in their white chairs, the processional music struck up. It was not the wedding march, but rather a Leonard Cohen song, "Hallelujah." Various *hmms* and *huhs* sounded from Kiki and Tobin, and some of the older generation of Whitby women. They wanted to make clear they noticed the nontraditional choice. Ms. Scribner— Susan—was sitting in the middle of the Whitby side with her new husband, an elderly man who owned a California almond farm. But Susan didn't join in on the clucking; she had never managed to break through with the family. Coming up the aisle first was Juan, just three and a half, and wearing a tiny gray suit with a purple tie so small it looked as if it had shrunk. He walked slowly by himself, fists clenched, concentrating very carefully on his mea- sured steps; his parents must have rehearsed and rereheared this walk with him. Shelley's heart swelled. She truly loved that child.

Walking up the aisle right after Juan was his mother, stunning in her long dress, beaming above her bouquet and below her short, pixie-esque haircut. A few cheers rang out from her side of the crowd, accented cries of "*¡Bella!*" and "*¡Hurra!*" The Whitbys giggled nervously. Esmerelda's dress was cream colored on top, but had a sheet of colorful flowers flowing down the silk skirt. Esmerelda's son turned around to her when he got to the end of the aisle and she winked at him, making the crowd coo. Then Juan ran to his father, who stood at the front of the crowd. Nick bent down, encasing his son in one long protective hug, before sending him toward the front row. Nick stood up straight again, gazing at his soon-to-be wife with sincere awe. He did look wonderful up there in his slim-cut gray suit. He was thinner than he used to be, and the innocent optimism he'd once carried in his messy hair and chiseled cheekbones was gone. It had disappeared over a decade ago, sometime after his long court case and the year and a half he'd spent in federal prison in Terre Haute, Indiana.

It was during the time that Nick was in prison that Shelley's mother had burned to death on the twelfth floor of the Beverly Hills Hotel. Elizabeth Saltman Whitby had been smoking in bed, having traveled to California for God knows what reason. A white Dixie cup had rested on her stomach as an ashtray—the hotel was entirely nonsmoking—and she had nodded away into a dreamless sleep. Within an hour she burned up in a bath of flames.

After her mother's death, Shelley took a leave of absence from work as a real estate broker and went to stay in Boston for the summer with Brooke and her wife and their two children, who were still small then. The summer spent in joyful and loud chaos in the house on Beacon Hill had helped a bit. The months following Elizabeth's death were low ones for Shelley, but curiously, even that time did not compete with the wretchedness that overcame her that summer after she'd dropped out of college, the summer when Grace Kamal got shot and Shelley got fired. A certain sadness had cast over Nick then, too, but it wasn't until he actually went to prison two years later that the exuberance and health of his youth had been permanently washed away. But along with his permanent melancholy came a calmness Shelley had never seen him possess before. That was how he looked as he stood at the front of the crowd at his own wedding: upright and grown-up, slightly weathered, and entirely calm. Yes, he was a quieter, sadder version of his old self. But he was still there.

"Auntie Shelley!" Juan exclaimed, turning in from the aisle. He climbed onto her lap, just as the plan went.

As little Juan parked himself on Shelley's knees, she squeezed his heaving body. His other aunt—Esmerelda's sister, Katy—sat in the chair beside them, and Juan played with a bit of blue crepe material from the skirt of Katy's dress as he focused on his two parents.

Nick and Esmerelda had decided to have no single officiant for the wedding ceremony but rather do it themselves, in a sort of group-participation model. When they'd told Shelley about this a few weeks ago, she had been dubious of how it would go over. But now as Esmerelda spoke—"Thank you all for coming to this special day, which has been a long time in the making"—Shelley got the impression that the ceremony might actually work out. Esmerelda was an elementary school art teacher, and both poised and authoritative before a crowd. Soon the aunts and uncles on her side of the family all stood up and read, in unison, a Frank O'Hara poem about love blinking between trees.

On the Whitby side of the dock there was some tepid, unsure clapping. It seemed there were no Scribners in attendance, other than Nick's mother. Susan had been estranged from her own family when Nick was young, and it appeared she hadn't made amends. Shelley ran a hand through her loose hair. She'd chosen to wear black blousy pants and a low-cut white top for the occasion, and was, she noticed, entirely comfortable in her clothes. It was her family's pending actions that were making her blood pressure rise. They all knew that Nick had a baby years before getting married, and Shelley noticed that they'd managed to hold their tongues about that topic throughout the whole ceremony so far. But honestly, for her extended family members, having to stand up and participate, to have to open themselves up to a laid-back, humor-filled public spectacle, to actually read a *poem* aloud, was brand-new territory. Shelley commended Nick on inviting all these buttoned-up, stiff-necked WASPs to join in on this hippie-happy, messy affair. But perhaps he'd asked too much of them.

Instead of aunts and uncles, Nick had reached out to some of the older half siblings to participate. Now Andrew and Tobin and Kiki and LJ stood up, clearing their throats and craning their necks down to their little printed-out note cards. They read a section of a Ginsberg poem carefully and quietly, as of course they would, nearly whispering the last line of "'Nude ghosts seeking each other in the silence . . .'" The rest of the Whitbys giggled again, louder and more nervously this time, at the clear fact that their side of the family had not done as good of a job as

Esmerelda's had. Thankfully, the de la Vegas cheered louder than they had even before, keeping the spirits up and making up for the poor Whitby attempt at joining in.

Shelley noticed that, conspicuously, Nick had not included any of the Whitby favorites in the ceremony, none of Roger's oft-quoted lines from Fitzgerald or other great American men. The wedding ceremony was very literary, still, but of course it would be. Nick and Esmerelda were now bookstore owners, right there in Red Hook. Nick ran it: a used-book store in the renovated bottom floor of a falling-down building, ironically named Mansion Books. She assumed that he'd bought it with the remainder of Roger's money that he'd been able to keep after signing the houses away, or with anything that was left after all the legal fees from his trial. But they didn't discuss that. She and Brooke and Nick tried to avoid the subject of money as much as possible, now. As the bookstore was just below their apartment, Shelley visited it nearly every time she was in the neighborhood. She was there just last week, standing directly under the Mansion Books sign and pressing her forehead against the glass-walled front. With two hands shading her eyes, she saw Juan inside, toddling through the free-standing bookcases with some kind of box with a strap slung over his shoulder. Shelley couldn't hear a word but watched the small boy curve around a corner and gallop toward Nick, who was leaning on the school desk they use as a checkout counter.

Shelley had come to return a plastic toy helicopter in her pocket that Juan had left with her when she was babysitting. As she was just about to leave the toy by the door and turn around, a thundering of tiny palms hit against the other side of the glass. He'd spotted her.

She pushed through the glass door. "You caught me!"

The sour odor of used books rushed up and Shelley sneezed, which made Juan giggle. Dropping the sling of his bag, he ran toward her, all thirty pounds of him overtaking her willowy frame as she mock-fell backward onto the floor.

Nick stared at Shelley expectantly.

"Juan left his helicopter in my jacket when we went to the park," she said. Standing up, she held the toy in the air, and Juan, singing, "'We all live in a yellow submarine'" now, gleefully snatched it up.

"Shelley!" Esmerelda's voice arrived before her body did. She emerged from the back room, her arms engulfing Shelley's waist as she balanced on the toes of her Converse sneakers to kiss the taller woman's cheek.

Juan, who had begun buzzing the helicopter through the air, landed it on the back of his mother's calf.

"Do you want to stay for dinner? The grown-ups are just having leftovers—"

"No, no. I just stopped by to bring back Juan's toy." Both women beamed at the boy. "I've got to be going, actually."

"Well, we'll see you at the wedding on Sunday." Esmerelda turned to her son. "Do you want to eat Elmo pasta right now, or in one minute?"

"One minute!"

Juan pushed his helicopter along the edge of a low bookshelf, and a young couple entered the store, college students most likely. Shelley often bought books there herself, insisting on paying something, although Nick and Esmerelda always offered them for free. In the back corner sat the nonfiction section. The store didn't carry any of the design books about Yousef Kamal, but it did keep in stock his narrative book, the one she had done the "research" for, the book published in 2007 entitled *The Master's Right Hand: The Golden Age of New York City and the Servants Who Inspired It.* Shelley had never bought it—never read it—although she certainly intended to, when the time was right. She knew that the work she did for that book, the relatively small number of weeks when she had trailed Mr. Kamal in and out of mansions, had pushed her to love real estate and to distrust men, and therefore still affected every day of her grown-up life. Perhaps she would learn something greater about herself if she read the book. But then again, maybe she already knew everything about herself that she needed. Before leaving the store that day, she lurked in front of the contemporary nonfiction section, but didn't pick it up.

As she sat in the crowd at the wedding now, she wondered if she would drop by the store on her way home and buy a copy. But no. It still wasn't time. Not yet. Nick and Esmerelda were on to the biggest surprise of the ceremony itself. They wanted everyone to sing. And to sing Bob Dylan's version of "Forever Young," no less, without any musical accompaniment. At the front of the crowd, Nick put his arm around his bride, and asked everyone to turn the programs over, where they'd find the lyrics. By the second verse, the whole Whitby clan, in weak and wobbly voices, were looking at one another in terror. But they croaked out: "'May you grow up to be righteous . . .'" Shelley couldn't help herself from chuckling. Her family, as uncomfortable as they may be, were making an effort. She was touched.

Shelley stood, taking a deep breath to prepare herself for action: she was up next. Although she was thrilled to be at the wedding, she had spent the morning wallowing in self-doubt. There is nothing like your sibling getting married to make you reconsider your own romantic choices. Ultimately, she was happy with her single life. Although she'd lived alone all these years, she wasn't some kind of shut-in. This wasn't some neat little like-mother-like-daughter tale. Yes, Shelley'd had her own romances: people she'd known as a child, someone a cousin or a half sibling had set her up to meet. These things never lasted though. The men would take her out to dinner or taxi down to the Film Forum, but when their attentions drifted to other women, even for a moment on the street, it was like a circuit cut inside her. She didn't get angry when that inevitably happened, but simply left, heading home. Then she'd silence their calls on her cell phone, or let the battery run out of the thing for a few days.

It didn't matter anyway. She couldn't muster up the care to buoy their egos or pretend to orgasm. She had been working in real estate for fifteen years, and after enduring the tedium of her early agent days spent walking through paint-stinking, empty rooms, apologizing for the lack of closets and the one window facing an air shaft, she was now a full-fledged broker. What she really loved were houses and buildings, the intricacies of their structures and context of their uses. In another life, she could have been an architect herself, or an art historian. But, on a daily basis, she was content with her actual job. She kept herself busy.

Walking to the front of the crowd now, Shelley grabbed both Nick's and Esmerelda's hands. She was very happy to be there, truthfully, and knew she was doing the right thing for her brother. And yet, for some uncanny reason, as Nick's dry skin rubbed against hers, and Esmerelda's sweat-moistened palm gripped her tightly, Shelley thought of Grace Kamal. After several stints of international aid work, Grace was now a lawyer and lived in Washington, DC, where she seemed to excel in her professional life but not do much else. Shelley knew this information from the internet, as they were no longer in touch. After Nick had disappeared on Grace, and especially in those months when Nick had been arrested and was awaiting trial, Grace reached out to Shelley, explaining that she loved Nick more than she knew what to do with, that it was ruining her life that he would not contact her. Shelley had nodded over several lunches and cocktails and truly tried to show Grace that she was listening to her. Grace's feelings were legitimate, inasmuch as they were unfortunate. Grace had to know about Juan, and surely she would hear about Nick's wedding as well, too. That was the way the world worked now: all events were public information. Shelley silently wished Grace the best, as she placed Nick's and Esmerelda's hands together so that they were clutching each other. She pulled her folded-up script out of the pocket of her silk pants.

"Because you, Nick Scribner Whitby, and you, Esmerelda de la Vega, have pledged your love and faith to each other, expressed pure dedication to each other before your families and community, and now sealed your vows in this ceremony . . . by the authority vested in me by"—Shelley smirked, as did Nick and Esmerelda—"by the Universal Life Church on the internet, I now pronounce you husband and wife!"

The de la Vegas let out joyous yelps and "¡Hurras!" and the Whitbys clapped demurely. Nick gave Shelley a grateful nod, then dived into Esmerelda and kissed her, leaning her backward while her arms flew into the air. Nick was married.

Shelley watched, and realized she'd never thought much about Nick growing up, as it had happened concurrently to her own growing. But now, she remembered twelve-year-old Nick, wondrous and big-eyed, in his gawky high-water pants at Grandfather Whitby's funeral; angry teenage Nick pouting with the hood of his sweatshirt up while sitting by the water's edge at Idlehour; the ecstatic twenty-one-year-old singing like a madman on the roof of Strong Place. She knew him in all his minutiae, each crevice and peak of his joys and flaws, and that's why she loved him. Her ridiculous, understandable brother. Nick, in his former boldness and his current peculiarities, in his troubles and triumphs, was a prime representation of their family. Loving him made her also love the rest of her complicated family clan, and her own place within them.

The meal portion of the wedding, the brunch, was held inside the high-ceilinged, enormous warehouse. Faux picnic tables were set up in rows in front of a long buffet, with a few signs instructing guests to sit where they like. The Whitbys all paused at this casual wedding detail; they were people who liked to be told where to sit. After some hubbub, Shelley found herself at a table with Brooke and Allie and their two now-teenaged children. The oldest, towheaded and pale Roger, who had a nickname that was pronounced *Rowgie*, and their younger daughter, Paula, who had skin as dark as Allie's.

"How's the real estate business going, Shells?" Allie asked in her direct-yet-kind manner.

"Good," Shelley replied. "The New York market is booming, but then, it always is."

"Michelle," Armond said, with a smile that was both warm and underwater-like, as he placed his sparsely filled plate on the table and took an empty seat beside her. He bit into a bagel with nothing on it. Nick and Esmerelda decided to have a New York City–food theme at their wedding: pizza, bagels and lox, and greasy lo mein. But they did have, to the relief of many, a station inside with dark-suited women serving mimosas and Bloody Marys. All around the room the Whitbys' seats were empty; they were on their feet, lining up in front of the bar.

As brunch progressed, several of Shelley's relatives stopped by their table—those who insisted on making the rounds, as if this event belonged to them. Shelley noticed that they conspicuously avoided Susan Scribner though, who was perched in a back corner with her husband and keeping to herself—even out of Nick's way—during the whole event. After Nick gave away most of the inheritance, Susan, in a fit of anger, admitted to him that she had pressured Roger to change the will in the first place. That move was too nefarious for Nick to get over, he'd told Shelley and Brooke over lunch so many years ago. He would probably never forgive his mother. It was kind of Nick to tell his half sisters this news. Shelley still, even at the wedding, felt a burst of relief that her father hadn't purposely tried to hurt her.

One young guy, a kid really, kept popping up at everyone else's table. His first time around, he introduced himself to all with a strong handshake and a wide toothy smile, including to Rogie and Paula. His name was Quentin and he was the grandson of Roger III, one of Shelley's half brothers from her father's first marriage. This kid was in his midtwenties, and, as he told the table several times, had just graduated from Yale Law School and was about to begin a clerkship with a federal judge in Manhattan. "Oh, yes, Michelle, known as Shelley." He grinned, ticking off some mental list he'd accumulated in his mind. "Now you work in real estate?" He had done his homework on all the relatives. "I'm very interested in a new districting law affecting New York State . . . ," and he took off talking a steady stream for over ten minutes, without taking a breath. As Shelley nodded at the kid and tried to maintain a focused expression, she noticed that he looked conspicuously like Nick had at that age. His broad shoulders and healthy heft of dark blond hair—not as curly as Nick's but as noticeable. What topic had he moved on to now? Shelley nodded and gave a *hmm*. This exuberance, he was surely gaming for a politician's post in the future. Perhaps he was what Nick could have become, had Nick made a few different choices in life. Perhaps this Quentin kid, jabbering on, was what Roger would have dreamed of in a son. Maybe there was hope for the Whitby future yet.

LJ, poor LJ, had come over and wrapped his two arms around the back of her neck, as if they knew each other well—as if they'd been close for even one brief moment in their lives. "The most stunning Whitby! How are you, Shelley-kid?" he asked. She murmured, "Good, great. Thanks," while wriggling him off of her. Several years prior, he'd moved on from Las Vegas to Los Angeles, following the same path as his father and grandfather, although at a significantly earlier age than the two men before him. LJ considered himself a businessman, and after several failures to make grand commercial real estate deals, ran into legal trouble and spent some time in a white-collar prison. Although slimmer, he was so much like Roger that Shelley tried to avoid any prolonged interaction with him, for fear of a triggering effect. That's what the Program advised her to do.

After most people had moved on to dessert—black-and-white cookies, from a local Red Hook deli—Brooke climbed out from her bench seat, kissed Allie on the cheek, and then, as she made her way up to the front of the room, tapped Shelley's shoulder, whispering, "Wish me luck!" One person had been asked to give a toast from each family respectively, and surprisingly, Nick had asked Brooke to do the honors. But then, in the past decade or so since Nick's legal troubles had ended, she had doted over him and fully pulled him into a little-brother role. Perhaps it was because of the little boy who died, who Brooke and Roger had loved so dearly.

Brooke, in her midfifties now, was stouter and more tired-looking than she was in her youth, but still very much the prim person she had always been. She was dressed more appropriately than the majority of their family, in a sateen yellow wrap dress and a brown cardigan sweater. Her still-blond hair (certainly from a bottle, now) was cropped close to her head.

In front of the microphone stand with a stack of note cards, Brooke smiled. "Hello, everyone, I'm Brooke Whitby, Nick's much older sister." The rest of their family grinned as well, fully aware of the fact that Brooke did not insert any kind of qualifier into that statement: she was not a half sister, or an adopted sister, she was simply a sister.

"I'm completely honored to be speaking today," Brooke continued. "And I could not be happier for both Nick and Esmerelda. These two have known each other for about the same amount of time that I have really known Nick—*haha*—and they've proven over the years that their love is not only solid and strong, but redemptive. But! I'll get back to that in a moment." Brooke flipped a card over. When did she get so confident speaking in front of a crowd? Shelley wondered if Brooke, when practicing this speech, had stood in front of a mirror and puffed her shoulders up and winked at herself, channeling Roger. But Shelley understood that Brooke was happier now than Roger had ever been. She had a loud and rambunctious family life in Boston, and although her own mother rarely left Connecticut and kept her cool distance from Brooke's children, Allie's parents had moved to Boston in order to be closer to them. Brooke had also been a nurse manager for years now, and although her life seemed exhausting, she appeared content. Fulfilled, even. She continued, "I've thought a lot about the most important thing to say today. And this is what I came up with: there used to be a funny rumor that there was a kind of scourge on our family, as if we Whitbys were prone to bad luck and undue disasters." The de la Vegas all chuckled, but the Whitbys, from their seats at the picnic tables, looked pained. This direct talk; it wasn't for them. "But the truth of the matter is that there was no scourge at all. Each action that formed the long and sometimes unlikely history of our family also came from an individual, free-willed choice that someone made. Sometimes these choices made other people happy, and sometimes they didn't. But as a family, we have been, and we are, simply blessed with the opportunity to have been able to make our own choices." Brooke was silent for a few beats too long. A chair screeched backward. A few glasses clinked. Brooke looked down and the tension in the air rose.

She looked up again, and dived back into her speech with a smile, to the audible relief of the room. "Our father, Roger, saw something special in Nick. And I'm so very grateful that he did. Because Nick is special. He is stubborn and insistent"—everyone from both families laughed now, kindly—"and he's brave. When he came into our lives, he led by example. He'd insisted on making his own, independent choices, and this allowed me, and our other siblings as well, to free ourselves from the old rumors and expectations, from the old curses, and make our own choices. And for that, little brother, we are entirely grateful." Brooke raised a glass to Nick, who sat at the front with one arm around Esmerelda's waist and the other over Juan's shoulders. He smiled sheepishly and nodded in Brooke's direction—more of a bow, really.

Brooke launched into the rest of her speech, covering how patient and kind Esmerelda had been, what a wonderful mother she was, a person filled with beauty and generosity. From one table over, Kiki, in her beige, formfitting dress that would have been more appropriate for a breakfast meeting than a wedding, smiled ostentatiously at Shelley. Kiki's children were in college now, two in England and one at Demming. She'd divorced their father five years earlier and had come to Shelley's table early to give a detailed account of her extravagant divorcée trips to Majorca and Fiji, being sure to include that she'd taken them on her ex-husband's dime. Now the Whitbys were always doing that: ensuring one another that any money that they did have was not, in fact, Whitby money. It was best to avoid the subject altogether; any mention of family money brought with it the suspicion that it had ended up in undeserving hands.

The party was winding down, with a few children dancing on the otherwise empty dance floor, to the jazz music that pumped out over the sound system. The Quentin kid was back, talking to Shelley again; she understood now that he'd had too many mimosas. He went on, "And really, if New York City wanted to fix the runoff issue, what the mayor should do is declare that residents can't use their toilets or sinks when it rains. . . . That's the solution to the sewer-overflow problem."

One of the de la Vegas shook Nick's hand and stood up from where he'd been chatting with him at the head table. In front of Shelley, Quentin said, seemingly out of nowhere, "Listen, I know you're my cousin or my aunt or something, but I just have to tell you: you are really, really pretty."

That was Shelley's cue to leave. She patted the kid on the arm, then beelined toward Nick to say her goodbyes. When she reached him, she said, "Well you've done it, Little Nicky. Everything always works out for you."

He grinned and pushed her hip, playfully. "Just like it works out for you too, Shells."

"I know," she said. Then she embraced him with both arms, whispering into his ear, "Esmerelda is the best thing that ever happened to you."

"I know," he said in a loud voice. "Best thing since meeting my sister."

Both Whitbys blushed. "Okay." Shelley turned. "I promised Juan we'd go to the Museum of Natural History this week," she said.

"We'll bring him up to you. Probably Wednesday," Nick replied.

Shelley nodded. "Congratulations on your wedding, old man."

He nodded back.

Heading south on Madison Avenue, Shelley rotated her shoulders and stretched her sides, her own walking yoga. She had taken the 4 train home from the wedding, in order to give herself the opportunity for a peaceful Sunday afternoon walk across the park. It was the first day that New Yorkers scaled the streets in zipped-up jackets and cashmere scarves, closing off the warmer weather, obscuring their bodily shapes. The hackberry trees had dropped their tear-shaped leaves across the sidewalks, speckling the pavement yellow. The wedding was her big event of the season, and now it was over. Soon the underbite of frost would coax maple leaves off their branches, mixing red and orange into the autumnal debris. Shelley loved this moment in the fall, the rush of beauty before the blankness. This rush is ephemeral: there and then gone. At Seventy-Second Street, she turned into the Grace's Deli to buy her usual supplies—two cans of tuna, a carton of soy milk, a package of Virginia Slims—and then entered the park. It had been sixteen years since Nick showed up on Strong Place and stayed for the summer, since Grace and all their crazy friends moved in. It wasn't just the wedding that reminded her of that time; she always remembered it when the fall weather began. In fact, it was the time of year when she tended to see Mr. Kamal the most.

She followed the path beside Terrace Drive to the center of the park, I ♥ New York bag swinging from her forearm, when she spotted him. He was shuffling along the sidewalk with his wife (always with the wife now), the aging but still pert redhead woman, leading him like a walking stick around Bethesda Fountain. His age was showing in the growing hump beneath his cardigan. Shelley had seen him often in the past decade and a half, frequently in this exact place, staring at him from across the park. Funny, this island of coincidences. The rage she'd once held for him had long since dissipated, and seeing him now oddly warmed her. It was reassuring, the fact that nearly everyone from her old New York was still there, machinating through their routines, tucked into crooks and cornices, hovering like ghosts. There were years when she'd wrestled with the idea of reporting him. Eventually she'd decided that although her days with the now-hunched man had shaped her, they were ones she did not want to relive.

Today, the sight of the elderly Mr. Kamal actually threw thirty-nine-year-old Shelley into a fit of tittering. The girl she had been when she worked for him had become a burning, and slightly endearing, memory. Sometimes Mr. Kamal's bellow would float into Shelley's head, asking the question *Just what is it that you are deprived of?* But she'd learned by now, and oh it took far too long to learn, that she had never been deprived of anything. As a child she'd assumed that someone else would make the hard choices for her—that someone else would lead her down a trodden path, announcing: *This is how we live, Shelley Whitby.* But the fact that no one was there to lead her didn't mean she was lacking, it meant she was human. How sweet it was, and slightly sad, to have grown up. She still lived in her childhood duplex, as Armond had managed to legally transfer both her and Brooke's properties before Nick's trial. But although her home hadn't changed, she had.

Shelley swung her plastic bag on her arm as she ambled up Strong Place and entered her apartment. When she was young she used to love being alone at the house on the Vineyard at night. She would walk out to the end of Biddy's dock, where she'd plunge both ankles into the ocean while bundling a fleece collar around her jaw and letting her stoned eyes blur the gemlike stars above. That was what she thought of as contentment, equilibrium.

It was noticeably chilly inside; the heat in the apartment had yet to be turned on. She shivered as she placed her soy milk inside the refrigerator and dragged the can opener along the edge of a tuna tin. She stepped lightly on the floorboards, but they creaked as she called out to Chloë and Zooey, her Egyptian mau cats who were already over a decade old themselves, and entering the twilight of their lives.

In the parlor, she set the cats' dinner on the floor before opening the hall closet. The sulfurous odor of leather boots and now-vintage trench coats wafted out as she pulled the plum Burberry coat off the hanger, the one that Mr. Kamal gave her all those years ago. It was in nearly pristine condition, as she never wore it out of the house. She draped the coat over her shoulders and sat down in the center of the long-repaired blue settee.

"Hello, sweet darling," she cooed to Chloë, who wound her gray body around Shelley's ankles, then rubbed her whiskers on Shelley's leg. One day, invisibly, you cross over from living through your days to living through your life. Bitter odds, she thought, but she had found it: stasis. Happiness. Shelley fastened all the toggles of the coat and, leaning back, let her frail body settle into it.

ACKNOWLEDGMENTS

I'd like to thank the fierce and fabulous Suzanne Gluck, my agent, as well as Clio Seraphim and Andrea Blatt. I am forever grateful for their generous faith in this story!

My greatest admiration goes out to my editor, Maya Ziv, whose brilliance and follow-through is nothing short of breathtaking. Maya, along with Maddy Newquist and the rest of the outstanding team at Dutton, has made this such a better book.

Thank you to my first readers and editors: Jeff Walker, Ali Bujnowski, Katya Apekina, Ann Roosevelt, Sarah Paule, and Jessie Singer. Your insight and guidance was invaluable. Thanks also to my greater community of writers and literary friends, including Kim Rossi and Steve Louie, and to Jaffer Kolb for his architectural expertise.

I have been so lucky to have had life-changing teachers who believe in the hallowed art of storytelling, especially Darin Strauss, Irini Spanidou, Bret Anthony Johnson, Karen Shepard, Michelle Wildgen, and my eleventh-grade English teacher Roger Stacey. Thanks also to Pat Hoy and all the minds that inhabit NYU's EWP, for giving me a home full of ideas.

Finally, thank you to my own wild and wonderful family: Mom, Dad, Kathleen, Jeff, Tracy, Rob, Colin, Finn, Danny, Barbara, and Aaron. Josh Fisher, my best editor, your existence is a miracle to me. And Gabriel Teague, oh boy, we love you more than words can describe.

ABOUT THE AUTHOR

Maura Roosevelt holds degrees from Harvard College and NYU, and she has taught writing at NYU and the University of Southern California. She lives in Brooklyn, New York.